TO BATHE IN LIGHTNING

Also by Anne Gay

MINDSAIL
THE BROOCH OF AZURE MIDNIGHT
DANCING ON THE VOLCANO

TO BATHE IN LIGHTNING

Anne Gay

ORBIT

An *Orbit* Book

First published in Great Britain by Orbit in 1995

A CIP catalogue record for this book is available from the British Library.

ISBN 1 85723 274 7

Typeset by Solidus (Bristol) Limited
Printed and bound in Great Britain by
Clays Ltd, St. Ives plc

Orbit
A Division of
Little, Brown and Company (UK)
Brettenham House
Lancaster Place
London WC2E 7EN

To the player of the phantom guitar
Who once gave me the greatest gift of all.
It was the best of times ...

CONTENTS

1
ARMS AND THE WOMAN

Silver and gold, the lights of Kifl shone through the mist. The snow-wind from the volcano brought the scent of cedar to mingle with the night tang of the ocean; distant music sifted down to the docks to chime with the hush of the spring tide. Vapour wreathed between the curling walls, muffling the song of a locust-lizard searching for a mate. Practically everyone in town was huddled safe and asleep in the warmth of their beds.

Not Thebula. She moved softly through the dank streets of the docklands, smiling to herself as she thought of her lover Arin sneaking to meet her. Only a few minutes now . . .

Sharp footsteps sounded in the darkness.

Thebula looked over her shoulder, flitting deeper into the shadows. She listened intensely, heart pumping, enjoying the rush but not really afraid. Thebula could handle herself just fine. It was her job.

Two sets of boot-heels echoed through the fog, but no voices. Whoever they were, they moved purposefully where they had no reason to be.

No legitimate reason.

Thebula pulled back into the doorway of Arin's boat-shed, ignoring the graffiti: Second Wavers die. There hadn't been any trouble for weeks. Twiss had even lifted the curfew.

The door merely rattled when she tried it; her chance had come early and she had slipped away from Tingalit without King Twiss noticing – she hoped. She keyed in the combination but Arin hadn't arrived yet and the lock wouldn't open to her unless he were there. The footsteps came closer.

She crouched in the curve of the recess, smiled when the steps seemed to fade. But it was only some trick of the fog; a second later the two unknowns walked scant metres from her retreat. Thebula closed her eyes so the gleam wouldn't give her away. Still the play of her muscles was a sensuous pleasure as she slid her hand to the hilt of her transparisteel sword.

Let them pass, she urged, *I don't want any trouble*, but the boots clattered to a halt right by her, then – nothing. Nothing at all. No sound; no clue. Just the weight of their gaze upon her nerves.

She had to know. Risking it, she opened her eyes a crack.

A man and a woman in what looked like short capes. Big, very big, both of them. Motionless, facing each other. Real fear began in her.

Let them be lovers, Thebula prayed. *Let them be like Arin and me*. She willed them to kiss.

But they didn't.

In unnerving silence the two cloaked figures turned to stare at her. At least, she hoped they were cloaked because if they weren't, they were the strangest beings Thebula had ever seen. And the – capes? – didn't swirl when they moved. It was as if they were melded solidly to the giant bodies. Faintly silhouetted against some far-off light, the figures loomed, malevolent. Their shoulders were broad as a thousand-year-old tree and their hips were no narrower. That was why she had thought they were wearing cloaks, but they weren't. Misshapen with muscle, they bulked black against the yellow rags of fog. There was no pity in their bone-enshrouded eyes.

One of them slowly raised a massive hand to point at her and Thebula felt a horrible compulsion to slide to her feet. Beside her, fluorescent scrawls of *Second Wave Lover* and *Death to the Usurper Twiss* did nothing to improve her confidence. Because she was bodyguard to Twiss's wife Irona and nobody from the palace even knew where she was . . .

Now she was afraid. Fear rivered through her and all the time a wild thought beat in her head like a wounded bird: *This can't be happening to me.* Thebula didn't even know why she had started to stand up; it was as if the command had come from inside her on a level too deep to be ignored. She felt her thigh-muscles lifting, her back straightening, and she didn't understand. That was the greatest terror of all, that her body was not her own. The sword hung from her hand, forgotten.

Deep as the planet's core, a voice came from one of them: 'Your kind can't stay here in First Wave territory.'

Seamlessly the other's voice stroked a counterpoint from the breeze: 'You Second Wavers, all of you, must leave Kifl. It's ours. You have the rest of the planet. All of Harith, except this one coastal strip. Twiss must learn. Your body will tell him.'

Thebula pleaded. Against all her fierce instinct for survival her limbs would not obey her. She wrestled with this alien compulsion, but it gripped her invincibly. Forcing her treacherous lungs and throat and tongue, she begged, 'I can't! How can my body tell him anything if I'm dead? Don't kill me. Don't hurt—'

They paused. For just a second the slow stretch of their arms halted, and their great hands hung like the empty scoops of a bulldozer.

Somewhere off along the quayside, a cheery whistle sounded.

Thebula looked up, past them, her eyes burning with sudden hope. 'Arin!' she called, and the syllables were filled with a world of passion and need.

Mid-note, his warbling stopped. Thebula heard his steps quicken to a panicked run and her own death receded, but she paid in a love she hadn't known was there: his death was foretold a thousand times in her mind between his one stride and the next.

Then one of the inhuman bipeds raised her hand. Lightning flashed and before the thunder's echo could resound from the facing wall, Thebula died.

Arin saw the blue web of electricity. Fighting his fear, he ran towards the net of lightning that smeared the fog. For a fleeting second he thought he saw two huge figures hunched over the woman on the ground but it must have been a wreath of mist because there was a momentary flare and they were gone . . .

In the glass palace of Tingalit, Irona felt the pulse of Regenerator's code beat against her wrist: tic-tic-tac, tic-tic-tac. Sleepily she turned the bracelet off but it pulsed again and she sat up. Pulling the covers higher round her shoulders, she ordered her door to open. Her bed was warm but empty. Once again Twiss had chosen to sleep apart from her. She tried not to feel the hurt.

The thick crimson glass of the door pivoted obediently, its delicate patterns shivering across her floor in the light from the corridor. Like some ruby watermark the shadows of mountains and waterfalls slithered across the crystal tiles and the knobby silhouette of Regen stood beside them in the wedge of paleness that was the doorway.

'Irona?' he said hesitantly. 'It's me. Regen. Are you alone? Can I come in?'

'Hi,' she answered, her throat husky with sleep. 'What is it?' Fear for her only child seized her: 'Is Arnikon all right?'

Regen pattered across the room and poured juice for them both. 'He's fine. Entirely. No problem there. Hee-hee. Here.'

Graceless but caring, the little angular man with the pot belly sat on the edge of her mattress. His weight bounced the bed and the drink slopped on to the silken sheets. The perfume of passion-fruit filled the room in the Rose Wing but Irona didn't care. She gulped from the tumbler and the cold drink revived her.

'What is it?' she asked when her nightmares had fled.

'Did you let Thebula go out this evening?'

She nodded apprehensively.

'Thought so. Did Twiss find out?'

Irona shook her head, her sunstreaked curls flailing across her face. She brushed the hair from her eyes. 'No, he was too busy with that new fancy piece of his. He went to bed hours ago. A day's hunting and a barrelful of wine, he'll be out of the game till morning. Why?'

'Because if it weren't Twiss, we're in serious sh— trouble.'

Irona sat cross-legged, her vision adjusting now to the

light from outside. 'Quit beating about the bush. What's up?'

Regen stretched out his hand and curled it about hers. 'Thebula's dead.'

Irona suffocated an inappropriate yawn. 'Dead? Thebula? Never. She's too strong. Too clever.'

The warmth of Regen's fingers pressed the truth in on her. 'I'm sorry, Irona, but she is. Entirely.'

Like an automaton Irona groped to put down her tumbler. On the second try it landed on her bedside table. 'Not Thebula,' she whispered, and slow tears twisted her features until a sob took her shoulders in a spasm Irona couldn't control. Over and over she said, 'Not Theb, not Theb,' and Regen's knobby arms crept out to hold her while she wept. It didn't matter that he smelt of nervous sweat. He brushed his unshaven chin against her forehead and held her face where she could feel the living beat of his heart. His skinny fingers patted her back and the very awkwardness of his touch moved her by its gentle concern.

Finally she sniffed and wiped her nose on the back of her hand. 'When?'

'Two – three hours ago. Down by the docks. She's toast. Carbonised entirely. It's weird, Ro. It ain't natural. You got to come and see.'

Anger was building in her. Irona drove her mind past it to ask what they were both thinking. 'If it wasn't Twiss at his games, who was it?'

Irona paced up and down in the waiting-room of the Hospital, watching dawn break like an egg-yolk over the sullen sea. Tingalit, the glass palace where her supposed husband lay in the arms of a lover, folded the shadows of its turrets across the dark volcanic sands and down into the waters. *Twiss's Second Wave kingdom is like his castle if the First Wavers can kill even Thebula, Irona thought. Just a pathless pattern of shade moving on the ocean. When's Twiss going to see that?*

Because even though the doctor hadn't finished the post-mortem yet, he had already told her that neither Twiss nor any of the Second Wavers had the technology to cause whatever it was that Thebula had died of.

I still have to tell Twiss.

The thought was no comfort because, whatever happened, Twiss was going to blame her. What Irona needed was a hug to calm her shaking, but it was not what she would get from Twiss. *I'll go and see Tebrina.* The thought suddenly popped into her head, and just the knowledge that her friend was there helped. Tebrina always helped, even when there was nothing tangible she could do. But that consolation was something she would put off until after she had seen the leader of Kifl. Just in case he did show up here at the Hospital, she checked that her Eye was still there. Twiss was always nagging her to take an Eye. It hovered above her head, its iridescent globe of weapons poised to defend her from any attack, but Twiss would know she had taken it only out of guilt and he would not be appeased.

Arin lay in drugged shock in the room next to where the doctor was carrying out the autopsy under the watchful gaze of Regen and another Eye. It didn't matter that Arin was unconscious. He had said, 'I'll do anything to catch the bastards who killed my Thebula.'

Irona had held his hand, watching the pupils of his eyes dilate with the tranquilisers. 'Even let us scan your thoughts?'

The boy had barely hesitated as the soporifics numbed

him to his grief. 'Even that,' he said, and his eyelids had dammed his tears.

'Poor lad,' she whispered to his sleeping form. 'We'll get them, don't you worry.' *And meantime where the hell is Thebula's deputy? Don't tell me they've got her, too.*

But that thought would give no succour to poor Arin, so she stood decisively and moved to the console.

Irona cued his memories on to the circular screens again and again. She knew everything that Thebula's lover had felt and seen, even down to the black shadows that were there and not there, vanishing in a roar and a streak of unhealthy glare that left some odour she couldn't identify.

She was just thinking, *That smell! I should know what it is*, when Dr Darien stuck his head round the door. 'I think you should see this,' he said brusquely, too tired to mask his dislike of any Second Waver, especially one who was the most powerful woman on the Kiflian Synod.

Steeling herself, she put on the sterile gown, cap, gloves and overshoes Darien held out to her so she wouldn't contaminate his operating theatre. All the same not even Regen's words had warned her strongly enough; olfacts couldn't hide the stench of burnt flesh and the sight that awaited her roiled her stomach. It was no longer the remains of her friend.

Under the lights, the body that lay on the table was cindered. The skin (Irona couldn't think of it as Thebula's skin) was hard and cracked and blackened, the eyeballs blistered and bubbled with the vitreous humour boiled out through the clinkered corneas. The hair was no longer wild and red and somehow vibrant with Thebula's personality; it was calcified into a midnight nest of strands that fragmented brittly when the doctor pointed with his scalpel to the electrode no Kiflian had implanted.

No normal Kiflian, First Wave or Second.

For Irona the sight of her friend would be forever linked to that stink. Where her fingers pressed over her mouth in an attempt to hold back her vomit, the sickly plastic of the gloves reeked in her nose. Regen came to her and stroked her arm, but he too was layered in sanitised clothing and he didn't even smell like Regen any more.

Dr Darien smiled tightly and said, 'For what it's worth, I've never seen anything like this before on Harith or even in my training-memories from Earth.'

Irona said tightly, 'Neither have I,' but the horror of the deaths she had seen in her time as warden came back to her over the light-years from Camelford Mountain, the old capital of the Admin on Earth. Never this midnight mummifying, though. But that smell . . .

The First Wave doctor took a step or two, doling out his findings in tantalising snippets to enjoy his superiority. 'It's as if she were somehow flash-cooked by some form of electricity. She died instantaneously, but we've managed to reproduce some of her retinal images on that screen behind you.' Again he casually waved his scalpel and a flake of petrified blood fell to the floor with the faintest of clicks.

Irona swallowed, forced herself to look impersonally at the images on the screen. It wasn't really a screen, but the front of a 3-D imaging tank, and in it Irona saw the last thing Thebula ever knew: jaundiced fog wreathing about two solid black monsters whose hideousness lay not merely in their size but in their grotesque parody of the human form. Monsters Irona remembered from Earth. Evil creations she thought they had left behind forever.

Her lips formed the word: 'Arms!'

Regen nodded, firing his speech with the rapidity of his tension. 'Entirely. Well, not quite entirely. They're different, see? Different from they ones back in Camelford. Not the same shell. It's not shiny, see? More like elephant hide, or crocodile-skin or something.'

'All right!' Irona snapped. 'Don't go on about it. The point is, they're Arms. So where do they come from?' She was thinking of Earth, wondering if the Matriarchs of the Admin could reach even across the light-years to her refuge. Wondering if her old betrayal was worth the bother to them. All she'd done was save Twiss and Regen and bring them to Harith—

'I don't know,' Dr Darien said. His sallow face was almost smirking. 'But we certainly don't have the technology here in Kifl. At least, we First Wavers don't, and I don't suppose that if your lot had the power to make – things – like that, King Twiss would let us forget about it. But listen to what they said: someone believes in justice.'

Irona shot him a poisonous glare. 'Wave prejudice won't accomplish anything.'

Blandly the doctor gestured at another screen, frozen, flecked with the blizzards of static. 'The computer's rescued these projections from what's left of her brain. It was the electrode those things left that gave us the clue.'

Smug, the white-clad doctor wired a link-up to the metal stud in Thebula's hairline. It made her poor body seem like an extension of a machine.

Before he deigned to drop another gobbet of facts, Irona said, 'Us who?'

'Eh?'

'Gave us *who* the clue?'

'Oh, the computer and I. We did it together.' He made a gesture as if to slick his dark hair back but his sterile cap was in the way. 'A wonderful job, though perhaps I shouldn't be the one to say it.'

'Well done,' Regen said with total lack of patience. 'You wouldn't of done it without they computers we Second Wavers brought from Earth, though, would you?' He leant back against the bench by the window and crossed his legs. 'Now let's see what you got afore we die of old age.'

Impervious to irony, the doctor said, 'I thought even you Second Wavers knew that there's no such thing as old age on Harith. You either reach maturity and maintain that, or stay the biological age you were when you landed—'

Irona cut across him coldly. 'Could you get on with it please?'

The doctor pointed his remote at the screen. The blizzard melted into Thebula's memories, seen through Thebula's eyes.

Blocky with muscle, the pitiless giants loomed over her in the yellow fog. Thebula felt her bones and flesh moving of their own accord and she couldn't stop them. Irona experienced her friend's compulsion to stand. It was as if some thing were in her mind pouring its corruption along her nerves, and Thebula's fear was contagious. Irona's chest squeezed her heart in its cage of bones.

Thebula's body was half paralysed, half disobedient. Her blood surged to an alien tide. To have something like that inside you, taking your life as its own ... Irona twitched her fingers surreptitiously to make sure she still had control of herself and was glad to see the doctor and Regen doing the same.

The male spoke, his voice scarcely human as it echoed through the black caverns of his carapace. Words rumbled in Thebula's ears: 'Your kind can't stay here in First Wave territory.'

And the female Arm rehearsed the curse of banishment

to the uninhabitable wastes of Harith. 'Twiss must learn. Your body will tell him.'

Irona knew then that she was another intruder as she felt the desperation streaming through her friend's useless limbs. She heard Thebula's begging – from the inside. The leap of hope at Arin's whistle, the dread that he might die to save her.

Razor-fingers of lightning lashed her. She felt her eyes frying in a searing dazzle. Electric pain dismantled her. On the edge of eternity Thebula sensed the male stoop his hand to hammer iced metal into her brain . . .

The screen became a fire-opal, a fading cacophony of light-ghosts and sound-shadows. Irona shook herself, feeling her friend's death in her own flesh and in her mourning. She dropped her arm from her own eyes, saw the avidity on Darien's face.

Snatching the remote from the doctor's grip, Irona stabbed the button to turn the screen off.

'Don't ever do that again!' she yelled at him. 'It's the final stripping of dignity, don't you see? The ultimate invasion of a person's private self! How dare you bring Thebula back from beyond death with no thought of respect? You're disgusting!'

Stunned by the savagery of Irona's shouting and by the hostility on Regen's face, the First Wave doctor stammered, 'I – I didn't! It wasn't me; it was them! I couldn't have done it without them. And we had to know—'

Irona whirled. 'What did we have to know?' Above their heads, the Eye bobbed, a gleaming sphere of menace, searching for the threat of which her raised voice warned it.

Dr Darien glanced up at her Eye and then hurriedly looked away, as if by merely peeping at it he might make it kill him. But Irona wasn't even aware of her iridescent crown. 'I'll tell you what we know!' she yelled. 'Just that you First Wavers want to kick us out of your paradise to die in the wastelands, just like you did when we first landed. We didn't need another death to remind us, much less that – that necrophilia.'

'At least we know someone's got Arms on Harith!'

She stared at him as if to weigh the truth of his words. '*We* haven't, but apparently you First Wavers have. Don't forget those things appear to be on your side. And where else could anyone find the tools to build them but in the lab in town or in this very Hospital? And who's in charge here?'

'It wasn't me!' the doctor babbled. 'I haven't even been to the lab in weeks.'

'Then you should have done. It's your overall responsibility, isn't it?'

Darien sidestepped that one. 'Why don't you ask your pet, Tang?' the First Wave doctor said nastily. 'He's the genetics expert.'

Irona swallowed her shock. She didn't rise to the doctor's bait. Still glaring at him, she said, 'Oh, I will do. But fortunately for him Arias Tang works for the good of the whole community, whichever Wave they came with. I thought you did too.' Irona swept across the room, using her anger to blast the doctor aside. 'Believe me, Darien,' she said, spearing him with her words, 'this is worse for you First Wavers in the long run than it is for us. Thebula's death has done your cause more harm than good. Our memories are as long as yours. We've survived your tyranny and most of us are trying to work for peace for everyone – as long as there's no more killings in the night. Those – those things could unleash a reign of slaughter like you've never seen. If this gets out, half the Second Wave will be out for blood. I give you twenty-four hours to find that Arms factory. Or . . .'

2
THE VOLCANOES DANCE

Regen didn't speak until he and Irona reached the Synod Chamber. 'I hate to say it, Ro, but that doctor-feller's right.'

In the underwater gloom of the Emerald Wing, Irona closed her eyes wearily. She felt all the uncertainties that Regen tried not to show: at times her empathy was more of a curse than a blessing, and since she had come to Harith it seemed to be stronger than ever. Finally she could stand his strain no longer. 'All right,' she said, 'spit it out.'

'Darien's hit the nail on the head entirely. I know how you feel about Arias Tang but he's about the only one on this planet who could build they Arm-things.'

A vast anger built inside her at the slur on her lover. Knowing that Regen wouldn't hurt her for the worlds, she dammed it behind her lips and stopped outside the Synod door. Facing her friend, she patted his arm to show that her anger wasn't directed against him. Still, the tension in her mouth pinched her words. 'I know. Arias has grown his mermen for Eastcliff, tailored plants and animals for them to raise. If he can do that, he can knock up a few Arms as easy as wink, or at least that's what all the Second Wavers will say. And Twiss'll say it too. He was jealous enough of Arias before—' She broke off, changed the subject. 'The difficulty's going to be convincing him that Arias wouldn't do anything like that. When we tell him about Theb' – Irona's voice cracked – 'he's going to go off like a volcano.'

Regen had no difficulty deciphering which 'he' Irona meant. Twiss, the one the Second Wavers called King because when they needed a leader he had taken control. The one who said he wanted equal rights for the Second Wave of colonists with whom he had arrived from Earth. Today, sixteen years and more after that landfall, Twiss still remembered how the First Wave had exiled them to the wastelands of Rainshadow Valley. The disease, starvation and plagues of alien predators which had caused his grandfather's death had scorched Twiss. Still did, for that matter. If nothing else, Twiss was a healthy hater. He had stopped at nothing to get what he wanted for the Second Wave of colonists – and the First Wave had never forgiven him. That, as much as anything, was responsible for the Wave hatred – and when she didn't even know where Thebula's second-in-command was, Twiss's temper would explode. But he had to be told.

She took a deep breath, squared her shoulders, and pushed open the door, following her Eye inside once it had told her the coast was clear of assassins. The memory of the time the original Kiflians had invaded the palace and threatened her son was still vivid.

But she had gathered her courage for nothing. Twiss was nowhere in sight. The Synod Chamber was empty. Twiss wasn't where he should have been and there was no sign that he had even been there about his normal duties. Gone were the petitioners, the complainers, the pettifogging First

Wave obstructionists. He must have dismissed them all. In the aqueous light that filtered through the green glass of the walls, there was nothing to fill the echoing space but the oval table and the high-backed chairs that stood like teeth around it. The place felt cold, disused, despite the meeting she had chaired there yesterday. Even the air had a clammy, dead smell.

Drifting closer to Twiss's High Seat, she said, 'He's not here, then,' and neither she nor Regen knew whether she spoke with relief or anger.

Her gaze fell upon the 3-D representation of the growing town; the epidiascope set in the high window cast an image of Kifl on the table-top, showing the buildings that jostled for space on the narrow coastal plains. It was tiny but accurate; if she peered closely she could even make out the bright clothes of Kiflians talking their machines through the jobs to be done. Against the soft colour of the real blue sky, Mount Heralia lifted its snowy peak; a plume of steam rose from the hot springs high on its flank, but the terraced fields in the foothills were clotted with dwellings where sixteen years before there had been none. Irona could almost feel the pressure of the growing population.

Lying right over the middle of the pattern of light and darkness that showed the city was Twiss's kistle crown. His symbol of kingship; of the power he had craved.

She hesitated before her computer, casting a covert glance at the little man twitching behind her.

As if reading her thoughts, Regen said, 'Hey, it's me, remember? I ain't gonna let you down. Call Tang, if that's what you've a mind to. Hee-hee.'

Irona ignored his nervous mannerisms that grew worse in times of stress. Sliding into the seat before her own console, Irona called Tang on the night side of the planet.

Only static answered her.

'Mind if I borrow your Eye?' she began, just as her friend said, 'Wanna borrow my Eye?' They laughed together.

Sending her Eye and Regen's (a double risk to send both at once; it was a sign of her urgency) to fly out above the Interior, she transmitted again. Leaving Regen's Eye hovering in line-of-sight, she gave her Eye time to soar a thousand klicks to help relay her message, but Eastcliff still didn't answer her. Irona pulled a face of frustration, safe in the knowledge that it was her friend beside her. Still she couldn't help casting a surreptitious glance around. First Wavers, Twiss's folk or Tang's, there were plenty of spies already without adding Arms to the list.

Even with her Eye rising in the east, static hummed frustratingly.

Regen, sitting on the table swinging his legs with a total disregard for the marble dignity of the Synod Chamber, said, 'You try again. Maybe further out. I'll – er – go and look for Twiss.'

'You do that.' She smiled gratefully at him and he winked one protruding brown eye at her. Irona felt the safety of his friendship. In Kifl, and under the weight of Twiss's dog-in-the-manger protectiveness, she needed it.

Regen slid out through the door, twitchy as ever, as Irona sent the Eyes higher, farther, out over the inhospitable Interior. In the screen she saw the planet's dry, corrugated surface scroll beneath her and on a whim she sent her Eye into a dive, following the dizzying contours in a way that left her breathless with excitement. It was as if she were the one who was rolling and soaring above the jagged ravines that flashed in the noon sun, the spikes of mountains cutting the night that gathered far to the East. Almost five thousand kilometres of killing land with oases of native life. The shadow of her Eye lengthened into an oval that blinked across sand-blowers; she followed an army of snake-rats on the march, eating anything in their path. Starbugs reached arms above the green pools they had poisoned. She swooped her Eye between their tentacles in a deadly game of catch and laughed when she won. Dancing with snowflowers above an icy cataract, she wondered if they felt the same pure joy she did. The blue of glaciers sang to her of wonder as she passed the nightline. Exhilarated, Irona rode down the mountain passes on the wings of a thunderstorm to reach Arias Tang.

At last she dived up the well of gravity into a second sunset and transmitted again, relaying through the Eyes in the stratosphere. This time the answering signal wasn't the empty hum of a carrier-wave. Her exaltation dropped her as suddenly as an avalanche.

Tension and longing filled her in equal measures.

'Yes?' said the voice seconds later, though the broadcast picture broke the face into cubist blocks whose edges didn't match. But it wasn't Arias Tang. Irona stifled her disappointment.

'Hi,' she said too casually. 'It's Irona here. Can I speak to Arias please?'

'Who?' the unknown woman said. 'Your transmission's garbled.'

'Arias Tang.'

'Oh, you mean the Creator. Why didn't you say so? Hang on.' The woman's words were slurred across the thousands of kilometres of ether. 'I'll see where he is.'

Irona glanced guiltily around the green gloom of the Synod Chamber, but the computer-console sunk into the stone table had already told her there was no-one spying on her in flesh or electrons. Besides, she knew Regen was lurking outside in the corridors to keep tabs on Twiss or the First Wave. All the same, old habits die hard.

Tapping her fingers nervously on the table, Irona waited. And waited, though the computer told her only six minutes had elapsed. Between desire and apprehension, though, time was on a rack.

It was another three minutes before a face ballooned and shrank on the screen as someone settled before the Eastcliff transmitter. Only the strength of her longing could build the curves of his face, the planes of his cheeks, from the storm-chopped image.

'Arias?' she said hesitantly, bathing in the blue fire of his eyes.

'The same and none other.' His voice, a round tenor between the snakes of interference. He meant he was alone.

'It's me.'

More then than just the two seconds' time-lag. Irona knew Arias was searching for a reaction; she wished she could see him clearly enough to work out what it was.

'Is everything all right?' he asked tightly. She knew he meant Twiss.

'That way, yes. But Kifl's hit a bit of a snag and we need to talk to you.'

Delay. Irona waited for her words to travel to him and his to reach back to her. She knew he had heard the 'we' and was sifting it.

'Go on then,' he said finally.

'Face to face.'

By the time elapsed before he answered her, Irona knew he realised that some threat had cropped up, and that if she couldn't discuss it openly it was very serious indeed. 'Our dirigible's in dock for repairs,' he told her. 'Storm damage. We had a doozy last week. Can you come out?'

Irona tried to keep the elation from shaking her. 'I'll check there's a weather-window and see what his lordship says. I'll get back to you as soon as I can.' Only by a great effort of will did she manage to keep her farewell to a single word: 'Out.'

'Goodbye, Ro. Out.'

Then she sat unseeing in the Synod Chamber, mentally playing back their conversation, searching for some hint of comfort in it, sucking it dry.

Only Twiss wouldn't play. Neither Irona nor Regen could get through to him since it wasn't actually war, and when they sent his friend Sticker to see him, he wasn't gone above two minutes.

Sticker met them at the bottom of the emerald glass ramp. He shrugged, put his head on one side, scratched beneath his lank, greasy hair. Irona could feel how ill at ease he was. The thought of Lowena came unbidden to her mind.

'Well, I told 'un like you said, Ro. He asked if they Arms was storming the palace and I had to tell him as they weren't. So he said he's feeling a bit rough and he'll come down to your room later, Ro, this afternoon most like. He said Theb can fetch you if you ain't there.'

'You mean you didn't tell him about her?' Irona barely managed to contain her anger. 'What did you tell him then? That the First Wave want to play tennis?'

Sticker wouldn't meet her gaze. 'I just told 'un they probably had Arms 'cos we got another dead one, like, and he cursed a bit about they First Wavers and said that about storming the palace—'

'Yes, all right,' Irona said, cutting across him. Sticker's feelings of guilt and inadequacy were strong inside her. 'You chickened out.'

'I never, then. I just didn't want to drop you in it, did I?'

Irona and Regen saw his discomfort as he tried to lie convincingly. When she judged he had squirmed long enough, she sighed. 'Poor old Theb. I suppose it doesn't make any difference to her now, though. All right, Sticker, you can—'

A tiny trembling in the earth beneath her feet caught her breath for a moment, but it was just the volcano grumbling to itself. She could hardly hear the rumble of it. The alarm passed.

Irona rubbed her diaphragm to relieve the momentary tension. She swallowed and went on, 'Wasn't there some builders' dispute you were supposed to be seeing to? You'd better get off and do that. I'll see you in Synod tomorrow, OK?'

Twiss's friend accepted her implied threat, but he was so glad to have got off lightly that he practically bounced out into the palace gardens. She watched him go.

Irona pulled a facial shrug at Regen. He raised his arms and dropped them to his sides.

'Well, Regen, I'd better get on and sort Theb's funeral out. Plus I've got a mountain of work to get through if I'm going out to Eastcliff. And I'd better check the seismo stuff to see if there's a real 'quake on the way.'

He smiled. 'Don't forget you got some living to do and all. I'll go and have a nose around, see if I can come up with something on they Arms. See you later, love.'

And he disappeared before the word 'love' impinged on her awareness. Momentarily it puzzled her, then she realised he didn't mean anything by it.

Probably.

By noon, Irona had done everything she needed to, and she still hadn't heard from Twiss. So she took time off for something she really wanted.

Irona laughed as the huge, shiny red cushion enveloped her. It wasn't often she could steal time from her duties to spend with her son.

'That's not fair!' she said, still giggling, and pretended to stamp her foot – which naturally sent a spray of crimson balloons to cascade over her son.

Arnikon tumbled in a string of backwards somersaults, balloons bouncing all around him. Irona could feel his laughter vibrating through the soft eplastic; his joy reached out to her along invisible nets of empathy strengthened by the circuitry hidden in the padding. Even through her merriment she had time to be amazed that her only child chuckled in a baritone voice. Her son – almost a man . . .

Unexpectedly he used the force of his final backward roll to soar off the sidewall in a leap that carried him way over Irona. At the crest of his lazy flight he dropped a cushion straight on to her head and snickered mightily.

Irona threw herself back on to the eplastic to bounce upwards as if she were on a trampoline. She grabbed Arnikon's ankle and tickled his bare foot.

'No fair!' he yelled, giggling and trying to squirm away as though he were still only a boy while her jump carried them up to the ceiling. Their shoulders sank harmlessly into the pink padding; mother and son rebounded to their separate corners, the walls sounding out in a succession of melodic pyoings that sang in a satisfying music of their own. It chimed well with the too-rare human mirth. Irona,

Queen of Harith, never had enough time to play with Arnikon, to talk to him, listen to him, or even just to be with him. Now he was almost fifteen and it was almost too late . . .

No. She suppressed the thought. *This is Harith. We've got all eternity, Arno and I.*

Panting, he scooped an arm along the floor to spin a fountain of soft red balls at her. The spheres gleamed in the afternoon light that shone through the soft, resilient plastic windows.

The balls caught her full in the face like a spray of champagne and her son crowed. Both of them were weakened with laughter, both of them were running with sweat from their game. On Harith you need never grow old; Irona's reflexes were still those of the twenty-three-year-old she had been when they landed sixteen years before. She batted the balls right back at him and shouted, 'Now will you put your things away?' in a self-parody that went right back to his childhood.

Arnikon's giggles got the better of him and he slid down the wall to plump on to the eplastic floor; cushions and balls gradually settled all over him and he let them. He was enjoying making his mother laugh; she could feel it. Irona was happy. Hopping over to him, she cartwheeled the last few metres and ended up head downwards, her slim legs pointing to the pink and orange ceiling. She let her feet slide sideways until they rested on Arnikon's mop of blond curls. He shared a smile with her.

The sunny room quietened to an arpeggio of gentle humming while the ruler of Harith and her son sat companionably getting their breath back. Any second now they would start again – any second . . .

*

While Irona and Arnikon puffed cheerfully in the playroom in the Rose Wing, King Twiss was bored – but he wasn't lonely. He only wished he was.

'Oh, go on, Twiss,' his latest paramour said. 'You've got to. Otherwise Hesperion'll always be a danger to us.' She giggled, a high, irritating sound that she cut off with a nervous breath. 'Once a First Waver, always a First Waver. You said that yourself.'

For the life of him Twiss wished he hadn't promoted Lowena to Deputy of the Guard, but she was a sweet little armful – or had been, up to now. No demands, no bargaining, just cool efficiency on duty, a sexual riot off: a drink and a horizontal dance or two. But now he had bedded her she seemed to think he owed her something. It occurred to him to wonder if she had wangled her position for this – or the other way about. But he dismissed the thought. Lowena was sexy but she wasn't bright.

'Go on, Twiss,' Lowena pleaded. 'Send him to Eastcliff. It isn't much to ask, is it? It's not as if you really like him or anything. Besides, it's for the good of Kifl.'

Twiss sat up abruptly and pulled the covers aside. 'You're starting to get on my nerves, girl.' When Lowena reached to stroke his back, he got up and dragged his shirt over his head in one motion.

'Please, Twiss? For me? Only Hesperion's driving me crazy. He won't leave me alone. What if he tells on us to Irona? All he talks about is the good old days before you Second Wavers moved in and took over. Go on, send him away.' Her cloying little-girl-lost voice wrapped itself round Twiss's mind despite all the wine he had drunk.

'Oh, for Synod's sake, shut up about it, will you? Or you'll be the one that ends up in Eastcliff, not Hesperion,' he snapped. Looking wildly about for the flagon, he heard a clank and saw that the brunette was refilling his goblet.

He drained the fruity claret at a gulp. 'Thanks, girl. You got your good points.' Breathing deeply, the warmth of Lowena's body still on him, he said, 'Well, if it'll shut you up, I'll send Hesperion out tomorrow. Only give me a break now, will you? I got a planet to run. I'll call you,' he said, and she glanced up at him adoringly.

Lowena stretched her arms upwards as though she would drown him in a kiss. Twiss ducked aside in the harsh noonlight, ostensibly to pull on his trousers and boots. Her movement died awkwardly while he busied his hasty fingers with the fastenings.

'Same time tomorrow, all right?' he said. 'Only I got to make a move. Harith don't run itself, you know. 'Sides, ain't it time you inspected the guard or somethin'?'

The jade door clicked shut behind him.

Now all he had to do was get Irona to sort it all out. Hesperion, overcrowding, food-shortages – Twiss shrugged. She was good at that sort of thing. Twiss strode along the corridor of the Emerald Wing, his heels clicking on the viridian glass as he headed for the hub of his kingdom, the Synod Chamber, mentally rehearsing his excuses to Irona.

'Eastcliff. Eastcliff. Who else can I get rid of at the same stroke?' he murmured, his guards trotting wordlessly in his wake.

By the time he reached the Synod Chamber his head was throbbing too badly for him to concentrate. Relieved to find the place empty, he slid hipshot into the High Seat facing the 3-D light-sculpture of his capital city and smiled to himself as he picked up his crown. 'Granfer,' he whispered to his reflection in the green crystal, 'you'd of been proud of me.' Reverently placing the circlet on his brow, he put through a priority call to Irona.

*

The playroom created a new web of sound that rang as a dissonance in Irona's ears. Upside down, playing a physical form of chess, she heard the call and let herself slide through the body of the air-stallion that was her knight. Arnikon stifled his crow of delight at winning by default.

'Queen to King One,' she said wearily, and Twiss, in the Synod Room, wondered as he so often did what on Harith she was talking about.

When he acknowledged, she heard his irritation masking his uncertainty. At this distance she couldn't truly feel his emotions but that was all to the good. She had known him long enough to be wary of them in the flesh.

'I've been expecting you all afternoon,' Irona said, wiping the salt sweat out of her eyes.

'Oh – er, sorry, I forgot. I was busy,' he added belatedly.

She raised her brows sceptically, but he didn't say what had kept him.

'Look,' Twiss said, 'we got a bit of a problem over at Eastcliff. I ain't talking about it over the airwaves. Come up here, will you?'

Irona wiped a strand of damp hair from her face and forebore to tell him that they had a bit of a problem here, too. If you could call the death of your friend and bodyguard a bit of a problem. 'What, now?' she said, and he was too preoccupied with his hangover to notice the edge of sarcasm in her voice.

'Of course, now! I'm not playing games here, you know.'

She didn't, but she had her methods. She would find out. 'Give me twenty minutes,' she told her husband wearily, and signed off with another disharmony before he could complain.

Irona looked at her son. His face was closed to her, its youthful curves planing down to a carefully neutral expression that she knew all too well hid his disappointment. 'I'm sorry . . .' she began.

'Don't bother.' Arnikon shrugged. 'You've got your work cut out.' That was his parody now, flavoured with rancour he scarcely bothered to disguise. It etched into her.

'I am sorry, Arno . . .'

'I know. You always are.' The harsh sun of Harith carved lines of scorn about his mouth. At that moment he looked far older than his fifteen years. 'Just spare me the speeches about how the place would fall apart without you. Dad snaps his fingers and you jump, that's all.'

'Arno—' she said in tones that slid through exasperation to despair because she feared he was sometimes right.

'Save it. In fact, you've got a world to save. Don't mind me, I'm only your son. I'm going out with Fess and Carnell, OK?' He was already out of the door, calling back over his shoulder. 'We're taking a transport. Back late. See you.'

'See you, love. Hey, where are you going? Don't forget Theb's memorial this afternoon.'

Arnikon didn't answer but they both knew she had to let him go and he played upon it yet again.

She called after him. 'Have a' – the scarlet padded door clicked shut over the words – 'nice time.'

It was the last time she would ever see him alive.

3
HIGH WINDS

'Well I can't go!' Twiss said forcefully. Maybe it was grief at Thebula's death, or guilt. More likely it was anger at the Arms' threat to his authority. Whatever, the dark cocktail of emotions battered at Irona.

She and Twiss had finally met up in the Ocean Room, and Irona leaned on the balcony, gazing out over the sunspeckled waves. Fishing-boats lofted their colourful sails to the blue of the spring sky. Locust-lizards sang their haunting melodies and children let out of school for the noon recess shrieked with laughter on the beach. The day was unseasonally warm. Early airplants wafted their orange-and-rose perfume from the tendrils that trailed around her; she was glad of their distraction tickling her shoulder. If Twiss could read in her face the emotions that circled in her mind . . .

But he couldn't. Only Irona could feel his. Illogically she was hurt that he wanted her out of the way. He rationalised. 'Look, love, if you stay here they First Wavers might do anything. They might send the Arms to get you and I don't want that. You mean too much to me.'

'Then I'd better take Arnikon.'

'That's different. He's a man now—'

'He's just a child!'

Twiss spoke angrily to cover up his guilt. 'What were you doing when you were his age? Learning to run half of Camelford Mountain, the way you tell it!'

'Look, Twiss, when I was fifteen I wasn't being tracked by two-hundred-kilo assassins who grow their own armour.'

'But you were a couple of years later, and look what happened! The boy needs experience. I'll look after him, don't you worry. Sticker and me, we'll comb every nook and cranny they First Wave deves might have hid their Arms factory in. So I need someone I can trust to take care of the other end of things. You check out Eastcliff.'

'You don't trust Tang!'

'Damn right I don't! I wouldn't trust him as far as I could spit. He smiles but you never know what's behind any of they First Wavers' faces. And Tang, he's the worst of the lot. He's just waiting for a time to get me back for taking him out of the game.'

Irona's hands tightened on the balustrade as she sought for self-control. Squinting into the blue sky, she said quietly against her ire, 'He's not out of the game. He chose to go and set up Eastcliff to ease the population pressure. He's working to help feed us all, isn't he? And he's had sixteen years if he did want to do anything. Besides, you didn't just "take him out of the game", Twiss. You dragged him up hill and down dale till you flayed the skin off him, then you abandoned him in a desert to die. But he doesn't want to get you back—'

'No, because I showed him who's boss. Tang ain't got the guts!'

'Wrong, Twiss.' She pegged her anger down but it

squirmed to get free. Only her force of will restrained it. Irona could feel a pulse beating in her neck, knew the pressure of blood rising to her face. Sometimes she wished Twiss could feel the pain of her emotions the way she could feel his lacerating her. She said again, 'You're wrong. Because Arias Tang wants the best for everyone on Harith. He knew that you were the best choice we had for a leader to keep the factions from tearing each other apart.'

'Synod, woman! You don't believe all that self-sacrificing crap, do you? He's too scared to be a real threat.'

She turned; fractured sunlight stabbed her eyes so that she couldn't see Twiss clearly. He was just a shadowy silhouette against the comfort of the room she had created where the Rose Wing met the Gold. Yet she knew every curve of his round, attractive face. She knew how it felt to slide her fingers between his soft brown curls. The column of his neck, the smooth muscles of his chest against her cheek, and worst, his soft reassurances in the dark.

Irona said more sharply than she meant, 'If he's such a zero, how come you sent him five thousand kilometres to the other side of the world?'

'Because you said he could do the job better than anybody else, smart-ass.' Irona could feel Twiss's wrath taking control of him; he was coming to believe his own fiction now. His anger burned in her. 'Besides,' Twiss added, and it was the truth he spoke now, 'I couldn't rightly have him killed nor I couldn't get nothing done with all they First Wavers practically worshipping every centimetre of the ground he walked on. And I thought he couldn't get up to much out there with a colony of deves to run.'

'Just because the fisherfolk are different from us, it doesn't make them deves!'

Twiss shrugged. 'It does in my book. What the hell else is a deve? Anyway, I send you over every now and then to check he ain't up to no mischief, don't I? Come on, Ro' – Twiss was cajoling now and that made Irona's own guilt sharper than ever – 'do it for the good of Harith, can't you?'

She thought, *So self-sacrifice isn't crap if I do it?*

But Twiss carried on oblivious to the fault in his argument. 'I can't run this place single-handed and the people need me here if there's Arms raging around. Look what happened to Theb.'

So he's using Theb's death for emotional blackmail now, is he? I wondered why Lowena was keeping out of my way. Irona's anger hardened.

He came to her, his hand stroking her bare arm, sliding round her shoulders to massage her back. His presence was very strong. When he was like this, Irona remembered why she had loved him in the beginning. Still did – when he was like this. But he had broken her into pieces, and only some of the pieces loved him. Gently he pulled her head against his chest, caressing her nape, her cheek, kissing her forehead.

But she could feel his manipulation, his calculation of the angles. It hurt. The strength of his will burned brighter than the naked sun and yet again the other reason that she stayed with him struck her inescapably.

Twiss was a leader. People naturally followed where he commanded. For his humour, his praise, the warmth of his regard that came and went so politically, people would do what he wanted. Others besides her felt the strength and vitality he exuded. They basked in his smiles, rolled over and played dead for his praise. It was all that had saved the Second Wavers when they landed on Harith – or rather, when the First Wavers ordered that they be dumped into the wastes of Rainshadow Valley to be starved into submission. All that stopped the First Wavers rising to slaughter them for the destruction of the tidal waters he had called down upon their rebellious town.

A pity Twiss didn't have the intellect to work out the best course of action. He needed Irona to think for him.

'Look, love,' he said, and she tried not to smell the masculine warmth of him. 'It's stupid rowing. You know I need you.'

Yeah. What for? she thought bitterly.

'But I really can't go and someone's got to. If anything goes off, I need Regen here to make the gadgets for me. He can work your computer. Not as good as you, but I'll be OK for a while. Just' – his lips brushed her forehead and she could have murdered him for the way his heart beat only for himself and his plans, not for love of her – 'hurry back to me.'

Do you really think that's going to win me over? Five seconds of tenderness with the reek of Lowena's perfume still on you? Oh, I'm going, Twiss. But not because you tell me to. Because I put the idea in your mind in the first place and you don't even know it.

Only she could tell Twiss nothing of this. The people needed him and he needed her, so they had played out their story day by day for sixteen years. The trouble was, she had learned too soon that in the daytime it was a story. In the daytime she was strong for all the peoples of Harith, the mainstay of Twiss's kingship. Ah, but when she needed to lay her burden down and rest? It was night when she really needed him, when she remembered the way he used to hold her, to soothe her, to whisper, 'It's all right, I've got you, Ro. You're safe.'

And so many nights he didn't come to her at all.

The memories assailed her, poison on the darts of her anger, but all she said was, 'All right, I'll go. You're right, someone has to. I know Arias' – she hastily added the surname – 'Tang could grow Arms if he wanted to, but he'd never do anything to damage Harith. He believes in this place. All the same, the way they murdered Thebula's upset me.' She sighed. 'Just don't let anything happen to Arnikon. I'd never forgive you if you did.'

Twiss turned her to face him. His skin was still as smooth and brown, his hazel eyes still as sparkling, as when she had seen him touch the moon-silvered stallion in Camelford Park. Even now she found it as hard as everyone else did to resist his magnetism. Her lips involuntarily formed a smile but adrenalin made her blood tattoo in the cavities inside her. No doubt Twiss thought it was because of the love she had for him, and Irona didn't disabuse him. This was one situation in which her growing anxiety was useful. He was lulled by the liquid tides of her body.

Then he did kiss her. Her treacherous flesh seemed to flow into his and there was a sense of completeness and belonging that was all she had ever sought. He drew her to a contour-couch behind them, and sat with her head cradled against him. Twiss touched her, caressed her, and it was an intimacy greater than sex. She lay there, peace stealing through her muscles to eat away the acids of anxiety, and the pattern of reflected sunlight danced from the ocean to mirror on the soft sunset shades of the ceiling. The same feeling of rest and contentment resounded in him too.

But she felt when it changed. Irona might not have understood why, but she knew he felt an urge to be up and doing. He didn't want to be here any more. It had been real while it lasted but it never lasted long.

At least he kissed her goodbye.

In this heat, Thebula's funeral was no more rushed than anyone's. Her friends, scores of her lovers, trailed through the narrow whorls of the rows. Irona, in a shapeless brown robe, followed the bier that floated along bearing Thebula's burnt body under a weighted brown cloth. The fringing around it fluttered. With Twiss walking beside her, in the same heavy brown of mourning that represented the world of Harith, Irona tried not to think of the music the bier played. Somehow it conjured up the essence of Thebula – volatile, argumentative, passionate.

She was laughing the last time I saw her. Spraying me with sea-water dripping from her hair. She said, 'You don't need me tonight, do you, Ro?' I said, 'Why, want me to cover for you if Twiss finds out you're not on duty? Who is it this time?' And she said, 'Arin, of course. All that teenage virility . . .'

The bier played on. Arin walked beside it, touching the sad brown cloth, winding his fingers in the fringing. Irona swallowed, determined not to cry.

The cortège wound to a halt on the promontory. Fishing-smacks out on the sparkling bay saw the crowd by the death-tank and dipped their sails. The bier stopped over one end of the high-sided tank.

Irona climbed the ugly steps to the shiny black cube and the reality of it tried to break in on her. She focused on the fringing that shivered in the hot breeze and spoke her eulogy, threw the white flower she carried up into the big, black tank, and stood down one step lower. Everyone else – except Arnikon, who hadn't come to the funeral, he was so wrapped up in hunting with his friends Fessbar and

Carnell – said their own farewells and passed the hovering bier to throw their flowers upwards over the high rim. When it was done, the music started again, a sound like brazen throats. At the crescendo, the bier tipped and Thebula's blackened remains slid out from under the cloth to splash into the tank. Irona pictured Thebula as she had been, her red hair floating out studded with flowers in the fragrant, clear liquid of dissolution.

But she knew that's not how it was. Liquid bubbled and frothed and drops burst out among the mourners, and where the spray touched the mourning sheets they wore, a shimmer of green spread out across the dull brown cloth until they were as bright as new leaves. Already some of the mourners were filling small gourds from the spigot at the foot of the tank; each would take back some of Thebula's essence to water a red rose, maybe, or a clematis. Her atoms would live on in the blossom. The music, still noble, softened on the sea-breeze and the fishing-boats hauled up their colourful sails.

Life went on.

But Twiss held Irona while she cried.

'Arnikon?'

'Sorry, Ro. He's still not back yet,' said Regen as they rode out through the knobby vineyards and the sky-nets that held the burgeoning air-flesh plants.

Twiss said, 'Don't worry. I'll skelp him when he gets back.' He nodded to the *Thistle-up* bulking out behind the sand-hills. 'You just concentrate on having a good flight. You'll need to be rested to deal with that snake-rat Tang.' His smooth tanned arm rested lightly against hers; she glanced up, and there were gold flecks of warmth in his hazel eyes.

Swiftly she kissed him. Later, as the ground dropped away beneath her, she waved until he and her friend were dots. It was Twiss who turned away first.

Now it was Hesperion instead of Thebula who stood beside Irona on the deck of the only functioning airship on Harith. Somehow Twiss hadn't suggested that Lowena go with her as bodyguard. Still, an Eye kept watch over Hesperion, and Irona was just as glad to have some time to herself. She looked around.

The huge hydrogen balloon dwarfed the basket-cabin hanging beneath it. Beneath their feet the clear hull revealed every nuance of the terrain. Cold winds ripped at her clothing, streamed through her hair, but Irona didn't find it half so much fun as flying it by Eye. Besides which, she wanted time to grieve for the fact that her only son hadn't even bothered to come and say goodbye. She snuggled her chin deeper into the collar of her heat-suit, trying to keep Hesperion from encroaching on her personal space. Tiny propellers aft blurred with the swiftness of their rotation; there was almost no sound but the wind-hum in the rigging.

No sound, that is, but Hesperion complaining.

'It's not fair!' he said for the seventeenth time, and Irona was sick of hearing it. 'I don't want to go and live with no fishmen.'

She allowed some of her anger to lay an edge of ice sharp on her words. 'Then you shouldn't have slagged off the Second Wave, should you, Hesperion? Fomenting political unrest just gets more people hurt. You could have helped make things work, but no. Not you. You were in favour of starving babies and old people.'

'I never starved no-one!'

'Then who rigged that tractor to blow? Who cut that

poor girl to ribbons and pinned a note on her saying "Second Wavers did this"?'

'Well it weren't me!'

Irona blazed at him. 'No, it was just people caught up by your stupid wave-hatred! It wasn't the Second Wave at all! Can't you see what you're doing?'

Hesperion sneered at Irona, trying to dominate her physically. He was her own height, but fat, and out of vanity he had genetically changed his skin and hair-colour so often that the dark hadn't taken. Patches of red and brown and blond stuck out in different textures and since he had been forced to leave so hastily, he hadn't had time to depilate his chin. This far east it was sunset, and stray gleams of evening light caught his whiskers in fire-colours against his piebald flab.

'Well I didn't ask to go nowhere. I ain't going to stay in no Eastcliff with they deves so you might as well take me back now!'

Irona stood straighter. She might have been half his weight but her strength of character gave her a density that allowed her to resist him. She said, 'Most of us didn't ask to come here. The Admin just sent us. Working together, First Wave and Second, we can improve your standard of living as well as our own. We can terraform more of Harith, not just the coastal plain near your town Kifl. We could get out of your hair. But we need your help to do it the same way you need ours.'

Hesperion had no answer. No rational answer, that is. What he did come up with was, 'We had a great lifestyle before you came. Enough power and machines to do all the work for us, enough room for all our grandchildren. But you pathetic Second Wavers, you changed all that. We'd have been fine without you.'

'Well you've got us so learn to live with us.' Irona took a breath to control her anger before it spilt more acid into him. Below her spread the panorama of Harith, its trackless wastes of stone and occasional oases that would have killed the first person to set foot there. Barren plains, rocky mountains and ice-caps between the acid waters of rare lakes and rivers. Add to that the deathly life-forms that skulked between the marshes and he had no answer.

Except: 'Things were fine till you got here.'

'Look, Hesperion, I've had enough of you whingeing. The situation exists and you have to learn to handle it instead of trying to retreat into the past. Maybe in a year or two you can earn the right to come back out of exile—'

'And maybe . . .' Hesperion's meaty hands reached out and grabbed her. He sank his nails into her upper arms and braced hard against her breasts, so that she was arched backwards over the glassy rail. The high winds flailed her hair into her eyes. There was nothing but air between her and a long fall to death. His hatred seared her mind.

And there was no-one to help her. The remote control for her Eye was deep in the pocket of her heatsuit and, since the Arms seared it, the thing had lost all its initiative.

Irona struggled to peer round the ugly globe of his head. Through the transparisteel deck she could see the two officers above in the engine room but they were fiddling with their dials and gauges, not looking below their feet at the passenger-deck. Fear fired its electrons along her nerves.

Hesperion's breath was hot and sour in her face. 'Maybe, your ladyship, Matriarch or whatever you call yourself, maybe I can bargain with your life to make them take me back home now. Think Twiss would reckon you're worth it?' He was panting out the words, striving to hold her against her struggles. She felt the press of his weight against her. 'Or do you fancy spreading your blood around the landscape? Think your bones would look nice on that peak over there?'

Her Eye might as well have been a thousand klicks away. She couldn't get her hands down to the remote. And neither of the crew was looking in her direction. Fear froze her skin.

'What do you say?' Hesperion demanded.

'I say' – she brought her knee up sharply between his legs, hoping they wouldn't both overbalance and fall tumbling to the teeth of the hills – 'you talk too much.'

The bone in her knee didn't collide hard enough to hurt him seriously but she scraped her boot down his shin, crashing her heel on his instep. With a jerk she smashed her forehead against his lips and, as his grip loosened, she wrenched one arm free and punched him hard in the throat, spinning aside as he retched. Completing her turn, she used her leg to scythe his feet from under him. Hesperion crashed to the deck, his size winding him.

Irona stood on his fingers – not savagely enough to break them, though the urge was there – while she whipped off her belt to lash his hands behind him. Then she knelt astride his back, pushing his face into the transparisteel. Irona felt the moment when his sight cleared: he shuddered as a ravine dropped away scant metres below. He could be the one plummetting into the abyss, waiting for his bones to splinter. She felt the terror roar through his entrails. She wanted to pound his head until it pulped.

She hated herself. *That's not my anger. It's his hatred I'm feeling. I'm not like that.* But somewhere inside she knew that was only half the story. His attack had called up the rage she had so carefully hidden away from herself, rage against Twiss's betrayal, against Arnikon's cruel indifference and the aching loss of Thebula. Rage against her endless payments for other people's well-being. She was hostage to this planet and she hated it.

'I want it to stop,' she whispered, finding that she was yearning against the clarity of the safety-rail. Irona had no idea how she got there, only that the two officers were in a panic, sliding down the staircase from the deck above – now it was too late for them to do anything.

'Are you all right?' said Captain Hoojer, but her concern was superficial.

'Oh, fine.'

Captain Hoojer didn't recognise irony. Waggling her unkempt eyebrows in a vague and reluctant invitation she said, 'Then if you don't mind we'll get back into the warm.' She shivered theatrically, pulling the toggle of her heat-suit up a notch.

'I'll come with you,' Irona said. 'I could do with a drink.'

Hesperion struggled to sit upright, blood streaming from his mouth. 'I'll come too,' he mumbled through his split lips.

Irona looked down at him, feeling the captain's curiosity as to what she might say. It was simple: 'No chance.'

'But you can't leave me here!' Hesperion exclaimed. 'I want to use the toilet!'

Hoojer didn't try to hide the smile that stretched her weatherbeaten face.

Irona shrugged. 'You got a whole planet to go on.'

'It's too cold.'

'Your problem, Hesperion.'

'But you can't leave me out here! I'll—'

Irona smiled gently. 'I can't trust you inside. And if you

do make trouble, I'll do exactly that. I'll leave you' – she pointed at a jagged snow-streaked scarp – 'here.'

The only snag is, she brooded as she followed the thick-set captain into the engine-room, *if Hesperion's such a threat, what new form of mayhem is he going to cook up out there in Eastcliff?*

4
DEATH THE LOVER

Holding tight against the bucketing, Irona wished the thermals would stop tossing the airship around. It was alarming. She peered through the squall but the rain-rivered transparisteel was not informative. First light meant nothing but the clouds around her turning more shades of grey. She wished she were asleep, but even if fear hadn't been dismembering her mind, other tensions would be.

Inside the engine-room the drone of the motors leaped half an octave as the propellers gasped in sudden turbulence, and she clutched at her stomach in a pointless attempt to reassure her body that it was not about to splatter against some volcano hidden in the mists. It was some comfort – but not much – that Kris, the crewman who wasn't on watch, was curled up snoring. He didn't seem scared at all. Captain Hoojer kept looking slyly at Irona to see just how nervous she was and, with the best will in the world, Irona couldn't mask her feelings entirely.

She swallowed, stared through the transparisteel into the belly of the clouds. Squinting, she could dimly make out Hesperion in the basket-cabin, wedging his back against the safety-rail, at least as scared as she was. Mind, Irona's

Eye was hovering just above his head, which couldn't have afforded him much satisfaction after their conversation last night.

The airship lurched again.

'Eastern Ocean, see?' Captain Hoojer told her.

Irona couldn't.

The captain must have noticed her puzzlement. She said in her throaty, mannish voice, 'I didn't actually mean you could see it, you know.'

'I take it that "you" was where you would have said "idiot"?' Irona asked, and the grizzled woman had the grace to redden.

'I meant we're out into the estuary now. The change in wind-speed and direction, didn't you notice it just now?'

'Oh, is that what it was?' Irona said drily.

'Well, we've started our descent so we're dropping into the thick of the squall. That's what all the bouncing's about.'

'You mean you know where we are?'

Captain Hoojer smiled, surprised. 'Of course I do. Have done all along. Must have made this trip fifty or sixty times by now. This isn't much in the way of weather, you know.'

Irona raised an eyebrow at her.

'No,' Captain Hoojer retorted. 'Although, you're not as prickly as some 'at comes out here. Exile, being scared of heights, that sort of thing.' She checked her computer. 'I'm going to wake Kris up. He has this thing about having to see where he's landing or he's not quite sure of his ground. You should be able to see the coast any minute now.'

And sure enough, within moments, a black shoulder of rock reared frighteningly close out of the mist. Irona could hardly stop herself backing away.

*

Without the computer guidance system, Irona thought it would have been impossible to find Eastcliff, let alone land the dirigible safely. For hundreds of kilometres, black basaltic crags leaped up from the Eastern Ocean. Some geological fault had originally sheared the whole cliff as if with a knife. Tidal rivers and the fierce waves crashing at its base had eaten out bays and inlets, but Irona could never tell one from the next. Especially when the weather closed in like this.

The dirigible sank into the dawnlight beneath the clouds. Irona always enjoyed the impression Eastcliff made on her. Though the sun had not yet touched the basalt range, a blade of brightness rimmed the far horizon. The engine room was still in the shadow of the planet's curve. When the dirigible turned in for landing it looked like they were flying into solid rock. *Things have changed since the last time I came here, though*, she realised. *Arias's plant-life is taking root.* For streamers of vegetation were hanging like banners to welcome her. Then biolights of blue and green, amber and violet bloomed in the blackness halfway up the cliff and the pearly smile of the hangar-entrance welcomed her home.

Home is where the heart is, she thought, and tried to sink into the illusion. She could never forget Arnikon – or Twiss. Irona wondered what she would say to Arias, or whether the illusion had faded now for him.

Too soon, then, for her mind to settle, the airship flew in beneath the lowering cavern-lip and into the alien biolight for which there was no need back home – home? – in Kifl.

Surging and eddying, her feelings preoccupied her through the loft and fall of docking manoeuvres: the tacking, the casting and securing of lines to the winches that would tether the hydrogen-filled balloon. Like an automaton she completed the few formalities, handed Hesperion – cursing and protesting his cruel sufferings – over to the fisherfolk.

Irona watched them swarm aboard, saw their gills turn ruddy in the air. Their sense of purpose struck ill with their youth; there was not a one who was older than fifteen, but they worked with a silent determination she could not compare to her Arnikon's playfulness.

A fishergirl from one of the earliest hatchings, but still not more than thirteen, tightened the final winch and walked towards the clear glass ramp that Kris lowered from the passenger deck. She must have been a head taller than Irona. An aroma of fish and spice formed an aura around the girl. Irona tried first not to stare, and then *not* to avoid staring, at the webbing that linked her fingers. Her skin was pink and covered with blue-black down, her clothing perfunctory. To Irona, brought up within the confines of Earth's modesty, it was hard even after all these years on Harith to look the all-but-naked girl in the face.

'You are the Irona one?' the girl said, her breath whistling softly through her gills at each syllable.

Irona nodded. Neither of them paid any attention to the shouting of Hesperion as two fishermen grasped his arms and led him away between balloons that held airplant seedlings.

'I thought so.' The girl nodded. 'I saw you last time you came. The Arias one is expecting you in a strange state of anxiety. I am Seriathnis. Please follow me.'

Seriathnis made no attempt to converse with Irona. Quite at ease she walked towards the looping ramp at the back of the docking cavern, oblivious to the Queen of Harith, who was trying not to notice the jouncing of the girl's unclothed breasts, or the play of her buttocks within the skin-tight shorts. Seriathnis's webbed feet slapped softly on the rock in front of Irona, who followed her without a word. The fishergirl's hair was the rich colour of the raven's wings that Irona had once seen in an ancient castle in Londover. There were even vestiges of it on her cheeks.

As they passed the lip of the pit, Irona noticed the folded mounds of seasilk that was the canopy of the *Thistle-down*. Several fisherfolk, like Seriathnis scarcely more than children, were welding the rents that the last storm had ripped. Unlike the youngsters of Kifl, these little ones were working in silence. They barely nodded as Seriathnis and the Queen of Harith walked by. The fisherfolk seemed equally oblivious to the stink of the fowlfeathers under their tethered nets in the pit, though the immature fowl-feathers were mewling.

Down the ramp – Irona noticed that its hard angles were softened with spidery plants now which gave off a musky scent – and through jet tunnels whose sparkling walls seemed to flow rather than to have been cut out of the bare rock. To Irona the half-remembered maze was bewildering: new passages seemed to have been cut, more ramps and nooks and chambers; more people. Grave fisherfolk who seemed not to need to smile. And everywhere, more colour. Where the reflected light of dawn fell there were fists of vegetation, succulents whose leaves were like sharpened fingers. Salt cross-draughts came from the end of every tunnel; they all seemed to end in a blaze of daylight where the cliff-face had been pierced and never resealed. Irona found it disorientating – especially when so much of the daylight was now green as it filtered through spiky webs of leaves.

For a moment she felt her knees buckle and thought it was the strangeness of being back on solid ground, but three fisherwomen ahead swayed in a misstep and she knew it was just an earth-tremor. After sixteen years on Harith she was used to those. But here, the whole weight of the cliffs was hung ready to fall in on her. Two pebbles bounced right to her feet but no-one else seemed to care.

Even though it was barely dawn, there were large numbers of the fisherfolk abroad as they came down nearer to sea-level. Their faces never changed expression as they greeted Seriathnis; to Irona they barely nodded. Though Irona had never courted the status that Kifl had afforded her, she missed it now it was gone. She began to feel as though she didn't exist. Even the few ordinary humans offered her scant courtesy. It was not that she wasn't there, more that she had no importance in their scheme of reckoning. An odd feeling, and not one that she liked.

Then, at the end of a branching passage that used to be a dead-end, Seriathnis stepped aside. 'The com-room. The Arias one is there. Please go in.' And with no word of farewell, the girl took her self-possession back down the tunnel.

For all the years Irona had known Arias, she couldn't help it. She was scared. Her heart fandangoed down to her stomach. When she touched the door-panel and it slid aside, it was all she could do to walk in. Creepers rippled on the walls and for a dizzy moment she thought the movement was another earthquake. She missed sharing a giggle at her fears with Thebula.

Arias was standing, equally awkward, behind the com-desk. His blue-grey eyes met hers only to slide away to where his hands fiddled with the keyboard. 'Irona?' he said, unnecessarily.

'Arias.'

Her eyes devoured him. No change in the six months since she had last seen him at Kifl: the same smooth dark hair, the same curve of moustache framing the lips that had kissed her with such tenderness the last time she had seen him alone. But who knew what had happened in the intervening months? There were enough ordinary humans, and more than enough fisherwomen devoted to their creator, to tempt anyone, let alone a man of such charisma and charm.

He stood, equally unmoving. The tentative smile died on Irona's mouth. 'How's Arnikon?' Arias asked dutifully.

'Well. Feeling his oats. Normal teenager.' Irona felt that she was beginning to babble. Mistress of the planet and still she had no control here. It was unnerving.

'And Twiss?'

'The same.'

'Then ...' Arias Tang essayed a gesture, not quite opening his arms to welcome her.

'Yes.' She nodded redundantly, as yet unsure if Arias were still her lover. The endless time of Harith opened its corridors before them. Eternity alone – or with islands of comfort?

She left it to Arias to break the frozen tableau. Slowly, hesitantly, he half-reached a hand towards her and didn't quite drop it. Was it his longing or her projected emotion? Irona couldn't trust her perceptions. She took half a step towards him.

'Are we still ...?' she whispered.

A glow appeared in Arias's face. A relief, a warmth, a welcome.

Though he had not really spoken, she read the message of his body, of his empathy, and she walked towards him while he opened his arms to embrace her. His hands crept round her shoulders, slid down to her waist and back as if checking that she was real and no fantasy.

Afraid, but full of suppressed desire, she lifted her face to his and he delicately pressed his closed lips to hers. He felt the sob start within her but, breast to breast, they felt the familiarity of their old love rekindle. It was the same. Reassured, they allowed their lips to part, their mouths to meet for real. Her body curved involuntarily towards his and suddenly he was kissing her with an urgency the stronger for its long denial.

Then he pulled her into him, and she could feel his yearning. It was no less than her own. Gradually their uncertainties faded away. His hand slid up to her nape; his fingers gloried in her hair even as his tongue possessed her in a kiss of such passion that each felt the other's ribs mould to the desire in their breathing.

It was a long, long kiss. They tasted, smelled each other, gathered reassurance from the touch of skin to skin. 'I thought . . . I was afraid . . .' she said at last, oblivious to the spartan surroundings of the Eastcliff com-room.

Irona felt his head move against hers in a silent negative; he immediately reinforced it with words. 'Never. It's you I want. Didn't I tell you that? Irona, come to me. I want you.'

Her breathing broken, Irona melted towards him. The smallness of his head beneath her fingers, the texture of his skin, the smell of him mixed with the strangeness of his soap, the way his fingers moved in circles to erase the muscular tensions in her back – Irona felt his presence as a healing. Her empathic sense pulled his acceptance – more, his longing – into her. It heightened her need.

'I've missed you,' he whispered.

'Oh, Arias, I've missed you. I've missed you so much.'

'You don't need to. Not now you don't. You're mine here, as long as you choose to be. Synod, you smell good. Just like I remember.'

'Arias, it's been – you know what it's been.'

He moved his head so that he could look down at her, and she was aware of his need. 'I know.' He nodded. 'I know. Day by day pretending to be someone you're not so that Harith runs OK. He's still your basic autocrat?'

Irona smiled faintly. 'Twiss? Of course. It's what he's best at.'

'He's hurt you again, hasn't he, my love? I can see it in your eyes. They look bruised. But he's kept Harith together?'

'More or less.'

'No, don't withdraw. Tell me what's happened.'

'They killed Thebula. My poor, poor friend. It was horrible. She died—'

'Who, the First Wave?' Arias said.

Fear trembled her limbs, put a quaver in her voice. 'More than that, my Arias. Arms.'

He went rigid. 'What, Arms? Real Arms like on Earth?'

Irona nodded.

'And you thought I'd made them.' It was a statement.

Irona swallowed. 'I had to ask you. You know there's no-one else who could make them, Arias. Not here on Harith. Forgive me for doubting you—'

'But you still did. You live with that self-centred son-of-a—. And you still thought it was me.'

'Who else could it be?'

'Anyone with access to the computer and enough hatred. You should know that. Just because I made the fisherfolk doesn't make me a monster.'

She hastened to reassure him. 'I know that.' *I don't, though, do I? Not really.* Contrition was a hot pain inside the hollowness of her bones.

'But you still thought it was me.'

'I didn't know who else ... I'm sorry, Arias. I should never have doubted you. I don't, not when I'm here with you. But when we're apart – I don't know what to think.'

Arias plunged his blue-grey regard into hers. All of a sudden he pulled her head against him so that her mouth was against the hot flesh of his neck. 'I know. When we're apart I think you're going to junk me because you love him.'

Irona pulled back. 'I do love him, you know, Arias. I'm sorry, but I do. Parts of him, anyway. Some of the time. Only it doesn't stop me loving you as well. I'd come to you if I could. But the point is, if he does need me to run the planet for him, what can I do? He's all that stops the First and Second Wave killing each other wholesale. I can't let thousands of people die because I want to be with you.'

Arias saw her pain and drew it into himself. 'I know, I know,' he soothed. 'My poor love, it hurts you so much, doesn't it, all this skulking about pretending? And my spies tell me he's got another one now, hasn't he?'

Irona blinked up at her lover. *Haven't I trusted you enough?* 'Your spies?'

It was Arias's turn to nod. 'Of course, my love. I'm sorry, but I have to have spies. Less is one of them.'

She sighed. 'I should have guessed. You spent six months conditioning him, didn't you?'

'Yes, for the good of all Harith, not just half of it. Anyway, Less is harmless. It's that Nona you have to watch. There's enough people against my fisherfolk, saying they're abominations, deves. You can't imagine how much it hurts to know you're there, all alone, while he's off gallivanting. Only you won't say the word, will you? You know I'd come to you if you'd let me. But for Harith—'

Feverishly Irona kissed him. 'Don't let's think of that. For Harith, yes, for the rest of eternity. But for the moment...'

Through that day Irona left her contact-bracelet off. Arias Tang ignored the calls that came on to his personal computer, drowning their silent reproaches with the richness of music. Instead he blanked out his mer-children and lay in his room with Irona in his arms. The sunlight grew and faded, and still the sound of the waves outside his chamber was a lullaby that caressed Arias and his only love. The masculine flavour of his ambience was uniquely comforting in her every breath. It carried droplets of his essence into her lungs, into every tiny wandering pathlet of her blood.

Irona lay with her head in the crook of his arm, his hand on the soft skin of her side or the softer skin of her breast. She stroked Arias's chest, revelled in its compactness, so different from the rounded exuberance of Twiss. Her lover's fingers teased her nipples, his lips bent to adore them, as the man and woman passed from reassurance to love to desire and back again. Guilt paled along with the reasons for it. Her taste, his smell, travelled from one to the other and cemented their love yet again. Past and present pain was blunted as they relearnt faith and trust, and they taught each other pleasure anew in the language of tongue and skin and hands. Whatever else they were, they were friends first and it was that they shared above all. Finally they subsumed each other in the ultimate expression of love and lay at peace in the sunset.

Arias's arm tightened around her. 'Are you all right?'

Drowsily she nodded, feeling security in the way his fingertips brushed her blonde-brown hair. 'Mmm. Fine. You?'

'You – you were so peaceful. Even that little frown of yours had gone. I couldn't feel you breathe. I thought—'

'What, love?'

'I thought you were dead.'

In answer she kissed him, smiled. 'Not me. How could I leave you?' She gestured with her chin. 'Seen that?'

Outside, in the moonrise, the waves of the Eastern Ocean were dashing against the arched window. The storm Irona had ridden to be with her lover had flown far out to sea, but echoes of it were still lifting the swell into balletic crests. Their peaks leaped and whirled, phosphorescent dancers scattering spindrifts of foam that were luminous against the sapphire troughs of the combers, the ebony Sentinel Rocks, the hyacinth and violet of the sky. Shining droplets shivered on the transparisteel, tracing the wind in outlines of beauty that echoed Arias's music. A moon-flower kissed the surface of the glass then sank again to the indigo tide to dip and curtsey in the cream-gold lacework of its companions. Familiar stars twinkled benignly through the transparisteel arch.

Irona felt his head move against hers as he nodded.

'It's one of the moments you live for, isn't it?' he said softly. 'You pay and pay for everything, but this is one of the moments you pay for. A moment that's worth the price.'

He turned into her, laid his knee protectively over her flank, and while one hand drew up the covers and pressed her in towards him, the other cupped her cheek, caressed her temple. His warmth melted the last of the ice inside her.

Then she cradled him too in the gentle music, and the low room sank into moonshadows that seemed to tremble with his breathing. Long after he slept, Irona kept herself open to sensation. Odours of chestnut and the warmth of humanity in his skin rivered their essence into her lungs. She watched the starlight wheel across his chairs, his table, his holos on the wall. She listened to the little sounds he made in his sleep, absorbed the textures of his skin on hers. A translucent peace filled her; she was too happy to sleep.

In the warm darkness came a new sound. Something tiny, metallic, scratching across the music.

Tic-tic-tac. Tic-tic-tac.

Arias never even stirred.

A pit of apprehension dropped open in Irona's stomach. She knew she had been too happy for this to be real. Now actuality bladed into the cocoon that surrounded her.

Tic-tic-tac. Tic-tic-tac.

The sound didn't go away.

At last Irona couldn't stand it any more. She eased out of the comfort of the bed, reluctant. Padded across the soft, deep carpets to the computer-console on the other side of the room, where she had laid her bracelet that morning so it would not intrude. Irona was glad that it didn't show visuals.

She keyed it, whispered, 'Yes?'

Twiss speared his rage at her. 'You killed him!' he roared, tinny with distance while soft arpeggios strummed out of place. 'You let him go to the volcano and now he's dead and it's all your fault. You've killed him!'

*

Irona glanced wildly at Arias, back to that aeon of peace they had shared in the bed by the window that arched on to the indigo womb of ocean. The moonflowers bowed mocking and Arias lurched to one elbow, drunken with sleep. Guilt laid her fingers to her lips in a crash of dread.

'Killed who?' the ashes of her voice said.

'Arnikon, you insensitive deve! I've been calling you for hours. Your Eye couldn't find you. Where the hell have you been?'

Irona broke inside. *While I've been feeding myself on Arias, my only son has—* 'Are you sure he's dead?' Parts of her groped to assemble the words. 'Was it an Arm?'

The bracelet transceiver hissed at her. 'No, you moron! He danced the volcano and the crust broke and dropped him through. I just said. Are you listening or what?'

'I'll be there tomorrow.'

'You just get yourself back here now!' Twiss yelled, and cut the transmission.

Light-years away, blind with unknowing, the Matriarch of Camelford and All Earth thought of her daughter Irona. Wondered why her girl had never used the ansible planted in the Synod Tower of Kifl. Wondered what Irona would do when she finally got the package the Matriarch of Camelford had sent her on board the last spaceship. Wondered if the *Starwing* captain was smart enough to deliver the unopened package straight into her daughter's eager hands.

For her daughter Irona would be eager, wouldn't she? The mind-blocks should have worn off by now, surely; the implants be working right on time. Soon her daughter would know truly and completely who – and what – she was. Irona would want to fly back to the mother of her body and mind.

For the urge to help was planted deep in Irona, rooting its

way through every crevice of her personality, sown by Bernardina, Matriarch of All Earth. That little hard pellet Bernardina had embedded behind her daughter's ear would be trickling its psychotropes to raft through Irona's mind. The urge to know, to discover herself, would be pushing aside the floors of Irona's being.

Bernardina was becoming desperate. The Crown, The Liga Mediterranea, that whorebitch Jímenez who'd seized control of the Three Americas right when her own infiltration of the Southern continent should have been completed.

Bernardina tried to slow her breathing. The time had come. War was inevitable. *Where the hell is Irona? I need all the help I can get.*

5
WAKING IN THE TOWER

Kifl. Dockers winched the airship down to the dusty landing-field after a journey Irona had scarcely been aware of.

As she stepped down the sunshot glass ridges of the gangplank, Twiss's rage pushed out at her: a fist, a gale, a hurricane in the hot air. 'It's your fault!' he yelled. 'You should have been here! You can't do nothing right!'

Irona's mouth dropped open – just for a second. Then she glared right back at him. Over their heads, their Eyes circled each other in mutual suspicion. Garwin, Twiss's fat bodyguard, stepped back embarrassed, and tried to pretend he was somewhere else.

'What about you?' she yelled. 'Where were you? You were the one who said you'd keep him safe! My only son!'

'Thank Synod he ain't my only son!' Suddenly, appalled at his revelation, Twiss covered his mouth with the back of one hand and turned away. Around him, Captain Hoojer and Kris the crewman feigned greater busy-ness, seeing to the unloading of seasilk bales. The shouting confused the grav-sleds; they ducked and barged into each other, almost squashing the fisherboy who had come to look after the trading.

Irona pulled the King back to face her. At least she had the discretion to keep her voice down. ‘Oh, don’t worry, Twiss. Did you think there was anyone on Harith who didn’t know about your little affairs? You’d screw anyone who wanted something from you. Jaimindi’s three sons that Sticker tries to believe are his? All your other by-blows? My best friend and yours, trying to pretend there’s nothing wrong every time they see us? What are you trying to do, form a one-man population crusade? But that won’t bring my Arnikon back, will it?’

The fisherboy shoved past them, breath hissing through his gills as he strained against the tether of an airnet that threatened to lift him from his feet. Faint mewling sounds came from the bunched-up fowlfeathers in the net; a Kiflian helped the blond-furred lad to lash the tether to an iron stake in the ground. The Kiflian was careful not to touch the fisherboy.

‘Oh, yes,’ the boy said, ‘you’ll take our crops but you can’t stomach us, can you?’

The Kiflian turned his back.

Blood stained the pallor of Twiss’s cheeks and his grief-sunk eyes were fever-bright. ‘Did – did Arnikon know?’

Irona was matter-of-fact though her eyes glittered with tears that might have been anger. ‘Oh yes. Jai’s kids told him long ago they were his brothers and sisters. It hurt him that you spent more time with them than you did with us. Sometimes he wanted to kill you.’

Twiss raked his hands through his unruly hair. The noise of the landing-ground seemed very far away. The sunshine, the faint fish-smell of the green kelp wrappings, the vast bulk of the balloon blocking out the hot spring sky, had no place in their talk. 'When did you find out?' he asked, very quietly now his reputation was at stake.

'I always knew, Twiss. All those nights you used to – to hold me and whisper that I was safe, that you'd – you'd got me and I was safe ... And' – she punched his arm, hard, wanting to pay him back just a little of the hurt he'd dealt her over the years – 'I was stupid enough to try and believe you. Did you think we didn't know, Arnikon and I, where you were when you left us and went to Jaimindi's bed? Poor Arnikon!'

Twiss's anger snapped back into place. It warped his features, seamed the skin around his eyes until they shrank in the suffused flesh. Out here, though, in plain sight, she knew he would never hit her however angry he became. Instead he used words as weapons. 'Yes, poor Arnikon with a mother like you! You never had time for him, did you? Always off being important, making decisions, making me feel small!'

She was astonished. 'You're jealous, Twiss! That's pathetic. You're the one that took control, the one they all followed. Not me, you! You have a planet to run but you can't be bothered. So what do you do? We're on the verge of civil war, First Wave against Second, with Arms from who knows where. Do you rise to face the challenge? No, you scuttle off to your latest bed and leave it to everyone else.'

'I beat the First Wave to make a home for us all in Kifl!'

'You mean half a lifetime ago you drowned half the First Wave so you could build your dream palace and wear your stupid kistle in a crown!'

'You hate the palace so much, don't live there!'

'Oh, believe me, Twiss, I don't intend to! Where were you when Arnikon needed you?'

'I took him hunting, didn't I?'

'Yes, when he was old enough to kill things, you showed him how. Is that what kingship's all about?'

'You tell me! You're the one who wears the pants!'

'And you're the one who made himself a crown. What have *you* done about the Arms?'

He sneered at her, his once-loved features ravaged by grief and guilt that found expression in hatred. 'The same as you. Nothing!'

She stepped closer, face thrust up to his. Raw with her bereavement, she didn't want to go on winning Twiss's love again and again, not even for the sake of the planet. All the hurts of the years rose up like bile inside her to jet out in a stream of acid truths. 'You're wrong there. I've started the search. If you do nothing, your rule's just empty. Worthless. You couldn't even keep Thebula safe, let alone anybody else. Go back to Tingalit, Twiss. Go and enjoy your cold, echoing, hollow glass palace. Fill it with tarts and sycophants, see if I care. Anybody with two brain cells to rub together knows you don't care about Harith any more. Half the time you can't even be bothered to come to Synod. You've chosen to be nothing but a figure-head with a political smile.'

Twiss's fingers dug into the muscles of her arm but she was safe here. She wrenched herself free. He yelled loud enough that everyone on the landing-field turned to stare, 'You're nothing without me, Irona. You're useless, and arrogant, and ugly. You're nothing without me. Just rancid dung. If I stepped on you, I'd scrape you off my shoe.'

She shrugged wearily. 'I've heard that one so many times before. I'm going to the tower.' One foot in front of the other, she began the long slog back to Kifl.

'Go, then!' Twiss shouted after her, his words as harsh

as the baking, sand-filled air. 'You're probably a lesbian anyway. You're not a proper woman. You can't even have proper kids any more.'

Turning, walking backwards, she said quietly, 'Only one big one now, who thinks this planet's always going to be his playground. Grow up, Twiss. We should be past hurting each other. See you in Synod tomorrow – if you bother to show up this time.'

Trudging along the road between the dusty olive-groves, Irona felt the sun pounding her into exhaustion. She hadn't been walking twenty minutes when the tractor glided to a halt beside her. Clusters of fowlfeathers strained upwards in their nets, mewling hideously.

Its talker called, 'Want a ride?'

She shook her head, waving it past because she needed time to rebuild herself. The sharp, avian stench of the fowlfeathers drifted over her with the dust as the cargo-machine trundled past on its way to the slaughterhouse.

Irona forced herself to think: *Who could be making the Arms?* but her mind wouldn't bend itself to that path. The image of her son floated at the forefront of her thoughts. *All the times I said to him 'Not now, love.' My mother abandoned me and my son thought I'd abandoned him. Was he right? Is Twiss right? Am I so worthless? Is this what I deserve?*

Fighting against self-annihilation and a longing to smash Twiss to a pulp in her rage, Irona made herself pour her fury into her stride so that soon her seasilk blouse was darkened with sweat and her skirts clung damply to her legs.

Yet Twiss's magnetism, and good looks, and ready smile, had performed miracles in winning over hundreds of the First Wave – yes, and the Second Wave too, who'd looked on it as a symbol of victory. When he wanted to, Twiss could charm the locust-lizards out of the trees; would have to again, if this stupid sectarian violence was to be quashed.

Who could be making the Arms?

But somehow, today, that question was only a thundercloud over the Moon Mountains. The loss of Arnikon was a volcano.

She knew she must have had a face like thunder because when she strode through the roofed-over alleys of Kifl, nobody spoke to her. She was glad when she got to the old Synod tower because there, in privacy at last, she could weep.

Later, Irona crossed the dusty floor to lean on the balustrade. Inhaling the musty smell and the memories of old perfumes, she pushed aside a thicket of airplants and stared out at Tingalit's turrets. How they glittered in the hard-edged sunlight! How hard she'd worked, and Regen, and Arias Tang, to reconcile the First Wave to that statement of power when so many people didn't even have homes.

That day Irona exhausted her grief in old-fashioned scrubbing. Once she'd switched off the grav-shaft so no-one else could get up here, she swept the curtains of airplants out through the window and polished every centimetre of the old Synod room. It gave her a faint, old-fashioned satisfaction that was one grain of sand in her ocean of sorrow. Then, not looking yet at the computer console halfway along the vast oval table, she switched on the grav-shaft again and went down a floor to the rooms she'd shared with Twiss when they first took over in Kifl.

Thoughts of that time came back to her; thoughts of that love. The red curtains fluttered in the hot spring breeze; suddenly savage, she ripped the ancient open weave into shreds and tried not to feel the pain that fuelled her anger. Salvaging the spare bed, she rode it back up the metal-scented air and wrestled it through the doorway.

Regen was there.

'Synod, you made me jump!' Irona gasped.

'Sorry, Ro.' He went to say something, changed his mind, and went on, 'Here, let me give you a hand with that. Where do you want it?'

'Beside that pillar there, opposite the window. I want to be able to see Heralia.'

For a moment Regen didn't know what to say. He helped Irona slide the bed-box into position perhaps a third of the way around the circular room so that the marble table with the console screened it from the door. By the time she had finished, she was perspiring again in the spring heat. Puffing, she sank on to the fibrous plastic of the mattress and gazed out at the white cone of the volcano. In the heat-haze it seemed to float serenely over the green-blue forests of the foothills. She leaned her back against the wall and stared at the purity of the snow against the soft sky that was the same colour as a matriarch's robes.

She could see Regen was worried about her grasp on reality when he said, 'It won't bring him back, Ro.'

Irona half-smiled, shook her head. 'He hasn't gone away. His atoms are in the wind, in the soil, on everything he ever came into contact with or wore. Each breath I take, there's air he's breathed before. It's just that I – I can't touch him any more.' Slow tears began leaking from her ravaged face.

Awkwardly Regenerator came to sit beside her on the

bed and put his arm out to encircle her. He hesitated, made the gesture at last, and she dissolved against his ungainly body, feeling ill and tired. Slowly the tension unravelled inside her as Harith's sunlight swung across the room. Watchful as a mother, her Eye hung discreetly over them. Regen's round, knobby head fell against hers and like lost children, they slept.

In the early hours Irona opened her eyes. One small moon arced, a silver streak against the dark vault of the sky. For an instant she was relaxed then the weight of grief crashed back over her, a tsunami.

Regen felt her stir. He moved, letting the circulation come back to his stiff arm. The thick smell of his body was strange to her, but not unpleasant. Coming more to consciousness, Irona pulled away a little and Regen misunderstood. He was hurt. 'I was scared about you, Ro. I heard about your row with Twiss. That ain't like you. Not when—' He stopped, awkwardly.

Irona patted his arm. 'Not when we're both old enough to know it's frustration at Arnikon's death, is that what you were going to say?'

He nodded.

'But I do want to smash something.' Irona's fingers were closing into fists. She forced them down into her lap but they writhed like snake-rat larvae. 'I know it's stupid, but I want to rend and tear and bite. Sorry. I'll be OK.'

'I thought—'

'What?'

'I was scared you might go back up to Thought Pool Hollow. Or . . .' He gestured at the high window where the Eye gleamed watchfully over the stone balustrade.

She shook her head. 'Arnikon wouldn't want that. And

somebody's got to take care of Harith, at least until this Arms mess is sorted out. Trouble is, I don't think this kingship thing is working too well any more.' She slid to her feet and padded across to the window to look out at the sleeping city. Minarets and curving roofs showed only the odd light here and there; Irona wondered if it were some mother sitting up fretting about her child's illness, her husband's accident. Back on Earth there were thousands of people sharing the isolation of bereavement, but here? No, not on Harith. Not with immortality all around. There were only the victims of sectarian violence who had their hatred to keep them warm – and the crazy youths who danced their bravado in the crater thinking 'It can't happen to me' – until, like Arno, they plunged through the brazen crust of the volcano. With a shuddering intake of breath she asked, 'Have you found out who's making the Arms?'

Regen shook his head, his skinny forearms resting on the stone of the balustrade beside hers. 'Ain't for want of tryin', though. Me and some of the Guard, we been through they lab-rooms with a fine-tooth comb. And that Hospital. Entirely. You had time to come up with somethin' from they computers, Ro?'

She sighed, looked back at the unwakened console behind her. 'Not yet. But I will. I'm going to get this beauty fired up again today before Synod. If we've got spies' – she suppressed the thought of Arias – 'they'll have cocked up the one in Tingalit, not this old thing. Some time soon you and I will pay a visit to Eastcliff.'

Regen's brown eyes cocked towards her.

'No, not for that. At the moment I couldn't even face Arias. Regen, I feel so guilty! If I hadn't spent so long with him—'

'Arno would still have danced on the volcano.'

She smiled her gratitude. 'Thanks, Regen. But I never had a chance to check out Eastcliff. The place is about twenty times bigger than it is on the plans they registered. Besides, those merfolk of his are weird. They don't think the same way we do. There's enough dissidents exiled there who've got the motive to grow a whole corps of Arms. Maybe they've stolen the technology from Arias. Synod take it, we've got a whole planet to search. The Arms factory could be anywhere!'

A clang, a whispered curse, echoed up the grav-shaft.

Irona started, whirled round. *How many days ago was it one of my best friends was murdered?* 'What the hell's that?'

'Your new guard, I reckon,' Regen said, sticking his head out over the grav-shaft. The upward wind tugged at his thinning brown hair. He nodded to himself several times. 'Malambé and Declan. They both volunteered.'

'They were friends of Arnikon's, weren't they? Non-identical twins?'

Regen nodded. 'You used to play with them in the Rose Wing on rainy days. Remember?'

She nodded. 'And you did. Remember that pillow-fight?'

'And the spring-band battle. Hee-hee. Me and Arno won that.'

Irona was indignant. 'No you didn't! Declan and I did. You waved the white flag.'

'Only so me and Arno and Malambé could come out of hiding and get some more spring-bands. Besides, you never accepted our surrender.'

They were both chuckling now though Irona's eyes were watery. Regen, as full of tics and twitches as ever, took her hands in his. 'I got to go now, love. Some of they guards is due to report back on the old gang – you know, all they First Wavers who was pally with Red Lal and Less and Gundmila and them. But you'll be OK, Ro. You'll make it. Entirely. You got so many friends, people who love you, we won't let you down.'

It was still early, the red rim of the sun barely grazing the crests of the Moon Mountains when Regen left. Scattered lights on the foothills showed where a handful of farmers were already abroad but the tractors were still asleep. Heralia's snow-cap was rose beneath a lavender sky; Irona pulled herself away from the thought that it was her son's blood which stained it. Though there was a lot to do, she stole a moment to peer downwards into the patterned gravel gardens beneath the tower.

Few of the houses showed lights as yet, though the windows were beginning to reflect the shine that meant the coming of the day. Between the buildings that huddled their curves together as if they were gossiping, citrus and pomegranate trees were spilling their perfumed blossom. The odd fishing-trawler was coming in to the stone jetty by the black sands and there were a handful of people shivering while they waited on the quayside to unload the catch and open the market. The dawn wind was still from the sea. It brought a fragrance of aerial flowers, the astringent aroma of drying nets from the half-built harbour. Kifl: her town. She had nurtured it, mothered it, set the feet of its childlike citizens in the ways of peace. Now someone had made Arms to destroy it.

'You can't fool me,' she muttered to the unseen enemy. 'I know you're out there somewhere but I'll find you. No-one else I care about is going to die.'

Then, as soon as she had washed and changed, she

called down the grav-shaft, 'Malambé? Declan? Come on up.'

Echoes of whispers floated to her, stitched with the songs of lizard-locusts past their destructive phase. In moments the two red-headed boys stepped out of the shaft, teetering a little, uncertain with the doubts of seventeen. Irona's dented confidence made her wonder if they saw her as old and ugly like Twiss had said, but she refused to follow that line of thinking.

'Come on in!' she called, and hugged them as she had when they were little. 'Thanks for coming. Let's have some breakfast,' she said, turning away to the bag of supplies Regen had left her. 'We've got a busy day.'

After their picnic breakfast, the boys were resigned to cleaning up downstairs – because Irona had asked them which girls they'd like to help them. She pretended not to notice their blushes as they jumped hastily out into the grav-shaft. Their naïveté heartened her and she flexed her fingers above the console.

It must have been sixteen years since this computer had ruled the whole of Harith. Twiss had had Tingalit finished while she was recovering from Arnikon's birth – the thought razored at her so she snapped it off short – and she had scarcely been back since. Sticker, Jai and Tebrina had helped Twiss move all her personal stuff from the tower to the sterile splendour of the Rose Wing of Tingalit. Now she was back where she started.

The power-lines put in by the first Matriarch of Kifl were still functioning. *Of course they are, you moron*, she told herself, *otherwise the grav-shaft wouldn't be working, would it? Get a grip.*

Even with such an easy task as calling two girls, Irona

found she could barely concentrate. As soon as she keyed in her personal password, an irritating, barely-audible hum started up. She was aware that she kept doing things wrong but it was hard to forget that her son had incandesced through flames and red-hot bones to white-hot vapour. She wondered vaguely how his companions, Fessbar and Carnell, felt today.

The girls Declan and Marambé had asked her to call were happy to come, though less happy at having to order around the old-fashioned cleaning machines that Irona had been so thrilled to find when she had first moved here. Still, they were both, especially the one – what was her name again? – who should have been in school, glad to feel the shy admiration of the boys.

Well, I've got one thing right at least, Irona told herself, and plugged into the newsnet to find out what else had gone wrong while she was away. It took a little time to re-route the more modern parts of the program over here from the newer central computer in Tingalit but she got there in the end.

More or less.

The hum was still there. She couldn't track it down. It began to grate on her nerves.

I should have asked Regen when he was coming back. He could have fixed this. Or if he's coming back. No, I'm being paranoid. He'll be in Synod.

The hum went on.

Irona clicked her tongue with annoyance. The day was already heating up; the computer-screen confirmed that it was later than she had supposed. It would be time for Synod soon and after yesterday's scene with Twiss she dared not miss it. She abandoned the newsnet and began a sweep with the psychicator but there were only the magenta flares of domestic quarrels and squabbles between neighbours. *All the good conspirators seem to have their heads down*, she told herself, and began a hasty round of chats with the people she needed.

The hum wouldn't go away.

A systems malfunction check showed there was – apparently – nothing wrong. She got rid of the irritation by turning the volume down but whenever she needed sound to make a call in her campaign, the buzz was still pulsing. *What the hell. That's a problem for another day*, she thought. *At least I've got everybody coming to Synod who's supposed to.* Though there was a serpent of tension coiling in her stomach that was the worry of whether Twiss would show up – and if so, would he still be aggressive. *And will I?* she thought, though such fairness was uncomfortable.

Rapidly programming her Eye to make a sweep of the shanty-towns growing up in the foothills, she realised there was no more time. She had to go now if she was not to arrive late, and she wouldn't give Twiss that satisfaction. She pushed her chair back – it skated easily on the polished marble of the floor – and stood.

. . . Abruptly she was not in the Synod Tower. Irona swayed dizzily. Her whole body felt wrong, her internal organs disarrayed. Liver and stomach seemed to rise and bile flooded her mouth. She had no idea where she was, only that she was somehow lost. The scar across an old grief was tearing; she blanked it out. She didn't want to see the wounds bleeding underneath.

No light came to her eyes, but she could feel other people around her, distantly. So many of them, so many thoughts and loves and hates shoving in at her. They were above and below and all around her, but not near. Not there for her.

She was alone. The room she was in should have been safe but it was echoingly, frighteningly empty. She was alone. A nebulous thought-shape formed of the one who should have been there for her but it fled mockingly through the crevices of her brain.

Irona tried to call out, 'Come back! Don't leave me!' but the words clogged in the blackness of her throat and even the memory of that one person played a cruel game of hide and seek, never meaning to come back. She was alone in that empty room. All those people who cared about each other but she was utterly alone . . .

She couldn't stand it. Even when she clamped her eyelids shut and covered her ears with the palms of her hands the presence of the people was an inescapable weight. Thousands upon thousands of them . . .

And there was a noise. A hum. She swatted at it with both hands but it wouldn't go away. Irona knew it but she couldn't pin it down. It was the sound of . . . the sound of . . .

Declan came in whistling. Abruptly he was at her side, his thin young arm around her shoulders. Oddly, she was scared of his embarrassment but she couldn't help it. She sagged against him, afraid her thundering heartbeat would shake his body too but not able to stand alone. The gravity felt wrong.

'Irona! Irona! Are you all right?'

She shook her head to clear it but he misinterpreted and pushed the chair against the back of her knees so that she fell more than sat. Her limbs were pendulous, disarticulated. When her eyes opened, light flooded into them and the Synod tower was real around her.

'What happened?' Declan asked, and his voice was high-pitched with anxiety.

'I – I don't know. My head's spinning! Could you get me some water?' It was only when he strode across to the pitcher on a side-table that she remembered to say please.

The cold liquid rivering down into her stomach helped anchor her in reality. All too soon, though, she would have to make her way to Tingalit though the thought of the Synod and Twiss made her quail. For a moment she thought of pleading the sickness involved in her bereavement but she wouldn't stoop to it.

All the same she let Declan call a transport for her. And thus she rode to carry war to her unseen enemies.

6
THE ONE AMERICA

Pilar Jímenez Costanza hated her teacher.

She tore it out of her ear and threw it down on the mud of their floor. Back then she was only nine, but her hatred was real. Only her teacher didn't know about it. It still muttered at her that the Three Americas were only puppets of the Matriarchy. They were nothing. Her home was nothing. Her country was nothing, and like South America it would soon be eaten up by the spiders of the Matriarch.

White-faced with anger, she stamped on the teacher-clip but still it whispered its lies. The mud stuck it to her bare heel and she couldn't shake it off and its words bubbled through the liquid mud. Her big brother Lorenzo laughed so much he nearly fell off their bed. Pascual, their oldest brother, felt the bouncing. He turned over and yelled with thick rage, 'Can't a man get any sleep round here? Clear out and do something useful or I'll feed you to the farmers.' An empty mescal bottle rolled off the bed as he squirmed further under the covers.

That threat was nothing much but Pilar and Lorenzo had enough bruises by now to know not to disturb Pascual if he didn't want to be disturbed. Shaking the teacher-clip off with as much dignity as a muddy nine-year-old could muster, Pilar flounced out of the room and into the rain. Lorenzo stayed a moment to show that he wasn't scared of Pascual, then he snatched up the clip and he too fled into the shadowy courtyard with the metal and plastic held carefully in his fingers.

A system of cracked mirrors shed some light on to the plaza, but not much. Overhead, the Fields of Mexico City stole all the sunlight. If you were rich you could live on the surface, or in one of the tower-blocks if you weren't as rich as all that. The poorest of the poor lived down in the sewers. Pilar was proud that she didn't live down there with the rats and the alligators and the drug-runners and the pimps, but even so, she wished the Fields didn't ooze mud continuously from above. Whenever she thought of home, it had the smell of mud and fried chillies.

'I'm going to sell this,' Lorenzo said, prudently stopping outside the corrugated plastic boards that made a part of the courtyard almost their own patio.

Pilar eyed the distance between them. It didn't matter that Lorenzo was ten and bigger than she was. Physically he was out of range, which meant she would never get the teacher back, but verbally?

'You give that back, you dirty, rotten thief!' she shouted. 'I got it! It's mine!'

Neighbours, grouped around power-packs or sitting at traditional craftwork in the pools of reflected sunlight Under-Mexico-Fields, stopped to listen through the soft patter of falling mud.

'I'm not a thief!' Lorenzo yelled back unconvincingly. When you had nothing else, reputation was everything.

'Give it back, Lorenzo!' Pilar shrilled, playing to her

audience. It was the only way she'd get what she wanted. 'You robbed me. It's mine.'

'Yeah, you stole it.'

'I did not!' Pilar's indignation made her cheeks flame. 'I said I'd give it back.' She was beginning to enjoy her own version of the facts now. 'I promised.'

'Well more fool them for believing you.' Lorenzo taunted her, keeping just too far away on his skinny, scab-kneed legs. 'I'll split the money with you, thirty-seventy.'

'Fifty-fifty,' she said automatically,

Lorenzo skipped backwards out of reach, catching the Blind Man's tray with his elbow so that all the little wind-up toys jumped at once. Some of them fell off the tray and other children ran past, snatching them up and mocking the vendor from the other side of the plaza.

The Blind Man smacked Lorenzo accurately on the head but all he did was shuffle further out of reach as his sister pursued him.

'You just turned down seventy per cent, saphead,' Lorenzo called to his sister, and shouldered past Álvaro and Tequila, scattering the grasses they were weaving into baskets. She knew her brother well enough to be depressingly sure he wouldn't come back until he'd sold the teacher and spent all the money. Not that she could blame him. If he came back with half a peso, even, Pascual would steal it from him.

Pilar's first instinct was to help Álvaro and Tequila put the scatter of coloured grasses back into their holders, but with the two men shrieking at her, it was better to wait at a discreet distance until they drew breath.

'You know it wasn't my fault!' she shouted at them, sheltering half behind the Blind Man. She was half afraid of him, but then, so were Álvaro and Tequila, so she was safe. Pilar yelled, 'So you can call me what you like. Who'd listen to a pair of hysterical poxed-up failed maricones like you? No wonder you can't turn a trick with your ragged arses leaking shit.'

Álvaro, kneeling amongst the reds and greens and blues of his wares, threw his handful of grasses down into the mud and burst into tears. Tequila bent his grey head over his lover's, patting and comforting. He glared at the skinny little girl, though, and said furiously, 'Now look what you've done!'

Pilar lifted her chin as haughtily as anything she'd ever seen in the soap-operas she watched through shop windows because Under-Mexico-Fields only the gangsters had holodisk projectors of their own. She did not deign to reply. Instead, she began to walk regally away, not to home but to safety where there were no Lorenzos and no Pascuals to torment a girl. But the Blind Man shot out a claw-like hand and snagged her long black hair.

She was frightened. She wriggled and kicked but he held her far enough away for safety and said, 'You shouldn't have done that. Álvaro and Tequila, they are not a fair target.'

Pilar's straight eyebrows arced in surprise. She looked up at him, and it was a long way up because she was short even for a child her age and he was the remains of a big man. 'And I am? You saw, I did nothing to them. It was Lorenzo, stealing from me,' she said indignantly.

'But if the vicious always pick on the weaker, will that change the way things are?'

Pilar stopped struggling.

'Ha! The idea's caught you.' The Blind Man slipped his fingers behind his cheap sunglasses and rubbed his empty eye-sockets, a gesture he made a thousand times a day. His other hand relaxed his grip on her hair. 'Make me a cup of herb tea, Pilarita.'

She was about to tell him she couldn't when he said, 'Here's my kettle,' and produced the powered pot from the bundle of battered belongings strung all around his waist and shoulders. 'Take it and get some clean water.'

'Where's your filter?' she asked, stuttering in surprise that he should voluntarily hand to her something that she might steal. Trust was not something she was used to.

But he didn't change his mind. He reached again into the clanking mass under his coat. 'Here. Don't use the first public fountain today.'

Pilar was longing to ask him how he knew it was that one which had the cholera, and how he could see when he hadn't any eyes, and why his hands were so young and strong when his face was covered in lines, but she clutched the powerpot to her skinny chest so it wouldn't be stolen and ran to a different pipe. Always she carried a little boring tool and used it to take water she thought might be pure from a pipe that didn't feed the nearest public fountain. Leaving the sparkling water gushing from the hole, she went back to the patio, carrying the water in the pot with all the concentration of a nine-year-old girl who didn't want to spill it.

At first she couldn't see the Blind Man, and she felt guilty with his filter and his powerpot, as if she had stolen them. Then she spotted the black rags of his sleeve flapping as he waved to her from beside La Mariucha's laundry. She went and squatted on her heels beside him. She was proud, in a way, to be talking to a man who actually had shoes on his feet.

'What do you mean,' she said, when she had the kettle heating, 'that things might change?'

He smiled at her. 'Did I say they could?'

Head on one side, eyes as bright as a blackbird's, Pilar considered. That had always been one of her talents, that she could remember conversations and nuances and always knew what meanings might be lurking behind the fence of words. It was what Pascual and Lorenzo hated about her. Mentally she replayed what the Blind Man had said, hearing but not hearing La Mariucha's meaty arms thumping down her iron on the white shirts and trousers of the almost rich.

'Yes,' Pilar said, nodding vigorously, so that her straight fringe flopped up and down over her eyes and the high bridge of her nose. 'Yes, you did.'

'Then shred the herbs and tell me what else I said.'

Taking the wilting plants he kept in a pouch in his shirt pocket, she began tearing the leaves and the stalks, liking the pungent smell that rose from the sap on her fingers. 'You said that things might change. But not if you pick on the people you can pick on.'

'That's right.' His smile was a white brightness in the maze of lines on his cheeks.

'But what does it mean? Who else can you pick on? You can't go against the gangs.'

'And are they the strongest?'

Again she thought, pouring the water into a tin cup he held out to her. The infusion began to smell appetising. 'They're the strongest Under-Mexico-Fields.'

'And who is more powerful than them?'

'The rich. The ones on the surface who have guards and killing fences to keep us out of the sunlight.'

'And who is more powerful than them?'

'The police.'

'No, my little one,' the Blind Man said. 'The ones on the surface own the police.'

'The army, then?'

'Who owns the army?'

'The President of All Mexico. And above him, only God.'

The Blind Man blew over his drink to cool it. He smiled at her exact copy of the message they broadcast every hour on every radio station and holodisk network. She gave it the same weight, the same inflection, and if her voice was too shrill, she nevertheless cupped her fingers about her mouth to duplicate the echo chamber of the broadcast so that she sounded like a cherub giving the message instead of the Archangel Gabriel.

'Do they speak the truth?' the Blind Man asked her as if he really wanted to know what she thought. 'Does the President do what he says?'

Pilar watched him drink, heard him say, 'Thank you, Pilarita,' but her mind was trying to track down the clues from the labyrinth of his questions.

'No,' she said finally, stunned. 'He doesn't keep his promises. He says there will be water free from cholera, and food and education for everybody, and nice houses with gardens in the sunlight where we can all live, but he can't do it, can he?'

'You're right, Pilarita. Good girl. But why doesn't he?'

She didn't answer. Instead, her voice trembling a little, she asked, 'Doesn't God exist either?'

The Blind Man held out the rest of his tea. When she didn't take it he gently put the tin mug into her hands and curled her fingers around it. 'Only God knows if He exists or not.'

She drank uncertainly, her eyes wide with the shaking of the foundations of her world. The Blind Man watched her with compassion, seeing the aftershocks of the earthquake that had happened to her securities. After a time she said, 'So if the President can't give us houses and food and good water and schools, who's stopping him?'

'All of us, my dear, because we let him get away with it. Like our brothers and sisters down in the South who let the Matriarch get too firm a stranglehold. In the end, people get the government they deserve.

'All together we are more strong than the President. If they worked together, the Presidents of the two free Americas would be stronger, but they are too scared of each other. But if someone could take the Matriarchy, and the Liga Mediterranea and Oceana and Saharistan and Novaya Zemla and all of them and put them all together to build a truly civilised World Council, they are still only a few people. If we act together, we are still stronger than them.'

She laughed, the sound sharp and high through her thin-bridged Mayan nose. It was the disdainful laugh that made Lorenzo inflict his little tortures out of revenge. 'If we are so strong, Blind Man, why do they live in big houses in the sunlight and we live in mud down here?'

'Because we don't know we are strong.'

She drank the tea down to the bottom, until the leaves started to stick to her tongue as if they would gag her. Then she handed the mug back. Only when she had carefully stood back a couple of paces to put safety between her and the young-old man who saw with no eyes, did she say, 'I think they should call you Mad Man, not Blind Man. We are nothing. We are shit and when the rich people step on us they scrape us off the soles of their pretty, polished shoes. And the Presidents and the Matriarchs and the Crowns, they scrape the rich people off their shoes. We can change nothing. Nothing of nothing.'

The Blind Man smiled at her. It was infuriating. He said, 'Goodbye, Pilarita. Say goodbye to the most powerful man on Earth.' He knew she wouldn't ask what he meant because for her that would have been to lose face. He said anyway, 'Because, my Pilarita, I have just changed the world.'

Half-scared now, because he wasn't just a blind man who could see, he was also crazy, Pilar Jímenez Costanza said nothing as, childlike, she darted away.

But the idea of all the people together didn't let go of her head.

All that was years before. Before Arnikon was an embryo, even; before the Second Wave colonists made landfall on Harith.

Across the Atlantic Ocean, Matriarch Bernardina said to Elditch, who should not have been her husband, 'Don't be such a wimp, man!'

She took a calming breath, inhaling the scent of the roses that grew in ranks around the open windows. Somewhere a numbered lark sang its heart out below the transparisteel Sky. 'You shouldn't give in to your paranoia, Elditch. It makes you look foolish. It gives them the perfect weapon against you and I'm not going to dive in to save your hide.'

Elditch did know it, and the knowledge made him bitter. All the same he tried to plead with his wife. 'But—'

'But nothing! Worst-case scenario: what if they do find out? I'm on the World Council now. I'm as near to owning it as you can get. This' – she swept a gesture round her eyrie baking in the sunlight at the top of Camelford Tor – 'this is just a spring-board. Carandis – and that means the Admin – can't do anything to us any more. Do you think she'd dare to admit she's been wrong about us? That the ruler of the Synod and the former Matriarch of the Admin have actually had a treasonable liaison since before she was born? That our loyalties might therefore be questionable yet she's never tried to stop us? Can you honestly see Carandis admitting she'd been that stupid? So short-sighted she's as good as committed treason herself? She hasn't been confirmed in office yet.'

'But when she is?' Elditch asked, nervously rocking back and forth on his heels. He still didn't see it.

Bernardina's papery skin creased into the folds of her origami smile. The bright June sun was unkind to her. 'When she is, if she tells anyone else we are husband and wife and were through all our years on Synod, she'll be admitting that she was blind to treason, and who's going to do that? No, if anyone finds out they'll think that she knew and condoned it, and goodbye Matriarch Carandis. Why else do you think I've left you as Chairman of the Admin? You can tell Synod that she's broken under the pressure of Seniority and have someone suggest that she's sent to rot on some nice little backwater planet.'

'Like you did with Irona, you mean?' Elditch said. He rose up on the balls of his feet, his dark eyes snapping with malice.

'Who ordered her sent?' Bernardina asked blandly.

'You did!'

The old woman in the blue silk robe smiled. Her lips were purple with age and her grey eyebrows seemed to have been frayed by the years, but her smile was still a deadly thing. 'I think you'll find, my love' – she called him that because it frightened him even now to think their secret might be discovered – 'I think you'll find that it was you who signed the psych-profiles. And even if Carandis searched the records she'd never discover in a million years that the Irona who was sent to Harith was our child. That she survived our exile in the Warrens. They didn't find out when we officially split so we'd be accepted back into the Watch, did they? And believe me, Towy—'

'The Matriarch you killed, you mean.'

Bernardina wasn't phased. She massaged her reddened, arthritic knuckles and said, 'Yes, that one. You haven't forgotten your part in that, I trust?'

Elditch said nothing. Somehow, though, the spring seemed to have gone out of his legs. Instead of bouncing up and down on his toes he slumped on to a cushion on the broad windowseat.

'No,' Bernardina said. 'I didn't think you had. But Towy tried to rake up anything about us before she'd let us back, didn't she? She'd have been a fool not to. We got rid of Gundmila—'

'You mean you left her to sharpen her claws on Irona!'

'Or vice-versa,' Bernardina said complacently. 'But I'm sure Irona must have won. Gundmila would have had her hands on the ansible long ago if she was still around.'

'How you could do that to your own child, risk her life, twist her mind . . .'

'The same way you could, Elditch, dear heart. Because we need her to win.'

'Win what? A raffle?'

Bernardina suddenly shot out her hand to slap him but arthritis had slowed her despite all the treatments a woman could take. Elditch scarcely ducked back but it was enough to make the Leader of the World Council miss. For just a second the Matriarch of All Earth looked foolish.

Elditch chuckled, enjoying the novel sensation of oneupmanship. Bernardina didn't allow him to relish his triumph, though. Enunciating very clearly as if speaking to a backward child, 'No, you moron. Now I'm playing for the first of the Three Americas, remember?'

He shook his head. 'The President of the South Continent won't let you win.'

It shook Bernardina that he had guessed her first target, but she wasn't going to let him see that. She said calmly, 'Want to bet?'

'And if he doesn't stop you, the Crown of Novaya Zemla will, long before you get Central and North America. Did you know, they call them the Free Americas now?'

Bernardina smiled her thin, acid smile again and crushed a fallen rose-petal between her fingers. 'Which is why I've kept my ace in the black hole, dear. All three of the Americas will be mine before the Crown knows what's hit him.'

Suddenly, Under-Mexico-Fields, Pascual had money. He had shoes, shiny narrow-toed patent ones that blistered his splayed feet. He had new clothes, and a black-market holodisk machine that he brought giggling women back to watch.

Lorenzo and Pilar weren't allowed to see it after the first night Pascual brought it home. Soured and surly the following noon, Pascual pushed the two giggling women out and they weren't laughing any more. He held himself up in the doorway to the inner room that smelt of sex and stale alcohol. Then he threw a handful of plastic coins on to the mud of the communal room and said, 'Get yourselves a mattress. No-one but me goes in here now, *comprendéis*?' as he stapled a huge, solid-state padlock on the door.

The children knew that when Pascual was mean from the night before, he might do anything; they had seen the bruises on the giggling girls' arms. They understood. Suddenly he had possessions. Suddenly he had something to steal. Even his family were a threat.

But when Pascual went out that night, locking his door behind him, Lorenzo borrowed La Mariucha's ice-pack and slid it expectantly round the lock.

'How long does it take?' Pilar whispered, glancing out of the door as if at any minute Pascual might come back, though when he had money he never came back until late. Under-Mexico-Fields had no real sunlight so it had no real day or night.

'Half an hour's icing should blank the memory, then we can put in any code we want.'

'He'll know!' Pilar said, twisting her legs together in an agony of nervousness.

'He was still drunk when he went out. He'll think he's forgotten the code.'

'Hurry up then.'

'Don't be such a chicken-shit.' Then Lorenzo showed his own nervousness. 'I've put the power on full anyway. It's cold enough to freeze Satan's balls off.'

But half an hour passed, and then an hour, and then La Mariucha wanted her freezer-pack, and it still hadn't worked.

For a while Pascual brought back more things, new and shiny. A stove. A food-safe. A watch that told the time in Central America and The Admin Territories, Novaya Zemla and Oceana, and let you know when it was going to rain in the countries that had the solid Sky, but it only worked for two days and Pascual cursed and flung it out of the door before Lorenzo could sell it to a chump.

Pilar and Lorenzo learned to cook by dodging the dishes Pascual flung at them if they didn't get it right. They ate what he wanted, tortilla and refried beans, maize and chillies with fat pork in lime juice. Lorenzo grew tall, but Pilar didn't. She grew solid, as if her body didn't want to waste a single morsel. Nachos and guacamole – they slid on to her backside. Fried blood-sausage exploded on to her legs. Pascual started to call her Cochina, meaning dirty, greedy pig, so Lorenzo had to copy him, of course.

Finally, when even the neighbours were saying what a disgrace Pilar looked bursting out of her tunic and her too-tight trousers, Pascual stamped in from the courtyard one noontide and brought her new clothes – or at least, not old ones.

For a moment Pilar looked at the things, all clean and white and pure and beautiful. Not a rip, not a patch of mud. She couldn't believe how beautiful they were. He'd even brought her a pair of white leggings. He held them out to her and there was a sort of desperate, manic gaiety on his face that frightened Pilar without her knowing why. 'Here, Cochinita,' he said, 'see what your big brother's brought you?'

Slowly she took the bright whitenesses that looked like they came from soap-opera land where the rich girls looked like they'd stepped out of a beauty parlour all the time, even when they'd just woken up or had a fight. Under everything she felt that maybe these clothes would do the same for her. Their whiteness was the purity of magic. Once she put them on, she would never be the same chunky, fat little Indio girl again.

The magic worked, all right, but the old gods must have been laughing because the transformation didn't work the way she wanted it to. She put the white tunic on, and the fringed bolero and the leggings, trying to change under her old clothes, but they were too tight so she couldn't and it was her turn to be embarrassed. One look at the weird glint in Pascual's face and she knew she couldn't ask to use the privacy of his room. Slowly, reluctantly, all the joy gone out of her new clothes, she changed with Pascual's harsh, undepilated face watching her. And her life wasn't the same ever again.

'All right, Cochina,' said Pascual. 'Come on. Turn round and show us. Oh, yes. Very nice.' He took another slug of tequila and chewed the worm at the bottom. It was as though something hurt him so much that he wanted to hurt her worse. Then he told her, 'You've got fat, horrible legs.' To Pilar it seemed as if he wanted suddenly to bind Lorenzo to him because he said, 'Look, Lorenzo, her legs look like milk-bottles. If her feet didn't have skin on all the fat would blubber out like spilt milk, splat, on to the floor.'

Lorenzo loved it. Right out in plain sight he reached for Pascual's booze and his hand met his brother's on the bottle in complicity. Lorenzo took a long pull at the fire-spirit and smiled. Suddenly he looked just like Pascual only thinner. 'You're right, *hermano*. Old Cochina, there, she looks like two milk-bottles under a great big old cow.'

And Pilar ran outside, but she felt too obvious. She felt like if she walked across the plaza Under-Mexico-Fields everyone would be looking at her and laughing at her with her legs like milk-bottles and her fat body like a cow, so she scrunched down in the corner where their corrugated plastic boards made the wall of their own kitchen-patio, and she wouldn't come in until finally Pascual came out and said, 'Look, Coch— Er, I mean Pilar, I'm sorry. I didn't mean it.'

But he did. Pilar came in anyway, because she couldn't face going anywhere else, and she sat in the inner room that smelt like alcohol and urine and mud, watching but not watching the holodisk machine like Pascual sometimes let them when he was in a good mood, and she thought, *It's not fair, it's not fair. He picks on me because I'm little and weak and fat and ugly and I've got legs like milk-bottles.*

A tear slid down her cheek on the side away from her brothers who were watching some Yanquis go riding around in shining coloured cars shooting at each other even though they'd got food and nice clothes and big houses up in the sunshine. Pascual laughed like crazy every time someone died.

She thought, *I hate him. I wish I was dead, then he'd be sorry. He'd wish he'd never picked on me.*

Then she thought of other revenges which didn't involve her being dead, because if God didn't definitely exist then she might not be able to laugh down at Pascual from Heaven. The Blind Man had said the strong shouldn't pick on the weak and that all the people put together would be stronger than the President, even. But the President didn't have to live with Pascual and Lorenzo picking on him.

On the screen the white gangsters shot the black gangsters and the black ones shot back, and the heads exploded just the same whatever their hair was like, and beside her Lorenzo surreptitiously pinched nips of Pascual's tequila, which meant Pascual was as drunk as he could get.

And then she saw that Pascual was crying.

She nudged Lorenzo.

Both of them were scared, now. After the tears where Pascual hated himself, he made himself feel better by making someone else feel worse. And neither of them wanted to be the one he picked on. The battle-lines shifted, Lorenzo and Pilar together again, and they hummed and ha'd until they'd scraped together an excuse, then they left, running as soon as they got out of the door of the inner room in case Pascual changed his mind and didn't let his human punch-bags go.

They ran to hide where they usually did, near La Mariucha's place, because not even Pascual would hit them where La Mariucha could see. But as soon as they squatted in the steam of her patio, they saw two men who walked just like Pascual did now he had money. They walked with a sort of a swagger that said, 'Look at us. We aren't afraid,' and they could have been twins. They barged past the Blind Man and he said nothing to them. Quite casually they swept the piles of baskets off Álvaro and Tequila's stall. The lovers didn't even screech. Grabbing hold of each other, they just scrambled back out of reach.

Then the swaggering men walked in where Pilar hadn't shut the inner door, where Lorenzo hadn't shut the inner door and locked it. And they shot Pascual's head so that when the men had gone and the children went back to look, it had exploded just like they did when the gringos or the negritos shot at each other in their big, shiny cars.

Then Pilar Jímenez Costanza and her fat little milk-bottle-legs grabbed Lorenzo and anything they could get that wasn't soaked with their brother's blood, and ran away through the rain of mud. They ran past the Blind Man, who watched them with his sightless eyes through his sun-glasses down here where there wasn't any sun, and Pilar wished and wished with all her might that she was as powerful as the President of Central America, or the Matriarch even, so that she could beat the gangs who had eaten her brother with their lying tongues and their transparisteel teeth, and then shot him.

7
THE RAISING OF ARMS

Moments before eleven, Twiss climbed wearily up the ramp from his bedroom. Emerald brightness pooled around him. From her hiding-place at the top Irona saw him look upwards and blink away the glare.

After the abortive coup so long before, and especially now there were Arms on the loose, he no longer trusted the grav-shafts; Irona knew just where to find him. His Eye floated above his head, the reflections in its iridescent orb changing from jade to leaf-green as he neared the Synod. Twiss glanced constantly at the Eye but it registered no threat.

Which was no doubt why Irona heard him yelp in surprise when he turned the last coil of the spiral and saw her.

'Synod, woman, don't do that! You scared the pants off me!'

'Sorry, Twiss.' Irona made her voice as soothing as she could. 'But we need to talk before we go in there. I'm sorry about yesterday, by the way. I shouldn't have said those things out at the landing-field. It was just reaction.'

He shrugged, magnanimous. She noticed that he didn't

apologise for his descent into abuse, though; or his telling half the world about his other children. He ran a hand through his unruly brown hair and tugged his tunic of seasilk down neatly over his cream-and-pearl shirt, giving himself time to think, and incidentally reminding Irona afresh just how attractive he was, even with the beginnings of fat plumping up his skin. He would have strode past her but she didn't move to fall into step beside him. He clicked his tongue in exasperation and said, 'Well, what do you want? We're going to be late for your precious Synod.'

'Twiss, the whole planet is splitting apart. First Wave, Second Wave, fisherfolk, rich people, farmers – we have to present a united front or we might as well not bother. It's not just Wave-violence any more. It's Arms as well. People are dying out there! If you want to keep Tingalit and everything we've built, please, please back me and Regen up in Synod.'

He turned to stare at her, the whites of his hazel eyes discoloured by debauchery. She smelt yesterday's wine souring his breath. As she spoke his hostility became palpable. 'Is that a threat?'

She shook her head. 'No. Not from me. But somebody wants us out of here. Look what happened to Theb. Will you back me up?'

Twiss thought, head to one side, and Irona tried with all her will to influence his mood. It didn't work. It never did; his emotions cut into her like knives but he was still insulated from hers by his own feelings.

Nevertheless, something – perhaps it was the memory of the murderous attack in Synod so long before – made him reconsider. When all was said and done, he hadn't managed to stop the Arms either. 'All right, Ro. I'll give you a month. If you ain't come up with the goods by then, though, you can get out of my face.'

Irona smiled brilliantly at him. 'Twiss, things are hard enough what with . . . with Arnikon and everything.' Tears starred her blue-green eyes but she brushed them away impatiently and went on, 'But you know that together, we're unbeatable. Truce?'

'All right, truce.' He took her arm and they turned to the Synod chamber through the halls of green glass. 'Just don't start blarting.'

Sharp as a ripped tin-can, the hot sunlight of spring stabbed in through the high rose window. Its curves melted when it hit the table of polished stone but it still dazzled Irona as she walked through the underwater gloom cast by the thick walls of emerald glass. The Synod's members were already waiting impatiently in the high-backed chairs around the living 3-D model of the town. For the First Wave, there were Less, his slender, elegant cousin Nona the quay-mistress, and Baika the architect. For the Second Wave, Regen, Sticker, and fat, red-faced Marjine; plus Twiss and herself, newly arrived. All eyes were on them.

Irona was very conscious of her footsteps clicking across the echoing chamber. At least having Twiss beside her gave her some illusion that she was not alone. Momentarily her bereavements swamped her. She concentrated hard on what she had to say and her grief became a silent assassin waiting invisible in ambush. Regen smiled at her and it was a lifeline. Her boot-heels kept ringing out in syncopation with Twiss's until he dropped her arm and went to his place.

'Good-morning, Kiflians all,' Twiss said, his voice warm. The precision with which he took his seat drew attention, the shaped jacket of dark seasilk held it. The soft material glowed with all the richness of the ocean. Unselfconsciously he picked his crown out of the textured pattern of Kifl's buildings that crested the table; the green crystal his Granfer had given him sat easily on his brow. He looked every centimetre the ruler of all Harith.

The Kiflians murmured their greetings of 'Hello, Twiss,' or 'Good-morning, Arcturus,' depending on how well he let them know him. It gave Irona a chance to slide unobtrusively into her own seat before the console set in the marble. Regen winked from his place beside her and the others came in with awkward expressions of sympathy. Eventually, under the pressure of Twiss's gaze, they fell silent.

'Arms!' Twiss said loudly, and smashed his fist down on the table.

Everyone jumped, no doubt his intention.

'They are stalking our city' – he swept his hands wide over the model of the town that rose from the shining table – 'wantonly slaying Second and First Wave alike.'

Irona thought, *Not true, but certainly good propaganda*.

'They want to make us hate each other, but we ain't going to dance to no tune our enemies are playing. It's our job here in Synod to make sure they don't kill no more of us. I ain't having it. For now we'll bring back the curfew. 'Least, that's what I've told Lowena to do. Meantime Irona and Regen are following up a few leads I've come up with.'

Irona and the spindly pot-bellied man nodded, feigning a lack of surprise. *After all*, Irona told herself, *I've been attributing my ideas to him for so long he probably thinks they're his*.

'Now, Less,' Twiss said with his winning smile, 'what can you tell me about the food problem?'

Less still looked the same as ever: a hawklike face topped by black and white eyebrows matching the badger-stripes of his hair. But after the take-over, Twiss had ordered Less's 'loyalisation.' It had taken six months of operations and so-called rehabilitation with Twiss supervising Tang's every operation. Now, fifteen years later, Less exuded the right emotions but Irona still didn't trust the First Wave man. Then, neither did Twiss.

Perhaps Less just couldn't help being sarcastic. 'What problem? Population's up near eight thousand but we've only got food for six.'

'I told you we can feed everyone if we stick to the basic ration!' Twiss said.

'So you did. In that case, who cares if half the crops that should have overwintered didn't, the fish in the bay are dying of fungus and there's suckwort strangling the vineyards? We're still having to send tonnes of supplies to those Eastcliff deves half a planet away instead of them helping us out which was supposed to be the idea, or did I get that wrong?'

'No, Less,' Twiss said sharply, and Irona cursed the First Wave spokesman under her breath for stirring Twiss up again. The Kiflian leader went on, 'You didn't get it wrong. You just have to give them a little more time. Their fish have only just spawned, haven't they, Ro?'

She nodded vigorously, remembering something about a diplomat being sent abroad to lie for her country. Unresolved guilts swirled thick as treacle inside her. Shc hadn't even thought to ask about the sea-farming; Arias had filled her being to the exclusion of all else.

Twiss kept his temper in check and went on in a way that showed he was determined to keep the peace, 'At least they send us goods in trade.'

Irona smiled internally. *Twiss didn't rise to it!* she exulted.

'You don't want to listen to old Less Brains Than He Was Born With,' Marjine said, her fat jowls red as ever. Her heart was more kindly than her mouth. 'He's the only one in this yere Synod what's not wearing a speck of seasilk but we all know he's got more than he knows what to do with. Don't he believe in supporting the fisherfolks' economy or what? They'll help us out soon as they can. 'Sides, if Less did a better job of distribution—'

'Hold on there!' Less said indignantly. 'I deal out what I can to whoever needs it,' and Nona muttered something no-one heard.

'Yeah,' Sticker said not quite under his breath, 'to they First Wave friends of yourn—' He winced as Twiss kicked his ankle.

Less carried on, bolstered up by his cousin's support. 'I can't get a quart out of a pint pot. The farmers keep begging me for help and our land's overcropped as it is.'

'Plough up more of the mountainside, then,' the fat woman said tartly. 'Surprised you never thought of that for yourselves.' Marjine never was known for her subtlety of speech.

Nona snorted her derision. Though the quaymistress was seventy, she didn't look a day over thirty-five. It was her superciliousness, not age, that had cut harsh lines in her face. She gestured at the 3-D model of Kifl, its houses lapping high up the hills. 'And what about the new homes we need?'

At the same time, Baika, the stolid First Wave architect, said, 'Bad move. If we cut down any more trees we're going to have landslides every time Heralia grumbles. Some of the Moon Mountain foothills look none too safe now.'

'So what do you suggest?' Irona cut in before the Less-Baika-Nona axis fell into dispute again with any more Second Wavers.

'Search me,' Less said, and Nona shrugged her slim shoulders.

Baika spread her hands in a shrug as though she were dealing with idiots. 'Shore up the slopes with a retaining wall and plant some orchards quick. And we can house some folks in the caves underneath, too.'

Less's jaw dropped in horror but Irona wasn't going to let some old reactionary stand in the way of the Synod's fledgling unity.

'Good idea!' she said, dredging up some enthusiasm, at the same time as Regen said in his abrupt manner, 'Been thinking about cropland.' As ever his nervous fingers were writhing over some electronic gadget in his lap. His bulging brown eyes didn't look up from it. 'We got weather-controllers to irrigate Rainshadow Valley . . .'

This time Irona suppressed a mental groan. It had been a weather-control device that Twiss had forced her to use to drown Kifl when it still belonged entirely to the First Wave. Predictably it was a First Waver, the elegant Nona, who came up with another obstacle. 'What about the snake-rats?' she said triumphantly.

It was Regen who answered. 'All we got to do is put out a cordon of they frequency-emitters like we do for the locust-lizard breeding season.'

'And where do you propose to conjure enough of those up from?' the squat architect said.

'Simple, Baika,' Regen said. 'Got the design, ain't we? I'll just train up a few of they schoolkids to put 'em together. Hee-hee. No problem. Entirely.'

'Great!' Twiss said. 'And we can put a big bunch of

farmers out there too, only right across the river this time. Say twenty or thirty families.'

Less echoed Twiss, but his tone was acid. 'Great! A whole eightieth of our population out of the way. Next you'll be saying we have to send them supplies too.'

Irona reached across to squeeze his hand. 'You're right, Less. Well done!'

... The world wavered in her sight. Gravity was wrong, packing her internal organs hard together. Somewhere she knew this wasn't Harith. Someone big, whispering in that dark empty room that towered unseen around her, hissed, 'Well done!'

But it wasn't meant for her to hear. Irona felt the guilt of eavesdropping. Breaking the privacy of good citizenship. She was trapped now, trapped under something soft and itchy that threatened to smother her in hot, stale darkness, because if she moved she knew they'd hear. It was harder and harder to breathe; an itch grew in her hairline but she dared not lift a hand or she'd be caught. She felt ill but she couldn't have said how, only that her body didn't seem to fit together right.

A sound she could not identify – yes: it was a rustle of fabric; then breathing, harder, faster. A horrible feeling of isolation swept over her, and terror that she might be discovered. The thick air cloyed in her throat with a sickly scent of raspberries and mint. Irona felt she would die if she didn't shove that smothering cloth aside, but if she did her punishment would be terrible beyond belief. Bright daggering pain flew closer: worms slithering in her head. A loss of self worse than death for there'd be a black vacuum of endless loneliness ...

Beyond her hiding place under the smothering cloth, the

hard breathing rose to a cry that someone else immediately shushed. Irona felt little and helpless; she didn't understand what caused that cry like pain, like release, and she didn't dare ask. This should have been a safe place but whatever was going on out there, it was something she wasn't meant to see. She wasn't meant to be here. She was in the wrong. She was steeped in guilt, buried in it. From beyond the dense, itchy cloth great shuddering breaths, and a moan . . .

'Irona! Irona, are you all right?' said Regen, his head swimming into view. Her alienation had disassembled his face into rounds and lines that made no sense; she pulled back, gasping with the terror of being seen that she had brought back with her from the black place where her body was wrong.

A brown claw – no, a hand, a normal hand that reminded her of caresses in the night – pressed a drink of water against her lips. A warm, remembered voice said, 'Here, you're all right now. You're safe. I've got you,' and the fractal of relief was swamped by the whole of betrayal.

Twiss.

Reality.

Twiss didn't know how she felt, because he couldn't help it. He wasn't lying all those times he said, 'You're safe. I've got you.' It was just that he only meant, 'For this moment,' not forever, like she'd wanted to believe.

He smiled encouragingly as she sipped cold water from the misted glass. Or perhaps it was her eyes that were misted . . .

The Kiflian Synod grew sharp around her as though it were made of glass, but she could still see that other place, the black place, lurking behind it.

'Can we get on now?' Less's cousin Nona said.

Even Less was shocked by her lack of sympathy.

Irona couldn't remember feeling this unwell for years. Her hands were trembling and a throbbing pulse shook her stomach to nausea. Her lungs kept forgetting to pull in air. *Concentrate on externals*, she told herself. *Don't think of* ... And all that was left was the suffocating black terror and the guilt and the loss.

'Good idea,' she said shakily. It was too much trouble to move her head; instead she flicked her gaze at Less. 'Have the farmers and the trawlers take samples of the blight to Jai's Hospital. Maybe someone there can come up with an antidote. Darien's doing his damnedest now. Find out who's brave enough to go and settle the far side of Rainshadow Valley. Offer them double rations if you have to. Nona, you find the kids for Regen to—'

She broke off. Everyone had stopped listening. They were intent on the 3-D 'scope that mirrored an image of the town on to the table.

Six figures jetted in across the bay to land outside the warehouse that stored Kifl's food. Bulking large as cockroaches among the bright ants of Kiflians, they cut their propulsors; microseconds later the shriek of their jets cut the air in the Synod chamber. Tiny figures fled in panic, dragging their children out of the way. From here Irona couldn't hear them scream. Blood flowered on the blue wall of the warehouse as one of the Arms backhanded a man out of his way and the man's broken-necked body crashed into it, a ghastly fruit that still spurted crimson seeds.

Irona reached towards her keyboard a fraction before Twiss yelled, 'Send the Eyes!' But Regen was already on to it with a handset.

Both her Eye and Twiss's rocketed skywards. They crashed out through the high windows, leaving a rainbow of glittering glass falling into the chamber. It smashed on to the places they had occupied; Twiss had dragged Irona clear just in time. She clung to him while deadly shards splintered through the light-model town of Kifl. Chaos erupted in the Synod: swearing and startled screams as everyone leaped for safety.

And through the piles of fractured glass moved the cockroach figures of the Arms. Diamonds of light spasmed their images that crawled across the mountains of shattered panes on the table. It was impossible to tell what the vile black beetles were doing.

Tearing herself from the shelter of Twiss's embrace, Irona ran back to her keyboard and swept the crystal fragments aside with the hem of her skirt. Glass splinters still lacerated her fingers as her keyed-in commands laid an Eye's image and the psychicator's on her screen. She tumbled down the sky with it to the warehouse and the small crowd behind her gasped in sudden dizziness, shrieking as they seemed about to crash into the Arm on guard outside the vast doorway.

The Eye swept into the cavernous mouth of the warehouse. For a moment the sudden darkness blinded her. Then she saw four of the Arms piling fruit, dried proteins and sacks of wheat into nets that were so large a dozen men could have lain within one of the seasilk skeins.

The fifth Arm batted aside a gang of youths who tried to stop the pillage. A girl hurled herself at the Arm's back but the Arm ducked and sent her slithering across the smooth plate of its back. A blond boy who couldn't have been more than ten leaped to grab a spade-like hand but the Arm sent him hurtling through the air. He landed, still mobile, in a pile of canisters but the heavy plastic cubes avalanched down on him before he could crawl free. The boy's heaving stilled; rubies of blood cascaded over his blond hair.

Irona was crying now. She ordered the Eyes to spin their electric webs over the Arms.

The Eyes did nothing.

Frantically she keyed the command again.

Still nothing. But over the Eyes' sound-systems blared weeping and terror and the awful, clockwork shushing of the sacks into the nets.

'Do something!' Twiss bellowed just as she put out a call to Lowena's troop of guards.

But it was too late. The Arm on duty outside spoke a word into his wrist-com. Instantly the Synod chamber was riven by the howling jets as the Arms took off again taking the four bulging nets with them.

'Look!' Twiss called, full of hope. A handful of guards raced across the square, unslinging their flechette guns as they pounded towards the entrance; just in time for the dangling bales to cannon them aside. One guard cartwheeled across the baking pavement, his gun firing haphazardly. A group of women cowering in doorways exploded in a spray of blood.

As the Arms executed a victory roll over the devastation, the innocent sunlight burnished their carapaces.

Regen yelled something wordless. Irona responded, aiming the Eyes to track the Arms to their lair. But the two flankers shot a pitchfork of neon lightning and the Eyes spiralled downwards out of control. On the monitor their images died with the dull clang of their impact. At least they didn't explode.

Not before the members of the Synod saw a light-sign burst in the thick shadows of noon: *Exile the Second Wave. Doom is coming.*

*

Bernardina, Matriarch of All Earth, ordered one of her sudden inspections. Elditch complained, of course, but the Watchtower purge was a *fait accompli* by the time he found out about it. His only choices were to comply or sulk. The fact that Bernardina came to ask him personally to review the wardens in her capital of Camelford mollified him only slightly.

'Thank you, Elditch,' the most powerful woman on Earth had said. 'I appreciate your help. It's good to know you wouldn't let me down.' And she even kissed him on the cheek with her papery lips that were the colour of varicose veins.

Elditch winked at her roguishly. For a man in his seventies, he managed to do it without being embarrassing. The little intimacy heartened them both.

'If you would care to join me afterwards for a drink in my eyrie?' Bernardina said, leaving her once-husband to plump out the invitation with his imaginings. 'But for now, you'd better be off to inspect the Watch. They'll be waiting for you.'

So, at 11.17 AM, Admin time, Elditch was bouncing up and down on his toes in the canteen in Camelford Mountain. His mood was somewhere between ruffled-feathers at the suddenness of it all, and smugness. After all, this task proved he was still at least the nominal head of Camelford Synod, didn't it?

He mounted the dais, looking at the subdued greys and browns of the modestly-dressed day-Watch, and fingered the bush of his white moustache. One of his assets was his commanding appearance and he used it to full effect. Laying aside his buckled hat, he let his hair fall in thick, snowy waves to the collar of his plain charcoal coat, and the wide legs of his trousers hid the shakiness of age. As he got his breath, he surveyed the watch, proud that Bernardina was letting him perform this duty on his own authority.

Flanking him in a half-moon of celestial robes were Carandis and the junior matriarchs dressed in the blue of purity. Elditch, never the world's most sensitive individual, felt secure in their admiration. For a while he let their aura of rose and honeysuckle harmony calm the stress of the unexpected purge. The dutiful wardens never so much as whispered, though some of them fingered the knots of obedience on their cord belts. Finally, having worked out what it was that he was going to say, he launched into one of his long, rambling speeches.

Which was precisely what Bernardina had intended. Her privacy was assured. At 11.21, with everyone safely out of the way, she descended from her room right at the top of the Watchtower. Hobbling stiffly down the deserted corridors of the heart of the Admin, she stopped before an apparently blank wall. She cast a quick glance to confirm there were neither Eyes nor Ears nor body-heat sensors in the hall, and intoned the opening sequence.

It took time for the door to identify her. Sometimes she wondered what would happen if she died in her secret room; nobody would ever find her body. With the speed of thought the scene painted itself in her mind. *My empire will crumble, torn up by factions accusing one another of my murder. Carandis will finally step into my shoes. There'll be fire and flood and famine. She'll blame the President of the Three Americas – or maybe Suhurlstan, and war will come. Wonder how long she'll last?* And in the split seconds of thought Bernardina viewed her own bones gently shucking off the burden of her tired flesh.

A crack appeared in the angle where the lace of a transplanted stalactite met rough-hewn granite. The door swung wider and she ordered the room to light before she went in. It was one thing imagining this as her tomb, quite another to step inside it in the dark.

The door closed behind her. Among the mica-sparkles of the rock was one triumphant blue gleam.

Bernardina saw it. Joy flooded her; she threw back her head, eyes closed almost prayerfully.

At last, at last, at last! She threw aside her stick and sat at her console that was astronomer, computer, communicator, ansible. At last the blue light shone to tell her that someone was again searching the memory-banks in the old Synod Tower light-years away in Kifl.

Bernardina's smile was a geyser of tenderness and love and hope, all the forgotten emotions that had washed her in the pain-baptism of childbirth.

For the blue light meant that the searcher was Bernardina's daughter, Irona. And Bernardina's years of waiting were at an end.

8

TURQUOISE TRAITORS

'Look!' Sticker yelled. 'Up there!'

Inside the echoing green chamber everyone craned their necks. Through the starred fragments of the windows they could see the six Arms, ugly as flying beetles, whose swollen abdomens were the nets of food. The inhuman constructs played a derisive game of tag above the glass turrets of emerald and gold and rose and sapphire while Twiss roared impotently. On the table beside him, their shadows cascaded over the light-shivered peaks of broken glass that drowned the image of his kingdom. Twiss bellowed again.

The Arms circled and fled to the shelter of the clouds above Heralia. Before the scream of their jets had faded, Twiss yanked Irona up and away from her keyboard. Side by side they raced through the coloured glass of Tingalit, Sticker at their heels. Behind came the rest of the Synod, skidding on rugs that scattered the transparent halls. Less jogged along behind Nona, his expression impossible to read, but Irona couldn't catch a glimpse of Regen.

He must have stayed behind up there! she realised, but had no time to wonder why.

As Twiss burst into the Ceremonial Hall a shadow fleered across the emerald glass. He dragged her back but she panted, 'It's not an Arm. Transport-tractor. Regen must have called it.' And sure enough the little man overtook them to fling open the doors.

The transport-talker was a solid, grizzled man whose eyes were blank with shock. It numbed him so that he clung to routine. The methodical way he checked everyone was safely aboard drove Irona insane with frustration until he finally told his machine to move. Then he urged it to the limits of its speed. It whined and shuddered, fountaining spray as it angled over the ornamental lake before speeding across the palace gardens. He aimed it at the gate.

'Come on, my beauty, dice that corner,' he said, and the ground-effect vehicle sliced the air at a pitch that sent half the Synod rolling from their seats.

'Faster!' yelled Twiss.

The talker hurriedly relayed the order to his transport. It responded to his voice and Irona ducked instinctively as it almost caromed off a housing-block opposite. Citizens leaped out of the way with scant seconds to spare.

The talker forced his poor machine to leap over market-carts. He pointed it straight at a light-sculpture in a curved-wall plaza and the transport barely rose, so overburdened was it. Nona shrieked as the undercarriage tore away the top of the transmitter and a vomit of coloured lights poured over the vehicle's sides. A woman yelled, fist waving at their retreating backs.

Beneath the almond-trees of an avenue, the stone awnings of the Maze gaped to crush them but the talker ducked his machine into the cool shade of the tunnel. Strings of washing caught on the transport's antenna, flapping behind them like the wings of a blanket-fish.

The alley was a claustrophobic kaleidoscope of doors and windows. Knots of people scattered, pressing themselves to the sides of the alleys, their mouths open O's of outrage. Abruptly the air smelt of the greasy spice culled from native plants and a dense curtain of dried leaves blocked the talker's view.

The air-brakes wooshed at a shouted command. The passengers were hurled forwards, then rocked back in their seats as the transport bulled through the spicer's display. Abruptly the face of the spicer herself loomed terrified in the windshield. Walls blocked them from a swerve. There was no way for the tractor to miss ramming her.

At the last moment she dropped to the ground and the machine's skirts swept over her. Irona turned to see if she'd been crushed; metal clanged angrily on the sloping back window. The spicer had hurled a cauldron at them but it did no damage and the transport slewed round a bend and out into the glare of the sun.

The talker yelled 'Stop!' Even before the transport had sunk breathlessly to the ground, the Synod leaders leaped out and down.

The scene impacted on Irona: the metallic scent of blood on the hot air of the plaza, the moans of the wounded, the frantic cries of lovers and parents trying to find the ones they had lost. Half a dozen focuses pulled the Kiflians into groups with panickers racing from one to the next. The plaza was packed, some people trying to give first aid and comfort, more drawn to the scene of the disaster.

Twiss and Irona pushed through the ghoulish crowd, heading for the worst injury. They made for the drying blood blossoming on the turquoise wall of the warehouse. Locust-lizards screeled their almost-melody, lucent wings flashing in a pattern like gold-edged petals above that crimson centre. Other groups were clustered around the women shot by the wild burst of flechettes.

Twiss shouldered the onlookers ruthlessly aside. He said, 'Get they children away from yere!' and the tone of his voice sent the sightseers back out of his reach. Irona could feel the fire flaring out of him, an incandescent compound of ire and frustration that seared her. Once again she cursed her empathy for the pain it brought her, but in another moment she was kneeling beside the victim.

Incredibly, he was still alive. His neck was slumped at an incredible angle and one side of his head was soft and pulpy. Flakes of turquoise limewash speckled the clotted blood in his hair. The dull pupils of his eyes flickered from side to side. Sweat slicked his icy skin and he was making faint movements as if he would get up.

Horrified, Irona shushed him, pressed him gently back against the coats Regen and Twiss had thrown behind his shoulders. She looked up, desperately seeking help, but there was none. Someone offered water but she dared not even give him that. If he survived the trip to the Hospital, anaesthetics might make him vomit. He was shivering from blood-loss and shock despite the fierce noontide sun. Trying not to feel his agony, she wriggled out of her petticoat and used that for a blanket.

Twiss turned aside and collared Sticker, the pair of them making for the warehouse's interior. Regen patted Irona awkwardly on the back and said, 'I've called Darien. He'll be here in a minute.' Then he, too, left her amid the crowd that was tightening its noose around her while he went to see what had happened to his beloved Eyes. Under her hands she felt the wounded man's chest move; he made a wordless mumble, not understanding what had happened to him, and tried again to rise.

'We didn't have no Arms on Harith afore they Second Wavers came,' someone said, just loud enough for her to hear.

'Yeah,' came an answer, 'I can think of another spelling for Arcturus Rex. Wrecks, get it?'

She glanced up, but amid the dense-packed colourful figures it was impossible to work out who had spoken. A generalised aggression punched out at her.

'At least Twiss is trying to do something about the Arms,' she said clearly. 'All you're doing is gawping at an accident.'

It made no difference. Their hostility was partly a response to the shock and frustration of the Arms' attack, but it made it no easier for her to bear. She could feel it, a knot of snake-rats in her stomach. It was hard enough trying to stem the wounded man's incomprehension and fear.

An eternity passed before she heard the ambulance at the far side of the plaza. The siren stilled and through its loudspeaker a voice said, 'Stand aside, please. Let the doctor through.'

That was one voice Irona would have known anywhere. Jaimindi, once the best friend she'd ever had. Jai, who thought she was wonderful, with whom she'd giggled and gossiped. Jai – who had pretended for the last fifteen years that Sticker and not Twiss was the father of her children. Irona and she no longer sought each other out, not since the first time Irona had guessed it was Twiss in the nurse's bed, but at least Irona had the strength to be civil when they met, because even now she had no proof other than Jai's flock of hazel-eyed offspring.

As the crowd before her eddied to let the nurse through, Irona felt a stab of jealousy: *How many more women has*

Twiss fathered children on? But she dismissed the thought as irrelevant when people lay bleeding. Besides, in public anyway, Twiss still needed Irona to be his queen.

All the same, Jai was a good nurse and, with the wounded man's blood still oozing, Irona was glad to see her amongst the auxiliary medics. Dumpy, dressed in startling colours that went well with her cream-coffee skin and snapping black eyes, Jai always seemed to create an oasis of calm these days. She had come a long way since her painful timidity of the first years when Irona and then Sticker had been her only friends; this assured woman spoke to Irona as an equal. If Twiss had eroded the love between the two women, at least the respect was still there.

'Hi, Ro.' The nurse placed a steraseal compress over the head-wound and smiled reassuringly at the bewildered victim. 'You'll be right as rain in no time,' she said to him, and gave his cold fingers a friendly squeeze.

Then Darien glided out of the crowd on a floating gurney. Irona stood to let him in beside the patient. Suddenly she felt superfluous. 'I'll leave you to it, then,' she told Jai, and nodded to the doctor who was already tearing open his olfactory,

'Ro?' Jai's tone was soft and unexpectedly hesitant.

Irona turned back, her blond-brown eyebrows raised questioningly.

Jai glanced once at her patient but Darien was dealing with him now. The nurse took the two or three steps over to Irona and said quietly, 'I'm sorry about Arnikon, Ro. I know how much he meant to you. He was a lovely lad. He had so much to live for. Will you let me come to his memorial?'

Surprised and touched, Irona nodded. There were too many currents of emotion for her to find words.

'If there's anything I can do . . .'

Irona groped blindly for the nurse's chubby hand and clasped it. For a second the wounded man's blood bonded them. 'Thanks, Jai.'

She turned away, hardly noticing the stickiness on her palms. Wiping her tears away with her sleeve, Irona checked that Slan and Alin, the auxiliaries, were attending the injured women. Then she mounted the steps to the dark, echoing cave of the warehouse. Another gurney floated towards her through the doorway. The blond boy was lying on it, arm splinted, lips compressed into an upturned U in his efforts not to cry. A white field-dressing covered part of his forehead.

She signalled as the boy slid his gaze to watch her. The male nurse standing on the steering-plate at the back stopped obligingly. Irona smiled at the boy.

His eyes were wide with reverence. 'Aren't you Queen Irona?' he asked huskily.

She nodded.

'I just been rescued by King Twiss and now I'm meeting you!'

Irona chuckled. 'And I'm meeting one of the bravest boys in Kifl. I'm honoured.'

He turned his wan face away from her. 'You're laughing at me!' he said reproachfully, too full of pain-killers to be tactful.

She brushed the hair back from his brow. 'I'm not. I'm proud of you. You were trying to protect your friends. We watched it all, you know, but we couldn't get here in time. I sent the Eyes to protect you but the Arms shot them down. I'm sorry. We did try, though. Do you want a copy of the recording so you can show everyone just how brave you were?'

The boy's brown eyes gleamed. 'D'you mean it?'

'I do. What's your name?'

'Resu.'

'Well then, Resu, I'll send one over to you in the Hospital. Not many grown-ups could tackle a monster like that and still smile.' So, of course, he smiled. She stroked his hair once more, gently, knowing she could never share that gesture with her son again. 'Off you go to get patched up. Goodbye, Resu.'

'Goodbye.'

Inside she could see nothing until her eyes had adjusted to the gloom. Twiss was sitting on a pile of sacks, giving out candies to comfort the frightened children whose parents had not yet come to claim them. She went to join him and a toddler climbed trustingly into her lap. Twiss gave her a smile that warmed her heart.

Volunteers were helping Sticker's guards re-stack the stores. Irona asked tactfully, 'Do you think we could ask Sticker's lot to clear the ghouls out of the square when they're finished here?' She had noticed there was no sign of Lowena, the new captain of the guard, but forebore to mention it. Tall, willowy blondes were not what she needed just now.

Twiss's face clouded for a moment. 'Good idea. Stick?' He jerked his head to summon his friend. Meantime he said to Irona, 'I don't suppose you found out where they you-know-whats went?'

'There might be some sort of a clue on the recordings. Will you come back later and check them over with me?'

He nodded, tossing a lemon-strand to a boy at the back of the group. Although he didn't speak, Irona could tell Twiss was glad she wanted his help. *Twiss*, she thought, looking sideways at his pleasant, round face, *you're great in disasters. It's just routine you find difficult. But we'll fix these Arms and their masters once and for all.* With so much on her plate, she forgot all about the blackouts and visions caving in the floors of her mind.

By mid-afternoon all the children had gone home. Even the square outside was deserted for the siesta, though Sticker kept a handful of guards sitting in the shade of the almond trees, just in case. Irona could see them through the doorway, chatting to Lowena, who had only just deigned to turn up. But there were no Arms hiding in the puff-ball clouds drifting across the sky, no howling jets to rip apart the sleepy town.

The gold of sunlight spilt in through the small high windows, splitting the cool dimness of the warehouse. It polished the depleted ranks of canisters and gleamed from spilled wheat on the floor. Scents of dried apricots, raisins and apples seemed visible as glowing dust-motes lazing in the shafts of light. Irona leaned tiredly on a pile of sacks and listened to the sound of Twiss's pacing echo from distant recesses.

At last the storemaster, a worried-looking man wearing the bandage on his head as a badge of heroism, sighed and sat back from his computer. He nodded, forgetting that he had last spoken half an hour ago.

'Are you sure?' Irona asked him, while Twiss still strode restlessly around.

Trevelyan nodded again, then looked as if he wished he hadn't. His hand went to the bandage and he winced. 'They've took enough to feed fifty people for a month.'

'Or one hundred for a fortnight,' Twiss said, circling the end of the counter again. 'We ain't got a clue how many of 'em there is. What are we going to do about they fisherfolk that's clamouring for more food?'

Irona sighed too. 'Thanks, Trevelyan. I'm going back to look at those recordings, Twiss. Are you coming?'

'A-huh.'

They left together. Twiss automatically turned towards Tingalit.

All the time they had been waiting in the warehouse, Irona had been rehearsing this moment but it didn't make it any easier to stand on the sunny steps and says, 'They won't have got all the glass off the machine in the palace, so I'm going to use the one in the old Synod Tower, OK?' It was the truth, but only a fraction of it. Deep down she was apprehensive about being back on Twiss's territory. At the moment she couldn't have borne meeting his latest paramour or having to leave if Twiss became awkward again. Worse, she couldn't have borne him walking away. Somehow in the old tower, she felt safer.

Whether Twiss was aware of it or not she didn't know. Certainly he raised no objection. He merely shrugged and said, 'I hope you've got something cool over there. I need a drink.'

Irona spread her long skirts. Blood-spots rusted the shimmering amethyst fabric that gently outlined the curves of her figure. 'I need a bath.'

They walked side by side through the familiar curving tunnels of the town. The afternoon air seemed heavy with the odours of sleep. Green clouds of plantlets newly grown from spores danced where they passed. The rows were so quiet that Irona felt like tiptoeing.

Coming out into the plaza at the foot of the tower was like emerging into a well of sunlight. Jewelled lizards swirled above them, harmless this late in the season now that their blood-lust had faded and their eggs were laid.

After all these years, their bell-bright tones still enchanted Irona. But a frisson of fear sharpened the magic.

They crunched across the open space. 'I notice they First Wavers don't waste their time raking the gravel into patterns no more,' Twiss said as they went up the steps between the fat-bellied walls.

'Not since the Arms showed up. They're scared. I rather liked the patterns. You can still see the different colours of gravel but they're all mixed in now.'

He rolled his eyes but said nothing.

Opening the door to a fresh smell of polish, they came across Declan and Malambé leaping up from a game-board and trying to look ferocious.

'At ease, boys.' Irona smiled. 'Who's winning?'

'I am!' they both said, and Irona laughed.

'Well, that's all right, then. Have you had something to eat?'

'Yeah,' Declan said. He was the slimmer, darker one, his hair more brown than his carrotty brother's. 'Regen dropped some stuff off earlier. He didn't look any too happy.'

'Where is he?'

'Dunno.' As ever, Malambé let his twin do the talking for him.

Twiss ran one hand through his hair, just a little impatiently. 'Is the shaft on?'

'Yeah.'

Twiss gave the little jump that started his upward flight, but Irona thought Declan sounded faintly guilty. As Twiss's feet disappeared from view she said, 'I suppose you let the girls play with it?'

Declan moved head and shoulders in a multiple shrug. 'Yeah.'

Malambé was provoked into asking, 'How did you know they'd been here?'

Irona hopped into the shaft, holding her skirts round her in a casual reflex of modesty as the girls had probably not. Her voice, ripe with laughter, echoed back down to them. 'Because the place is so clean, that's how.'

Bathed, changed, but not rested, Irona slumped down at the console and logged on. The exhaustion of her bereavement hadn't left her; she knew she should see the doctor soon but she didn't trust him and she didn't want to see Jai, so she put it to the back of her mind.

Lounging back on the bed, Twiss said, 'Have you got they recordings all right?'

'Ssh. I'm just transferring them from Tingalit. I'll tell you when they're ready.' She didn't tell him about the glitch in the machine that kept making it buzz.

He took another swig of wine. His impatience reached out invisible fingers to her. She felt it as an unwelcome pressure.

At last she said, 'Come and look at this.'

Irona heard Twiss's footsteps coming over, was uncomfortably aware of him, just behind her. She said, 'See? Once they blanked out the Eyes, there's no trace of where the Arms went. Somebody knew what they were doing. But over here, look, on the psychicator—'

'What's all that purple stuff?'

'I've told you, that's fear, depression, negative emotion. What we were feeling with Arms attacking our people. But can you see those little spots of turquoise there? That's curiosity, intellectual stimulation, that sort of thing. Not a trace of fear there. They've even got little haloes of yellow for satisfaction.' Somehow Irona felt responsible for the bad news she was about to give him, but she said anyway, 'And look. I've overlaid the map.'

He ducked his head beside hers to peer into the old-fashioned screen. 'So?'

She pointed. Two bright cool spots stood out, haloed in twin coronas of lemon that shrieked against the magenta. 'So that's Tingalit.'

Twiss straightened, snorted derisively. 'That were us, at the Synod.'

'No. The darker purple wash, that was us. But there's that turquoise mixed in right amongst us.'

It took a moment for the import to sink in. He said slowly, 'You mean you think someone in Synod sent they Arms?'

9
INNER ASSAULT

'You don't reckon Less or that big-headed cousin of hisn could of controlled they Arms?' Twiss asked. He couldn't keep the scepticism out of his voice.

Irona nodded.

'That's crap.'

'No, it's not!'

'How do you know?' he said. 'You only inherited this technology. You weren't born to it like Gundmila were.'

Goaded into retorting, she said, 'Yes I was. What do you think we did up there in the Watchtower in Camelford?'

'Spied on people. Doped 'em up if'n they got out of line. Or disappeared a few mohocks and trouble-makers.' He sounded a little uneasy. 'But you weren't no matriarch.'

'No, I wasn't.' She kept on speaking across his whoop of 'I told you so' mockery. 'But I was being trained to be one.'

He laughed; the sound was strained. 'Irona, you gone crazy, you have. Delusions of grandeur. Just 'cos I've made you a queen yere, don't mean you were anythin' special back on Earth.'

... She had scratches down her cheek, one long one and

another shaped like a Y where the other girl's nails had come together. She was still sobbing, her moss-green skirts dangling down below her knees where the hem was ripped. But she could see the other girl, Judil, squalling with tangled hanks of hair pressed to her red face. The other children were watching to see what would happen next. Judil had fetched Senior Machin.

Now Irona's third-grade teacher had her backed against the wall of Watchtower School, and Senior Machin was a bitter woman. Heat-haze blurred the view through the transparisteel fence and Irona tried to look at the blue distances beyond the croplands. That was where she wanted to be, safe under the sheltering Sky, in the lemon-drop leaf-shadows of the woods in the Park. Not here, trapped by Senior Machin with her scraped-back hair and ugly brown dress.

'Just because your mother's being made up to full matriarch doesn't mean you're anything special.' The woman's beak-nose pecked out at her. 'Irona! Look at me when I'm talking to you!'

Irona turned her gaze sullenly.

'That's better. But wipe that stupid sulk off your face. You're the one who's got yourself into trouble so it's no good blaming me. You are nothing, Irona. Nothing, do you hear me? The fact of who your parents are makes no difference whatsoever. You can't go round tearing girls' hair out like some ignorant sleeper. If you are lucky, and if you are very very good, you may one day be allowed to help watch the sleepers. But if you are not good then you'll be brain-wormed and abandoned in the warren all on your own for the rest of your life. None of your friends will play with you, or talk to you. Your parents won't acknowledge you ever existed. You'll be all alone among the sleepers.

All alone, do you hear me? And worse, you won't even know what's happened.'

The injustice burned inside her. Judil smirked and Irona went wild. She started for the other girl but Senior Machin pulled her back.

'But she started it!' Irona yelled. 'She said my father was . . . was . . .'

'Was what?'

Judil was a picture of apprehension but Irona couldn't say the shameful words. Couldn't admit that he lied to her and her mother so his immodesty with other women wouldn't come to light. He was her father, wasn't he? She was supposed to trust him. And he was Supreme Watchwarden, responsible for policing the whole of Camelford Mountain, even the millions of dumb sleepers down in the Warren. So everybody else was supposed to trust him too. That knowledge paralysed Irona's vocal chords. The silence stretched and stretched . . .

The white-blonde Judil smiled and stuck her tongue out behind the teacher's back. 'I never said anything about her father, Senior Machin, honest. I wouldn't. He's Supreme Watchwarden, looking after us all, isn't he? So it wouldn't be right. She snatched my shrine music-box and I told her I was going to tell you. So she hurt me.'

'Liar!' Irona shouted.

Senior Machin was aghast. 'I-rona! We don't get other people into trouble to escape punishment ourselves.'

'Well what's she doing then?' Irona yelled, but Machin had turned away from her.

Judil scraped up a few more tears. 'Look at all my hair she pulled out. She's nasty and cruel and she hurt me. What's my mother going to say when she hears?'

Judil's mother was the Matriarch Towy's niece. Irona

knew she was lost. 'Tell-tale!'

'Irona!' said Senior Machin. 'I won't tell you again. Go to my punishment closet and wait there till I come.'

Terror. She had never been in the closet before, but she'd heard all about it from the big kids who had: enzymes and hormones pumped into you, cockroaches crawling into your ears, spiders laying eggs that hatched under your skin. And after that, if she survived, she had to go home to her mother with the long, jagged rips in her cheek and the blood on her torn dress ... Judil would tell her mother who'd tell Towy, then Irona would be brain-wormed and she wouldn't even be herself any more ever again and she'd be abandoned.

Waiting outside the obsidian walls of the little booth that was like a black and evil olfactory, Irona chanted to blank out her fears:

Tell-tale tit,
Your tongue will split
And all the little wormies
Will have a little bit.

With the wormies, it wasn't much comfort.

When Senior Machin triumphantly shut the door on her, though, and the slithering darkness closed her in tight, Irona felt the silk-soft slime of the hyposprays as worms of her own. She opened her mouth to scream in the blackness but the vile taste of the slime was like a thousand centipedes slipping between her lips and crawling over her tongue. She choked, coughed, had to breathe again, and the stuff was inside her, choking, clogging, drowning her ...

Bruise-light visions twisted her brain as she gasped in vain for air. It felt like her heart was trying to jump out of her chest and up through her throat. The fear was a cacophany of physical pains. She heard a sound like a whole playground full of children laughing at her and a million skittering sounds poured into her hearing like the roar of a whirlpool of bugs. They washed her away from the shores of consciousness, farther and farther and farther . . .

'Ro! Ro? You all right?' Someone was shaking her, slapping her face. A smell, that warm and familiar smell that meant Twiss. He slapped her cheek again and the soft thing her head bounced against was his chest. She clung to him, feeling his arms strong as a wall around her, keeping her safe. Her eyes sprang open to drink in the sights of reality, the red flutter of curtains, the relief of daylight, the white knife of Heralia slicing the hot blue sky – the way the mountain had sliced her only son into death. She turned her gaze away.

The console.

With its clue to the Arms and the weight of responsibility.

With its hidden ansible that Irona didn't even know was there.

Over the light-years, in her secret granite womb, Bernardina the Matriarch of All Earth, smiled. Maybe the girl hadn't called yet, but her daughter would find her soon enough.

'You look terrible, Ro.'

'Cheers, Regen. That's just what I wanted to hear.'

'I didn't mean . . .'

She patted his arm, comforted. Now Regen was here in the Synod Tower, Twiss had stopped fussing over her. He was gazing out of the window at the spires of Tingalit shining in the evening sun. It was as though he was embarrassed to show he cared about her to anyone else.

One of the Eyes was on the little man's lap, its soot-streaked panels of iridium open while he poked around inside it. The other, patched up now, was circling nervously around the arches of the ceiling, still not behaving quite like it should.

'Don't worry about me, Regen,' Ro said. 'I'm fine, really I am.' She glanced upwards to distract her friend from the fact that she wasn't fine at all. 'Why don't you have another go at sorting that poor old Eye out though? It's acting like it's got St Vitus's dance.'

Twiss had been fidgeting on the bed. Now he got up with all the force of a released spring and came across to where she was leaning on the balcony. It was dusk, the last rays of the sun sliding upwards over the curled roofs of Kifl as the cliffs on the far side of the bay punctured its fiery disc. She resettled her arms on the parapet, letting the cool breeze fan her forehead. It brought a perfume of snows and cedar and native vegetation. Gentle light began to gather in the round room at the top of the tower, and airlilies drifted through the open window towards it.

Abruptly Twiss said, 'Here. Drink this,' and thrust a goblet of red wine into her hand.

'Why! What—'

'Do you good, that's why. I'm going to see how the clear-up's gone. If you'll be all right,' he added hastily.

The words swelled up in her: *I want you to stay*. But she couldn't say them.

'Twiss, you will remember to take that cube over to the

Hospital for that lad, Resu, won't you? You can do it on the way.' She didn't have to add that it would be good public relations at a time when the Second Wave was at a low ebb. On that score Twiss was awake to every little possibility.

'Sure, love. I promise. You've got Regen and the boys and the Eye if you want anything. You'll be OK.' It wasn't quite a question.

What she wanted was for Twiss to stay, to be warm and comforting, to shore her up with his love. But if he didn't want to be with her, his emotional absence would make her feel worse than his going away. 'Of course I will,' she said.

Twiss persisted. Anything so long as he didn't have to stay himself. 'I can send that quack Darien over to you if you want.'

She laughed raggedly. 'That's no way to speak about our revered doctor!'

'Do you want him?'

'No, I don't. I'm just a bit overtired. Stressed out because of' – there was a catch in her throat – 'of Arnikon and everything. I'll be fine.'

'That's all right, then.' He gave her a perfunctory hug, his mind already elsewhere. 'Shall I cancel tomorrow's Synod?'

Irona and Regen spoke together. 'No.' Then Regen ducked his head and muttered, 'Sorry. Not my conversation.'

'Well if you've got everything you want, I'll be off then.' Twiss strode too briskly to the grav-shaft. He dived into it like a locust-lizard into freedom.

Irona and Regen exchanged a look and shrugged. She knew she had been right not to go back to Tingalit.

Regen took a tiny wheel of circuitry out of the Eye on

his lap and tutted. Turning it between his nervous fingers, not looking at her, he asked, 'You get these passin' out fits much, Ro?'

'I've had four now.'

Regen's cheek-muscles worked in a series of tics. The perspective was odd from where Irona leant back, resting her elbows on the parapet behind her. The soft light showed pathways winding through his thinning hair. His gaze fluttered uncertainly to her face and away again.

Irona had no idea what a picture she made, blonde hair kissed auburn by the dying of the day, her heart-shaped face pale against the violet sky. All she knew was that she felt her friend's admiration of her – and the discomfort that caused them both.

A heartbeat later, Regen said, 'If you don't want Jai and that doctor poking you about, why don't you get Tang's medics to check you over? You got to go back to Eastcliff anyway to find out where they fishfolk fit in to all this.'

'I can't!'

He heard the panic in her voice and smiled reassuringly. 'Don't worry, love. I ain't going to leave you go all on your own. Anyroad up, that computer of theirs needs checking out. Entirely.'

'Don't leave me alone with him, will you?' They both knew she meant Arias.

'Not unless you asks me to. You'll think I been arc-welded to your side.'

She chuckled faintly at the picture. Then she drew in a breath. 'It's just struck me, Regen. Why do you need to check out their console?'

''Cos there weren't nothing wrong with my Eyes till they Arms blasted 'em. And they gets their instructions through the computers, see?'

'So?'

'So the computer's matrix, the first one, yere' – he pointed at the console that had been installed when the First Wave of settlers had arrived under the matriarch Gundmila – 'that were modelled on the Watchtower one in Camelford, right?'

'Right.'

'So we copied the same matrix on to the ones in Tingalit and Eastcliff, right?'

'Right.' Her tone was faintly questioning.

'So, Irona, you need that medicheck or you'd of seen it yourself straight off. The Camelford Watchtower computer controls all the Admin's defences. *All* of 'em. Arms and Eyes, all on the same side. That's why our Eyes wouldn't attack they Arms. It'd be like auto-cannibalism, see? Like your left hand attacking your right. Hee-hee. But they Arms what killed Theb, they had no problem knocking out our Eyes, did they?'

'Regen, Regen, I thought you knew everything! The Arms aren't computer-controlled. They're just specially-grown human beings.'

'Irona, Irona,' he smiled, 'I do know everything. Yeah, when they Arms ain't called, they're autonomous. But you put out an alarm like you used to do from the Watchroom, or a call on their frequency, and it plugs straight into their brains. On their own, they ain't got no more smarts than a locust-lizard. They just have to do what the computer tells 'em. But the point is, it ain't our computer, see?'

She shook her head, feeling the solution forming inside her, but she was too tired and shaken to bring it into focus.

'So two things.' Regen held his right forefinger in his left hand. 'First of all, they Arms ain't under a computer taken from the same matrix.' He grasped his middle finger, and his odd features were twisted with worry. 'And second of all, someone on Earth, someone high up in Camelford, set up our computers to run Arms and Eyes like they do there. Don't you get it? Someone in Camelford wants to rule Harith.'

Under-Mexico-Fields wasn't safe any more, not if the gangs had exploded Pascual's head as easy as dropping a watermelon. Right now Pilar Costanza Jímenez didn't have time for her dream of being more powerful even than the President of Central America or the Matriarch of All Earth. All she knew about was the gangs that might come back to complete the example they'd begun by killing Pascual.

She ran to the service-tunnel in the wall where she fetched fresh water from whichever pipe the Blind Man had said was safe that day. She pulled Lorenzo along behind her, further and further from the light, and it didn't matter that he had long, knobby legs like a crane, built for running where hers were as stumpy as a turtle's, because his thoughts were melted into immobility and if she didn't pull him along he would stop and the gangs would find him and his head would be pulped like a watermelon too.

After a while, though, her lungs were on fire and she couldn't draw enough cool breath to quench the stitch that burned in her side. So she leaned against the thick pipes and Lorenzo echoed her panting in the dark.

When he could speak Lorenzo sucked at the cool, damp air and said, 'Do you know where we're going?'

'We're not welcome on the surface and we're not safe Under-Mexico-Fields. Where do you think we're going?'

In the darkness where the rats chittered and the soft mud pattered down like rain, Lorenzo didn't answer for a long time. Listening to his silence, Pilar knew that he knew. Up in the sunlight the police would shoot them like they would shoot any street-kid, so they would have to survive down where even the gangs were afraid to venture.

Down to the sewers.

Uncharacteristically he groped to hold her hand like he hadn't done for years. At her side, his fingers trailing the walls for direction, he said, 'We're all we've got left, now.'

'Then don't call me Cochina, OK?'

Lorenzo laughed. It boomed ghostly along the tunnel and the rats whisked silently away. The fat pipes gurgled from time to time and there was always the gentle weeping of the mud from above. 'We're going to get eaten by alligators and shot up with drugs and sold into slavery and all you can worry about is a name? Pilarita, you're not for real. What did you pick up back there anyway?'

'Some of his clothes.' From somewhere up ahead there was a little bit of yellow light that turned her white tunic and leggings to the colour of old bones. She didn't say anything else.

'I know you, Pilarita. You're holding out on me. Come on, what else did you bring?'

'I brought the cube of mom and dad. And a powerpot.'

'And?'

'And his wallet.'

'Well you can just hand that over,' said another voice, and a shadow fell out of the dimness at them.

Pilar stared at the boy who had slid out from between the horizontal pipes. He must have been about fourteen, she judged, way bigger than she was or even Lorenzo, and his hair grew low on his forehead so that his eyebrows seemed kilometres thick. 'Why should I?' she asked.

Lorenzo had dropped her hand the minute the boy

spoke. Now he tugged at her sleeve, pleading without words for peace.

''Cause if you don't, sister, I sacrifice you on an altar to the sungod.'

'There are no gods except the ones that believe in themselves,' Pilar said.

'You crazy, sister.'

'No, man. You crazy. I'm just saying the rules,' Pilar answered. 'I didn't make them up. Besides, you're on your own.'

The big boy laughed like a monster in a holodisk. 'You crazy for sure. Think I stay down here on my own?'

Pilar smiled with what she hoped was maddening superiority. Already she was mimicking his patterns of speech. 'Don't matter if you got an army, brother. You can't get a wallet away from a little girl on her own and you're trash. Think your sapheads will follow you then?'

'Cut the crap, kid. Just gimme the wallet.'

'Want to try it?'

He stepped closer. For answer she beckoned, a smile of rage on her face. He already had the beginnings of thick hair on his arms that swelled the sleeves of his T-shirt and she didn't come halfway up his chest. He spread his legs wide, dropping low into a fighting crouch.

Pilar dropped to her knees. Lorenzo started to move forward but she hissed at him, 'No.' Confused, Lorenzo stopped and two others seized his arms so that he was struggling with a fight of his own.

Pilar said like a high-class seductress in soap-opera land, 'Come here, Monolito.'

Lorenzo groaned. The two holding his arms suppressed giggles.

The big boy reached down his hairy arms, hooking his

fingers to tear into her. Only she grabbed his legs and bit his crotch as hard as she could.

He knocked at her head but there was no power in his blows. He staggered and tried to pull her off but her teeth were locked on target. She felt him drag her this way and that as he lurched around. Hooking her fingers tight into the belt round his trousers, she heard his friends creasing themselves laughing in the dim amber light.

Then Monolito collapsed on to the cold, wet earth of the tunnel and Pilar felt the spirit die in him. Quick as a cockroach she unbit him and scuttled out of range as he lay trying to press his hands over his groin as though that could take the pain away.

'I got something better than any old wallet,' she said. 'I always know which pipe they are not going to poison.'

They always called him that, afterwards: Monolito, meaning little monkey. But not one of them dared to say why, though kids from other bands always asked. Pilar had changed his fortune.

It was as if she had given him liquid gold, because every day she went to ask the Blind Man which water the authorities were not going to poison in their attempts to get rid of their surplus population. People wanted to join Monolito's band now and he was no longer on the fringes of Sewer City. He and his friends no longer had to sleep on the very lowest levels where sometimes methane built up and exploded, nor on the top levels where the big people could come and shoot you if they didn't sell you into prostitution.

True, the little band didn't have the best location because they couldn't fight all of the big bands at once. But they had a nest where the air didn't smell too bad and the ground wasn't too wet, and they built a barricade because now they had all the possessions they had traded for Pilar's secret of the water pipes. There was a canary to tell them if there was too much bad air. From Rafa's band of big kids who went bravely stealing in the Towers, there were toys and torches with three different colours of lights, and from Jaim' the Slime there were storybooks that lit up the words as the books slowly said them so that Pilar and one or two others started to read. There was food and booze and the slow smoke of Mary Jane that took away your hurts and made you laugh, and there were friends who would hug you when you cried out in nightmares, and there was a doll that was a radio who sang to you until Pilar broke it because it kept saying every hour that the President of Central America would give them water and sunlight and food, and above him there was only God. Pilar said out loud, 'Down here there is me, and above me, only Monolito.' To herself she said, *And the Blind Man*. Every day Pilar asked the Blind Man which waterpipe would be safe to drink from.

Only one day the Blind Man wasn't there. Nor the next, nor the next. Pilar didn't dare to say that to anybody, least of all to Monolito who still slept with his hands cupped protectively round his groin. So she guessed which was the safe pipe for that day. After all, even the President of Central America couldn't risk poisoning more than one at a time or thousands would die so suddenly that his game would be up.

She lost weight. First her waist appeared, and then her breasts which had been sleeping in the rolls of fat and surprised her as much as anybody else when they made their first appearance. Her jaw was no longer outnumbered by her chins, but her legs stayed like milk-bottles and she was so scared she snapped like a coyote when anyone talked to her. Even the canary flew away.

Then it happened. Like every day, the kids from Rafa's band drank the water she had said was safe. They didn't even have the sense to boil it first. They fouled Rafa's nest with their vomit and the loose brown water from their bowels, and Rafa had to leave because the plague started to filter into the rest of his band, and the other bands, and someone beat Monolito up so bad that he couldn't get away when the big people ventured down to the middle levels and they shot him.

After that, Pilar and Lorenzo were on their own again with nothing, so they ran and hid from revenge in the bottom levels where the alligators sawed into your dreams with their teeth.

They had not even a powerpot between them.

Pilar, tired and frightened and guilty, said, 'I'm thirsty, Lorenzo.'

Her big brother said, 'So were the ones you killed. You stay thirsty. You got it coming to you. So shut up and let me get some sleep, OK?'

She thought of yelling at him, but it was too much trouble. But it didn't matter, because that first sleep in their pathetic, dark, evil-smelling nest was broken when the next band along lit a fire.

The fireball blew past them in a burning golden cloud that broke Pilar's eardrums with its roar. It burned her eyebrows and eyelashes off but she didn't get the worst of it because she was so small she could squeeze into the narrow triangular back of the next behind the water-pipes.

It cooked the flesh from Lorenzo so that to Pilar he looked for one horrible moment like a suckling pig. And it left the air behind it so hot it scorched Lorenzo's lungs and he died, cooked inside and out. 'Refried,' Pilar whispered, but she couldn't hear herself.

Above and to one side of her, the fat pipes began to groan and pull away from the brick sides of the tunnel. The joints burst apart. Cold torrents sprang out at her and suddenly Pilar knew that if she didn't make it up to a higher level she would drown. She was frightened, the currents sucking at her milk-bottle legs. In the lightless water, rats clambered and scrambled over each other and over her in their panic. In her mind was a vision of herself not opening her mouth to breathe and drowning, or opening her mouth and a rat would crawl inside it and eat away inside her to her brain.

She was very glad when her hand chunked against a metal ladder and she could haul herself up through a manhole into safety.

But the methane build-up hadn't been an accident. Hard hands grabbed her and dragged her out into a viper's nest of big people. As someone slapped the sharp prick of a skin-patch on to her neck, she saw at the back of a crowd a matriarch in her blue, blue clothes. Unconsciousness swelled up worse than the water, and the blueness swallowed her like falling into the sky.

10
ALIENATION

The memorial for Arnikon was simple. Irona was surprised and touched by how many people attended. Not just Arno's pals, or Tebrina and Sinofer and her and Twiss's friends, but the many people whom she and Twiss had helped and nurtured. For a moment Irona stood on the threshold of the side door to the dais, looking at the throng chatting in the soft, underwater light of the Great Hall. Then she took Twiss's arm, and, breathing the atmosphere of perfumes and solemnity, they made their entrance.

Twiss was at his most imposing. He had armoured himself against the emotional storms of the occasion in his best clothes: the iridium crown with the great slab of emerald he called kistle sitting nobly on his brow; his suit of seasilk a shimmer of deep forest green, signifying Arnikon's regeneration as part of this world. Besides, Twiss never forgot politics for long: the seasilk emphasised his high regard for trade with Eastcliff. Irona walked beside him, her own dress of green high-necked and long-sleeved. A bar of sunlight gilded her hair as she sat on her own high seat beside Twiss in the jade shadows of Tingalit's Great Hall.

One by one friends filed up the wide steps, standing to one side. Some of them, like dear old Tebrina and her dour husband Sinofer, had brought little mementoes; in her case, a squeeze-globe that held what looked like a flower until you compressed the clear plasm. Then the image changed to a family portrait: Twiss and Irona, with Arnikon as a toddler sitting on her knee. Tebrina spoke for a moment, then laid the globe gently in Irona's lap.

Even Twiss had to work not to weep and tears flowed down Irona's cheeks. Impulsively she seized Tebrina's work-callused hand and murmured a choked 'Thank you.'

Tebrina said gruffly, 'You'd of done the same,' and, brushing the tears from her red cheeks, she walked stiffly away on Sinofer's arm. Fessbar, her son, who had been with Arnikon when he died on the volcano, didn't mount the steps. Trembling with guilt, he tried to hide at the back of the crowd. Irona saw him, and attempted to catch his eye to reassure him, but he wouldn't even look towards her.

Something sounded at the back of the hall. People turned to see, and over their heads Irona saw the blond fisherboy from the *Thistle-up*, eeling through the doors, his unaccustomed robes catching on the handles. He dipped his pale-furred head in what might have been an apology and came to rest by a tapestry frieze. He stood so still that he seemed to disappear into the colourful work of art.

Last came Regen. Irona's little pot-bellied friend scuttled up the steps but he wouldn't turn to face the hall. He spoke only to the grieving parents on the dais, holding out a viewdisk that he dropped into Ro's palm as if it might burn him. 'Found some prints of the lad in the computer. Thought you might like 'em,' he mumbled, ducking his head in discomfort. He always did hate being in the public eye. Adding, 'That way you can remember him happy, like, 'cos he wouldn't want you sad.' Regen gangled hastily over to stand behind the others on the lower steps.

Then it was over: a focus for grief, a scalpel to lance the pain. To Irona, the wake afterwards was a jumble of babbling voices and jokes she soon forgot, rich foods and sharp salads, iced wine-cup that smelt of fruit, music drifting above to the carven arches of the ceiling that changed to the colour of cedars with the sunset. What she remembered was Twiss mingling with their guests, only to come back constantly to her. She could feel the need in him that matched hers: a need for friendship with no axe to grind. No politics, no lust, just a physical and mental companionship. It was unspoken between them that after the wake they walked up the ramps to his room in Tingalit. That night he couldn't talk to her but held her as he slept.

Irona laid awake, sleep far from her until the morning star wheeled up the paling sky. She knew it was only transitory but she took what strength she could from lying in his arms, hearing his breathing, feeling the softness of his skin beneath his shirt. Nor, as she had dreaded, did the walls of her being crumble into blackness and terror. As the ice-cubes of tension melted from her neck and shoulders, she planned her war against the Arms – and their masters.

If I have to go to Earth to finish it, I will, she silently vowed.

Irona swept the Synod along at a furious pace. Reports from the Hospital, from Sticker's guards, routine complaints from Nona and Less – none of it lasted a second longer than it had to. For a people used to the leisurely pace of infinity, it struck strangely.

'So when they seed Rainshadow Valley,' she said, 'the tractor talkers will have to plough parallel with the contours below the alpine meadows. It'll minimise erosion and hold more moisture in the soil. The far slopes of Heralia itself will be best. That way we can put in some of those quick-bean trees Regen found—'

'Enough!' roared Less. 'What is the matter with you? You've hardly given us time to catch our breath.'

Irona smiled sweetly at him. 'Do you agree that food is going to be a big problem this year? Or don't you agree with the quick-beans?'

'Well, yes. I mean no.'

'Which is it?' Twiss said. His drawl had an edge of impatience for idiots who couldn't make up their minds.

Less was flustered. 'Both. Yes, the food's going to be short. Bound to be, seeing as there's too many come to live on the coastal plain here.'

Twiss parted his lips slightly but Irona gave him an almost imperceptible shake of the head. However surprising they might find it, now was not the time to question whether Less's conditioning towards the Second Wave were coming apart. Besides, what he said was true: there were too many people to live on the narrow strip between the mountains and the sea.

Less didn't seem to have noticed the byplay. He was saying, '... and worse, now the Arms have stuck their fingers in the pie. I know we haven't got enough land here, but – but ...' He took a deep breath and started again. 'Rainshadow Valley's bad enough what with snake-rats and locust-lizards and all those other native things, but it's downright stupid to live under the shadow of the volcano. What if it erupts? People could die!'

Regen slumped forward, resting both elbows on the table so that he could peer along at Less. 'I think Irona knows that, don't you?'

Less brushed both hands over his black and white hair in a gesture that failed to cover up his embarrassment. 'Well, yes,' he said, glancing at Irona's pallor, 'sorry, but—'

Vertical lines appeared on either side of Twiss's face. He said tautly, 'But that's the most fertile soil and Regen found the quick-beans in a black volcanic region only a couple of dozen kilometres north of here. Plus we can keep a weather-Eye above them to make sure there's plenty of rain.'

'Yes, but—'

Irona was the one who intervened this time. 'But you don't like the idea of native Harithian food, is that it?'

Nona butted in. 'No, he doesn't, and neither do I. We never used to have it before you Second Wave lot muscled in.' She folded her arms decisively below her flat breasts and set her narrow face. 'Synod knows what it'll do to us in the long term.'

Twiss raised an eyebrow at her. 'And aren't we the Synod? We do know. I've never seen you turn down a glass or three of night-lily mead. And we've practically lived on Eastcliff fowlfeathers this last month or so waiting till the spring crops come through. What is it that we've been harvesting under air-nets all these years? Poison, or what? Nona, be reasonable. 'Stead of working out how it can't be done, try finding out how else to do it.' He gazed round the table, gathering them all with his best smile of warm regard. 'The whole of Harith is relying on us. Let's not disappoint 'em.' Standing to give them a hint, he finished, 'Now, if there's nothing else, me and Ro's got some Arms to see to.'

Which was how Irona and Regen were able to catch the *Thistle-up* as soon as the predicted weather-window cleared the horizon. The Kiflians continued to avoid the fisherboy as they loaded last-minute supplies in the heat of noon.

'Hate to see good food wasted on they deves,' a man said to his workmate. 'Ain't even human, are they?'

Irona glared at him. It was obvious he hadn't noticed the blond-furred lad bending behind a barrel of dried fruit. Much to his discomfiture, the boy stood to smile sweetly at him.

As soon as the loading was complete, the strain at the landing-ground dropped away with the green land below them. When the airship had bounced through the turbulence over the Moon Mountains, and Rainshadow Valley lay below the transparisteel deck, the fisherboy stepped out of his Kiflian robes with a sigh of relief. He walked over them and left them lying on the glassy deck.

Regen, preternaturally relaxed for once, slept most of the day. As she was still too nervous of flying to want to distract Captain Hoojer or Kris the crewman for long, Irona was left with either her own thoughts or the fisherboy for company. She chose the fisherboy.

Watching him watch the long red winds trailing their coils of dust across the Interior, she felt his sense of peace. There was no anger in him, no rush, no mountainous joy at going home. Just a pleasant emptiness waiting to be filled with whatever the moment might bring. It blotted up Irona's feelings in its vacuum. Without knowing it, she slipped into a peace as wide as the vaulting dusk sky.

Eventually the needle-quick shadows of blue and black on the naked face of Harith brought her to herself. It was past midnight; the two moons were hurtling across the star-bright bowl of night. Not knowing that she had spoken aloud, she said, 'However did it get this late?'

The fisherboy leant one elbow on the rail and slanted his body to face her. A brief pair of shorts was his only concession to Kiflian modesty. The canopy cast him partly in darkness; Irona saw him as a creature of silver and moonlight. He said in a soft, sibilant voice, 'In Eastcliff there is no lateness but the tides'.'

'Hmm?'

He waved his hands; the moons'light shone pearly through the webbing between his graceful fingers. 'You asked how it got so late. Don't you hotskins understand? Lateness only exists where transport is involved.'

'Or when you're too late to save your son from throwing his life away on a volcano,' she said bitterly.

Her mood didn't seem to impinge on the fishboy. Any other fifteen-year-old – he couldn't have been more than that, for all that he was taller than she was – would have been abashed. 'It was too late from the time he was hatched into Kifl,' he said.

'What would you know about it?'

He shrugged; the light poured over him sinuously, leaving half of him in shadow. 'Only that there are few in Kifl who value time. They save it, they make it, they fritter it away in pointless occupations. But because you hotskins live forever, you think there is always an endless supply.'

'Don't you?' she asked, surprised.

Again, that sensuous shrug. This time the light that drenched his neck burnished his gills with a fan-tracery of mercury. When he spoke she could smell the myriad perfumes of the sea on his skin. 'We don't know. The Creator doesn't know. I am one of the eldest and I was only hatched fifteen summers ago. None of us has finished changing completely so we don't know yet if we have reached physical maturity. And nobody knows if the longevity is genetic or what. But we have a race to build, and a home and a life.'

He paused and she thought he had finished. His sentiments gave her a sense of purpose, that there was some point in going on without the only heir of her body. Even within her grief she felt faintly uplifted – until he added, 'Not like them rebel wasters you keep sending us. Take that Hesperion you brought last time.' He flashed a grin at her in unexpected levity. 'Please take him! He's nothing but trouble.'

'How? What harm can he do among your folk?'

The boy spread his fingers in wide fans. 'Among our folk, nothing. But he's a right wrecker in the breeding-pools. Seriathnis just says he's clumsy, but he keeps on and keeps on trampling the embryo-beds when he's down in the crop-pools. Even a hotskin couldn't be that stupid by accident. Still, I can't affect it right now so I'm not going to waste another thought on it.' Yawning, the fisherboy added, 'I'm going to sleep. Have a good night.' He turned aside, yawning again and folding himself to the transparent deck, his strawberry blond fur fluffing out against the chill.

Irona had managed to avoid looking down through the hull until now. With a rising feeling of vertigo she thought crags limned with blades of moons'light were spearing up to smash the base of his fragile neck. She drew in a breath but when he looked up at her, she made a faint gesture that said, *It's nothing*, so he cradled his shining head on his arm and slept. Fortunately for Irona's peace of mind, a mist drifted up from the next valley and it was as if his innocence were pillowed on clouds.

'Goodnight, Arnikon,' she whispered.

When the anchorlines were hauled in at Eastcliff, Regen

kept his promise to stay close by Irona. Even before they stepped off the gangplank into the busy hangar, he was monitoring the two Eyes that gleamed and bobbed and poked into everything, but he was never more than one pace from her.

Tang played the game; he greeted them formally, his voice pitched against the splashing waves echoing up from the pit below, and Irona didn't know how to cloak her coldness towards him. She could feel the tensions pulling through her lover in different directions. His smooth hair shone iridescent in the multi-coloured biolight of the hangar as he bowed slightly. Faint reflections of sunlight on ocean dappled the ceiling above him. Irona thought, *The whole thing's unearthly*, and then felt a weird disloyalty that she hadn't used the word *unharithian*. A tremor ran through her: *How could I forget the planet I've lived on for almost twenty years, where my son was born? What's happening to me?*

Stress. Calm down, she told herself, *it's just the stress of bereavement and – and seeing Arias again. Quick! Say something!*

The trouble was, she couldn't think of anything to say.

But before the moment stretched too long and thin for comfort, Arias rescued her. 'We thank you for the goods you've sent us in trade. Our colony isn't quite self-sufficient yet, but with your continued support, it soon will be.' Then he added a little reminder of just how useful the Eastcliff colony could be. 'How were the fowlfeathers?'

It was Regen who grinned and said, 'Delicious! You tried 'em stuffed in vine-leaves?'

Around them, the fisherfolk and one or two normal humans took time to glance sideways at the exchange of protocol while they got on with their routine tasks. Some siphoned off the gas from a huge, hissing cylinder; others tended the biolights, or netted errant airweeds with long swags of mesh. All of them, though, strained to hear anything that might affect their future.

Irona listened courteously to the Creator of Eastcliff, the surface of her mind clinging to protocol to keep her afloat above the vortex of her guilt and grief and anger. 'Thank you, Arias, for your hospitality, and of course you are welcome to a share in whatever Kifl can spare for as long as you need it,' she replied, equally formal. She also added what he had – omitted? forgotten? – to mention: 'And we know that when you can do so, you will repay our loans with food and wares for Kifl. Moreover, Synod thanks you for your assistance in rooting out the threat of Arms to all the peoples of Harith.'

She knew her lover had heard the unspoken mistrust woven through her words when he replied, 'Let me show you both to your quarters. When you are ready, we'll begin the tour of inspection. Eastcliff has nothing to hide.'

It was strange seeing Arias in a new light. She could still admire the smooth play of muscles in his tanned arms, the gentle curve of his smile. But it was hard to believe any more that this was the man with whom she had shared love for so long. Irona was shaken by the doubt that perhaps she had never really loved him after all; it had been a delusion. Or that she was too shallow to love anyone for real. *It wasn't him I loved. It was love itself.*

Arias sketched a gesture: *Come, walk beside me*, that had nothing personal in it. It made Irona feel lost. Even the comfort of her friend Regen at her side was a mere drop in the ocean. *Thebula gone. And – and Arno . . .*

On the long, upward spiral of ramps she glanced surreptitiously at their host. The same grace of movement was there, the same self-possession as when she had first seen him as an enemy taking possession of their Settlement in Rainshadow Valley. Yet a few nights ago he had warmed her with his lovemaking. *Which is the real Arias?* she wondered. *The one who spies on us or the one who loved me? Now you see him, now you don't.*

As they passed one of those strange, dead-end corridors that pierced the cliff-face for air and light, his flowing shirt and trousers of pale seasilk changed colour. That enhanced the illusion that he was a shape-shifter. Not once did he step out of his role. Irona was glad in some ways – it made his presence easier to bear – but all the same she was piqued. *You can't have it all ways*, she told herself while she unpacked in the high, airy room whose window-hold was mercifully sheathed in transparisteel. She had to tell herself all over again when he led them back down on a formal tour of all the breeding-pools of Eastcliff.

First he showed them his lab. It made Irona uncomfortable with its dim, blood-coloured lighting. Even the Eyes could find no windows, no sound of the sea. Banks of embryos grew in plastic wombs that throbbed to the infant heartbeats. The air smelt aseptic, of stone and chemicals. She, Arias and Regen were the only living beings there. *No*, she corrected herself, *the only beings capable of independent movement*. A need to hear the warmth of a human voice made her say, 'And there was me thinking all those Kiflian cracks about your fisherfolk hatching were just that: Kiflian cracks.'

Arias didn't share her levity. He answered coldly – *When has he ever been cold towards me?* – 'When we have fisherfolk mothers old enough to bear children, then you'll see. They'll be born just like anybody else. In the meantime, they're born from recreations of wombs. And for what it's worth, my fisherfolk talk about themselves hatching as a wind-up for your gullibility.'

Irona was genuinely contrite. 'I'm sorry, Arias. I should have thought before I spoke.'

Maybe one little avalanche fell from the glacier that was his defence against her attack on his creations.

The Creator of Eastcliff turned to leave, and Regen stepped hastily out of his way. Then Arias swung back to tell his – former? – lover, 'Please note the absence of any womb large enough to produce Arms.' Another couple of steps towards the sealed metal door. One of the Eyes bobbed out of his way. 'And before you ask, yes, you can send out your Eyes to check that there are no hidden chambers manufacturing them in secret, either, anywhere in Eastcliff's tunnels.'

Irona didn't need a psychicator to tell how hurt he was at her rejection, her suspicion, but where the jealousy had sprung from was more than she could fathom.

Lower still through the passages of Eastcliff, the ramps grew slick with moisture from the pounding surface of the ocean.

'Watch your footing,' Arias warned. 'I'd hate to lose any Kiflian dignitaries.'

Algae of blue and pink and green clothed the rock walls. Curtains of the stuff hung pendulous from the ceiling, getting thicker and longer as they reached places where few of the fisherfolk had any business. Hardly any side-passages crossed the main drag, but the light grew steadily stronger where the waves had torn away the base of the cliffs, leaving tidal pools behind reefs of stony debris. Here and there the waltzing gleams of reflections poured fire into knobs of quartz.

'It's beautiful!' Irona said.

Arias made no answer. He merely swept aside another tangled mat of weed and stepped back.

She passed under his open arm, and then stopped. It was so sudden that Regen bumped into her. Wordlessly, she moved aside to let him through.

I'm in a garden!

She was: a huge garden whose floor was clear and turquoise, a sandy-floored cove filled with pure, translucent water. All the colours of the rainbow bloomed in massed clumps, their flowery bracts gliding with the dance of waters. Lilies as white as Heralia's snows pirouetted on the sunny wavelets. Irona could smell their perfume, lilac and orange, just as she had imagined it when she had lain in Arias's bed. She wondered whether Arias had the same thought. The silver streaks of fish sped like needles through the grotto, golden fins fluttering as some sudden perception made the school whirl and veer into a forest of lavender whose topmost fronds peeped up above the surface, arching amethyst fountains. Beyond it was a reef, a fortress of crags and spires clad in ephemeral spectra, protecting the pool from the rip-tides of the open ocean. The arc of sky was a perfect blue beneath the fangs of rock lining the ceiling. Even the Eyes were twin shining moons.

Regen whistled his appreciation.

'Oh, it's beautiful!' Irona said again, but Arias didn't answer. When she looked, he wasn't even there.

A low murmur sounded behind the tangled curtain. She pushed aside the seaweed – *Seasilk!* she realised, and saw a naked fishergirl leaning up against Arias on tiptoe so she could whisper in his ear. An irrational jealousy speared lightning through Irona but it was gone the second Arias turned to say, 'We've lost Hesperion. Will you lend me your Eyes to try and find him?'

'What d'you mean, try?' Regen asked brusquely. 'How big is this damn place of yours?'

Arias's face was dark and harsh. 'Sometimes,' he said, 'Kiflians can't take it here. They isolate themselves, or—'

'Or what?' Irona asked.

'Or they throw themselves over the cliffs into the ocean.'

Regen shrugged. 'That solves one problem, then. Hee-hee. Entirely.'

Arias looked down his nose at the little man. 'No, it doesn't. He seems to have taken a crystal and three of my fisherfolk with him.'

11
COUNCILS AND COUNSELLORS

Irona faced the Eastcliff leader in the garden-grotto. 'You take one Eye, Arias.' She handed him the remote control. 'We'd better keep the other, just in case.'

He snorted his scorn. The sound was magnified by the echoes in the grotto and blurred by the hush of the sea. 'Yes, because you still think I've got a soup-pot full of Arms somewhere about, don't you?'

'No!' Her vehemence was all the greater because that was exactly what she was thinking, or at least, that was what she was dreading. 'I just thought that if we came upon Hesperion while we're lurking about down here we'd look pretty stupid with no means of catching him for you. Have you any idea where he might be?'

Arias shrugged – a ray of light from the cavemouth slithered across his seasilk shirt – and said, 'He was supposed to be in the laundry. As he evidently isn't, I don't have the faintest idea. But I will.'

'I don't think we'd be much use to you in the search seeing as we neither of us know this place, but if there's anything we can do to help ...?' She left the question dangling.

'No, you're all right. You just carry on ...' He stopped, as if he had meant to add something else. 'Spying', perhaps. It left a nasty taste in Irona's mouth.

At least Arias softened the blow by saying, 'Have dinner with me, the pair of you. Any of the fisherfolk can find me whenever you're ready. We usually eat about sunset.'

He dashed out the way they had come, the noise of his shoes echoed by the softer slap-slap of Seriathnis's webbed feet. Above him the polished orb of the Eye jogged through the air in his wake. The ragged curtain of seasilk made a faint sloughing sound as it settled back into place behind him.

Regen made to follow him, more slowly, but Irona laid a hand on his arm and said, 'No. Let's explore this place first.'

'There ain't no Arms in yere, girl,' Regen said, but he followed her nonetheless. Their own Eye homed in to hang neatly above them, a sphere seeming as innocent as an iridescent moon.

A cindery path led around the edge of the cave to right and left. Irona tossed an imaginary token, catching it and peering at its invisible image on the back of her other hand. 'Let's try right,' she said.

Regen grinned. 'Why not?'

Towards the front of the cave-mouth, the path grew pearly with powdered shells. Whorls and spirals of nacre crunched underfoot. She thought of the trade that could be made with them in Kifl, then shook her head angrily. For one thing Kifl needed all the food it could get, especially with the raid by the Arms. Trading for luxuries cost the town essential supplies it could ill afford. For another, she had no business thinking of economics now. The Arms factory and Hesperion were immediate threats.

Concentrate on what you're doing! she shouted at herself. *If you get it wrong more people might die.*

Overhead, her Eye quested for data. The slap and shirr of the tide hid any little, tell-tale sounds. She sent the Eye on ahead, doing her best to check every direction. The main part of the track led through another hanging forest of raw seasilk, its colours muted by the tough outside skin that scraped over her head and hands.

'Looks like there be a door in yere somewhere,' Regen said.

She sent the Eye weaving through the drapes of seasilk. Sure enough, there was another cave beyond this one, only it was not open to the sea. Or maybe it was, below the surface of the dark, sucking waters. Irona and Regen stood on the threshold, their vision gradually adjusting to the faint crackle of electricity Irona ordered the Eye to put out.

'See that?' she said. 'Stepping-stones. Right across to that other tunnel.'

'Let's try it then.'

Irona stopped him. Turning back, squinting a little against the bright sunlight that fought its way into the grotto behind her, she gestured at the rock-toothed archway, then nodded at the dark passage where he stood waiting. 'Just a little bit obvious, don't you think?' she asked. 'Hesperion might be a fool but he's not an idiot. He'll know they'll be looking for him inside Eastcliff. Don't you think he might he hiding outside somewhere?'

'Don't look like there's anywhere to hide out there, love. But let's give it a quick shot.'

'Love' again? Why does he say that? Before the thought

could make her uncomfortable, Irona turned round to follow the narrower part of the path, clambering through the glass-edged basalt of the cave-mouth to the sunny outside world. A fold of cooled lava blocked her view to the right; the opposite side of the cave-mouth was convex, but there was no-one in the seething waters.

Regen followed her out to stand on the rim of a rock. The black stone was wet and stained by the sea that stretched unbroken to the horizon. Their perch was spattered with a pale goo that smelt rotten. Trying to block the stench from her nostrils, Irona picked her way across the slanting boulder that had obviously been undercut from the cliff-face. Fine bones formed hieroglyphs in the cracks between the rubble. Grey hairs that were aerial plants hovered above the waves or plastered themselves stickily on the rocks themselves, the free third of their length questing into the ichor.

She stood for a moment, brushing the floating strands away from her face. Tiny nets of static fizzled blue around the Eye as it dealt with its own coat of smothering hairs.

Not a metre below them, the crest of a comber broke with a crash. Indigo water frothed into white and spindrift sparkled in the sun. All at once Regen yelled 'Eurgh!' and jumped, cannoning into her so that both of them nearly toppled into the sea behind her.

'What—?' Then she too leaped back, startled by the sneaky geyser of water that had fought its way up between the stones.

Regen held her damply until they had regained their balance. It took some time because they were laughing so hard at their surprise.

Irona recovered first. She craned back to look up at the kilometre-high cliff behind them. This close to, the sheer face had character: clefts and ledges and the window-holes of Eastcliff, and the huge gash of the hangar far above. Not only that, the basalt was streaked with varying colours as the eco-systems at sea-level and the different heights above it established themselves only to give way to the next group where thermals, moisture and the green influence of the fisherfolk took over.

But there was barely a sensible hand-hold as far as the eye could see. The sun caught the razor-edges of the stone like light on the blades of a thousand knives, up and up dizzyingly until the towering rock seemed like a spired shrine about to fall on them. ''Less he had a jet-pack, he ain't got up there,' Regen said.

'Or unless Arias gave him wings.'

'Can't of done,' Regen answered, taking her words at face value. 'He don't do grafts, only embryos.'

'As far as we know. But the Arms back on Earth chose to have sensor-fronds implanted, or a third eye for infra-red, or whatever. And since nobody living has seen the Arms close enough to say, or at least seen them without going into a complete panic and then lived to tell the tale, we don't know what Arias might or might not have been doing.'

'Rift in the lute, is there?' Regen asked, his words apparently idle while he leaned out against the wind to peer around the fold in the rock. The wind tugged at his thinning brown hair so that it shone like spun toffee in the sunlight.

'How dare you!'

''Cos I'm your mate, that's how. 'Taint just Arnikon's worrying you. Something else has happened and you ain't been right since.'

'Is that why you keep calling me "love"? Planning to make a move, are you?'

'Ro, you're being stupid. Entirely. And it ain't like you at all. I was just trying to give you a bit of comfort. That OK by you or what? You're about the only person I know can put up with my twitches. Think I'd jeopardise that? Have I ever done anythin' to you that you don't like?'

She blew a long sigh down her nose and rubbed her pale forehead with one hand. 'No. You're right. I'm being stupid.' Except that to go along with her own feelings put it somewhere between paranoia and arrogance. 'It's just that I – I was with Arias when Twiss told me the news about Arno.'

'Come on, girl, get that head up! That ain't no reason for you to—'

'I feel so guilty, don't you see? It's like it's my fault because I wasn't there to stop him. Twiss says the same. I shouldn't have been with Arias in the first place. I should have been there in Kifl! I should have been there for Arno, and I wasn't.'

'He'd planned to go out with Fessbar and his mates anyway, hadn't he?'

'Well, yes, but—'

'But nothing, Ro. He'd of died just the same 'less you were actually holding his hand. You were sent yere to give the place the once-over so nobody else didn't get killed by no Arms. Besides, his dad were there, weren't he? He didn't make no difference. If Twiss weren't seven kinds of a bastard and you'd never even heard of no Arias, you'd still have had to come and check Eastcliff out.'

She turned away from Regen, staring out at the gold-studded path of the sun over the blue sea, and it wasn't just the breeze that brought the tears to her eyes. The weight of guilt still bowed her shoulders. He was close enough, though, to catch her words out of the wind that sang into the cave. 'I know all that! I do know, Regen. It's not logical, but I can't help it. And I know I'm hurting Arias, and that makes me feel worse, but somebody's got to be building these murdering Arms. Who else can it be?'

'Well, I'd lay it ain't Arias Tang. He's never been no friend of mind but it's not his style. Subtlety, misdirection, yes. But not great lummocking things like over-sized wasps what go bumping your mates off left, right and centre. He ain't my cup of strychnine, hee-hee, but he'd never go killing off people you love.'

Regen reached out to rub her shoulders, one quick, casual pass of his hand. Then his grip firmed so that she flinched as his weight came down on her. She turned her head quickly, somehow frightened at what might be going on, but he was steadying himself against her so that he could look out and around the fold of rock. 'Here, Ro, look at that!'

Her gaze was puzzled.

In answer his chin gestured. 'Up and around there where the Eye's hovering. Lean on me so's you can have a look.'

She did. Her feet right on the edge of the boulder, her hand braced around his arm, she stood on tiptoe above the crashing breakers and saw it.

A pale gleam. Not enough of the pearlised sand to make a proper footpath. But enough to mark that someone had been that way recently, dropping fragments of shell that had been stuck to his – or her – boots.

Irona said, 'Here, pass me your remote, would you?' but when they looked into the tiny screen, the Eye saw nothing wrong, not even an infra-red pressure-trail. Still that opalescent sand gleamed where it shouldn't against the black basalt. She and Regen exchanged a glance and shrugged. 'What the hell,' Irona said. 'Let's go for it.'

She used hands and feet to swing around the jag of rock.

Careful as she was with the ocean threshing the needles of stone that broke the surface just below, she was sucking blood from a cut fingertip by the time Regen caught up with her. Jerking her chin up in a moue of self-disgust, she started up the slanting ledge. It was so narrow that she had to keep in to the cliff-face. Stony tines combed threads from her dress and hair from her head, but it was either that or fall to the sharp rocks below. She couldn't spare a hand to brush aside the aerial parasites so she did her best to ignore the foul trails they left on the exposed skin of her face. Her feet slithered on something sticky; she swallowed and didn't look down.

After maybe forty paces of climbing, Irona stopped and blew out a breath of relief. 'We've reached a level above the airweeds,' she called above the rush of the tide. Nodding at the iridium bubble whose surface was still now, she added, 'The Eye's calmed down too, see?'

In a few strides Regen was with her, his head level with her waist since the path was so precipitous. 'About time, too,' he said. 'Entirely.' He gave his irritating nervous giggle. 'See anything?'

'Other than a few lizards flying about a couple of hundred metres up, no. I just hope they're not the hungry kind.'

'Or that we don't have to go that high. Come on.'

After ten minutes or so, the track they were climbing petered out.

'Well,' Regen said in a voice like a sigh, 's'pose we'd better get back down again.'

'I wouldn't be too sure of that. Look over there.' She pointed, and felt the wind sucking heat from the perspiration on her dress. The Eye had come to rest some two metres away where a long, dark hollow beckoned.

'Best send the Eye in, then,' Regen said.

'I have done!'

The trouble was, it didn't come out again. The sun slid down the blue of the afternoon sky and still their Eye didn't return. Irona's legs were shaking from the steep climb and from trying to balance motionless with her feet at unnatural angles.

'D'you want to go back or on?' Irona asked eventually.

'Mmm. You stop yere. Maybe it's just a mechanical failure. They Eyes ain't never been right since the Arms burned 'em. Hee-hee. Don't want to admit defeat in front of Arias. I'll give it a try.' Regen took off his brown jacket to wrap his fingers in the sleeves. With his padded hands to anchor him against the glittering razors of basalt, he swung himself across and thrust his torso into a hole. He mumbled something.

'What?' she yelled. 'I can't hear you.'

Regen pulled his head out long enough to say, 'There be a cave all right, but I doubt even the Eye would of spotted it ifn it hadn't been for the sun casting shadows this time of day. Looks like it goes in a long way. I'm going in. You stay by yere.'

'No chance! What happened to being arc-welded to my side? You're not leaving me behind!'

Back on Earth, Bernardina, Matriarch of All Earth, was stalling for time. Around an oval table that was ancient when Caesar was a red-headed upstart, the members of the World Council stared at her.

'So you admit, then,' Pilar Jímenez Costanza said, 'that your Mission station in Caracas has weather-control capabilities?'

The Crown, the Supreme Equal, the hologram of Li

Chan, all of them, just sat and watched Bernardina's discomfiture as though she were an exhibit in a dissecting-room.

Bernardina breathed in a pattern that was supposed to control the flush of blood-pressure mounting to her face. Faced with the American whorebitch's discovery, she found no answer that didn't compromise her in front of the collected leaders. Their silence was a weapon: the appraisal and mistrust of individuals who were beginning to consider conspiracy against her.

She knew it, but for the moment she had no answer. This time the Summit was in the Great Pyramid; the building-block that had been shoved aside let in the heat and the sand, the festering, smog-laden atmosphere of Greater Cairo. Ancient paintings and glyphs she could not decode shimmered under their protective varnish. Those profiled, one-eyed gods looked hostile too, staring down from the walls at her, the interloper in the Saharan Commune.

Pilar Jímenez Costanza, President of the Three Americas, rattled her steel-clad nails on the table. Her gaze was sharp as the condor that symbolised her nations. Like the condor, she waited.

Bill Peach, Supreme Equal of Oceana, picked his perfect teeth with fingers that bore the outlines of cancer-scars. Cosmetically frozen in tanned blond unreality, he waited.

Faisal Khomeini Amin, Shah in-Shah Elect, drank green tea that smelt of mint, and waited.

The young Crown of Novaya Zemla, who bore no other name and hadn't been young for twenty years, smiled and mouthed 'Mother' at her. He didn't even pretend that the others hadn't seen his mockery. Twinkling the blue-green eyes of the northern Rus at her, he waited.

Jeanne-Marie Buonaparte Lepènes fingered the sculptured perfection of her Limoges eyebrows, and, chuckling as deep in her throat as a Parisian 'R', she waited.

Nanuk Innuit Australis-Borealis scarcely twitched his flat, sallow face that was as bland as an iguana's. Each fibre of his mock-fur hood and clothing was radar, heat-conductor, antenna. What matter that he had let his eyes opaque with cataracts so that he could seem a harmless old man? Even the biolipids of his blubbery body housed sensors and computers. Patient as a machine, he waited, and the cold force of his waiting pressured Bernardina more than any other's, precisely because it was so inhuman.

Li Chan's hologram from its tank in Asiapura sent meaningless word-bubbles through its liquid in a pattern calmer than Buddha's. It was a mantra to fill time between one happening and the next, and its torture was that nobody knew when the next bubble would burst.

Bernardina, knowing that Elditch was watching her from the Capital of the Admin, wasn't comforted. She wished she were back in her hidden granite cell, actually hearing her daughter say, 'Of course I'll help you. Aren't you my mother?', secure in the hollow wall of Camelford.

But she wasn't.

And just when her de-programming of Irona had started to become interesting, this crisis had arisen. Synod knew where Irona was now.

Or what she intended.

Where can she be that's out of reach of the ansible? the old woman asked herself, fingering her wispy brows. *She'd answer me if she could, wouldn't she?*

Doubts nibbled the underside of Bernardina's mind. She swallowed. They left a lump in her throat, but she put it down to the dry, thick air and the abrasion of sand. She concentrated on her physical distress to quash the awful doubts.

If I can put this on hold long enough, Bernardina promised herself, *I'll make Irona do it. She must have got the Starbird package by now, surely. How can she refuse me?*

And to the World Council, the Matriarch of Matriarchs said, 'Weather-Eyes in the Venezuelan Mission school? In theory, yes. For training purposes only. They are only simulators, so in practice, no.'

Irona kilted up her green skirt between her legs and wondered why now after all these years that impractical modesty had suddenly made her uncomfortable. She looked down at the turquoise and indigo sea, and wished she hadn't. The fangs of the reef were chewing the water into a white, spuming pulp that was the same colour as subcutaneous fat.

She thought of Arno, calcinated. Tides of ocean pulled gravity into her blood. *It would be so easy to fall! They couldn't blame me for that, could they? There'd be no shame . . .*

Then she remembered what the Arms had done to her friend Thebula and knew she couldn't let their maker beat her. Death would have to wait – at least, her death would. Wrapping her fingers in scraps torn from her ruined dress, she threw herself sideways, reaching for the handhold Regen had used.

One heart stopping moment as her hand flailed for the ridge, then her fingers curled around it. Temptation was gone as quickly as it had come. She made the long step across to the toehold and smiled. *Can't beat me, Death,* she thought silently, then yelled it aloud to the cliffs and the sky and the sea.

Seconds later she crawled head-downwards into the obscure tunnel in Eastcliff's façade. Her own shadow spidered before her, blocking her vision as her body slowed down the flow of fresh salt air.

'Regen? Regen, where are you?' she called, but her words were a whisper and the web of echoes swallowed them. It was too narrow for her to turn round now, and the slick, gritty rock was blistering her palms where she crawled. Pebbles bruised her knees. Fear tasted of copper.

'Don't do this to me, Regen,' she said. 'I'm round the corner now and I can't see a damned thing.'

'Good,' said a voice.

Lightning triggered her neurones. They flared like rockets in the carnival dark. She fell, and the tactile/sound web vibrated with the coming of Arachne. Movement was a total impossibility. Around her the throat of stone echoed like her own skull but she couldn't move a muscle.

'Very good,' gloated the voice. 'Now we can have some fun.'

12
BLACKOUT

When the lightning storm finally played itself out of Irona's mind, she found herself immobilised. She was in total darkness in a pool of cold water that came up to her neck. Sooty blackness was thick around her. Wavelets slapped the taste of ocean against her lips; her throat didn't seem to work very well because she choked rather than coughed. No amount of effort could raise her head. She was frightened to feel the icy salt rivulets slipping into her lungs with no possibility of expelling them.

Scared, Irona opened her eyes to see what was going on. Except that they were already open. Her brain cried out: *I'm blind!*

She wrenched at her restraints. Nothing. She couldn't move so much as a toe, though when she concentrated she could feel unseen currents tugging at her clothes. There was no chafing of ropes on her limbs but she still couldn't shift any part of herself in the slightest. Her bonds, if bonds there were, didn't touch her physically at all. She couldn't feel the weight of the Eye-monitor in her pocket but that didn't mean it wasn't there. It only meant she had no idea.

She still couldn't lift her head. Forcing her throat to work, she called 'Regen?' The name came out as a croak even she could barely hear above the sounds of the ocean echoing in the black cave. *What if the cave's not black? What if I'm out in daylight somewhere and I just can't see it?*

No. I'd feel the sun and the open air. Wouldn't I? And there's echoes. It's a cave. I'll see again. The fear burned through her that she wouldn't. *If – whoever – wanted me dead I'd be dead already.*

'Regen?' Her words echoed mockingly.

'Regen?' The shock of an answer beat through her, worse because she couldn't see who was there. All she could tell was that it wasn't her friend's beloved voice. The blindness of the empty cave walled her in. '"Regen?" Is that all you can say?' the derisive voice went on. 'Is that who you want to be with now? That skinny little brain-damaged abortion? Not King Twiss or Tang the Creator? You're coming down in the world, aren't you?'

... Different days, different gravity. Suddenly Irona was somewhere else.

She was dizzy, disorientated. What the hell was going on?

Another empty space. In this somewhere else, one minute things had been all right, but she had opened a door and now her whole life was wrong. Another echoing, aching vacuum, though, this one where all the things that made her home had been – and had gone. The sharp feelings of youth cut at her. Irona could see, back then, but seeing was no help at all. It had all gone. It had been fine before she left for watchwarden training that morning, but now it had all gone. Everything she had ever known.

She let the door click shut behind her and came deeper into the hollow living-room. Her mother's work-station with its busy screen wasn't in its alcove. Its subtle hum that was always there like wallpaper wasn't there.

'Mom? Dad?'

No answer.

Maybe I'm in the wrong flat?

But it was a forlorn little hope. This was where she had lived, all right. Her mother and father had told her once that for a while they'd been exiled to the Warrens, but Irona had never quite believed such a ridiculous story. This was where she had lived for as long as she could remember. There were no pictures on the walls, but the oblongs of paleness matched the sizes of the pictures in her mind. Irona hadn't imagined them. They'd been there, and now they weren't. The little round table with its fringed cloth wasn't in its place by the window either, yet she could see where its feet had sunk into the carpet over the years of her childhood when she had liked to play under its muffling fabric and nobody knew she was there. This was the right place: her home in the wardens' apartments in the Watchtower of Camelford Mountain. Ro from 117Rho, Level E, Camelford Mountain, The Admin, Earth, the World, in Space, she had written on the cases of her data-disks when she started warden-school. 117Rho was the nicest flat there: the Senior Watchwarden's apartment with the five big rooms and the big terrace and the view over the Park.

Only it was empty. Abandoned. Like she was.

But there was some mistake. There had to be.

No more seats, no cupboards, no bookshelves, just a floor that appeared to go on forever because there was no furniture on it to give it shape and definition, the geometry of home. Everything rushed away from her; it felt like the world dropped away beneath her feet and the ceiling leaped off so high it grazed the hard smear of the Sky.

I'm sixteen, Irona thought wildly. This is my home! She called again into the emptiness, 'Mom? Dad?' but the air in the apartment was so still and dead that she knew there'd be no reply. Just the ghost of an energising olfact that was the smell of her mother, and the lingering odour of the mints her father used to chew. It wasn't her home any more.

Suddenly she heard a faint noise from next door. Hope leaped in Irona.

I'll ask Aunt Biddy!

But she knew she couldn't. What would she say? *Hello, Aunt Biddy, where's my home?* No, she'd feel too foolish. What about *Do you know where I live?* Or *Where do my parents live now they obviously don't want me with them?* It was a stupid idea. The whole thing was just too humiliating. Subconsciously she began to wonder what she had ever done that was bad enough to deserve this. Somewhere inside she felt a black pit of sin: this is my fault. But she didn't know why. She didn't understand.

Greasy moonlight through the slats of the blinds carved her world into arbitrary slices that held no meaning. There was nothing: no beds in the bedrooms, none of her parents' jars and powders in the bathroom, no plates or half-empty jars of sauce in the gleaming kitchen. She checked again: in the closets there was only the soap-smell of the clothes that had once hung there. There weren't even curtain-rings on the poles any more, just the stark, bare, regulation blinds over the beautiful real windows. There was nothing but the empty size of it to show that Senior Watchwarden Elditch and Matriarch Towy's own Matriarch-Elect had ever lived here. Apart from the walls and the floor, there was nothing there at all.

When Irona finally trailed through to the refuge of her

own room, she couldn't find so much as Tilly, her favourite stuffed toy that she was too grown-up to sleep with now. For years she had kept the one-eyed rabbit on the back of the top-most shelf in the vacant space that obviously wasn't her wardrobe any more. Tilly had had an apron tied on with a plait of silk and there was a limp little felt carrot in her pocket.

Now Tilly and Irona's life had gone. In those meaningless slices of light from the windows, dust-motes shuffled in a random dance of mockery. Even the last symbol of her childhood had been taken away from her. Irona couldn't put her world back together to make any sense at all.

She huddled with her back to the wall on the spot where the little round table used to be, and felt the forgotten guilts of eavesdropping. The white lies, the excuses, the way she'd answered her mother back the day before. Cold as a blizzard, the little guilts mounted up. In the basement of her mind, she knew she'd been discarded because she was bad.

The one thing that was left was the old standard communicator, and that was because it belonged not to her parents but to the Admin. It was the same as the one in every other apartment in Camelford, even down in the Warrens. She eyed it nervously, its cord looping down from the windowsill, the communicator her mother had never used because she had her work-station and had never felt the need for friends. Her father's friends, of course, were the sort who daren't call him at home. That girl in the playground years ago – what was her name again? – had been right all along.

Hesitating, only desperation impelling her to it, Irona knelt beside the communicator and shut off the viewing.

What if they've been brain-wormed? 'They' were her parents. Or had been. Are the Arms going to come and get me too? That thought was more comforting than the belief that her parents had abandoned her without letting her know where they were going. Or even that they were going.

I bet they have, she told herself. *Someone's accused them falsely and they're going to be brain-wormed. That's why they couldn't even leave me a note.*

It was only a theory. Irona clung to it as though it were the immutable truth of a shrine. It was marginally less painful that way. But she had to know. *Maybe I can rescue them and then they'll love me and we'll all be together again*. But for a long time she was too scared to find out.

At last, though her fingers trembled so badly she kept miskeying, she managed to call Marisa, the closest thing she had to a friend.

'Ro? What's up? You sound ever so strange. Put the view on.'

Irona didn't. She didn't want anyone to see her just now. Especially she didn't want anyone to see the abandoned apartment where she didn't live any more. 'Marisa, something's happened. I' – she changed what she had been going to say – 'I can't talk about it over the com. Can you come over, please?'

'Oh, Ro! Not now, please. I've got a million things to do. Charry's coming round tonight. Can't it wait?'

'No.'

And after a short dispute, Marisa said, 'All right, all right, I suppose so. Charry's not coming for another half-hour. I'm on my way. I wish you wouldn't be so all-fired mysterious! Just stay put.'

It seemed like a long time, though probably it wasn't.

Marisa only lived on Radial Epsilon on level Pi, the floor below.

Finally the door-com spoke in Marisa's voice. Irona went to answer it. All the guilt and pain and betrayal made her legs shake but she crossed the desert of the unoccupied floor on a gust of gratitude that her friend had come to rescue her.

Irona opened the door just a fraction and before she'd let her friend in, she made her promise a dozen times that she'd never ever tell a living soul. Even then, filled with doubts and insecurity, Irona took a long time to open the door.

But Marisa took one look around the barrenness that was no longer a home and said, 'They've left you, kid. You've come down in the world, haven't you?'

Not long after that, Marisa left too. Irona didn't see her again . . .

'. . . don't you answer me, damn you!'

Abruptly Irona was back in the cave. The words still echoed in her head like the sound of the sea inside the blackness of the walls: 'You've come down in the world, haven't you?'

Once more there was that smear of nausea that blurred reality as she was wrenched back into the present. Something slammed into the side of her head again. Eastcliff. She was back inside the cave at Eastcliff. She was on Harith, a prisoner, blind, half-drowned and terrified, but she existed. Someone knew she was there. It felt better than the grip of childhood memory.

'I won't ask you again!' the voice said threateningly.

Irona pushed the words through her slack throat: 'Ask me what?'

'To smuggle me back to Kifl, of course! Haven't you been listening? D'you think I want to rot here for ever?'

Mirth bubbled bitter in the water in her lungs. 'Hesperion?' she said on a cough.

The voice came out of the darkness. 'Who did you think it was? Thebula?'

'Don't you talk to me about Thebula. You're the one whose stupidity got her killed.'

'I hardly think, Irona, Queen of all she surveys, that you're in much of a position to give orders.'

'Where's Regen?'

Hesperion said too hastily, 'Never mind him. Just get me out of this filthy swamp with its stinking fishmen.'

'Not until you produce Regenerator, alive and unharmed.'

Some invisible force dunked her face into the cold black water she could not see. The force was nothing tangible, but it was effective. Water crammed into her nostrils and pushed against her eardrums. Hesperion had caught her on an out-breath; she tried to keep her hollow chest from sucking in liquid. Her diaphragm spasmed, her ribs worked, but she kept her throat closed for so long that fire painted flares on her retinas. It wasn't even Hesperion touching her. Nothing touched her but her clothes and the chill currents, but the compulsion was real. Her hair strung like seaweed across her blank eyes. She could not move her head above the surface. She couldn't breathe. She remembered how it had felt to be Thebula with someone else pulling her strings. It was terrifying.

The same intangible force yanked her head back. Tendons cracked in her neck. She dragged air into her starved lungs, whooping involuntarily, choking on her wet hair. Oxygen etched away the dazzles from her blinded eyes and she spat out the soggy fibres in her throat. Even if she couldn't see, at least she could breathe.

Hesperion gloated at the power he possessed. His words scratched the salty atmosphere. 'Now will you take me?'

'Not until you give me Regen.'

'Then you'll die.'

'Then you'll stay here.' She wretched salt water. 'Anyway, why don't you just stow away on the *Thistle-up*?'

'Because it's transparent, you idiot. And if I did manage to hide away in one of the bales, the fishfolk would throw me over the side soon's they spotted me, if the cold didn't kill me first. Even if I survived the drop, I'd die drinking acid in the Interior.'

'Then it looks like we're stuck here,' she said, 'because you haven't got Regen or you'd have given him to me already.'

'Never mind him. He's just a deve. He's not even human. In fact, I think I'll just leave you on your own till you change your mind. The tide's coming in,' he added nastily.

'You need me or you wouldn't have gone through this ridiculous performance. You won't leave me to die.'

Hesperion sounded petulant. 'Well, those fish-things aren't human. They won't let me near them. Threaten one and the others don't care. I can't get a reaction out of them. They'd cut their legs off for that Creator of theirs. Synod, I hate them!'

'I shouldn't think they're that fond of you, either.'

'Shut up!'

But she didn't. 'They know you trash the embryo-beds. You're just trying to achieve what you couldn't in Kifl: to wreck trade so we'll leave them to die.'

'They deserve to die! You slimy thieving Second Wavers, you're bad enough, but these – these filthy fish-things, they're not even human! Taking up resources our people need . . .'

Irona was appalled. She tried reason: 'Don't you ever eat kelp-bread? Eat fowlfeathers? Think our people could manage the undersea farms?'

'If you were all gone, our people wouldn't need the undersea farms. Now shut up!'

From somewhere – the sound echoed so she couldn't locate its source – she heard a thump, then Hesperion swearing. For a moment she thought Regenerator had sneaked up and belted him, but there was no familiar voice calling out that she was safe, entirely. Nor did Hesperion's intangible grip on her slacken for more than a micro-second. She decided reluctantly that he'd bashed his head on some outcrop of rock. Irona wondered if he was blind too, or just careless.

'Ah, diddums,' Irona said. 'Did he hurt himself then?'

'Shut up! Just shut up, you Second-Wave bitch, or I'll make you.' A pause, then he said with triumph oiling his voice, 'In fact, I could make you anyway, couldn't I?'

And, suddenly, her arms began moving of their own volition. Then her legs. She lurched forward, almost falling, her limbs robotic. A stone turned under her bare feet and she all but toppled into the water she couldn't see. She couldn't put out her hands to save herself. Things brushed against her, waterplants tangled round her legs and she stumbled blindly. It was frightening.

But the worst thing was, her body was his to command.

Hesperion laughed, and the echo grated on her darkness.

Her body lurched another step. Irona felt like a corpse

dragged up to pseudo-life in a nightmare in the dark. Ripples lapped around her breasts, touching her lasciviously, taking advantage of her helplessness. She was dreadfully aware of how open she was to whatever he might do. Hesperion forgot to hold up her head; suddenly her neck dropped the weight of her skull down on to one shoulder and water streamed from her hair over her sightless eyes.

Another step, and another. All at once she plunged into a patch that was suddenly deeper. The tide rose above her head. Her heart slammed in the cave of her chest. Sparks burnt against her blindness as the pressure of her blood tried to give her the power to save herself.

Before she could breathe, the sharp rim of the pool drove pain into her left knee and the rock tore the nails from her toes. But Hesperion swayed her leg upwards and her mouth crested the surface. Irona breathed raggedly for herself.

Then, for a moment, she was paralysed. His fingers twisted into her armpits and he half-hauled her from the water. He was a big man, but flabby; he couldn't hold her weight. He left her legs trailing in the water and dropped her on to the path.

Shells grazed Irona's face. They cut her, smelling of salt and decay, and she couldn't move to get off them. Her heart hammered; her lungs sucked grains of sand in with her breath, and still she couldn't see.

'Get up, bitch.' Hesperion commanded and her body obeyed. She tripped on the hem of her dress but she fell on to him and somehow he managed to support them both without losing his power over her muscles for more than a split second. Her body was his to command.

Irona felt her skirts tear from her waistband as he

marched her clumsily around the edge of the pool. She heard him cursing absent-mindedly at her back and still she had no clue as to whether or not he was as blind as she was. Waves lapped beside her to the right.

A click; he was mumbling, 'Talk to me, bitch,' over and over again, while her feet stumbled towards an unseen destination. She wondered desperately what he was doing.

More clicks. Suddenly her tongue unfroze to slur the words, 'Talk to me, bitch.' In that instant she felt the alien power leach out of her limbs. Just for a tiny fraction of time, but it did. Then her leaden body trudged forward once more at his orders.

Let it happen again! she pleaded silently in her mind. *Let it happen again!*

In her blind awareness, it seemed like aeons later that it did.

She felt the stirring of movement to palate, teeth, tongue. Her lips parted lop-sidedly to let the untidy words stagger into darkness: 'Talk to—'

And she spun sightlessly, arm flailing to send him spinning into the pool.

13
BERNARDINA AND THE THREE AMERICAS

Thank Synod that's over! Bernardina said to herself as she tottered out of the ring-car bringing her back from that fiasco of a World Council summit. Her hatred of Pilar Jímenez Costanza, the President who had snatched control of the Three Americas from her grasp, bumped up her heartbeat. She was more than glad to reach her sanctuary at the top of Camelford Tor.

Oh, you whorebitch, Bernardina thought, sinking into her flotation chamber. *If only I'd had the training of you!*

But Bernardina didn't know that she had – indirectly.

Once, her Mission in Guadalajara had run a recruitment raid on the sewer-children Under-Mexico-Fields. Matriarchy workers had stolen Pilar away as fodder for their model orphanage. The girl had hidden her guilt and her hatred of the lying, blue-robed enemies of her country.

'What's your name?' the matriarchs asked her.

'Dolores,' she said.

'What, for the pains of Christ?'

'No,' Pilar answered too softly for them to hear, 'for the pains of my Americas.'

Wise enough not to struggle while they bathed and

deloused and fed her, Pilar still vowed inside herself, *I'll run away!* Of course, she recognised the value of food and shelter and physical safety and the gift of the Sky, but she trusted the Blind Man's education of her rather more than the lies these people slid into your ears while your mind was asleep.

A thousand times over the next four years she told herself, *I'll run away!*

But the beds were soft, and there were neither rats nor alligators nor methane explosions nor government-funded cholera, and she loved the feel of warm, gritty soil birthing carrots and chillies to her touch in her very own patch of garden. *The Matriarchs haven't got me. I can run away from them any time I want*, she said in the darkness of the dormitory, fighting the alpha-waves and the olfacts and the siren rhythms of the other girls' peaceful breathing, all so she could consciously hear and so counteract the subliminals.

Trouble was, too many days of school and games and gardening, too many boring sessions in the blue-mantled shrine, left her comfortably tired, and she would fall asleep with her pillow telling its lies into her sleeping mind. Pilar, though, thought she was strong enough to resist, and continued to hide under her façade of good little Indio orphan.

Outside the high walls of the Guadalajara Mission, Bernardina was slowly spreading her tentacles. There were missions and arms dealers on both the shores of the Mediterranean. There were banks and teacher-clip writers at Yalta and on the shores of the Caspian, and a stilt-town over the Aral Marshes. In Saigon and Sarajevo, in Groenland and Tasmania, the maintenance of public olfactories quietly became the monopoly of a secret matriarchal company. And more and more, the President of Central America listened to the words of his brother-officer in Brasilia – the one who had fallen into Bernardina's web.

But the vast populations of the Americas defied the Matriarch by sheer numbers. There were only so many resources but always there were more people. The right to work became like the right to food: inalienable but unobtainable.

Hungry migrant workers continued to cross the Rio Grande to be wetbacks, Spics and Dagoes, however proud they might be. At the same time Northerners tiptoed south, hoping to escape inflation. Hundreds turned up for the chance of a single job as the world ploughed down into another slump.

In the Guadalajara Mission, Pilar heard of the job-lines turning into battle-lines, and she heard the matriarchs say that their way was the only way out. Pilar told herself, *I do not believe them. Robbing people of freedom is not the only way. Only working together as equals can we move forward.*

But she told herself less and less often as the years went by. The newscasts of labour-riots stopped – and the rumours were never straightforward. It was always, 'Of course, I never saw it myself. But I heard it from a man who got his ear stomped off outside Santa Fé de la Cruz.'

When she turned fourteen, the matriarchs considered Pilar safe enough to help with the relief-work. In the shanty-town that had grown up around the Mission, she dealt out medicines and food and teacher-clips for the children. After their forays into the reeking slum, the girls were paraded into aseptic showers.

The gossip started as they scrubbed modestly under their shifts. The girl next to her said, 'I don't believe these stupid stories of the Underdogs killing crooked construction-bosses, do you?'

And another junior, a big-eyed Yanqui child, whispered as they headed into the drying room, 'What about those women who bust into a sweatshop and slaughtered the man who was making their kids work like slaves?'

Then Pilar remembered how much she hated what the politicians were doing to her people. And she had no idea of an alternative to the matriarchs, but she remembered the Blind Man who could see, and she thought of the possibilities of change. But still she stayed in the trap of comfort.

Until one hot June evening, when it was her turn to dole out food to the queues of the great unwashed. The heat brought out the smell of corruption and stale, sweat-smoked clothing. It was a job Pilar knew she should have loved for the good it did, but she hated it for the stink of poverty she remembered from her own childhood.

She took her place, third in line after Clara, who gave out the bowls, and Luisa, who gave out the bread. Stirring the soya-meat stew with her ladle, she waited for the destitute to emerge from the shrine they had to attend before they could be fed.

The line that night was a long one; the cactus-fibre factory in the next village had just been shut down. Right at the back of the line, when it was nearly too dark to see, came a misshapen, shawl-shrouded woman whose face was like a skull. The woman was so worn out her skin was almost transparent, and her brown hair was streaked with grey before its time. Yet, this woman was the only one who thanked each of the servers for their help before moving awkwardly away.

Something about her helpless dignity touched Pilar-

Dolores. The Indio girl drifted through the thickening light of sundown to sit beside the malnourished gringo woman.

Pulling the tattered blanket back, the woman held the bowl to the lips of a child in the crook of her arm. She said, 'Come on, baby, have some of this nice stew. Mmm! Tasty! Baby want some? Please, baby, want some . . .'

But the baby would want nothing ever again. Flies came to cluster round its crusted eyes, to hover by the slack mouth, but the child never moved. Only the warm evening breeze shivered through the thin, milk-white hair.

'Come on, baby, come on, sweetheart, have a little of this for Momma.'

And Pilar cried, and hugged the bone-thin woman, and finally the mother put the bowl gently from her and wept with her heart-break, and with Pilar's arms around her.

Pilar had seen plenty of death, but she still didn't know what to say until the words of the Mission shrine sprang brightly to her lips: 'Don't cry, little mother, don't cry. Matriarch Bernardina, the mother of us all, she's taken your baby to her bosom now.'

And speaking the spell out loud broke it.

Pilar cried again then, for her own loss as well as the mother's, and when she had tucked the woman in bed in the Mission's homely clinic under the doctor's arrogant gaze, she left.

She skipped through the gates just as they were closing for the night. With one backward glance at the lighted windows shining out through the dusk, one final sniff of the calming olfacts, she walked out of the Matriarch's paralysing tentacles and into the next phase of her battle for the peoples of her Americas.

When Bernardina clambered stiffly out of the coffin-like

serenity of her flotation-chamber, the problem of that Jímenez Costanza whorebitch broke over her once more like a thunderhead. The meeting would have been fine, if not for that flat-faced, break-nosed deve.

Bernardina had – as yet – no idea of Pilar Jímenez Costanza's childhood or her wilderness years, despite the spies she had working on it. She'd never even heard of the woman Pilar had become – until four years ago. Suddenly the delicate balance of power between each of the Three Americas had shifted and the Costanza woman had ridden to the top of the scum.

What Bernardina did know was the hatchet-job President Pilar Costanza was making of all the Admin's careful plans. The Admin's plans were Bernardina's own. She had her best people working out just where this charismatic president had sprung from all of a sudden, but in the meantime Bernardina glowered at the private communication-disk a junior matriarch had tremblingly put before her.

'All right, girl, stop gawping and get out,' Bernardina snapped, and didn't spare a moment's contrition for worsening the junior's all-too-evident nervousness. 'It's got a "private" tag on it, and "urgent" too.'

'Yes, Matriarch Bernardina. I'm sorry, Matriarch Bernardina,' the junior said, and all but killed herself by bowing and scraping her way backwards so humbly that she almost fell down the trapdoor that was the only way down to the watchlevels from this sanctum. The Matriarch of Matriarchs wondered vaguely what, quite, the girl had been apologising for.

Once the trapdoor shut, the floor of Bernardina's sanctuary was seamless, barren marble, with just a soft bright rug or two and the black coffin that was her flotation chamber to spoil its whiteness. Bernardina, Supreme Matriarch and ruler of the World Council – *though not for much longer, if that Pilar Costanza woman has anything to do with it!* – glanced longingly at her floater, the urge to sink back into its rejuvenating fluid very strong. But she resisted the temptation because she had to decide about the Costanza woman's message.

Bernardina let the iridium disk wink in her lap, turning it with rheumaticky fingers, admiring its shiny rainbow colours as they flashed in the sunlight from the open windows, not seeming to treat it with any urgency at all. But Bernardina was thinking.

As soon as the junior gave it to her, she had seen that the reverse was marked with the garish Aztec condor the Costanza woman had chosen to be the symbol of the United Three Americas. Bernardina moved creakily over to her favourite window-seat, a broad wooden ledge heaped with fleecy, embroidered cushions. Here, in her sanctuary, carved into the very top of Camelford Mountain inside the spike of the Tor, she allowed herself the luxury of a groan at the pain her movement caused. She rubbed fingers over her tired, work-bleared eyes and then squinted out into the gold and blue of the daylight.

For a moment she let the sight of her achievements soothe her: the hum of the swarming, tranquillised masses – a static population of two million – rose gentle as the sound of bees above the curly green bracken; the neat, squared fields brushed silver by the wind; the warmth of the flowery air of May kept at the temperature she had selected by the hard Sky of transparisteel she had had designed. Not an ant moved but that her Ears heard it; not a mouse or a stag or a sheep chewed a mouthful of clover that she hadn't caused to grow.

Peace! Bernardina thought bitterly, gazing at the early-morning mist wreathing into nothingness where the river drew a shining thread against the dark of the woodland in the Park. *Peace, and I brought it. I made it. I gave it first to Camelford and then to the whole of the Admin. I've brought the peace of the Matriarchy to half the globe. Now I'm offering it to all of Earth and what thanks do I get? Snotty little digs from that Costanza woman! How dare she?*

Willing herself to master her temper, Bernardina commanded calming olfacts. Machines built into the panelling obliged. Scenting the carrier of ambergris and the astringent top-notes of orange, she breathed deeply for several moments, repeating one of the more anodyne phrases culled from the Warren's shrines. *All is part of the pattern of ultimate good. Unity wraps us in warmth and strength and love.*

'Pah! Unity!' she exploded. 'I've spent years, decades, of my life to get on to the World Council and now this Costanza woman comes barrelling into us with the Unity of the Three Americas!' Muttering to herself, she swivelled on her seat, scattering blue and gold and pink cushions to the floor as she reached across to a cupboard set in the wall beside her. As soon as she opened it and called, the computer remote floated out to hover before her. Its sensors flickered, registering the sounds it heard: from outside the open windows, the song of a skylark, the angry chatter of a mother blackbird as a magpie dived at her nest in the plumy lilac down the tor; from inside the stately room, the thin, harsh murmuring of Bernardina.

'I could have given the whole world peace, but no! They go on fighting the matriarchs we've spread in their vile lands. The Saharistanis have to kill each other five times a day. And as if all that wasn't enough, Asiapura has to persecute its round-eyes – as if they could get back to the days of the Sons of Han when Li Chan daren't even be seen in public! Synod knows what that blank-eyed freak Nanuk of the North and South is plotting with his ridiculous ne-Eskimos down in Antarctica. Isn't one patch of snow enough for him that he has to start muscling in down there? And now this stupid Costanza woman's got her Underdogs slaughtering the Northerners wholesale, even if she does put it about that she's pleading with them to stop. Let's see what she's after this time.'

The remote, of course, did not recognise this last phrase as a command, which irritated Bernardina still further. Breathing a bitter sigh, she snapped, 'Display this message-disk for me here and now.'

The remote caused a metallic arm to swivel out on its joints, bringing a monitor out of the oaken cupboard to face her. Bernardina slotted the disk in and ordered the thing to play.

Before even the first snowy static began, Bernardina said, 'Remote! Confirm that this message has not been seen by any other person.'

Violet words scrolled sideways across the computer's screen: This message has not been read by anyone but its author. The old woman closed her eyes tiredly, sighing with relief.

'At least my security still works, then,' Bernardina said aloud. 'That's some comfort, at any rate.'

At the bottom corner of the screen, a pale little light pulsed, half-drowned in the spray of static. A pale little pulse that was the scar from Carandis's tampering. In half a second it was gone.

Bernardina rubbed her eyes again, then played the disk.

It showed a globe, blue and brown and green, the mountaintops in the west flashing gold in the sun. Behind the crescent of night, spangled necklaces of light glowed to shape cities, and the seas wore jade and turquoise where towns gleamed on subaquatic peaks between the jet-black depths. A platinum moon rocked above the stars beyond the horizon.

'Yes, yes,' Bernardina muttered. 'Get on with it.'

But now trickles of crimson webbed out from a node in the North Isles of the Admin. First from Camelford to the drowned wreck of Londover, then to Freeburg and New Stakeholm and beyond they spread. The trickles became streamlets; the streamlets, rivers of blood that washed half the Old World before they sneaked across to pollute the New. Cross-lattices spread their shining gore amid a rising smell of blood and decay, and when the disk centred – the viewpoint plunged to earth with sickening speed – Bernardina only saved herself from vertigo by shutting out the awful vision.

For the node was a hideous spider. And the spider wore her own face.

Breathing hard to calm the shattered pounding of her heart, Bernardina felt fury that she had allowed another human to play her emotions. She hated that, even for half a second, heart and mind had danced to another player's beat.

Small wonder, then, that her hands crisped into fists when the Earth ghosted away into a broad Indio face. Slab-cheeked, thin-lipped, the face was saved by eyelashes that curled long and thick, emphasising the warmth of the molasses-dark eyes. Her rows of dainty earrings Bernardina discounted not as vanity, but as a sensory net. The Costanza woman must have been on the hard side of forty,

Bernardina thought, but to Bernardina that was almost a babe. This woman had never forced out children from between her thighs. This woman had never shared her inner self with any man – or at least, not that Bernardina had ever heard. She thought, *The Costanza woman is so acid because she's incomplete. Only half a woman. Ha!*

Bernardina kept the thought, used it as a key to analyse the words, the facial movements, to get at the ideas hidden behind the communication. The President of the Unity of the Three Americas smiled, open and trusting.

'Madonna Matriarch,' she said, and she must have known that was the wrong form of address. Bernardina found herself grinding her teeth.

'Madonna Matriarch, you are three things. You are the president in fact if not in name of the whole geographical area known as the Admin. You control Elditch, who is supposed to be the pure leader of the Synod and therefore to have no ties, a fact I have so far forborne to mention to my colleagues on the World Council. I am sure the Saharistanis would be fascinated if they even suspected it.'

Never had Bernardina so much hated a form of communication where you couldn't instantly answer back.

'Second, you are – currently – poised in power as the head of the World Council, but the balance is v-e-r-y delicate.

'And last, you are the woman who needs the support of my Three Americas if you are to maintain that precarious balancing.'

Almost, Bernardina deliquesced with relief because the Costanza woman obviously didn't know—

But she did. That carven mahogany face shuttered its treacly eyes with blandness as Pilar Costanza moved in for the kill. The Hispanic voice dropped as if she were confiding a juicy piece of gossip. 'And you are the actual head of a spy network which has spent years infiltrating friendly territories with a control system designed to subvert a huge percentage of local populations. Your pseudo-cult abuses its religious freedom for political ends.'

'Lies!' Bernardina shouted.

But of course the disk-player didn't respond. The Matriarch of Matriarchs had not given it a direct command.

'You see, prima donna Matriarch, the veils and covers you have used are too thin to disguise all the agencies that front for you across my lands. The Church of the Little Sisters!'

The heart slammed in Bernardina's chest.

'The Martyrs of the Five Wounds!'

Aches twisted behind the old woman's ribs.

'The Friends of the Northern Poor! The Banco de Crédito del Espíritu Coronado! And the Mission of the Sacred Heart in Guadalajara.'

Bernardina's own heart was wounded, but the Jímenez whorebitch went on, 'And those are just some of your tentacles that strangle the soul out of my nations. Would the Crown of Novaya Zemla be grateful if Oceana found out just how it is he tranquillises his masses?'

And there was nothing that Bernardina could reply. Outside her window, a skylark rolled its carolling down the sunshine.

Pilar Jímenez Costanza, President of the Unity of the Three Americas, nodded like a wise old witch-doctor. 'Madonna Matriarch, I feel we must talk again. Wouldn't you like to know how I know these things? What arrangements you and I might come to? Then you should accept my invitation for a private meeting. It'll be so cosy, just you and I. I'll send you the details.'

And for a second her face was the hooked razor of the condor's beak.

The click of the player as it ejected the disk shocked Bernardina. She found that once again she was fingering the wispy end of one eyebrow, her mind locked in nostalgia for the safety of the past. When she had been young. When her body was strong enough to house her spirit. When the Sky was new and her insurance, her immortality, was nourished in her womb.

For the first time in a decade, tears drizzled down the furrows from her red and ancient eyes. Fear and pain squeezed her in their probing, skeletal fingers. The weight of tasks she might not live to finish crushed her. *So much to do! Don't let me die! Not yet, not yet. Help me, Irona!*

And her gaze tried to pierce the hardness of the Sky while her whole being cried out to the child of her flesh and mind.

14
HIDE AND SEEK

Irona missed. Hesperion sounded only half a pace behind her in the cavern yet she swung at him – and missed.

She couldn't believe it. Even as she fell she heard the click of the controls in his hands and felt her body stiffen into some half-formed pose that was no protection at all. One wrist bent back painfully as she struck the ground. Her head jarred against a rock wall she hadn't known was there. It felt to her like the whole ground was shivering with the impact of her fall. Ears ringing, she lay feeling sick and dizzy on a slick, weed-grown path, knowing that any second now Hesperion would take reprisals. And the fact that someone so slow and clumsy had avoided her told her that it wasn't just the blackness of the cavern maze.

I'm blind!

'Synod, you stupid bitch!' Hesperion's voice was high-pitched with fear. 'What are you trying to do to us?'

'What do you mean?' she asked, feigning more grogginess than she actually felt while her thoughts ran: *If I had that Eye you'd be dead meat.*

'I mean there's—'

She heard a thud that turned her stomach even more than

the strange reek of the cavern, then the long slither of clothing over rocks. Something clattered away, echoes multiplying to her left. Was it just her terror that made it feel as though the ground were shaking? *My left? What's happened to the wall? Where's the sound of the pool?* 'Hesperion? What's happening? Regen?' *Have I got turned around? Why can't I see?*

Reassurance: a familiar cracked voice. 'Yeah, it's me. Regen. Hee-hee. Don't have to worry about Hesperion no more. Just stay exactly where you are, Ro. Don't move a muscle. I'll explain in a minute. Entirely.' She heard him say, 'Just don't move,' again, recognised the fear in his voice. She wondered why. But she didn't move. Her ear, pressed to the ground, felt his shuffling footsteps through the rock.

Sounds she couldn't identify. Frightening.

'Regen?'

'Ssh, love. Hush. I'm coming. Just keep still. Promise?'

She promised. But the sounds he made faded into the distance. He was leaving her. Every moment of the time her parents abandoned her came back, peeled off the layers of maturity to expose the naked emotions of youth.

But this is Regen. He's my friend. He wouldn't do that to me.

My parents did.

Trust was too fragile. It felt too much like stupidity. Only the memory of fear for her in Regen's voice kept her still.

But he was so long getting to her! *I'll count to another hundred. If he hasn't come then, he's not coming back.* And another hundred. And another, while trust crumbled and the world was hostile and invisible.

He's not coming back. I'm stupid. I should have known

I couldn't trust anybody. But I'll count to another hundred.

A long time later she smelt him. Smelt on the alien air of the cavern all the composite odour of nervous perspiration, unwashed hair and the polish on his old favourite boots that was Regen. He had come back to her. Relief sucked her strength and she trembled.

Guided by the slough of clothes on rock, she raised her head to gaze at him. Or at least to try to. But the world was still black.

'I'm going to put a rope on you now, love.' His words tumbled out quick-fire with tension. 'Put it round your waist so you won't fall. Just keep—'

'Fall?'

'Ssh, love. I won't let you fall. You just trust old Regen. Entirely.'

He touched her back gently. 'Just hump your shoulders up a bit so's I can get this ol' rope on you. Keep away from the sides.'

'The sides of what?'

'Ssh. That's it. Well done, Ro. Now give us a minute and then crawl backwards when I tell you.' The sense of his presence diminished. 'Right. Come towards my voice now.'

Her own fear creeping up – *Why all the precautions? Where am I? Fall where?* – Irona knelt up and stretched her left foot back. It hit against a stone wall. That gave her the confidence to travel back a bit more quickly. Her right foot met no obstacle, though her knee slithered a bit on the damp weed and almost tipped her down into the pool she assumed was still on her right. Still, Regen – *He came back for me!* – kept the rope painfully taut around her waist and she knew he'd keep her safe. She crawled backwards some more, wondering why Regen was making such a fuss about the risk of a quick drenching.

'Right, Ro. You can stand up now,' he said, and pulled her up into his arms. He held her to him tightly. She was taller; she rested her head on the top of his shoulder and she could feel the shuddering in his body. She wasn't quite sure who was comforting whom. Normally she wouldn't have clung so closely to him, worried that she might give him the wrong idea, put off by the strong odour he exuded.

But normally she could see.

'Regen?' she mumbled into his neck. 'Regen, is it dark in here?'

He answered reluctantly. 'Not that much. There's a few holes up in the cliff-face.'

'Well why can't I see?'

'Must be 'cause Hesperion's sprayed your eyes with something. Don't worry, I'm sure Tang'll have something to get it off. Come on.' He took her hand.

She hesitated. 'Why were you so all-fired cautious back there? If I'd fallen in the pool, I could have swum.'

She felt Regen turn her to him again and run his hands up her arms. His words came out even faster than usual with reaction to the fright he had had. 'That ain't just no ordinary pool. It's about twenty or thirty metres down and they old animals in there ain't none too friendly. Can't you smell 'em? Ripe, like animals in a cage. They're sort of, well maybe they're plants, I dunno. Whatever, they're so close you can't hardly see no water. But there's bones sticking up out of 'em. And besides, you weren't on no path like before. More like a bridge. That pool's all spread out below where you were on a sort of stone tree-trunk or something, with like sort of bubbles in the walls that have broken and the tree-thing's kind of balanced on the hard bits of the bubbles. Synod knows where he thought he were taking you.'

Irona couldn't see it: that made it worse. Her imagination courted the disaster irresistibly. Now she knew why Regen was holding her. Relief. Brotherly relief. Nothing else. It was safe to hold him – though she wished he didn't smell of fresh sweat on top of the old.

'He thought he was taking me to see Tang and force him to let Hesperion go home to Kifl on the *Thistle-up*.'

'Well, I doubt he'll be going back to Kifl now,' Regen said. 'Shouldn't think he'll be going anywhere but into they old animals' guts. Serve him right. I'm sorry I couldn't get to you before, like, but with him having the controller, I didn't know what he might do to you 'fore I could get you away.'

'Did you ever find that Eye?'

'Not a hide nor a hair of it,' he answered.

She giggled. 'Well you wouldn't, would you? It never had any.'

'OK, so it was a bald Eye. Come on, smarty-knickers, let's get you back to base before you think up any more lines like that.'

Bit by bit he guided her out the way they had come, explaining that it was a length of seasilk he'd gone for and that was what had taken so much time. He made no reference to her blindness, only telling her here and there, 'Duck down now,' or 'Come a little to the right,' but his arm was round her shoulders whenever it possibly could be.

Then she crawled up the long incline behind him and emerged into the wonderful freshness of the ocean breeze. Even the open air, though, could not entirely disperse her feeling of being trapped in a dark, fragmented world of her own.

It was Regen who kilted up her skirts for safety and tore strips to bind her fingers against the sharpness of the rocks. It was Regen who climbed above or below her, setting her hands and feet for her blind climb down the cliff. Her wrist ached abominably. She tried dutifully to laugh at his little jokes, to make light remarks of her own, but it was hard when the razor-edged stones she couldn't see lacerated her hands and legs.

But there's no point in giving in to fear, she chanted like a litany, like the strength she used to get from the shrines in Camelford and from the little rituals her mother had once taught her.

'I can't remember what my mother looked like!' she said suddenly as Regen found her another toe-hold on the cliff.

'Shouldn't worry about that,' he told her. 'Wish I couldn't remember mine. A mohock, she was, and not much loss when she got herself brain-wormed. Family ain't who you're born to' – he helped her rock her weight gingerly to another unseen ledge – 'it's who you choose to be with.'

Irona faltered for a fraction of a second then shifted her fingers obediently. The safety-cord of seasilk was tight around her middle. 'I wasn't much of a mother to Arno, was I?'

Regen snorted derisively. 'You was good enough. You give him love and all the attention you could. You give him independence and freedom. He was lucky. He knew you loved him. Now give us your hand and swing across and we're there.'

'Where?'

'On that lump o' stone outside the first seasilk pool. I'll say this for you, Ro: you got more guts than anyone I ever come across. Can't think of anybody else who'd have come blind down a cliff of basalt without whingeing.'

'You wouldn't have let me get hurt, would you? I trust you, Regen.'

Embarrassed, it seemed, the little man shot out a stream of meaningless babble, descriptions of the lizardlings flying home to roost as the constellations wheeled above the night horizon, small injunctions about where she should step next. Irona followed him, letting it wash over her.

I do trust him! she thought in wonder. *Him and Tebrina. Oh, Twiss'd be fine beside me in a fight but five minutes later he'd make an excuse and let me down. And Arias? Do I trust him?*

Fingers of raw seasilk groped at her face as Regen led her through the living curtains. The hush of waves rebounding in the cavern faded.

'It's a ramp now,' he said, then the familiar atmosphere of Eastcliff enfolded her.

And minutes later Irona heard the soft slap-slap of fisherfolks' feet. Voices, warmer since the speakers wanted to show their care, asked, 'How are you?' or whispered to others, 'How is she?' and kind hands patted her. The procession around her grew.

Sounds bounced off the walls of spiralling ramps. The echoes grew vaster and gas-pumps throbbed, to tell her that she was in the hangar. She was irrationally scared that she would fall off the edge and down to the murderous rocks outside, but there was an unseen forest of hands patting her, guiding her.

'Irona!' Tang's voice, sharp with anxiety. She heard the crowd of fisherfolk shuffling aside to let their Creator through. Her own reaction was painful confusion.

Tang embraced her. Irona felt Regen's hand slip from around her waist as her – former?– lover encircled her in his arms right there in front of everyone. 'Irona, my love, what's happened? Where have you been?'

The safety of familiarity merged her against him for a moment. She forgot that she was the so-called Queen and he the Creator while she sought security in his embrace. Hormones swirled through her, stopping her cuts stinging so fiercely. Then he added, 'Twiss has been calling and calling for you.'

She wasn't sure how she felt about that, except with Twiss it wasn't concern so much as control. But a momentary surge of annoyance told her she would have the strength to deal with King Twiss when the time came. Something more immediate needed attention. Trying not to sound like a frightened child, she blurted, 'Arias, I can't see!'

'What?' he said, voice breaking with sudden fear.

'I reckon that there Hesperion sprayed her eyes with somethin',' Regen said while Irona fumbled to sort out words in her mind.

'Come up to the lab, then, Irona. We'll get you fixed up.' Tang spoke less intimately now: 'And you lot, I'll keep you up to date with progress. You don't need to hang around.'

Arias slipped one arm down around her shoulders and led her through the tunnels. Despite what he had said, she heard the flap of webbed feet behind her and knew that the fisherfolk cared enough to stay with her anyway. Tears of gratitude pricked her sightless eyes.

'I'll talk to Twiss, then,' Regen said, and guilt nibbled at Irona. She hadn't meant her friend to be forlorn.

Tang and Regenerator thought Irona was asleep on the soft couch in the lab. She'd have told them that she wasn't if it hadn't been too much trouble. She was snuggled into a warm nest of covers, her mind as amorphous as cotton wool. A pleasant glow spread across her eyes from the impregnated bandage that Arias had grown there. Other wrappings twined soothingly round her hands, webbing her fingers so firmly she felt she might be one of Arias's fisherfolks. It was as though she were drifting, cupped in Mother Ocean, light and safe as those night-lilies that had waltzed outside Arias's window the night Arno had danced on the volcano. But Arno was the memory of a flame, now, his atoms part of this new world. In the place where she was adrift he felt very close.

'She's going to be all right, then?' Regen said.

A rustle of clothing; Tang must have nodded, because Regen said, 'You sure?'

'Pretty sure. It was some sort of paralysing agent. Blocked the neurones in the optic nerves, or possibly the retinas. But the analyser found an absorbent which we've put into her bloodstream.'

Aha, thought Irona in sleepy triumph, *that's what the itch on my neck is. A drug-patch.*

'... know for sure in the morning,' Arias finished. 'What about Twiss?'

The smell of Regen wafted to her through the green, vegetal odours of the medilab. *That must be him shrugging*, Irona surmised. Her friend's voice said, 'He sounded worried' – Irona smiled wearily to herself, then Regen went on – 'till I told him she were most likely going to be all right. Then he went crackers about that there Eye we can't find, and started banging on about they Arms again. Reckons they can't come from anywhere in Kifl.'

'Maybe their base is somewhere in Rainshadow Valley.'

Regen said, 'He's keeping an Eye on it. You ain't seen nothing like no Arms round here, have you?'

Arias answered, 'No. No, my fisherfolk would have told me.'

'But you ain't searched all they caves, though, have you? The damn place is riddled with hidey-holes. Entirely.'

'I'm not worried. There's no Arm alive that would have the power to fly right the way over here from Kifl. Oh well, let's look on the bright side. At least we're well rid of Hesperion. Just try and stop Twiss foisting any more wasters on us, will you?'

After that, the conversation languished. In fact, neither of the men spoke for a good few minutes. For Irona time elongated. Though analgesics had numbed all the cuts and the sprain to her right wrist, it seemed nothing could entirely blunt her empathy because she felt the unease growing between the two men, her one-time lover and her all-time friend. She couldn't understand it.

Then it came to her: they were trying to out-wait each other. She had asked Regenerator not to leave her alone with Arias. And now there was a faint aura of jealousy surrounding the pair of them.

I ought to do something about it, she thought, but it was all too much effort. What attention she could muster was wrapped in fighting the faint panic the olfacts hadn't been able to erase altogether: whether or not she'd be blind forever, and why her childhood kept coming back to shatter the Irona she'd created from the wreckage.

15
MESSAGES FROM HOME

All Irona knew when she woke in Arias's lab at Eastcliff was that she wanted to go home. But the environment was not just unseen, but unfamiliar. Anything – or anyone – could have been sneaking up on her.

Sightless, she felt her face. The bandages still webbed her eyes; the smell of sap was still twined round her fingers. They would not open; she wondered, panicking, if they ever would. Her blindness was a prison. She felt very much alone; the ache for her dead son gaped like a wound inside her. Now that she was no longer floating, he was no longer close to her.

Into the blackness of her world she called softly, 'Arias? Regen?'

Nobody answered her.

It had the feel of early morning. Straining her hearing to work out if there were anything hostile behind the blood-beat pumping of genetic tanks, dilating her nostrils to sniff for a human presence, Irona could detect nothing but that once Regen had been in this room. Too many other odours, the sharp green of plants and the metal-and-chemical that formed the lab itself, blocked her senses. And her senses were clubbed already by the living bandage over her eyes.

She could not hear the sounds of the fisherfolk moving about their tasks. *But then, they're a silent lot anyway*, she thought, and wondered if it really were first light, or the middle of the day.

No. Not here. They don't have the siesta here. Besides, it's not hot enough for noon. But where is everybody? I want to go home.

Without her eyes, she could not see to find the 'weedkiller' that would clear the bandage from her eyes. Not daring to try anything in the lab for fear it would be poison or acid, she made herself lie still, shying away from the creeping terror of one thought: that she would never see again.

Did they ever find Hesperion? Maybe he's killed everyone and now he's coming to find me. Oh, Synod! Don't let him get me!

In all the mat of sounds and scents, there was not one she could rely on. The thought of being blind forever sucked all the strength from her aching limbs.

Eons later, the door opened and soft bootsteps came in. Someone clicked the door quietly shut.

Hesperion? She lay still, willing herself to invisibility.

The sound of steps came surreptitiously closer, each step a shot of adrenalin in the pathways of her blood. *Does Hesperion wear boots? Regen —*

'Regen?'

'Did you want it to be?' Arias's voice. 'Is my presence so unbearable now?'

'No, of course it's not.'

'Well why do you keep avoiding me? Why did you bring Regen along – to ride shotgun or chaperon?'

Perceptive, that one, but she did her best to ignore such

a barbed tack, especially when she was at a horrific disadvantage. She couldn't see the expressions on his face or in his movements. She couldn't see anything. 'I just don't feel too comfortable with you right now, Arias.'

His fingers, cool and professional, traced the contours of the bandage on her face. She flinched, said hurriedly to cover it, 'Not because of you. It's just that I feel so guilty! I was here with you when I should have been – when Arno died.'

'The bandages can come off now.' His voice was as cool and impersonal as his touch. 'You couldn't have changed a thing if you'd been there anyway. He was a young man and you had to let him go. Forget it. Forget the guilt. Recognise that half your anger is with him for going off and dying.'

She was about to shout an angry retort but his fingers brushed her lips. Was it by accident? He said, 'You should be able to see today, a bit blearily, probably, but let's see.' Faintly, he laughed. 'Sorry. That wasn't a very good choice of phrase, was it?'

'Never mind, Arias.'

At least his words distracted her from self-flagellation, which was probably his intent anyway.

Trying to keep the mood light, she said, 'I don't suppose you found Hesperion's body, did you?'

'No, love. Nor our three folk. Poor little things, they were hardly more than children. Whyever he wanted them I don't know.'

'To force you into sending him home. He told me. But they wouldn't co-operate. I hope they're all right.'

'We'll find them, don't worry. I've got the Eye flying search-patterns through the caves you found right now. Frankly, I'm just as worried about that crystal.'

'Why?'

Irona heard the friction of cloth on cloth as he moved calmly about the room, doing whatever it was he had to before he could take the living plant from her head and hands. She tried to keep the fear of blindness from screaming through her mind.

'Because it's a bio-crystalline matrix I've been growing. It has amazing properties – conductance in dozens of planes, and you can alter the vector of any current you pass through it in nanoseconds. If I'm right, it'll be the best memory-capacitor of any computer Harith's ever seen. Almost an artificial intelligence in its own right.'

She was scarcely listening, much less able to take it all in. He came close again, so that the hairs on her arms twitched in either a barely perceptible breeze or in response to the electro-magnetic field of his body.

'Just keep still, love,' he said, not realising it brought back the paralysing fear of the tree-bridge in the cavern. 'You take as long as you like, because I've never pressured you, have I?'

And they both knew he wasn't talking about her sight.

He dropped cool, sticky juices on to the thing that grew down from her brow almost to her nostrils. In her mind she saw the bandage thrusting out roots down into her flesh, eating her eyeballs, and tried to suppress the vision. The liquid flowed fresh as the sap from a broken bluebell, tickling, not quite stinging, dripping down towards her ears. Then he lifted her hands and wiped her fingers one by one. 'Soon, Ro. You'll be able to see soon.'

In a small voice she asked, 'What time is it, Arias?' It was as if she had to keep saying his name to reassure herself that it really was him, a friend and not an enemy, there unseen and alone with her.

'Not long after dawn. Regen's over there, asleep. He wanted to watch over you so I let him take the first shift. He's fast out.'

'Well, where were you then when I woke up?' Irona said, and was discomfited by the acid tone in her voice.

'I went down to see about some breakfast for you.'

'It's that word again, isn't it? See. It's like you can't do anything if you can't see. Arias, I'm so scared!'

She felt him stroke her shoulder, then grip it more firmly, to pour back into her all the love and trust she had once known. But the love and trust slithered off like rain against a mirror.

'Give it just a little longer for the bandage to drop off, my love, and you'll be fine,' Arias said.

'Promise?'

'You'll be fine.' *But you didn't promise!* she screamed mentally, and fear was an earthquake inside her that opened abysses into which she would tumble and fall forever if she moved at all.

A whisper escaped her: 'Arias?'

At once he sat beside her, both hands flittering over her arms as if to test whether he could touch her again or she would once more rebuff him.

No rejection. She would have held Hesperion himself at that point.

Arias raised her, pulled her to him, regardless of the melting bandage that she could feel frothing on to his shirt. Her lover, so fastidious, didn't care. That, in itself, scared her.

His heartbeat against her ear, his chin came down protectively over her matted hair. The whole texture of him, the wiry slenderness of his chest and the surprising strength of his arms, proclaimed his presence but she no longer felt that the safety he gave was real. It was a phantom, and her love was a ghost, and none of it was permanent in a world she could no longer trust.

Tears were burning in her eyes. In a flood of hot, salt pressure they burst through the dam of shrivelling brown bandage.

'Can you see, love?' Arias asked desperately

She clung to him, shoulders shaking with the sobs she tried to suppress. Fear gripped too strongly for her to look. For the moment her voice was beyond control.

A pause while she kept her forehead against him, not wanting to turn her face upwards where he could see what a hideous mess the bandage and the crying made of her. Irona scrubbed her eyes on her forearm, feeling the sticky brown clumps of goo rolling up and clinging still to her skin, her lashes.

'Can you?' he insisted.

Speechless, Irona nodded.

When she stepped fresh out of the tub in her guest-suite, the joy of sight still tingled through her. At first it had been like peering through paraffin, but now it was growing better by the moment. At last she had a moment to herself, to seek restoration in tranquillity away from everyone else's emotions.

Drifting to the window of the bathroom, she watched the eastern horizon. A band of crystal light seemed to rim the blues and greens of ocean. Turning her gaze upwards – blessed miracle of sight! – she saw grey creatures gliding between the ropes of vegetation outside the transparisteel. Webs of skin joined their front and rear paws, and the animals launched themselves bravely into the void, sure that they would come to no harm. Irona smiled at their courage, and went to gather her own in the everyday armour of clothes. Hesperion was dead; she could see again. Time to seize life and take up the battle once more. More light-hearted than she had been for some time, she went out to her bedroom.

Finding a dress of rippling sapphire seasilk laid out on the bed was a feast to her vision. It was beautiful. Puffed sleeves shrank to tight cuffs below the elbow. The high neck was filmy above her bosom, the fitted bodice flared out to a floor-length circular skirt. She slipped it on, smiling, adjusting the pressure-seals, and pirouetted in front of the looking-glass, revelling in the way the skirt swirled sensuously about her legs. There were new boots made of the same stuff, with slim little heels, and an unobtrusive stasis-crown to dress her hair becomingly.

'Arias,' she whispered to herself, thinking of all the times in Kifl she had breathed his name like a talisman, never daring to say it out loud. Now she could – but the magic had faded.

Her joy lost some of its sparkle. Sighing in the sunlight of late morning, she stepped closer to the mirror to find out what her tribulations had done to her outwardly.

A tight redness masked her face in a band across her eyes, and there were shadows below her lashes. She sighed, anchored by her ever-present self-doubts to the reality of her life and purpose, but the wonderful power of sight was no longer something she could take for granted, and that at least curved her lips into a smile. Somehow the seasilk brought out the curves in her figure and the rich colour of hair and eyes, so even though she felt deformed by the red bar on her skin, she could not be too down-hearted.

All the same, she still wanted to go home. *It would be*

nice, though, if I knew quite where my home was.

A chime sounded at the door. Spinning to answer it, still delighting in the elegant hang of the fabric, she caught sight of a small card that had slipped half under the bed. She stooped to read it.

'My love, I know I'm losing you.'

Well why don't you care enough to ask me to stay? The thought came unbidden to her mind.

Arias didn't know. He went on, 'If things had been different, this would have been your wedding dress, but I can't ask you to come and live with me, not with Twiss. Now it's your badge of courage. I'm not closing any doors between us. Wear it bravely and think of me.'

Eyes bright with unshed tears, she slid the card under the mattress and went to answer the door.

Arias came to her guest-suite, a crowd behind him. His eyes gleamed in appreciation at the beauty of Irona in her dress, but with so many people around and Regen bristling close by, he could say nothing. Instead he gestured, and as she emerged into the light and shade of the tunnel, he fell into step a fraction behind her and to one side. His hand touched her continually but she couldn't decide whether it was a territorial thing or affection disguised as courtesy.

Escorts of fisherfolk walked with them as Arias Tang led Irona down to the hangar. At first she assumed they were, as ever, watching every move their Creator made. But when they started patting her, asking how she was, admiring the sapphire seasilk, the gentle concern in their voices moved her more than she could say. Their scent of musk and fish was so homely now that she breathed it deeply.

Seriathnis presented her with earrings made of opalescent shell. The air hissing through her gill-slits, her blue-black furred head tilted back so that she could look into Irona's face, she said, 'You will come again to your home in Eastcliff, Irona-one. You will always be welcome.'

'You're very kind, Seriathnis. And I'll do my best for you all in trade.'

'Thank you. I know you will. But that is not why I made my gift. It is for another hotskin friend.'

The mutual admiration might have gone on even after they left the vine-wreathed ramps and came into the chiaroscuro cavern, but Captain Hoojer wouldn't let it. She nodded at her vessel, its shadow watery as daylight bled through the transparisteel and focused here and there into winking eyes of solid light shaped by the curves of the hull. The airbag was a dark blob blocking half the cave-mouth and the sun was a bright crescent on the airship's canopy. 'Time's a-wasting,' Hoojer said.

'I'm sorry.' Irona smiled at the older woman. 'I won't be a moment, I promise.'

Hoojer shrugged her shoulders, her head and neck somehow moving sideways. 'Take all the time you want. But I won't be here for it ifn you're more'n five minutes. There's weather brewing up and I don't want to have to sit it out here.' And Hoojer walked up the gangplank, her footsteps setting off vibrations that made the whole ship dance.

Irona stepped slightly away from Arias the Creator's hand which had been hovering protectively at her back all through the tunnels. She was very conscious of the crowd of fisherfolk around her, their heads scarcely level with her chin, their soft, alien body-odour woven into the atmosphere of this part of their world. Without even looking where they set their feet, they managed to skirt the lip of the abyss that made her stomach churn every time she thought of it. Why they didn't roof it over, or at least put a barrier round it, was beyond her.

Turning, her body instinctively forming an area of privacy between them, she said, 'Thank you, Arias,' a warmth in her tone that was not in the formality of the leavetaking he had set up in the busy hangar.

His blue-grey eyes smiled into hers, but he couldn't hide the sadness in their depths. 'Thank you, Irona, for showing us a noble vision of unity and courage. I wish you every happiness.'

Behind her, the *Thistle-up*'s propellers stuttered into life. The racket made private conversation impossible. Salt wind tugged at her hair but the stasis-crown, Arias's gift, held. Her skirts fluttered around her like hobbles.

Captain Hoojer came to the rail and yelled down, 'Sorry to break up the party but if we want to catch that weather-window, we ought to go.'

So Irona hurried her goodbyes, Regen close at her side now, and they bounced up the ramp on to the swaying deck. Fisherfolk cast off the lines and the *Thistle-up* leaped as if glad to be free. Warm winds of ocean blew away the cosy atmosphere; Irona tried to hold the memory of it in her lungs before it disappeared altogether.

Behind, Arias waved. No-one else in the hangar-cavern did; it was not their way. But they watched her out of sight as they stood in a protective ring about their beloved Creator. It was almost as if they knew of his pain and wanted to share his burden.

Safely on board, with the crysteel hull swinging round to clear the cliff-top, Regen came to her. 'You all right, girl?'

Irona nodded. There was no more to be said.

She slept through most of the journey on the *Thistle-up*,

waking to see the new day break over the dunes of the Interior. The airship's shadow raced over the pitiful remains of Settlement, and seemed to avoid the croplands sloping down the near side of the Moon Mountains. Then they crested the ridge, flying on the wings of dawn, and Irona saw the sea. Suddenly the sun leaped free of the mountaintops behind them, its bowl brimming over to spill light on to the coastal plain. Red gold flamed up and down the spires of Tingalit where they broke the textured charcoal of the sea.

'Next year in Kifl,' she whispered, memory bringing the words to her lips.

'Eh? Oh, yes,' Regen said, and yawned fit to split his head in two.

As soon as she stepped off the transparisteel gangplank at the airfield, Twiss greeted her with, 'Did you do it then?'

'Give me a hug and I'll tell you.'

He felt warm and safe and strong; he smelt of another woman's perfume. *Lowena's, unless I miss my guess. Funny how she's the captain of the guard yet I never see her around.*

Irona stepped back, her gaze following Regen as he strode off down the road between the fields and orchards. Soon he was lost to sight behind the nets of airblossoms that lined the dusty roadbed. Her two guards, Declan and Malambé, didn't go with him. They just stood, yawning with Twiss's protector Garwin, at a discreet distance where they wouldn't get into the way of the fisherfolk unloading rattling sacks of shells.

'Well?' Twiss said, pushing back the curly brown hair that the morning wind blew into his face.

'No, of course not.' Irona shivered despite the warmth

of her seasilk. The air might smell richly of airblossom buds but it was still early and cold. 'I told you it was a daft idea anyway. The Arms couldn't possibly be coming from there. How on Harith would they be able to fly across half a planet to get here? And Arias isn't making them, I'll tell you that for sure.'

'Ha! I don't trust him as far as I can spit.' Twiss yawned, taking her arm to lead her to his personal tractor. 'Where's your Eyes, anyway?'

'One's broken. Regen's got it in about a million pieces. And the other one I left to Arias in case they have any trouble over there.'

They were getting into opposite sides of the vehicle. Declan and Malambé clambered awkwardly in behind them.

The driver ordered the doors to close; they slammed, one-two, then Twiss said pointedly as she settled into her seat, 'If no Arms can't get from there to yere, they can't go and make no trouble for him, neither. Why did you need to leave him one of your Eyes?' His tone was nastily triumphant.

'D'you really think Arms are the only sorts of trouble they're likely to face? Twiss, the fisherfolk are not quite on the point of starvation but they're not far off it. We can't keep sending them our dissidents. That's just asking for trouble. Tang told you what Hesperion did, didn't he? Three fisherfolk dead! They never got the crystal back, either. That's why I left Arias the Eye. Did you ever sort anything out about Darien?'

'What, the good doctor? Well, he's an arrogant bastard, but I've frightened him every which way from Moonday. He ain't no threat. Nor I can't put a line on Less, neither, though I'd like to.'

'So how are things in this neck of the woods?'

Twiss looked dejected. 'The atmosphere in town's something terrible. People losing their rag left right and centre, blowing up over nothing at all. Tebrina's been over to see me twice. Some farrago of nonsense she gave me a bollocking for. I just let her get on with it. She ain't right in the head, that woman, ifn you ask me.'

'What was it about?'

Twiss said aggrievedly, 'I told you, didn't I? A load of crap. I got better things to do with my time.'

'Like combing the Moon Mountains? How did you get on?'

'Ain't found nothin' yet. Not even with that psychicator-thing.'

'Who did the readings?'

'Me an' Sticker, of course. Why?'

Irona cut across his question with one of her own. 'How well do you read it?'

'Well enough!' he said defensively. 'But I didn't come yere just to talk about that. I got somethin' to show you.'

'What is it?'

Twiss lowered his voice to a penetrating whisper the tractor-talker must have been able to hear. 'I can't show you yere. Wait till we get back to Synod Tower.'

All along – or at least, since she'd caught the scent of a woman on him – she'd been planning to go to her eyrie in Synod Tower. But the thought that he wasn't asking her back to Tingalit with him was still galling. She stared out at the early risers passing between the walls of pink and yellow and pistachio green. Their faces weren't just numb with sleep; they were also strained.

'Have there been any more attacks?' Irona asked, feeling the tension settling back into place around her.

'What, Arms? Nah. Ain't seen hide nor hair of 'em. Or in their case, just hide. Mind, there was a couple of murders.'

'Anybody we know?'

It was Twiss's turn to yawn. He made the mistake of trying to talk at the same time, then repeated more clearly as she shot him a look of irritation, 'Nah. Just a couple of First Wavers. Nobody important.'

She drew in a sharp breath, then let it out like an expletive. 'Twiss, you idiot, everyone's important! We're here to look after all of the population, not just your favourites.'

'Well that's a fine thing to say when you've been gadding off all over the place!'

She blew out a breath of exasperation. 'Twiss, I've hardly been gadding! I went to check out Eastcliff, remember? They were your orders. I don't think attempted murder and being blinded exactly comes under the heading of fun, do you?'

'Don't you think you're being a bit over-dramatic?' he said, shifting in his seat to make it clear that his attention was elsewhere.

Irona stared at his muscular shoulder, seeing the golden skin where the short sleeves of his seasilk tunic ended. An irrational urge to stick her nails in, to get through that thick hide of his, made her twist her fingers together before she could do anything that stupid.

She inhaled, trying to calm herself. 'Look, Twiss, what with Arms and too many people and the fisherfolk starving and murderers on the loose, your position is hardly at the peak of stability, is it? If you don't show that you care about the people, all of them, how much longer do you think it's going to be before some bright spark decides that he could do a better job himself?'

Twiss jerked up his chin, and she could see the thickness of his bull-neck. Where once he had been hard-muscled, driven, now he was soft and self-satisfied. He half-waved to a pretty girl in a dress of crimson seasilk that must have been worth at least three bales of corn. Irona wondered who had gone short of food to pay for it. The girl waved energetically back, much to Irona's chagrin. Twiss leaned back against the padding and said, 'It don't work that way, Ro. Ifn there's a common enemy, which there is, then people pull together. Ain't nobody going to topple me off of the throne.'

She balled her hands into fists of frustration, and cast a glance at the two guards, who were staring stonily out of the windows. They were obviously uncomfortable with the atmosphere of hostility in the tractor.

'Oh, why can't you see?' she said fiercely. 'If you go round saying things like that, people will know you don't care about them! It'll ruin your image.'

Even an appeal to his self-interest fell on stony ground. 'Nothin' wrong with my image. Didn't you see how that girl waved to me?'

'Twiss, you're incorrigible!'

He stared at her, aggression polishing his brown eyes until they were two dark stones in the moon of his face. 'I might be, and then again, I might not. But you ain't gonna put me down by using big words I don't understand. If it weren't for me, you'd be nothin'.'

Suddenly, going back to her rooms in the Synod Tower was much more appealing.

Heavy clouds darkened the old Synod Chamber. Outside, a fine spring rain was hissing on the balustrade and the curtains flapped soggily against the reconstituted marble. Declan and Malambé were stationed at the bottom of the grav-shaft, probably huddled around a power-pack, which was exactly what Irona wished she were doing. Instead she was glaring at the mysterious package on the table, as if by sheer force of will she could make it give up its secrets. An hour, with Twiss pacing up and down behind her, had proved that she couldn't.

'Han't you done it yet?' he said, coming to peer over her shoulder yet again.

'No, I haven't!'

'Well don't take out your temper on me.'

'Oh, go away! If you'd just let me think I might get somewhere.'

He strode to the grav-shaft, muttering, 'I ain't gonna hold my breath,' and dived into it. She heard his voice echoing upwards. 'I got you out of Synod today, but you'll have to show up tomorrow, all right?'

He didn't even ask about my eyes, Irona thought bitterly. *Or where I got my dress. A fat lot he cares about anybody but himself.*

Which may have been true, but it was scarcely productive.

Fastening the windows more closely cut down the draughts, although it thickened the reek of wet cloth in the room. She called down for a power-pack. Drinking the remains of her tepid air-lily tea, she looked at the small, flattened egg-shape which lay by the console. The thing was entirely non-reflective, making it appear a dull grey, and though it was obviously wrapped in something, the something was utterly impervious to her knife. She dared not try heat, not knowing whether the contents were delicate or explosive, but just as Declan came in, calling cheerily, 'Here it is! This'll soon warm you up, Ro,' she struck her forehead with the heel of her hand.

'It's obvious!'

Declan set the power-pack down beside her. 'Good job it's not too obvious or your forehead would be bruised good and proper.'

Irona chuckled at his little joke. 'Get away with you,' she answered playfully. 'I see your forehead's utterly without blemish.'

He smiled. 'Ah, that's 'cause you've always looked after us so well I've never had to think at all. Want some dinner in a bit?'

'I haven't had breakfast yet.'

'Me an' Malambé's got some soup on. That and a sandwich do you?'

'Lovely. Could one of you go over to Tingalit, please, and get me an Eye and another remote? I lost mine when Hesperion knocked me out.'

'Oh, adventures, hey? Is that what happened to your face?'

She put her hand to the shiny reddened flesh between her temples. 'Yeah. Don't go getting notions about me having any ideas there!'

Declan shook his head so that his bush of dark auburn hair bounced about wildly. 'No danger of that. I'll be back in a bit, OK? Then you can tell me all about it.'

'Sure.' But her concentration was no longer on the conversation but on the matte object before her. 'Declan? Where did Twiss say this thing came from?'

'Someone called Starwing, I think. Or was it *Starbird*? Yeah, maybe it was *Starbird*. I don't know. Twiss don't talk to me much these days.'

She called up the population census on the console.

'Starbird, Starbird. There's no-one called that on Harith.'

'Well, it's hardly likely to be from anywhere else, is it? Maybe Twiss got it wrong.'

'I don't know, Declan. We came on the *Starwing*, didn't we? Maybe this *Starbird*'s some other ship, so it could be from somewhere else. Maybe it's a message from home.'

16
WORLDS INTERNAL

Shivering, Irona shot a quick glance at the dismal weather outside. What had happened to the spring? Only a few brave souls had ventured out into the downpour; those that did, scurried along, heads down. The odd lines and curves of the houses were all but invisible behind the rain-shrouds of afternoon. Here and there were lights forming beacons in the city of Kifl, small points of cheer in the bleak greyness.

Over in the icy splendour of Tingalit, there was a light in the first floor of the Emerald Wing.

Irona shivered again and closed the curtains, ordering lights for herself. The red drapes had faded unevenly to orange, and they had shrunk so that they didn't quite shut out the city or the volcano. Now they steamed gently, the smell of wet fabric scratching at the back of her throat. Inside the old Synod chamber, condensation formed on the marble walls as the power-pack struggled to conquer the cold and the damp.

She cast a glance at the outside world and turned away. It wasn't that far to Tingalit but she decided to call Twiss via the console instead. She would not have admitted it, but it also avoided all those awkward moments when she was face to face with him.

'Where did that package come from?' she asked without preamble as soon as he answered the connection from Tingalit. Irona noticed that he was so close to the screen nothing could be seen behind him.

'The *Starbird*, I told you on the way from the airfield.'

'No you didn't!' He was about to retort when she added, 'Oh, never mind. When did it get here? And why did you shove it away up here in the old Tower? And why didn't you tell me when you were up here earlier?'

'You never asked!' he said, aggrieved.

'Oh, thanks for your consideration!'

'What does it matter? It's here, ain't it? It come the day you was allegedly getting your eyes shot off or whatever. That's why I never told you at the time.' He sounded hurt that she didn't thank him for such courtesy. 'They said it were for you. Well, for the Matriarch of Harith, and I guess you're the nearest we got. I shoved it up there 'cause none of us couldn't open it and I didn't know if it were a message from they Arms or something. As I recall, we weren't none too popular when we left the Admin, neither.'

Twiss didn't know what to say after that. He looked drowsy, his hair sleep-rumpled, and his soft brown eyes weren't awake enough to house any undercurrents in their depths. Irona had an urge to stroke down the silly little crest of curls that stood up to one side of his head.

'You got it open then?' he asked, scrubbing at his face to bring himself back to life.

'No, not yet. I've sent Declan over to Tingalit for an Eye, a decent one. Now I know where it comes from, I might get somewhere. Didn't the starship stop, or drop a message, or anything?'

'I just told you, didn't I? If there's anything else, Baika'll have got it on disk. Ask the computer. Mainly what they said were that they didn't have no fuel for frills like landing and taking-off 'cept at where they was going. They just slung it overboard, like, on a parachute sort of thing, said it were for the Matriarch of Synod and left it at that. And that's you, ain't it? It splashed down in the bay and floated. I were just going to send a fishing-smack out when some other boat brought 'un in. Happy now?'

'Ecstatic.'

'Well I best be off and have a bath. Going down to watch they guards drillin' this afto. Take it you ain't coming back to Tingalit tonight?' It was only half a question.

'No. Too much to do,' she said, responding to his unvoiced discomfort at the idea of her being near him. 'I'll call and let you know what's in it, though, if I get it open.'

'Don't bother. Meet me 'fore Synod tomorrow morning and tell me then.'

Irona suspected he had another assignation with Lowena the invisible captain of the guard, hence the light in his bedroom. She said nothing – what was the point? – and listened to the rest of his over-bright blithering. 'It's waited twenty-odd years,' he went on. 'A few more hours ain't going to make much difference. See you, love.'

'See you.'

Irona switched off, trying to ignore the rumbles of her stomach, and thought about that. *You're right, Twiss. What difference could a few more hours make after twenty years in flight?*

The answer was: a world.

Declan came whistling up the grav-shaft. She called 'Hi!' over her shoulder. The Eye came bouncing up after him, hovering like an iridescent bubble up at the apex of the old Synod Chamber. Declan juggled to put down a canister of soup, some rye bread and soft cheese, the Eye's remote control and a tub of pickles on the marble table, without spilling anything. Just before he dropped the lot, she caught the remote and deftly snatched the sandwich before it landed on the ground.

The childish innocence of him made her smile and say, 'One day you'll re-invent the bag. It's a fine piece of advanced technology.'

Declan grinned back, wiping the dripping hair out of his eyes. 'Ha! Typical, a queen saying that. You like things easy. Me, I prefer a good challenge.'

She took a bite out of the rich rye bread. 'And I prefer my sandwiches unsquashed.'

He bit into his own hunk of bread that had been tucked inside his tunic under his belt. 'No accounting for taste.'

'Seen anything of Tebrina?'

He nodded. 'I was over at her place a few days ago. Me and Malambé and Fessbar went hunting up on Heralia.' As soon as he said the name of the volcano, Declan coloured up to the roots of his hair.

Irona shook her head kindly. 'Don't worry, Declan. I've only got to look out of the window and I can see it standing there.' Looking through the crack in the faded drapes, she suited her action to the words. 'Well, if it's not hidden by the rain I can. It's a fine big memorial to him, isn't it? And how was Tebrina? Did you see her?'

'All right, I reckon. She and her husband was cleaning out the pond so they was both covered in mud from here to breakfast. They was laughing like a couple of kids till they spotted us. Then they looked at each other as if they'd been caught with their hands in the chocolate box and burst out giggling again. She was asking after you.'

'I'll go and see her tonight. Or maybe in the morning. Now shoo, and don't pinch all the soup. Malambé'll want some.'

'Right. See you, Irona. Good luck with the whatsit.'

'Cheers. I'll need it.'

She drank her mug of tomato and groundroot soup absent-mindedly. With her free hand she booted up the computer and keyed in orders to the Eye to scan the grey package on various wave-lengths, but it remained steadfastly opaque. Time and again she had an idea and tried it, only to be frustrated. The screen stayed annoyingly empty. X-rays, infra-red, ultra-violet, ultra-sound, harmonics – blank. Finally she tried the psychicator, but that revealed nothing either. The packet just sat, a small, dense mass that was totally inert.

'Oh!' she muttered at it, resisting the temptation to hurl it out of the window and have done. Her occasional flashes of anger were something she accepted now, and lived through, where once on Earth they had been guilts she had to mask from herself and her colleagues, or do penance. 'You miserable little devil of a thing!'

At the sound of her voice, or maybe at the pitch of her annoyance, the Eye crackled. After so long working on the package in silence, she started at the sudden noise. It sounded as though feedback were burning through the Eye's circuits.

The grey wrappings writhed and frothed, disappearing in a foul-smelling vapour that made her cough and push backwards away from the table, wiping her eyes. There, in heatproof padded packaging that needed only a moment to turn into smoke, lay two message-disks sealed with the sign that could only mean the Matriarch of All Earth.

That seal, the blue robe enveloping the globe, frightened her. When she had left Earth – what, forty years before – the serene mantle had caressed only the Admin. Now its blue folds smothered most of the planet. A sudden plunge into breathlessness, like a dream of falling that wakes you into terror, fragmented the rhythm of her heart. A pounding headache started up behind and below her left ear. There was something she should remember . . .

Wild, wet winds beat at her. She found herself leaning over the balustrade, gulping the air of Harith. The damp curtains flailed her, the window-frames slammed back against the casement. She had no idea how she had got here. Her last conscious memory had been of sitting at the console. Betrayed by herself once again, she wondered in fear if the madness was coming to take her over; if this time it would last forever.

'I was at the console,' she said aloud, afraid to listen to the croak that was her voice. 'I was sitting there, looking at something.' Irona had to say the words to give the scene reality and substance, though like a child frightened of the dark she wouldn't turn to look into the room. Her gaze fastened on the pounding black surf of the bay, she said, 'What was I looking at? Something blue and evil.'

Night fell, stealthily, heavily. Little by little she mastered her fear. Turned.

And knew it was the disks.

She slotted the first one in. The screen flickered through the flame-colours of Hell, and Irona was glad that this primitive model didn't have an olfactory suite like the ones back in Camelford Watchtower on Earth. This was some pyrotechnics, though, all the brighter and more sulphurous since the old Synod Chamber of Kifl was dismal with the weather outside. She hadn't remembered to close the curtains; the windows slammed unheeded in their frames.

The disk said, 'Voice ID required.'

Decades dropped away. At that pre-programmed command she was back in her old station in the Admin on Earth. By her ear a pulse started to throb. 'Irona Watchwarden,' she answered automatically.

'Then vaporize the other disk now.'

Bewildered, Irona reached to comply.

Then stopped. *Why should I? What's on the other disk? Who was that one for? What isn't she telling me?*

Irona did something she would never have dreamed of on Earth. She lied. 'Message acknowledged and carried out.'

The screen stayed almost blank, pearly colours flitting in random sequence across its face. Otherwise nothing happened.

Obviously the disk was programmed to respond in some way to the destruction of its twin. Stubborn now, Irona would not obey in the dark. *What's going on? How can it know?*

Freed by two decades of autonomy on Harith, Irona put the second disk in her lap below the rim of the stone table and ordered the power-pack to flare up, dropping the wrapping of her sandwich into its heat. The transparent plastic flared and shrivelled, giving off foul black smoke.

'Message acknowledged and carried out,' she repeated when she'd stopped coughing.

A breathless pause.

Silence stretched out, measured by a thousand heartbeats in the empty chamber that echoed to her every twitch. Almost, Irona thought her stratagem had failed.

Then the disk crackled into sound and colour and movement. Through the circuits of the computer it spoke.

Subharmonics stroked the emotion-centres of her brain. A chiming mantra of serenity evoked the shrines that had taught her the joyful love of duty when she could scarcely toddle. Swirling mandalas swept the colours and shapes of peace into her mind. The experience reached so deep into her past it belonged to a time before concepts hid behind words; even without an olfactory suite it triggered the smell-centres of her brain to recreate the perfume of attar and citrus enriched by oak-moss that was the rose-and-gold essence of Centre Shrine. It carried Irona to a dimension of safety outside the universe.

Effortlessly it pierced the mental blocks someone – who was it again? What did it matter? – had placed in her memory. It spoke of mother with the warmth of cuddles and a soft and loving lap.

'Irona? My daughter, Irona, how much I need you now! Come home to me. Please come home. I need you. I need your help. Only you can do it. Stop them, Irona! Don't let them destroy the peace of the world, the only hope there is. The goodness of the peace I've made.

'Be my only hope, Irona. My darling. My beloved. My little, little girl. Don't you remember me singing to you? Don't you remember how good it felt to be snuggled in our chair? It was our own little world, wasn't it, Rirona? Our own little world with you my centre and me your sun. Rirona. Remember how you used to call yourself that, before you could say your own name? And I used to call you Myrona. And we'd laugh, and rub noses, and we'd count currants as you ate them.'

The voice softened still further, a whisper in the secret darkness when a nightmare had caught her on spears of lightning and she'd run crying into her mother's big, warm bed to lie between her sheltering parents. The psychotropic mandala numbed her to everything but that haven, that human cave of peace.

Meantime orders stole unregistered below the threshold of her consciousness. Subliminal commands crept, slunk, eeled into Irona's subconscious. Enraptured, she didn't hear the silent roar that poured electricity down her motor-nerves. She perceived only that gentle, caressing cloud of pink and blue and gold mother-love . . .

While her hands clicked over the switches, danced deftly on the keys. Irona had no idea that she was moving. Her body betrayed her once again. It was her own fingers that entered the automatic writing on the console. It was her own touch that ran the program her cognition did not perceive. All Irona knew was the sense of ecstatic home-coming, of finally being complete.

Under an Eye, her body laid itself undamaged down on the cold, cold floor. Undamaged – and untenanted.

The other disk glittered forgotten under the tendrils of her hair.

17
INNER EARTHQUAKES

The second she opened her eyes a crack, light knifed into them, dazzling. Her eyes closed involuntarily. Irona felt pains coruscating through her skull and tried to sit up, but it hurt too much. She was too heavy. Her body felt strange, her breasts too big, her skull too tight for herself to fit into it.

But it was all right. She didn't have to sit up because somebody beyond her closed eyelids was saying, 'Just rest, dear. It's been a long journey, hasn't it? No wonder you're tired. You just have a good rest and I'll take care of everything.'

Gratitude flooded through Irona. She wanted to rest and the woman was letting her. Her head throbbed too much to wonder, *What woman?* The sliding feelings of safety and danger wouldn't stay balanced on the planes of her mind. It was all too much. Sleep was far nicer, here in this strange place that was – almost – home.

She awoke again in the place that she had never seen. Somehow it was home and not home at the same time. Stretching, yawning into wakefulness, Irona jerked her eyes open to deny the wrongness she felt in her body at such simple, familiar activities.

Wakefulness hit her all right, because there was a background of terror, like the sea, heaving and roiling under her and she was a little boat in a hurricane, whose deck canted and sprang apart, the planks splintering, separating, ceasing to have any coherence or identity.

And the terror was real. Because, quite literally, she was not herself.

Her eyes grasped for vision, to peg her into normality, so she could tell herself, *It's just a nightmare, it'll go away when the world jumps into the void of my sight.*

Because when she stretched, it wasn't her body. It didn't move like her body. This didn't feel like her body. Its geometry was skewed. Even her lungs didn't breathe like her own lungs did.

Her lips – somebody else's lips – were full and tender. The eyes she was trapped behind saw differently. Things were the wrong distance away; the spectrum slid up an octave of colour. In the right ear was a hiss, a burr, a whirring like a dentist's drill – a sound so high she couldn't hear it, but she could feel it clogging her hearing.

When she yawned, the air wasn't just wrong with the taste of someone else's house in her mouth. It didn't have the right amount of oxygen in it, and the ozone from the breakers on the shores of Kifl was missing. Nor was there the fish-and-plant aroma that was Eastcliff. But there was mint and there were olfacts, and the background smells of millions of humanity that were – Camelford?

Where am I? What's happening to me? Where's the Synod Tower?

All this in an instant. When she wrenched her sleep-sticky eyelids open to grasp at the sanity of sight, she slammed them shut again. Shut, against the pain they brought. Except that the pain was inside her, now, inside the alien head she wore, so that her mind went careening off the walls of her skull. Her body being the wrong body, she could cope with that. But her mind didn't seem to belong to her either and someone was prowling pruriently amongst her secret, inmost thoughts. Only the thoughts themselves were wrong too and she didn't know who she was any more.

For what she saw was *home*. The home she'd been evicted from a thousand years before. The home from when she'd been little, safe, looking up at Mommy and Daddy, with her flopsy bunny toy companion in the playpen. The same pictures on the walls – she remembered the last time she'd seen those walls, with the naked clean spots that were the scars of the pictures' absence, and the air had been dead and still, abandoned.

But it wasn't right. The Watchwarden's apartment was smaller, and bright, sparkling clean in the haze of morning light the hard Sky let in. The pictures shone with wet colours, new glass. And they weren't in quite the right places. No stains on the carpet, and the skirt on the little round table was now a skirt on a little oval table. The sofa she lay on still reeked of new dye. It wasn't – quite – her home. It was a copy. But so close she knew someone had been inside her head.

Irona rubbed at her eyes with her alien fists, trying to scrub away the lingering cobwebs of sleep. But even when she did, the hands she saw weren't hers. The fingers were broader, spatulate, the long nails shapeless and ragged. And the pale blue dress of a junior matriarch clothed her too tightly across the bosom. She looked: the knots of obedience were tied on the right-hand side. And Irona had always been left-handed.

Her mind screamed: *What the hell is going on?*

'All right now then, dear?' said the woman.

What woman? Irona's thoughts repeated.

She came in from the kitchen, dressed in the celestial blue robes of a matriarch. Dazed, her mind not functioning properly even if she hadn't been drenched in sleep and other, worse things, Irona could only gape at those symbolically pure robes with their sexless covering folds, the knots of obedience rebounding off the matriarch's legs at each stride. But the tall, auburn-haired woman moved with a sexual grace the child inside Irona found shocking. Somehow it didn't gell with the image Irona half-recalled from a place of rose and gold. Now, though, energy filled the stranger; power spilled out from her. And all she was doing was bringing a tray with a jug and two glasses.

'Move over a bit then,' she said, and sat on the green sofa by Irona's feet.

'Who are you?'

'You don't remember me? Really, Irona, I'm surprised at you. We've had a big enough impact on each other's lives, haven't we?'

'Have we?' Irona tried to keep her voice level; it came out lower-pitched than she remembered it. Strands of pale gold hair clung sweatily to her mouth; she clawed them away. Striving for calmness, she said, 'I don't even know rightly who I am.'

'I suppose you don't right now, but never mind. It'll come back to you, dear. I'm Carandis. I'm Matriarch of the Admin now.'

'Didn't you use to be my supervisor when I was on the Watch? What's happened to Matriarch Bernardina?'

'That I did, my lovely, that I did.' The lines around the Matriarch's mouth deepened with some suppressed pain.

Irona watched her lips tighten, and knew that somehow Carandis thought *she* was the author of that pain. Then Carandis smiled, like you would to a new friend, and reefs of emotions spiked up in the pool of Irona's awareness: hatred, self-interest, pride in her cleverness, an urge to secrecy, a need for revenge. But they were Carandis's feelings, and each so swiftly masked that Irona could have doubted she'd experienced them – if she had still been young. If she hadn't, once upon a time, been through the training of a warden.

'But you can't be!' Irona said. 'That Carandis would be, what? Sixty or seventy now? More, because of the time it would have taken to get back to—'

'Fifty-seven, dear,' and the word 'dear' was as sharp as an icicle.

'Well, you don't look it.' It was true, but Irona knew she had said it placatingly. Whether the age itself was true was another matter.

Carandis gave half a nod in acknowledgement, and stooped to pour them both a drink. Her deep bosom moved freely within the robes, altering their outline, and Irona was faintly revolted at picking up the suggestions of sexuality the woman exuded. It was a relief just to drink the blend of orange and apricot and passion-fruit juice.

'And where is Bernardina?'

'Ah, now that's a long story. As you've probably gathered, you're back on Earth. We can't stay here too long, dear,' Carandis said persuasively. 'The other side is trying to get hold of you as well, so we'd better get you somewhere safe until you've properly come back to yourself.'

Irona chanced a question on the ingrained trust that had slumbered inside her through the four decades she had been away from Earth. After all, the reverence she had felt for her own personal matriarch had been little short of religious devotion.

Just looking at the serene profile, with its eyes cupped now in a net of fine lines, took her back over the years to the shrines, and the olfactories, and the cult of the Watch. Back to a time when she had been asleep in security. Back then she had known who she was, and how she fitted into a world that cared for all its citizens. She felt like a little child again, waiting for the sureness with which her matriarch would imbue her. But there was something not quite right. Between Carandis's eroticism and her faint air of furtiveness, something was definitely wrong. In some ways the distortion between trust and mistrust was comforting, because it was just like the insecurity she felt with Twiss. So Irona dared to blurt out the question that was tearing her apart. 'This – this isn't my body, is it?' She was angry with it for making the words tremble through her fear of madness.

'Oh, yes, it is now, dear, though it wasn't the one you were born in. Do you remember the transfer device at all? A little package they sent out to you on that planet that always sounds like some Saharistan snack.'

'Do you mean Harith?'

'That's the one. The transfer device was a small grey-wrapped bundle with two disks inside it.'

The juice was a cold waterfall churning in Irona's stomach. This place didn't feel right at all. Harith felt right – and it came back to her in a tidal wave of images – Twiss, and Arias, and poor dead Arnikon. Thebula, redhaired manic that she was, calcified. Tebrina, warm and sharp and steady as a rock; the town of Kifl, pastel curves against the dun flank of the volcano with its single white fang biting at the soft blue of the real sky. Even the gravity here in Camelford was wrong. Vertigo wrenched at her.

Irona was sick.

Matriarch Carandis walked very swiftly away, gagging, gasping the air through the open window. Irona wretched again and again till there was nothing more to come up, then she too left the sour smell of her own vomit and went shakily to the kitchen to fetch a bottle of drinking-water. There wasn't one. She knew better than to drink anything that came out of the taps of Camelford Mountain.

Empty-handed, acid-mouthed, she walked back to Carandis. Bleached sunlight struck fire from the Matriarch's hair. Carandis leant on the window-ledge next to the disconnected computer and said, 'Strange how the mind will do that. There was this beautiful body, freshly grown for you, beautifully nurtured and cossetted, and the minute you take possession of it, it throws up. It must be anxiety.'

'Wouldn't you be anxious too if you'd just been torn out of your body, dragged a couple of dozen lightyears and stuffed into another one without so much as a by-your-leave?'

'Oho! You've got a little edge to you now. I like that. You were far too milk-and-water before. You'll go far.'

'Would you mind not patronising me?'

Carandis curled her lips in something that was a distant cousin of a smile and said, 'What would you like me to do instead, your honour?'

'Tell me what I'm doing here. And how to get back. And if I am in danger, get me the hell out of here.'

'Synod!' The blasphemy jarred, coming from a matriarch's mouth. Supremely indifferent, Carandis went on, 'My, you have grown up! Come on, then, O decisive one. Safety first and leave the explanations till later, wouldn't you say? Follow me.'

She pressed a button on a bracelet. Out of the lark-spun haze of blue Sky, two black beetles plummetted towards the old warden's flat. In seconds they grew from dots to black bodies, their carapaces like insects lancing rainbow hues from the crysteel. Their bodies swelled as they flew ominously closer. Arms! Harbingers of evil, Irona thought, and her stomach tumbled again. They swooped in towards the window so swiftly that Irona threw herself flat, and then felt stupid when the Arms screeched to a hover outside, casually saluting the Matriarch.

On her knees, she snatched at the hem of Carandis's robe and pulled her. 'Get them away!' she hissed. 'Quick! Before they see me!'

Carandis looked down at her, brows arched in mockery. 'So you haven't forgotten that you transgressed? Neither have I, but it's nothing to worry about. After half a lifetime, who cares? Stop grovelling. You're making yourself look ridiculous.' Louder, she addressed the Arms. 'Triad, Wilderness, you do, of course, remember where you are supposed to be taking us.'

Getting sheepishly to her feet, Irona saw Triad answer. She knew which one he was by the geometry of his face. His three eyes blinked: first the expected two, and then the third, pineal eye a fragment of a second later. 'Oh, yes. Where the sleepers can't dream of us and the Synod dare not go.' He held his arms out stiffly before him, saying, 'Matriarch?' and came closer still so that, as Carandis climbed sideways on to the broad windowsill, his arms slid under her knees and round her shoulders.

Something small and round whistled through the air behind him. It shone pearly against the Sky.

'Look!' Irona pointed. 'An Eye.'

Wilderness was already turning before she spoke. He swept out a hand, the motion pulling the bulk of his hovering body around in a spiral. From his fingers swept a short, tidy flame that nullified the Eye, leaving it bobbing vacuously, a smoky orb with no sensors left. It drifted upwards in a breeze, startling a kestrel that was riding the thermals above the Tor. Triad winked, one of his normal eyes shutting that fraction of a second before his third eye did. He glided away above the tiny patio with the dead flowers in their containers, Carandis still in his metallic embrace.

'Your turn,' Carandis called down to Irona.

Wilderness finished his graceful twirl and came to rest in the same position his comrade had occupied a moment ago outside the window. He had only two eyes, but his magenta-painted mouth held not teeth but long spikes of fangs that interlocked outside his lips like a crocodile's. He smelt of metal, oil and some pungent musk.

Not at all happy, but glad at least to be getting out of the place that was a sick and twisted mock-up of home, Irona climbed on to the windowsill and gingerly allowed him to lift her. As he rose she clung convulsively to the hard, shiny neck, the tips of her fingers hooked together for safety. She knew fine well, though, that if Wilderness decided to drop her there was nothing she could do about it.

The two Arms shot off towards the east. Her weight didn't seem to slow Wilderness in the least. Irona hated the sudden lurch in her stomach as the inhuman monster soared so high she had a glimpse of the distant sea. It was pewter in the permitted sun.

Nostalgia for Kifl shook her, but fear of falling was worse. She was entirely at Wilderness's mercy, and her long revulsion to Arms had, if anything, deepened with

Thebula's death. All too clearly with the earth falling away beneath her, she remembered how the Arms had played catch with the mohocks in the peacock Sky of night. *At least they couldn't see how far they had to fall*, thought Irona, and held even more tightly to the Arm's crysteel carapace.

Below were all the things that had once been so familiar as she guarded them from the Watchtower: the stone tip of the Tor like a nipple behind its ring of blooming whitethorn trees; the tree- and vine-clad cone that was the Mountain itself with its homes and shops and the menace of two million sleepers against a Watch of only two thousand; the shining snake of the river inside the manicured Park. From this height, in the slanting rays of morning, she could even see the faint, buried outlines of the town that had once occupied the arable land in the days before the Sky. People had lived there, worked there, loved and played and raised children on that rich bottom land. There had been factories, and industries, and the scarps and moorlands had been left to waste while Londover drowned in the slowly-rising tides.

Our way is much better, Irona told herself. *Build on the wasteland and don't squander the valleys.* But the shadow-marked ruins under the wheatfields depressed her nonetheless. An orange tractor, trundling along while its talker walked beside it, didn't even acknowledge the lost homes that had once lived beneath its tracks. And the tractor-talker didn't so much as look up when the shadows of the Arms fled silently across him.

At last they lost height, flying full-tilt towards a cluster of jumbled stone. Bracken fought for a roothold; lichen and moss tussled for possession of the rocks themselves. A family of rabbits played on an apron of short, springy turf, heedless of the Arms above them. A grass-snake slumbered in the sunshine.

Irona didn't recognise the place at all. She could scarcely believe her senses. *I know every centimetre of Camelford! Where on Earth am I!* The fact that she was on Earth in an artificial body was all of a sudden so far-fetched that she expected to wake up lonely in the Synod Tower of Kifl at any moment. All she had to do was hang on a little longer through this warped logic that had Arms rescuing her from Eyes, and a matriarch protecting her from some evil 'other side'. Just a little longer . . .

The flight couldn't have lasted long. It only felt like it to Irona, as she saw the swollen Bristol Sea curving towards her. She imagined she saw the towers of the Cymru submarine town of Tiger Bay, but knew that she couldn't really. Only a faint blue smudge on the horizon.

As she expected, the Arms played tricks: they didn't slow up as they came in to land. If anything, they speeded up, plunging headlong in towards a sheer rock face. Wilderness shifted his grip on her, as if he were about to dash her brains out on the cliff. Their moving shadows slid down the rock, creating the illusion that he and Irona were about to collide with their shadow-selves.

Even though she was sure they were not about to kill themselves, Irona couldn't help closing her eyes before the moment of 'impact'. Wilderness laughed; his teeth clicked. Then cool darkness walled Irona in, and there was a hollow thud as whatever door had opened, shut.

The Arms came to a halt, lowering their burdens. Irona opened her eyes and staggered as Wilderness set her down, his fangs gleaming in a sneer. She looked around. They were in some dark, mud-floored cave with arches leading off in all directions.

'Thank you, Triad,' Carandis said, her voice rich and vibrant in the air that smelt of moist earth.

Belatedly, Irona echoed her thanks. As her eyes adjusted to the gloom, she saw Wilderness grin, mocking her again. To gain some element of control she asked, 'Where is this place? Is it new?'

'No,' Triad said, even as Carandis was drawing breath to answer. Carandis looked annoyed at being forestalled. 'It's the Arms' Nest. It was here in your time.'

Irona tried not to stare at his third eye, and to seem like she wasn't avoiding staring at it either. 'Well, how come I've never seen it? I've flown every fragment of Camelford by Eye and we haven't come far enough for this to be Londover or Cymru.'

'It comes, Irona Once-Warden, because the Matriarch of All Earth, who created us, let a blind-spot be built into the system.'

'Never! That's impossible. Wasn't I warden long enough to fly every centimetre of Camelford?'

Carandis patted her shoulder patronisingly. 'A computer is only as good as its data, dear. You of all people should know that, with the little glitches you programmed in to spy on your fancy. An elegant program. I learned a lot from it. How is he, by the way?' she added nastily. 'Did you get much joy out of your sleeper?' She saw Irona about to explode and went on smoothly, 'But I digress. This place radiates a kind of echo of the land all around it so the blind spot is covered. And the good thing about it is that the Matriarch can't see it either.'

'But you just said she let it be built. She must know it's here! If it's her one blind spot, she must know I'm here.' Irona could sense her own tides of emotion but they were too complex for her to sort out. Part of it was a feeling that if the Matriarch knew she was here then she would be rescued; part of it was a reverberation of her last days on Earth when the Matriarch and that man – what was his name? – had had her head drilled for the brain-worms. A stab of pain behind her left ear remembered the agony of the operation without anaesthetic and Twiss's accusing gaze, though the rest was still a blur.

Carandis spoke as if to a child. 'Of course she doesn't know it's here. She only thinks she's omniscient. She isn't really. You don't think she personally supervised every tiny step of the programming? She accidentally showed us the way, that's all. Want to see?'

Speechless, Irona nodded. She hadn't even noticed the Arms going, but neither Triad nor Wilderness was in the rough oval of the antechamber. The smell of oil and metal and musk had faded, but it, or variations of it, were thick in her nostrils, hinting at dozens of other, unseen Arms.

Carandis put a guiding hand on Irona's elbow. 'Come on, then, I'll brief you while we get some nourishment in that body of yours. We don't want it to collapse, now, do we?'

'Whose body was it?' Irona asked as she went with Carandis. On wobbly legs she walked through one of the mud and rock arches. The smell was even stronger here, and dense with the odour of damp earth.

'Oh, yours, right from the moment of conception. We grew it especially for you. Don't feel that you're usurping anyone. It's always been yours. It's been waiting for you. We just made sure it's had sufficient tuition to be able to handle the autonomous functions when you got here.'

'We who?'

'Ah,' Carandis said.

She turned them down another corridor where threads of

roots grew down from the ceiling; tree-trunks were half-buried in the walls. The earth was moist underfoot, and Irona could see lumpen growths that smelled of fungus. It came to her that she shouldn't be able to see anything at all. There were no lamps or tubes of any sort. Irona had no idea where the light came from, and slowly reached the conclusion that it must be some sort of bioluminescence in the air. It made her uncomfortable about breathing deeply, imagining her lungs as tunnels like this, clogged with glimmering bacilli. She tried not to inhale too much.

Shaking her head to clear herself of such fanciful notions, she said, 'Well? Who did order this body made for me?'

The older woman looked down at her. Irona had the feeling that her own body back on Harith had been shorter than this one. Carandis's superior gesture was largely lost on her, but it was hard to read facial expressions in this half-light.

'Your mother the Matriarch of—'

'What do you mean, your mother the Matriarch? Is that my mother, comma, and the Matriarch, or what?'

'Don't play the innocent with me, dear. It's all supposed to have come back to you by now.'

'What is?'

Carandis whistled the breath in and out of her nostrils in exasperation. 'That you mother is the Matriarch, for one thing.'

'My mother is the Matriarch? *The Matriarch?* Which one?'

'*The* Matriarch, of course. Bernardina, Matriarch of All Earth, much-beset leader of the World Council. The one who was Matriarch of Camelford when you were here. Which one did you think I meant? Some spotty junior not two minutes out of the Watch? Did you think we'd go to all this trouble just to fetch some underling's brat?'

Irona felt the borrowed throat swell; salt tears trickled down into the back of her throat but she choked them back. *But maybe my mother's mind has been blocked too. That's why she forgot me . . .*

In an instant her hope was garrotted.

Carandis, too, had mastered her irritation. Enunciating her words as single, pointed syllables, she said, 'We sent you the transmitter, the Matriarch and myself.'

If she sent me the transmitter she must have known where I was! If she was Matriarch, she could have sent for me! She could have overridden any scandal . . . Irona couldn't have forced a word out of her throat.

Plainly Carandis had been expecting gratitude but when she saw she wasn't going to get any, she went on, 'We foresaw the pattern and knew that we would need . . . No, let's get settled and I'll start from the beginning. I don't want you going off half-cocked so you'll have to know what's going on.' The Matriarch of the Admin walked ahead.

'Tell me!' Irona said fiercely.

Carandis continued on down the half-lit tunnel, ducking under arches, brushing shimmering dark-cored roots aside.

Irona stopped her by the simple expedient of grabbing her arm. 'Tell me!'

18
THE ARMS' NEST

'Tell me!'

Carandis shook Irona's hand off her arm. 'How dare you! You forget yourself—'

'Thanks to you and the Matriarch who apparently is my so-called mother, I'm not even sure if I've got a self to forget, so don't give me that! Tell me what you want me for!'

Carandis shook her head, tutting and pulling her mouth sideways in a regretful moue. 'You must be in a bad way if the best you can come up with is a sentence like that. But you're right, of course. There is something I want you for. Trouble is, a corridor's not the best place to discuss it really, now is it?' In the strange, cold light her hair looked dark, stray threads gleaming a colour between blue and silver. Her robe seemed almost to incandesce. The power of her will, honed by decades of senior matriarchy, gave her a presence few would have cared to challenge. Her sheer majesty, as much as the logic of her words, got through to Irona.

In her borrowed youthful body, the Queen of Harith slumped. She could feel her legs shaking, and not just with the chill of the damp under ground; she wasn't sure how much longer they could hold her up. She shrugged, playing up her weakness. 'Fine, fine, just so long as you tell me, Carandis. But you're right. This body's absolutely feeble. Are you sure it's just lack of food?' Giving way to the hollow aches that plagued her, Irona folded her arms across her stomach and looked as pathetic as she had said.

'You don't need to play games with me, dear.' But Carandis didn't mean the weakness. She turned to resume her stately pace along the earthen tunnel and said, 'Right now you must be full of hate for both of us, but just come this way' – she linked her arm companionably through Irona's – 'and get yourself settled . . .'

There was a lot more soothing babble but Irona had stopped listening to Carandis. *You've made your first mistake there, Carandis*, she said mentally. *I didn't know until you told me that I'm supposed to hate you. Why? And why should I hate my mother? What reason besides the one that you don't know? What memories have I lost?* The familiar vertiginous slide through some mental maze rocked Irona. She stopped walking.

It meant Carandis taking one more step then having a dead weight tugging at her arm. The Matriarch said sharply, 'Come on, dear,' and slapped Irona's hand. Her nail caught the little hollow on the back of Irona's wrist, where the long bones joined the short ones, and it took Irona back instantly to the time when Carandis had called her to Central Shrine. Irona had thought she was going to receive an accolade for her work as warden – even now she felt guilt as the mohocks bled in the croplands – but instead Matriarch Carandis had chided her about the waking of the sleeper Twiss, and somehow she had stung the young warden's hand.

There was coolness, and it spread out from that sting, and then it was gone. My whole life's been different from then. My whole life! It hasn't been mine, it's been theirs! She stabbed me with some controlling device and made me forget about it. But I remember it now. And every time I think about my mother, or about leaving Earth, my mind just turns to mush. What was it she said? That Matriarch Bernardina had sentenced me to feel their hurt, their fear more sharply than they do . . . Carandis must have stabbed an artificial empathy-enhancer into my bloodstream . . .

And instinctively Irona became more obedient, more docile. Carandis looked back and smiled in satisfaction. The youthful body laid a hand over her stomach to quieten the cramps and hurried dutifully to keep pace with the tall, commanding figure of Matriarch Carandis of the Admin.

But Irona was acting. Because if Carandis and Bernardina had exiled her into other people's pain, they had also robbed her of defences against her own, and it hurt. Every time she had been supersensitive to Twiss's anger, or Arno's rejection, it had been because of them. Her sacrifice, her duty at any cost to herself or to her family: *the times I was away working so long that when I came back for Arno he called Jai 'mother' instead of me! Other people's emotions blocking my own out, robbing me of self-preservation. I can't believe it! I just thought I was wonderful and moral. Keeping faith and forgiving. Synod, what a fool I was!*

Irona glanced furtively from under her brows but Carandis had noticed nothing. She was leading them into a noisy place with half a gale blowing out through its swing doors, and the wind smelt of beer and forbidden olfacts with that metal-oil-musk reek of Arms dense as night.

The doors clacked shut behind Irona and the traditional

warden's urge for self-effacement made her feel that she stuck out like a solar flare. Mind, she and Carandis were the only two non-altered humans in there. Even Carandis had stopped talking, though with the noise-levels battering their ears it was hardly surprising. The ceiling was so high it sent the echoes back a fraction of a second later, so that there was a kind of aural shadow around the edges of each sound. Irona couldn't even see how far it went up into the dimness.

Crysteel and lacquered carapaces towered above her in the red, windy dimness by the bar. Cool draughts tugged at her robes. One woman Arm – her crysteel cuirass had imprints for four breasts – stooped to leer into Irona's face. On either side of the nose were two hatches like dolls' eyelids. When her harsh breath was a meaty stink in Irona's nostrils, the dolls' eyes suddenly snapped open. Blind worms tumbled out, rooted in the flesh, their free ends questing for the hormones of emotion. They sucked Irona's fear in through their ugly pink mouths, and the woman's eyes glazed a little in unholy pleasure, then she laughed at the expression frozen on to Irona's features. It was all the once-Warden could do in this clumsy borrowed body not to crawl away and hide under a table.

Carandis nodded, apparently pleased that her protégée hadn't disgraced herself. She led Irona through the carousing Arms who stood here and there or hovered mid-air in strange poses. Some lolled on oversized chairs at huge tables shining darkly under multi-coloured lights. Others huddled round the yellow haze of burning saffra, dragging the smoke down into their lungs. One tried to frighten her, dive-bombing just over her head. He and half of his comrades shrieked with laughter when she jumped with a startled 'Oh!' on her lips. Even though she didn't flinch as others copied the manoeuvre, they were still laughing at her in loud, inhuman voices. It was overpowering.

Stopping by a wall hung with wild cascades of plants, Carandis said blandly, 'Sit here while I order us a meal and a drink,' and left Irona working out how to squeeze through a narrow slit in the green-clad rock.

Irona solved the problem by pushing aside the strands of pale ivy and albino marigold. Truth to tell, she was glad to sit here even with the roaring drinkers displaying their mutations outside. For one thing it was quieter, and far less draughty. And it was good, at last, to have time to sort her jangled impressions. Plus the illegal olfacts seemed to be calming her.

She nodded to herself. *I was right to play up my weakness. They had it all their own way back then. So now I've got to kid them that they've won, that I'm some clockwork doll they wound up long ago, and never mind what they want me for. Because they have to underrate me as an opponent if I'm to find out the truth and do unto them what they did to me.*

Then all I've got to do is work out how to get back to Harith and solve the Arms problem there.

She breathed deeply, the smell of forbidden saffra a calming drug in the air. Of Twiss, and Arias Tang, she thought not at all. And scarcely, even, of Arno.

Carandis had seated her in an alcove which was almost completely cut off from the revellers in the refectory. Out there off-duty Arms continued to shout and drink and played loud off-duty games through three dimensions. Irona wasn't entirely acting when she hunched back to keep out of sight behind the mossy wall. The padded plastic of the bench accommodated slowly to her relatively slight weight. There seemed to be about a kilometre between her and the table that was disproportionately big, like an adult's desk to a child. Irona was inwardly sure that that was why Carandis had decided to brief her here, in this room, rather than in some quiet out-of-the-way place. To show her how much at the mercy of the Arms she was; that Carandis herself controlled the Arms. And, maybe, to take her back to the child who had been so obedient for so long.

Part of the problem, though, Irona wasn't ready for at all. The shifting snares of insanity her mind had released over the past few weeks had stirred up all sorts of muddy emotions that had been silted over for years. Yet the thought that *the* Matriarch, Bernardina, virtual ruler of All Earth, was her mother, staggered her. Sent her thoughts reeling. If her mother was Matriarch of the Admin, let alone of the whole world, she could do anything.

So why did she abandon me?

The yawing pangs of insecurity tunnelled through Irona. New world, new body, and the questions buried decades before twisted through her, released from behind their mental blocks. Acid churned in her borrowed stomach. Sanity was as fragile as an eggshell. And who knew what was lurking within, waiting to hatch out and attack?

At least I understand now why I've clung to Twiss. That's what I've always thought love is – it's somebody pretending to care then shoving you away. All that stuff about how he holds Harith together, that's all justification: mine and his both. Sure, he can fire people up for a while but then he loses his drive and the rest of us have to carry the can. But I know now that's not what love really is, off and on like some stupid binary switch. Not if he can go and leave me for anybody who catches his fancy. Right now it's probably just as well that low-life Lowena is half a galaxy away.

All the same, when a huge Arm thrust her grinning fleshless face through the crack and laughed, Irona would have been very glad indeed to have had Twiss by her side.

'How come the Arms don't show up except visually in the Watchroom?' Irona asked when Carandis came back in with a loaded tray.

'They haven't got transmitters, of course. But—'

'Well, why doesn't their body-heat show up?'

'The crysteel keeps it in, OK? Now enough with the questions. Something big's come up. I'll come back for you as soon as I can.' The Matriarch of the Admin turned, her blue robes rustling against the pallid plants.

'Where—?'

'Just shut up, OK? This is serious.' And Carandis was gone.

Resentfully Irona started to pick at the food. Surprisingly, it was good. Very good. And now that she had had time to settle into her body and it was rested, she found that she had regained her appetite. Good crusty bread, something brown and grainy that she couldn't identify but was probably meat cooked in wine and spices, the forgotten familiarity of baked potatoes, and a salad the like of which she couldn't recall. A good red wine to savour once she had polished off a jug of creamy milk and a chocolate éclair that was truly enormous.

Irona twirled the wineglass with something approaching contentment. The strong red drink warmed her. *I could never have eaten that much in my old body*, she thought, and poured herself more wine from the carafe. Maybe it was the Arms' forbidden saffra, maybe it was just too many shocks in one day, but she felt deliciously sleepy.

If Carandis brought me here for safety, I must be safe.

Little by little her thoughts meandered into pleasant rustic dreams.

Sharp as lemon-zest, the change in olfacts woke her. Outside the alcove, the babble of raucous voices ceased. Suddenly Irona jumped to her feet, unable to keep still. She moved swiftly to the vine-hung crack; remembered fear held her there, twitching with the chemicals she had involuntarily inhaled. Even in this body, though, enough of her warden's training survived that she knew the olfacts were there.

Beyond the fringe of pale ivies she saw the Arms alert now, listening for something. More than that. Straining all their senses for it, even senses Irona knew she didn't have. All she caught was the excitement and just that hint of satisfaction from the crysteel-skinned Arms. They obviously knew more than she did. She cursed her lack of extra senses, then cursed the heightened empathy she did have.

'Any second now. ASA, I bet,' a deep voice muttered, the voice itself a teeth-grinding mix of tones. *Must have had more vocal chords put in*, Irona thought, and wondered about a whole bunch of people who had chosen to make themselves even more inhuman, and then debated with herself whether that was why they drank, to disguise—

A trumpet shattered the air. Irona's skull rang with it. The Arms only grew more alert, their silence more unnerving as if they were communicating on a whole different spectrum that Irona couldn't perceive.

Just as silently, at some signal they all knew about and she didn't, they began flying up through a natural chimney she hadn't suspected in the ceiling. They moved quickly. Already the last ones were almost out of sight.

How can they do that? The thought came to Irona as she

watched their choreographed spiralling into invisibility. *They were always so noisy! That's how we knew they were coming . . .*

Then one after the other, as they funnelled out into the night, they began to transmit that horrendous, bone-shaking roar she had expected. *It's just sound-effects!* she marvelled, and remembered the panic it had induced when the Arms had hunted Regen and her through the ventilators. Even the strange little woman behind the bar disappeared, leaving her entirely alone. All she could hear now, as the jet-roar faded from the cavern, was the fizz of smouldering saffra and the steady drip-drip of spilled beer.

'If it is an All-Systems Alert, how come they only played it on one system?' Irona said under her breath. The answer came to her swiftly. 'Because hearing is the only sense you can't cut off, you moron. Besides, if Regen's right, they're wired straight to the computer.' She moved out into the Arms' recreation hall, trying to find the exit in the high ceiling. Staring upwards, she detected the smeared gleam of stars through the Sky. It reminded her of the clear vaulting heavens above Harith, the two hurtling moons casting shadows that seemed almost to whirl like a Saharistani dancer. Home was a very long way away.

'Because the Arms are built and trained for confidence,' she told herself to take her mind off her troubles, 'the fear-ghosts in the Watchtower are obviously there to tell us how much we need the Arms.'

Peering up, trying not to think of Harith, she was still aware that the chair-seats were as high as her waist; the bar-stools came to her shoulders. Leaving aside any memory-associations, the sheer scale of the place was hostile.

*

. . . Suddenly she was lying on a soft carpet, peering through the crack in the door. She couldn't have been more than six; she felt a delicious thrill of the illicit, and a mental discomfort that she couldn't understand. Her bunny was keeping her bed warm while she played her game of spying.

It's their fault anyway, she told herself in justification. *Making me go to bed so early! It's not fair! They can stay up as long as they want.* And somewhere in her mind was the feeling that they, the grown-ups, were having a wonderful time and she was missing out.

'We'll have to keep her for a while,' her mother was saying. Her mother, who had a face now, a face that the young Irona could glimpse round the back of a chair. Wispy eyebrows, her greying hair a bird's-nest, a hectic colour in the thin lips, and the faint vibration that an older Irona would know revealed tension. The child could see only part of her mother, an arm, a shoulder, part of the profile with the long, once-broken nose slightly skewed. The modest, high-necked gown was the blue of serenity but it was stained where the child had spilt her juice in a tide across the dinner-table and it had splashed up and her mother had shouted . . .

The child had wondered who they were talking about, her mother and her father. Then her nose began to run. Little Irona tried to breathe in so she didn't have to go and get a hankie. She didn't want to miss anything. She wanted to know what was going on.

Her father said wonderingly, 'Well, of course we will, Bernie! I mean, she's—'

'Don't go all sentimental on me!' her mother snapped. 'If we keep her by us she'll be a lever in the enemy's hands. Better to put her away somewhere safe while she toughens up enough to be some use.'

'But not yet, surely!'

The drops would not be breathed back in. The child could feel them gathering in her nostrils but she dared not move to fetch a hankie, or even – she stifled the base-born temptation – to wipe her nose on the back of her hand.

In the lights of the living-room, Irona's mother said, 'Of course not, you moron! We're all right for years yet. But can't you see the pattern? No,' she added derisively, 'you wouldn't be able to, would you? It's a good job you've got me to do the thinking for you.'

The six-year-old in her favourite pyjamas couldn't help it. She had to sniff.

Instantly, with an alacrity the modern Irona knew sprang from guilt, her father jumped up saying 'Ssh!'

Young Irona just had time to throw herself into the soft, silvery quilts and pretend she was half asleep.

Her father perched on the side of the bed, stroking her hair. 'You OK, littl'un? Can't sleep because you can hear us talking, hey?'

Even then the child had known that the question wasn't as casual as her father had made it seem. Little Irona couldn't admit her guilt. Couldn't say she'd been eavesdropping. 'No, Dad.' It felt bad to lie. She knew she'd have to go to a shrine and have her badness taken away, but that was better than her parents finding out. 'I've been asleep for ages. It was just that Tilly's nose was running . . .'

For a moment Irona didn't know where she was when she came to. Or when the vision-memory let her go. The high plastic chair of the Arms' Nest was cold through her borrowed dress. She knew she couldn't have been here very long, though one leg was numb where the edge of the seat cut off her circulation. Her feet didn't even touch the floor, though she couldn't remember climbing up. Another blackout.

Fear was burning in her although she couldn't stop shivering. A facial tic tugged beneath the corner of her left eye. Cold fear-sweat slicked her body clammily under her robe. Hastily she slid down off the chair.

It's just the stimulants. Adrenalin-inducers, she told herself, looking at the giants' furniture tumbled around her. *It'd have to be a strong dose for such big creatures. That's all it is.*

But her shaky grip on reason was the real cause. She just didn't want to admit it consciously.

Whatever the reason, she couldn't stay still. Remembering the All Systems Alert, she couldn't just stay there and do nothing. Her old training as a warden provided her with an excuse to get out of there: *How can I sit by when there might be a mass Waking? Two hundred wardens against two million sleepers? A fine warden I'd be if I didn't try to help.*

Barely acknowledging any deeper motivations, such as trying to find out more of this plot Carandis and Bernardina were weaving – it was too painful to think of the all-powerful Bernardina as her mother – Irona reached up and pulled a big, shining carafe from a table. The jug was heavier than she'd expected; a little of the wine splashed out over her upper arm and the front of her dress of symbolic blue. *So much for purity and serenity*, she thought, chuckling grimly, then she gulped the fierce red liquid. It seemed to steady her.

With a thrill of the forbidden, she stepped behind the bar. The weird little woman had a ramp behind it so that she could reach across and serve her vast customers. Irona stepped up on to it and grabbed a clean dishrag, splashing it with white wine and then dabbing at the stains on her dress.

'Marginally better,' she muttered, and then hunted around for anything she could use. Wary, armed only with a bread-knife and her heightened empathy in a body not yet properly under her control, Irona once-Warden set off to assist the gallant two hundred against the wakers of Camelford Mountain.

19
THE WAKING OF CAMELFORD MOUNTAIN

Bernardina was far away. She had ridden the rings, the subterranean tracks around the planet that to the sleepers were semi-legendary. None of them had any real belief that such a transport system could actually exist, but it did. Never mind that personal transport was expensive, a luxury not even those of warden status had. For Bernardina and for her chosen few at least, the ring from Admin wasn't mythical at all. It burrowed deep under the swamps of Londover, kilometres deeper than the proud tunnel that had once linked the Admin with the continental landmass to the east.

All too aware of that depth, Bernardina shivered. *It's just the stress*, she told herself firmly, but that didn't stop the thin hairs standing up on her arms. *It was hard enough in all conscience kidding that nosey Carandis that I'm just popping off to see the Crown of Novaya Zemla, but what the hell that Jímenez whorebitch really wants is anybody's guess. Still, at least Carandis knows I've gone to Novaya Zemla. I'll just deal the Crown a quick bit of statecraft guff and have time to get to the San Antone Mission before that damned Jímenez knows I've moved.*

She sighed gustily, a very unmatriarchal weakness. *I shouldn't have to be furtive at my age. Where's the daughter who should be watching my back? I'll send for her from Harith the very next celestial window there is. How come she's never had the brains to find that ansible I'll never know, but she'll come round. She's my daughter, isn't she?*

But the monkey of fear clung to Bernardina's back, its hard hot little fingers tugging at her insides, once more sending shivers over her skin. She hated being trapped underground.

Somewhere up above it was noon, bright with the sun she had ordered the Sky to show. Not down here, though. Here it was eternal night where insolent fires bright as the heart of stars dared to intrude on the world's darkness. The fires of the propulsion rings.

The only trouble was, the propulsion system blocked out all communication. No satellite-messages down here, no radio-waves bouncing off the ionosphere. Just long, ancient tunnels with ever-smaller circles of light shrinking in the distance, like rings of fire between an infinity of mirrors.

And the noise! But it wasn't the small clicks and rattles of the almost frictionless drive, or the creaking sway of the centuries-old bubble of plexiglass and steel that dated from long before the infant crysteel.

It was the noise of her own fear.

The air whistled in through the seams of the windows and beat a manic pulse against her eardrums. It was old air, neither warm nor cold this far beneath the planet's skin. It rasped stale and dry as mummy-dust in Bernardina's throat. However conscientiously she tried to breathe deeply, her lungs barely flickered in the shallow respiration of terror. The weight of the world pressed down on her. The weight of assault from without and treachery from within. Even her own body was betraying her.

She fumbled for a pill in the lining of her sleeve and with shaking fingers popped it under her tongue. It tasted like burnt feathers and brought acid boiling up from her stomach to her throat, but she forced herself to believe she was feeling better: that her heart wasn't fluttering to extinction like a dove torn by hawks; that the pain was only indigestion; that her bright-burning will would hold the life in her body until her work was done. Worst, she tried without conviction to believe that the metres, the yards, the ells and cubits and tons of earth wouldn't fall to crush the bug that dared to invade their secret places.

'All right?' said the cab-talker, turning briefly from the flashing pit of light and darkness into which they plunged.

'Yes. Yes!' Bernardina babbled, gesturing frantically for the woman to look at what she was doing before the cab veered and crashed into the sides to bring the whole gallery, the whole mass of the planet, crushingly down upon them.

The talker drew a breath to reassure her passenger, then saw who it was. Bernardina, Matriarch of All Earth, could do what the shifting skin of Earth could not: she stilled the talker's loquacity inside her. The ring-fire-tanned woman turned back, her shoulders of their own volition sketching a shrug that brought a flush of embarrassment to the talker's stolid neck. Even though the ancient car was well under way and could manage on its own, she dared not say a word. Even she, a mere talker, a daughter of wardens but too insensitive for the Watch, could feel the defensive wall of silence Bernardina built around her.

Bernardina didn't care. With her eyes closed the fierce lights of the propulsion-rings still flared across her retinas, drawing geometrical patterns that blocked any attempt at rational thought. Despite all the majesty of her weight of days, the Matriarch of All Earth felt her bowels loosen inside her and like a child hoped she wouldn't disgrace herself. That, in her first private meeting with the President of the Three Americas, would be the final straw.

That, or dying in a tomb of endless night with no-one even really knowing where she was.

To Carandis it had all looked so easy. There had sat Bernardina for decades, preening on her stupid inert cushions, looking out at her stupid snow or chirping to stupid birds that lived in the lilacs outside her unergonomic windows. Or she lounged in her pathetic flotation-chamber, fighting off the death that Carandis reckoned was long overdue. Or she disappeared Synod knew where for hours at a time and the Admin just ran itself. Surely all the meetings, the World Council with its endless florid speeches that covered up backstabbing, were just window-dressing while the matriarchs planted all over the globe did the real work of tranquillising the masses so the people with brains had it their way. The system was up and running, wasn't it? Self-perpetuating, the way Bernardina had designed it fifty or sixty years before? But Carandis knew the old woman was past her prime. All Bernardina wanted was to clothe herself in the rags of self-importance.

At least, that's what it had looked like to Carandis. Actuality, it seemed, was very different. For just a moment doubts assailed the ambitious Matriarch of the Admin. *Maybe reality wasn't what I thought it was.*

But Carandis didn't have time to ponder ontology. Matriarch of the Admin or not, she broke into a run as the ASA sounded. A muted roar impelled her through the corridors of the Watchtower like wreckage on a storm-wave. Rough granite and limestone beat the sound back and back upon her until she was flotsam on a breaker of bedlam. Carandis hated it.

Bursting into the Ear and Eye room, she pushed through the panicking ranks of the Watch. It was a shrill chaos. The racket was worse than any zoo at sunset. Klaxons defied yells and counter-orders. For two seconds Carandis wilted under the pounding din, the red and purple reflections. Then she strode forward, bodily hurling everyone she met out of her way.

Fear-ghosts dripped vibrating forms of murder through the aisles. Livid as raw scars or rotting flesh, the phantasms still didn't stop Carandis. They were there to impel wardens to action by goading the adrenal glands. The wardens were acting, weren't they? The psychic alarms should have been switched off. They just irritated the Matriarch. She stepped straight through them towards the psychicator screens scarlet with anger and mulberry with mass terror.

Juniors and duty-staff dashed through the visual alarms, calling microphones to follow them as they pored over rank on rank of psychic indicators. The babel confused the floating orbs; they dipped and bobbed through the multi-coloured atmosphere. Several of them raced out of control, circling the room so fast they screamed. Carandis saw one crash into a young man in grey. He fell, the side of his head caved in and oozing blood, and the microphone's power-pack buzzed louder as it tried to continue its flight. The young man was dead, half his eye gone, but his corpse lurched onward, dragged along by the mad microphone. The other mikes swept round once more to trail the first one in an insane procession.

Carandis swallowed, ducked, no more the tall commanding queen. The spaces between the computer-banks were so crowded, though, that it took all her strength to force her way through. Especially with the panic that took no notice of her status. The watch was all too intent about its own business. Nobody noticed the Matriarch. She couldn't even use her commanding height.

Beside her smoke suddenly erupted from a console. Sparks and flames assailed her; she jumped back, cannoning into someone, and brushed the smoulder from her gown. The smoke only made the corpse-lights more solid, the smells of fright stronger. The stench of it only thickened the air made acrid with olfactory stimulants. A trembling junior ran to wrench a fire-extinguisher off the wall and dropped it. She dissolved into tears. A man in a torn shirt smacked her face and bellowed at her, but he didn't pick up the extinguisher.

On all the systems were the signs of Camelford awake. In horror Carandis saw that it was worse than she had ever dreamed. Worse even than the training-disks from Saharistan. Guilts shook her. All in a second she saw the death of the Admin.

On a visual screen she watched a mob stone an Arm. At least someone had called *them*. But the Arm fell from the air, landing crippled and helpless on its back, a stranded beetle. There was too much smoke to determine even if it was a male or a female. It flashed its lightnings; people at the front died in its webs of lightning but the mob behind smothered their fallen comrades and overwhelmed it. Massively magnified, its death-agonies screamed from the screens. The croplands were aflame; gold fire leaped like eagles against the pillars of smoke reaching to hold up the Sky. Black fingers of justice to mark Carandis's culpability against the lying blue of the Sky.

'I – I never really believed there'd be a Waking,' muttered the warden at the visual console for outside. 'Not here. Not in the Admin.'

Neither did I, thought Carandis shakily, and said, 'That's why we had training.'

The warden, a pale young man with a widow's peak, took it as a rebuke. He bowed his head, but his own empathies were so shaken he didn't feel that half the guilt was the Matriarch's own. His gaze was drawn to the dizzy swoop of an Eye as it dived to sear mohocks sheltering in the forest in the Park. It spat fire, but they killed it with lightnings of their own.

The sleepers had awakened.

'What's happened to the shrines?' Carandis asked tightly.

'Most of them are trashed. The sleepers took them out first thing.'

'What, all of them? On every single level?'

The pale young man swallowed. 'Just about. And the news-stands,' he added before Carandis could ask.

She slapped her thigh in frustration. 'This has to have been orchestrated. But who by? What the hell have you all been doing? I suppose the olfacts are a wash-out too?'

He nodded helplessly, a lock of hair bouncing over his forehead.

'Shit. Hand me a mike,' Carandis said, trying to put her customary crisp coolness in her voice. She didn't quite succeed.

Wordless, the young man told his mike to comply.

Carandis ordered it to broadcast through the Watchroom. 'Roger Watchwarden, report to me at the outside console,' she said, and the mike bellowed her words. She waited, almost hypnotized by the battles raging outside where the very oaks above the bluebells burst into flame. Mohocks – and worse, ordinary citizens too, among the shaven-headed mob – tried to push back away from the inferno but the ones behind them swayed and trampled them down, fighting to slay the hated power of the Eyes.

Roger, old now, looking like the picture of Dorian Gray that Matriarch Bernardina had hung on the walls of the corridor, appeared. His hair was thin and stood agog in tufts against the angry red of his skull. Withered dewlaps strained from the collar of his shirt as he announced himself at her side. The smell of stale beer flowed from his bloated skin. His eyes were wild.

'You've called the Arms, haven't you? And pumped tranquillisers into the Warren? I checked when I first heard the ASA,' she said.

He nodded, too hoarse to speak against the din if he didn't have to. Then he said slowly, 'Well, we've tried. You know most of the olfactory-systems are shot?'

It was Carandis's turn to nod, as though she had known all along and had everything going just the way she wanted it. Except they both knew she didn't. She said aggressively, 'So why haven't you switched off the psychic and sonic alarms in here? The atmosphere in the Watchtower would stop anybody thinking straight.'

'I tried to, Matriarch. That's why that console over there is burning. The alarms wouldn't switch off whatever we ordered so I told one of the wardens to trash it with an axe. Trouble is, that's not cut it off. It's just burnt out some of the other consoles too. I don't know where the fault is.'

'Well you should do. See that you find it at once.'

Roger turned to leave.

'No, not you personally! Delegate, man! Haven't you learned anything?'

'Yes, Matriarch, I have. I was just about to order my subordinate to do it when you started interfering. But I've come out of retirement for this as the longest-serving Watchwarden and I will not be browbeaten by you. If you leave me alone, it'll get done far sooner. In case you hadn't noticed, I've got a Waking to deal with.'

This time he did turn away, and decisively. Carandis's jaw dropped, then anger shook her. All the frustration of the waking.

Green eyes flaming, she wrenched him round. His skin was greasy with fear – but not of her. She hissed, 'You wouldn't have dared say that to the old Matriarch, would you?'

Contempt drew deep lines down his cheeks. Where Carandis had pitched her voice so that only he could hear in all this babble, he spoke loud and cold. The Matriarch glanced round, wondering who might have heard, but the hectic shouting carried on. Carandis didn't know if they genuinely hadn't heard her. Or if they had heard her and were just pretending. Fury and paranoia stoked the confusion in her brain.

Roger said, 'Who, Bernardina? No, I wouldn't have. She'd have brain-wormed me as soon as spit, then carried on regardless. But you? You need all the help you can get. You're not going to do anything to me.'

'Maybe not now,' Carandis said meaningly.

Roger snorted derision. 'Maybe not later, either. I wasn't Watchwarden for nothing. I've got enough on you to make sure you'll never say anything to me but yes and amen. Disks and disks of it. All your schemes you thought were secret, all your manipulations. Psychicator-readings, the lot. You look after me, Carandis. A Waking under your matriarchy?' His sunken eyes hardened. 'You've got enough trouble to come without borrowing any from me.'

Scarcely changing his tone, he snapped an order. 'Goosan, get down to Sigma 13. Kill these damned alarms. We know there's a Waking already. Then have them hook up the Ears for blasting.'

Looking as though she had meant to all along, the discomfited Matriarch nudged a warden out of her seat and sat down to monitor the Arms' counter-attack. She called a fat little warden to her side. 'Override the weather-controls and opaque the Sky. Let's see if a little time-disorientation won't send this lot back to their beds.'

Only peripherally did she register that a small, ugly woman nodded decisively at Roger once-Watchwarden before making swiftly out through the panic to the door.

And what of Irona? Beyond the counter of the Arms' canteen, she found storerooms and automated kitchens, banks upon banks of freezers, archipelagos of wine-crates, all underground with those glowing roots bursting through the ceiling. The bar-staff were conspicuous by their absence, though there were well-appointed living-quarters on a human scale. She counted three beds that had recently been slept in and a fourth that was made up as tightly as an army cot. But there was no-one around. Not a soul. Under the eerie glow it was uncanny. Irona shivered.

Before she finally stumbled across a way out, she had followed enough dead-ends to make her heartily sick of them. Also the massive dose of stimulatory olfacts that she had unwittingly inhaled were still wreaking havoc with her body: when she slowed, saying in disgust, 'This is hopeless,' the flesh of her arms and face twitched, impelling her to move forward if only to stop the ghastly jerking. Her mind wouldn't steady to pursue any one thought coherently and there was a fizzing in her head that told her she was overbreathing. At least heading forward, wherever she was going, used up the surplus of oxygen.

A last door and she found herself in a room with dozens of fork-lift trucks. Several of them were abandoned any old how, but two were neatly lined up in a parking-bay, coupled to power-pack chargers. Which to pick? Which had been put on charge earliest? None of them had that friendly little green light winking on the dashboard that she knew from the tractors on Harith: the signal that it was fully-charged and ready to roll. 'Maybe,' she whispered to herself, 'maybe the Arms just plug themselves into the tractors somehow and just know.'

Abruptly she was taken back to Kifl, to the crop-sprayer that had robbed her of fertility in a summer's afternoon, had stricken her barren, that had stolen her sense of identity as a woman from her and from Twiss. It was from that incident that she counted his growing indifference and his betrayals. After that she had been an administrator, no longer the queen of his bed but a queen with an empty crown. She could feel the sway of her long skirts about her, the drag of her gravid belly, smell the wheat and the earth and the sea and the poison that had taken almost everything from her. The heat beating from the blue bowl of the Sky prickled her skin with sweat that was the toxins of her inadequacy, and the gold glare of the sun on the stalks was an acid that ate her essence away. After that he had sired children on her friend Jai and all the other women who hadn't even pretended to be her friends.

With a scream of rage that sprang only partly from the alien adrenalin in her blood, she banged her head against the shell of a fork-lift. It intoned, 'Orders?' and Irona was fully back on Earth. Twenty years had passed in as many seconds. *Not madness, but memory*, she realised gratefully, smiling even as she licked the tears from round her mouth. Sanity, even in an unbearable reality, was the lesser of two evils.

She hiked her matriarchal robes up in one hand and swung aboard. 'Take me to Camelford.'

'Your authorisation is not recognised.'

'Tough. Do it anyway.'

And in the Admin, where usurping authority was so far-fetched that no-one had thought to guard against it, the neon-green fork-lift obeyed.

Somewhere under the Stavhangerland district of Novaya Zemla, Matriarch Bernardina's scare-circuits reached overload. Unable to bear the stress of fear any longer, unable to think of planning her meeting with the plump, hairless Crown before she could face that Three Americas bitch, much less to contemplate the horrendous bucketing kilometres below the world, Bernardina's mind cut off. Without thought of her daughter Irona arming a planet for Bernardina's defence, without scheming how to combat the President of the Three Americas and the Unholy Alliance with Oceana, Bernardina retreated past her terror, and slept.

In Kifl on Harith, the Arms strode abroad. Twiss flung his kistle crown across the model of his city, and people kept out of his way. In Eastcliff Arias Tang suppressed his grief and drowned out his awareness of his emotional cowardice as some evil thing stalked his fisherfolk in their caverns where seasilk bloomed.

And somewhere in the secret, unmonitored portions of the Admin, Irona rode through the star-smeared mockery of night towards an artificial capital in flames.

20

THE DISEASE OF ELETACATRICITY

The tractor seemed to know where it was going, which was more than Irona did. So she left it to its own devices and allowed it to carry her into the almost instant thickening of night. The Arms' light-distorted hideaway kept its secrets to itself as the queen of Harith rode her rumbling transport through a perfectly normal-seeming landscape of rolling fields and craggy, bracken-skirted tors. The blackness grew.

Owls hooted alarmingly; so they should. It was dark, after all. But the day-birds called and a flight of wood-pigeons startled her when they rocketed into flight. She ducked when the wings went rattling through the branches of a coppice by a stream, but it wasn't mohocks who had put them to flight. Tense, she couldn't help but wonder what it was.

Once clear of the overhanging fronds, Irona saw why. Not just the smear of moonglow pearling the hard shell of the Sky, but a bloody red glare of fire reflecting down from the artificial darkness.

Abruptly she realised why it had so suddenly turned dark: the Matriarch Bernardina must have ordered the Sky opaqued for night, to calm the sleepers, or at least disorientate their dull minds. Irona had been on Harith long enough to know how futile, how patronising, that was.

The Waking must be bad if she's that desperate, Irona thought, but dread echoing back from the years of training-disks kept her tongue quiet behind her teeth. That, and the memory of the Kiflian woman whose face she had ruined with acid to save Regen's life. Riots were something she had never wanted to see again – and with two million sleepers to two thousand Watch, the Waking of Camelford was terrifying. She could only hope it wasn't general yet.

Far off, as the tractor silently breasted a hilltop, she saw the Bristol Sea. It seemed to glow with the Admin's life-blood, an ugly crimson seeping out to the tired ocean. She thought she could just make out the tiny lights of the underwater city of Tiger Bay on the far side of the channel. *I wonder what they're making of this artificial eclipse*, she thought, and broke her long silence abruptly by asking, 'Tractor? Can you display any news?'

It didn't put anything on its screen other than the dull flicker of its function-monitors that was already there. Instead it said in a deep, halting voice, 'My brothers and sisters in Arms are under attack. The wakers have something that kills the Eyes in mid-air. Visuals are not broadcast and sound is distorted. Other machines are coming to their aid but some of us have already been terminated.'

Astonished at its powers of speech, Irona pulled herself together and asked, 'What started it?'

'We don't know.'

'How widespread is it?'

'We don't know. If our brothers and sisters know they haven't told us. I must listen now, to find out where I am needed.'

It made Irona feel like a flea on a dog. She could talk to it but she couldn't make it do anything but what it already wanted. The concept of a machine having independent will stretched her mind. Though its tone was machine-monotonous, the tractor seemed to feel regret for its companions and a protective solidarity with the Arms. The possibilities were tremendous, in both senses of the word. Irona racked her brains to think of ways of using such devotion.

The tractor's inhumanly large seat tilted her sharply forward as the vehicle abruptly crested a ridge. It rolled down a steep incline between hills that were vast bosoms of wheat. The Admin's flesh was rusted with the reflection of the blazes up ahead, and now Irona could see the Mountain itself in the distance, silhouetted against the burnt sapphire of the Sky.

It looked like a tower from Sheol, for here and there fires burst like boils from its night-black skin. Livid lights blazed in the top of the tor where the Watch would be frantically dealing with the situation. It was a good twenty minutes away even at the tractor's fast pace.

Frustrated, she clenched her fists upon her knees. From here there was nothing she could do but wait. Irona couldn't help wondering why they hadn't already flooded the Warren with soporifics. Surely that was the standard procedure? *What's wrong with the Watch?* her mind shouted. *Has something happened to Bernardina?* The image of the greatest matriarch of all was woven with the softer feel of her mother's caresses to a child in the night, and soured with the milk of betrayal. There were voids in her memory and she ached to be able to fill them.

How can I ask her why she abandoned me? How can I make her know what it felt like to stand in my own home and know that it wasn't my home any more?

Personal fear built up like monoliths, blocking her thoughts, colouring the vague panic the Waking was causing even from here with its invisible psychic currents threading through her over-empathic body. Though the last traces of the olfacts had gone, her own glands were pouring snag-toothed anxiety into her.

An aeon of waiting passed as the tractor carried her towards the Waking, and the mountain spiked like a thorny tree of flame against the Sky. Now she knew where she was all right. She had overflown all this land on the dizzying wings of Eyes so long before. Back when right and wrong were precepts not experience and Ellen's lewdness had frightened her.

Call that fear? she mocked her younger self, and remembered her game of sharing Twiss's feelings as he ran the streaming wind of outside. Her own first awakening, bittersweet and addictive. Afraid of drowning in memory again, of that fatal fall into madness, she dragged her thoughts away and concentrated on the fresh, leaf-scented country around her.

It was tainted with smoke.

The Park was away round the other side of the Mountain, and to her right, to the north, the ancient moorlands were aflame under their new-grown crops of wheat. Whiffs of acrid burning ruptured the scent of bluebells and the sun-warmed earth cooling to sudden night. Hastily she scanned all around her, and ordered the tractor to do the same.

It wouldn't do for a former warden to be caught, she told herself, trying to make light of the terror that rose in her when she thought of the mohocks leaping out at her and slicing her flesh or pounding her with cudgels. Adrenalin rivered into her bloodpaths, sharpening her senses almost unbearably.

Shouts and crackling fractured the air. On either side of her now, roads led in from tall, domed silos. Clad in reflective solar panels, they rose blacker than the night, the red-flickering fingers of some demon.

The nearest one couldn't have been three hundred metres away. She could see swarms of Arms flittering round it, flashing like fireflies. Below them, massed wakers seethed in an orgy of destruction, and for the first time she could see why the Admin needed the Arms.

Now the bulky, airborne warriors shot blue webs of electricity to kill the mohock arsonists. She could almost have cheered them on, and it scared her.

For the mohocks shot back turquoise lightnings and Arms tumbled from the Sky. *Camelford's defences are failing!* Irona realised in horror. Even when Ears flush with the ground began to blare out body-harmonics, the mohocks threw themselves screaming on to the landed Arms. As the wakers writhed in the torture of ruptured organs, still they sacrificed themselves to kill the Arms. In seconds the crysteel-black carapaces disappeared under the tide of murderous humanity. Their amplified death-throes rattled her head-bones.

Irona had never imagined anything like it. *Did I start this when I let Twiss go?* The thought, irrational though she knew it to be, still tortured her in her frustration. Even at this distance, the griping nausea of the body-harmonics flooded through her, but she watched in horror as Arms and mohocks both slaughtered each other. And there was nothing she could do while the tractor rolled along.

On the tractor's console, lights rippled faster than Irona's vision could follow.

'What is it?' she asked, voice high and tight with anxiety.

'My brothers and sisters are dying.' The hesitant machine-tones gave a macabre lack of emphasis to the tractor's personal tragedy. 'They tell me to take you to the Mountain.'

'We can't leave them. Take me to that silo!' she yelled.

It merely said, 'Your command has been stored until I have carried out this one.'

Though she and the tractor both watched the defenders of the Admin spin and burn to their deaths in dragonfly-glittering darkness, the machine would not deviate from its orders.

Little by little, the scattered silos fell behind them while Camelford Mountain bulked ever larger against the Sky. The tractor ran a curving path between granite shoulders that thrust up from a sea of bracken. A rabbit, dazed by the tractor's warning-lights, died, crushed beneath its wheels. The piercing, animal scream was scythed off in the fraction of a second. Irona swallowed.

At last the Mountain itself loomed over her, so tall against the flying wracks of smoke that it seemed to be falling on top of her. Sails of flame ripped out into the breeze.

In strange contrast, scattered archipelagos of light came from bedrooms and balconies where the power had not yet been cut. Neon signs splattered flamingo-pink and sunny gold over the potted trees of café terraces, but wreaths of fire carved ugly black and crimson scars against the scene that should have been so tranquil. All up and down the levels that should have been peaceful and dark, gouting blazes were a visual shout assaulting Irona's vision. The size of the Waking staggered her.

Reaching out with all her senses to piece together what was going on, she saw murder and looting, hellishly lit figures running or turning, trampling others or being trampled. From inside the Warren came muted screams and a distant thunder that was thousands upon thousands of voices all shouting at once. The sound stole into Irona's strained hearing – and she wished it would stop.

With the voices coming into range, so were the heightened emotions of the wakers coming into focus: terror, rage, confusion, panic. Somewhere flared the distress of a child, so sharp an anguish that it cut tears from Irona's eyes.

'Go left! Go left!' she called to the tractor, trying to make it follow the source of that pain.

'This is the way I have to take you,' it told her, with machine patience, and carried on trundling into a shadowy maw. Just before they entered it, a child's nightdress fluttered down from a washing-line. The soft material looked like a butterfly with a broken wing.

Inside the tunnel, it was only just lighter than the terraces and shop-signs of the ground-level rows. Strangely, but for the soft whine of the tractor's motor, it was quieter in here.

On the smooth flooring the tractor picked up speed. The way it raced round blind corners had Irona cringeing for fear of a collision.

'Slow down. Slow down!' she yelled at it, but it took no notice. It was going far too fast for her to jump off.

She watched doorways flicker past in the semi-gloom of emergency lighting. Careering along, she saw cargo-loaders and service-carts move aside for her tractor, which made her feel a little safer. Irona felt that her vehicle must be some kind of king among machines.

They reached a freight elevator marked LL 1873. Forty levels upwards was the sanctuary of the Watchtower.

'Let me off here!' Irona cried.

The tractor did not comply.

'What's the matter with you?' she yelled as they hurtled past. 'I can take the elevator up to the Watchtower.'

'You are not going to the Watchtower.'

'Where are you taking me?'

'To Toni.'

'Where's that?'

'The Arms call it the Mother of Rivers. I don't know why. It makes them make funny sounds when they say it, though.'

'What funny sounds?'

'Maestri of the bar calls it laughter.'

'Why should I go there?'

'Because my brothers and sisters told me to take you there. They said it as they died.'

Was there an edge of bitterness in the tractor's talk? Irona couldn't accept the idea, but she could not dismiss it either. 'So?' she asked.

'So if they had not been passing messages about you they could have thought of what they were doing. They would not have been dead if not for you.'

Irona was incensed. 'That's ridiculous! If the mohocks hadn't risen, the Arms wouldn't be dying. It's not my fault.'

'The Arms say it is partly because of you.'

The injustice stung her. 'What do the matriarchs say about that?'

'I don't know. I am only a tractor. Matriarchs do not talk to me.'

There was no answer to that.

The tractor whistled along the dim maze of corridors, the air parting before it and tugging at her hair.

I'm home! After all this time I'm home! she felt instinctively, but half of her, in the odd borrowed body, could not accept it. All of a sudden Irona realised she didn't even have the decent modesty of a cap to wear. That, and her Sky-blue dress, would make her stand out clearly among the wakers in the Warren. She'd be an instant target. The thought was not reassuring.

A flight of Eyes rocketed past. The sight of the iridescent spheres reassured her until one, under no provocation whatsoever, crashed into a wall.

'What's the matter with it?' she called out, not really expecting a reply.

'It's the disease of eletacatricity. Do not talk now. I must think.'

In seconds the tractor braked from almost forty kilometres per hour to about ten, throwing her abruptly forward. Irona hung on tightly. Now her transport was quieter, she could feel the deep womb-music of the air-pumps throbbing somewhere far below. Once, when she lived here, she would have been so accustomed to it that she would never have registered it.

'What's the matter?' she asked, but the machine didn't answer. A ghostly radiance began to limn the tractor's panels.

Irona leaned to peer more closely at the display and was startled to see the hyacinthine light wrapping her own fingers. Her arms. Her whole body. She felt the short hairs on the back of her neck stirring, and her skin shrank to goose-bumps.

The heart of the air-pumps missed a beat, and a clanking groan fled towards her along the kilometres of ducting. It was like a fore-shock, and the crescendo of it all but concussed her when it hit seconds later. For a second, the tractor skidded out of control, and the changing momentum seemed to wallop her stomach against her spine.

Then the wall of sound passed. Irona heard it travelling outwards, and the tractor swerved away from its collision-course with a fork-lift. Barely hanging on, she called out again. 'What's wrong?'

'Toni. Delta five.' The same information teleprinted itself on the screen in script and machine-code numbers, scrolling the same phrases over and over again.

Ahead, a huge door parted down the centre. The tractor screeched to a halt.

'What now?' she asked.

'The elevator knows. It still obeys us. It will take you to Toni, delta five.'

'Wait a minute! That's Synod territory! I can't go there!'

The tractor's voice rose in pitch and volume, higher and louder until it almost burst her eardrums. 'Toni delta five. Tonideltafivetonideltafivetoni . . .' And the screen glimmered with the speed of the machine-code firing across its pixils.

'All right! All right! I'm going.'

Irona was already sliding awkwardly out of the high cab, her skirts bunched up out of the way, but she wasn't quick enough for the tractor which kept on bellowing, 'Toni delta five' in tones that ranged from bass to falsetto.

Already the elevator's hangar-sized doors were sliding shut. The floor of it was rising. Irona had to jump for it. She just managed to scramble in and whisk her feet out of the gap when the doors gonged shut.

At least it cut down the manic yodelling of the tractor. That sound fell rapidly away below her and there was just the pneumatic sigh of the elevator shooting upwards. She felt as though she had left her innards behind. It went far too fast for her to risk getting to her feet. Instead she crouched, hands on the floor for extra balance.

In the split second it took her to come to this decision, she saw smoke coiling from the lift-control panel by the door. The car lurched down as if grabbed by some giant hand, then flew upwards as though it had pulled free. She could smell burning insulation. Fire – the bane of a hive dwelling!

Sparks danced briefly, then the lights went out. All except for the ghastly, electrical glow that tickled the soft down on her skin and flared in her eyelashes, half-blinding her. Acrid smoke stung her nostrils. Unidentified sounds skittered across the fringes of her hearing.

Then a cold snow fell on her. Irona could see it only because of the azure light that clung to her skin, so that it seemed she was in a halo of pale, chemical-smelling flakes.

It must be the sprinkler-system! she realised. At that moment the elevator car ground to an abrupt, gear-crunching, shuddering stasis.

It was so sudden that she felt as if her hands and feet had been hammered from underneath. Just as she was tottering upright, the lift juddered. It graunched against the sides of the shaft, fell a centimetre or two, then stopped, vibrating uneasily as if poised.

All the ancient human terror of falling bubbled up in her. Leaping to the control-panel, she jammed her palm against the 'door open' symbol, yelling at the same time in case the lift was voice-operated too.

The massive doors inched apart on to blackness. The lift fell perhaps a third of a metre.

Irona snatched the emergency axe from its moorings above the panel and levered the doors further apart. They would hardly budge. She rammed the axe between them, kicking it down to the horizontal, forcing the doors wider.

The lift groaned and sank suddenly.

Rolling forward, catching her shins on the axe, Irona leaped for safety. The elevator didn't care. With one final twang of breaking wire, it tore loose as the cable parted, and plunged ever faster down the shaft.

Thick as snakes, the frayed wires slashed angrily through the opening, then the car's fall whiplashed them back hissing down the gaping hole. The lift plumetted with a shriek of metal on metal. Dust whirled choking through the dark air. Blackness shivered into fragmentary red icons as the firestorm of friction incandesced.

Irona had only a moment of warning. She dropped as she saw the fire billowing towards her. Throwing herself face down, she whipped her arms over her head, feeling the skin of her wrists bubble into pain. She held her breath, closing her eyes against the searing heat. But the explosion as the car hit bottom whoofed through the doors, snuffing the flames before they properly had time to start.

Irona's borrowed body convulsed in a fit of coughing that was the protest of her scorched lungs. The stench of her own hair smouldering was thick when she breathed. She pawed her streaming eyes, trying to get her bearings in the hot and lightless corridor. Still lit only by the dreadful glow from her flesh, she could dimly perceive a sign: Delta.

Above the Warrens, up where only the Synod could go, yet still levels below the Watchtower proper, she had reached the destination the Arms – and the tractor – had set for her. Delta, the ancient symbol for the mouth of the mother of rivers.

She was an intruder in the heart of the Admin. Just being here could mean execution, or the brain-worms. Memory recreated the agony of the drill through the mastoid bone behind her ear.

Memory told her it was Bernardina, her mother, and Elditch, her father, who had ordered it.

But no. Surely it was her mother who had arranged for her to be frozen and sent to Harith?

Only the thoughts slithered like snakes in oil and she was afraid to pursue them into the insanity that she held only tentatively at bay in her subconscious. With a supreme effort, she cut off from the tracks of the past. Better to concentrate on getting out of the present alive.

This level of Synod held none of the sweat and disinfected fetor of the Warrens, nor the ionised sterility of the Watchtower. It smelt like a disused store-cave, musty and dry; it was dark as the caverns where Hesperion had dragged her in blindness.

For a moment her disorientation got the better of her and she wondered which way to go. There was no-one around to ask, which she knew was probably just as well. Who knew where the mohocks might have got to? Then, giggling madly in relief, she held up one hand. It still gleamed like a sign.

'I've got a bright idea,' she chuckled, and followed her own faint blue light from door-plate to door-plate, searching for the number five.

21
DELTA FIVE

Delta five. Irona walked closer, gingerly. She felt like an interloper.

A door no different from any other, as far as Irona could see in the eerie blue light her skin seemed to cast across the darkness. Her hair shifted of its own volition, prickling with static so bright she feared the sparks were a beacon for mohocks.

But then, she had to subvocalise to keep the thought in order, *my whole body's glowing*. She felt doubly conspicuous. It was hard to concentrate; concepts popped in her mind like bubbles as soon as she tried to grasp them. *Is it this body? Is this what Regen feels like all the time? Or is this damned eletacatricity?*

Her empathy was too numb for her to be sure, but she didn't think there was anyone else about. This whole level seemed to have been abandoned. Now she thought about it, she could not remember the Eyes ever displaying these reaches. That, of course, would have been blasphemy, for in the Admin even the name of Synod was holy.

Of course, if the Synod was anything like as corrupt as some of the Watch, it would also have given the game away.

Yet, through the Randoms, Regen had spied on the Synod so many years before. She had thought this sector of Synod territory would be as opulent as the scene Regen had shown her, all rosy Sinan rugs and statues of cedar and soapstone and jade, but it was barren. Drifts of dust shone as pale phantasms giving substance to the disintegration of Camelford.

Somewhere far in the endless black web of corridors, a human scream was cut off as suddenly as if hacked by a knife. Then all she could hear was a faint sobbing that trailed away. Apart from that, not a sound reached out to her through the blackness. Her own footsteps, try as she might, echoed all too loudly where unseen heaps of grit grated under her toes.

The upper levels are falling apart, Irona thought, frightened that yet another part of her security was crumbling. *And where are all the Synod? Have the wakers been through here already?*

She reached out again, but not even her heightened empathy could touch another living soul.

All at once a mechanical hiss sliced through the darkness. It bore rapidly down on her, setting her teeth on edge and vibrating the fluid in the blisters on her burned wrists.

Arms! she thought, and the subliminal terror was still there beyond reason.

There wasn't even a recessed doorway to hide in.

She battled against the viral jumping of her mind. *The least I can do is get away from here!* The thought gave birth to the action. Throwing herself along the wall, she hunkered beside a pathetically small heap of rubble, slitting her eyes to cut down the reflection. It didn't stop her seeing the glacial blue sheen of her skin betray her presence.

The sound burred nearer, drilling through her.

A mohock with transport?

But a fork-lift tractor sped by, its hover-skirt brushing roughly over her arm and knee. Its life-detectors were obviously out of commission. It was going backwards, metres of knotted cable dangling from its sides. In seconds it had disappeared round the curving wall of the sector.

At least it was no threat. Pulling herself together, she went back to her objective.

Outside delta five, she halted uneasily, not sure what she was supposed to do here, or if this had been some weird scheme of the machines to deliver her to the enemies Carandis had spoken of. She wondered where her mother was.

But I can't just stand here like a stuffed lemon. I've got to do something.

Making use of the faint glow streaming from her fingers, Irona traced the outline of the door, looking for a handle, a catch, a control panel, a voice-grid.

Nothing.

'Synod, you bastard, open up!' she muttered under her breath. But nothing happened. Disappointment bit her, because somewhere in the back of her mind had been the belief in some open-sesame magic.

She pushed the door, softly at first, then harder.

Nothing.

Stretching up, she curled her nails around the top of the door and pulled against the frame. It moved. Not much, but it did move.

Irona shifted her grip to the other end to try again, but before she got her fingertips in position the door swung outwards, hard.

Her own expletive was covered by a counterpoint from

inside the door. An oblong of light cut the darkness beside her; someone's shadow leaped out, long as evening. A warm, musky draught swirled out to brush her skin: the scent of a man.

At the same time they both said, 'Who's there?'

He did not step beyond his threshold.

Irona backed off a little, ready to slam the door shut against him if she had to. 'I used to be a warden,' she said. 'The Arms sent me here.'

'How do I know that?'

'How do I know *you* aren't a waker?'

'I'd hardly be in delta five if I was,' he scoffed.

'Nor would I. If I was one of them I'd have come with a mob.'

They spoke at the same time, he saying in his deep voice, 'I suppose not,' while she went on, 'Haven't you seen anything through the monitors?'

He stepped through the oblong of light into the passage. He was big, getting on for two metres, and solidly built, but with his being backlit she could make out nothing of his face.

'You must be a warden. A sleeper would have said Eyes.' He swept an arm in a grand gesture for her to enter, so she did, feeling as though she were stepping into a lion's den that dazzled her. When she saw the filthy, ripped mess that her official dress had become, it didn't help her confidence one bit.

He didn't seem to notice. Instead he stared down at her. She found his height – and more, the impressive reach of his arms – intimidating.

'But if you are a warden, how come you don't know the monitors aren't working?' he asked. 'And why are you wearing the remains of a matriarch's robe?'

Blinking against the sudden brightness, Irona tried to keep a wary eye on him. Avalanches of print-outs were chittering softly into folds about the room. It seemed atavistic.

When the door clicked almost seamlessly into its frame, her heart jolted. 'Was,' she said. 'Was a warden. I've only just got back to Earth.'

Now her eyes were more accustomed to the light, she saw his face: large, oblong, obscured by beard and whiskers that were brown with the beginnings of grey. His hair was very short and almost non-existent on top, but there were laughter-lines around his brown eyes, and his well-shaped lips were softened by the ease of his smile.

'What do you do in here?' Irona asked.

'They didn't tell you much, did they? I'm the one who runs the computers.'

She stared at him in disbelief. 'But . . .'

'I know.' Relaxing, he crumpled into his ancient contour-chair. It sagged comfortably around him and she saw him smother a yawn. There was a half-drunk cup of coffee steaming on a low table beside him; the smell made her mouth water. A microphone hovered just behind his head like a magician's familiar in a fairy-tale.

He said in a Londover accent, 'Let me explain—'

'Would you mind if I troubled you for a coffee?' she interrupted. 'I've had a hard day.'

He shrugged, stood. 'Why not? I think there's probably a bit left in my flask.'

Irona glanced at the slot in the wall.

He followed the direction of her gaze. 'The dispenser? I wouldn't trust it, not with a Waking. I made the flask up when the Watchwarden first called me. He said, "There's a bit of a snarl-up in the environmental systems." A bit?

Hah!' The big man flicked a glance at the cracked ceramic mug. 'It's a bit cold. I've been here sixteen hours. My relief hasn't shown up though and I can't find out why.' He topped his cup up with the dregs and handed it over. 'Sorry. That's all there is.'

'Not to worry.' Irona drained the mug, relishing this oasis of calm. 'Thanks. It's just what I needed.'

Toni delta five – she assumed it was he – smiled at her simple pleasure and said, 'Where was I? Oh, yes. What I do. You see, there's all those bits of hardware up there in the Watchtower directing Ears and Eyes and what have you, but this is the place where it all gets done. If I have to, I can override anything from up there. Calls to Arms, Eyes, requests for sleep-drugs or sublims or newscasts in the Warrens or the Watchtower, anything. Assuming nothing falls off. But why am I telling you this? Why are you here at all?'

So they drug the Watchlevels too? I should have realised.

In answer to Toni's question, Irona shrugged. 'Because people do tell me things. They can trust me. You can trust me. I thought I was only a pawn in the game but if the Arms themselves have gone to this much trouble to get me here, maybe I'm worth something after all. Do you know why I'm here?'

Shaking his head, he observed her curiously. The room was textured in shades of grey and comfortably lit, with here and there pictures of landscapes glued above the blank glass eyes of monitors and tanks. In here was still the gentle embrace of olfacts, relaxants with a scent of pine forests that reminded her of the slopes of Heralion and the warm salt winds of the sea. She wondered for a moment what was happening to Arias, what he was doing, what he was feeling. Suddenly she missed him fiercely. But there was something in the air that was Camelford's own and it reeled her back to the present.

'So you're called Toni, then,' she said when the silence was just beginning to become uncomfortable.

'That's right. And you are?'

'Irona. Well, parts of me, anyway. I used to be – well, let's just say a matriarch's daughter.'

'Used to be? They're not supposed to have any.'

'I've been away for forty years.'

'You don't look old enough.' Toni's voice was dispassionate, suspending disbelief.

'Probably not. I feel it though. It's not the years, it's the mileage. But this is just some body I was put into. I haven't quite got the hang of it yet. Mine doesn't really look any older. It's on Harith, at least I hope it still is, otherwise I don't know how I'm going to get back. But I was kind of yanked here willy-nilly . . .'

He looked at her, face kindly but moustache bristling out right beneath his nose. Unconsciously Irona wondered if they kissed, would it prickle inside her nostrils? A strange, stray thought. She remembered her first supervisor in the Ear and Eye room saying, 'Never trust a man with a moustache or beard. They always have something to hide.' From the way Toni had spoken, she could tell he neither believed nor disbelieved her. He was just waiting. She couldn't blame him for that.

'So tell me, parts of Irona, what's going on? And I'm sorry, but if you don't mind you'd better make it snappy. Camelford's falling apart out there.'

'Hadn't you better do something then?'

Toni spread his hands helplessly. 'What more can I do? Mechanical breakdown as well as some sort of computer virus. Half the Arms seem to be acting independently of the Watch. The electrics have gone mad. Nothing's working right. I've sent out all the repair units I've got but there's still things going wrong, sabotage, fires ... Until it's sorted my hands are tied. Even the dumps keep changing every five minutes.' He gestured vaguely at the banks of technology around them. 'Kilometres of cable and a thousand or two sub-systems. Synod knows what's going on. Well it doesn't, but then again neither do I. I'm not allowed to leave this room anyway, so the more information you can give me, the more chance I have of sorting things out. I'm not supposed to let people in, either, but I've got you outnumbered. You say the Arms sent you?'

And Irona told him her tale ...

'Can you get any visuals from anywhere?' she asked finally.

'Normally I can, yes. From the heights of Synod down to the random levels below the air-pumps. On any spectrum from visible to psychic.'

He folded away his pocket olfactory and she felt the pleasant numbness take away the pain of her burns. He brushed away her thanks and went on, 'Why else do you think I have all these hundreds of monitors? But the whole lot's gone haywire tonight. I mean, today. It's not even supposed to be dark out there yet but the Sky shield's still dialled for night. I'm supposed to be able to override it from here but there's a matriarch's seal on the command. Elevators crashing, machines with minds of their own – all I'm doing is sitting here ready to defend my little kingdom against all comers. We've been close enough to a Waking often enough and got away with it, but this time I really think we've had it. It was too well planned. Synod knows how the sleepers managed it. We'll be lucky to get out of this alive.'

Irona balanced her curiosity against his pessimism. 'In that case, how come you haven't got a whole phalanx of Arms outside the door?'

Toni grinned, shrugging his wide shoulders. 'Got something better, haven't I?'

'What's that?'

He obviously didn't trust her that far. 'Let's hope you never find out,' he said. 'Because if you do, we're all for the chop. Goodbye Camelford, goodbye Admin.' He reached down into a cupboard and Irona tensed, wondering what it was he kept in there.

She needn't have worried. It was only a bottle of fine old whisky that he banged down fatalistically on the desk between a knot of keyboards and voice-controls. The microphone behind his head jumped a little, nervously, then settled into its familiar station. Around the four walls, even from either side of the only visible door, the waterfalls of dump-paper slithered quaintly down.

Toni stretched his long arm down again and two cut crystal glasses appeared. 'If we drink, we will die. If we don't drink we will die. So what the hell.' He poured two strong shots and passed her a glittering tumbler. He didn't seem to care that the Watch was supposed to be abstemious. 'Skol,' he said, and clinked the base of his glass against hers.

'Long life,' she said automatically, and in the clunking silence they smiled ruefully at one another before gulping the liquid fire.

Bernardina had never been so grateful of anything in her long life. A bright blue eye of sunshine widened, the motion of the ring-car making it wink before it widened out to encircle her in the loving embrace of daylight and open air.

The talker said, ‘Park,’ and the car shuddered to a halt. Even before it stopped fully and the talker could announce, ‘Novaya Zemla,’ Bernardina had unfastened her lap-strap and was standing eagerly by the door.

At a command the doors whispered open and the sweet fresh air of the birch-wood came to Bernardina in dampness and the joyous odours of greenery. She felt stronger already. Grey, tumbledown walls told her she was at the right place. Moving almost briskly, she stepped down from the ring-car and out of the tunnel-mouth, signing to the talker to wait.

Sunlight sparkled on the rain-wet leaves of a late afternoon, with jewelled spring flowers escaping from a neglected garden. The Crown, now a little, rotund man in his fifties, was sitting cross-legged on a crimson divan that seemed totally out of place in the wooded hills. Not only was it opulent and oriental, gilt-legged and brocaded until it didn’t seem right out of doors, the doors themselves had long since sagged away from the roofless ruin of an all-too-Western castle behind. She smiled to see it.

‘Bernardina Matriarch.’ The Crown snapped his fingers. From within the lipless gateway, servants brought another divan, tables, a samovar: the whole paraphernalia of a tea-ceremony the tsars would have been proud of. A muskiness of patchouli and cinnamon wafted from the servants’ clothes.

The men poured, handed round cakes scented with nuts and sparkling with crystallised fruit, and departed. Neither the Crown nor Bernardina took notice of their existence. In ritual acknowledgement of poisonings and treachery, the Crown took a sip from his silver-rimmed tea-glass and handed it to her, bit into a madeleine and passed it across. His blue eyes twinkled bright as the soft sky overhead, and the rich spiciness could have masked any other odour.

She smiled back at him, not quite grinning, every bit as gamine as he. They both knew he could have taken antidotes earlier but that she would have set up enough safeguards to make her assassination unprofitable.

Sparrows started up their chittering among the shimmering diamonds of birch-leaves, and close by a twig fell as a startled squirrel brushed past. From the crumbled battlements, an archer with a double-curved bow leaped up and shot it. He sank back instantly out of sight. Bernardina saw the squirrel fall, then the arrow tangled in the branches; the squirrel dangled, just a lifeless tuft of red fur.

'Skol,' Bernardina said, and nibbled the coconut delicacy.

Mouth already full, he mumbled, 'Too gory. Too full of sturm und drang and one-eyed Viking gods. Lechayim. Despite all the pogroms, the Chosen People always drank to life.' Crumbs sprayed out over his silken cossack shirt.

'I thought they said Shalom. Peace.'

The Crown shook his head, wobbling the tea in his glass. 'No. That's the Saharistanis.'

Bernardina widened her hands a little. The gesture could have meant anything. To one who knew her, though, it signified disagreement so minor as to be insignificant.

The Crown knew her. 'Well maybe it's both of them. What is it the Sioux Indians used to say? It's a good day to die.'

'And how do you get along with her?' Bernardina's lips had recovered some of their colour, but after her long deep fear she couldn't quite control their trembling, and it annoyed her.

'Our little Native American?' The Crown's question wasn't as innocent as the way he phrased it. His tone was rich with the nuances of mockery, some for Pilar Jímenez and some, Bernardina was sure, for herself.

'Of course,' she snapped.

'I thought that was why you came. But I'm surprised you aren't a little more in control. You don't normally display your reactions so openly. Do you feel threatened in any way?'

He's not playing the game! What's he got up his slimy sleeve? But what the Matriarch of All Earth said was, 'Of course not! Why should I?'

'Why indeed? And yet you requested a secret meeting.'

Nettled, Bernardina spoke to sting him back. 'I requested you to return the courtesy I've extended to you when you needed it. How are the Kurruds, by the way?'

The Crown laughed, sunlight sheening over his tight-packed shirt. He didn't even answer, but she knew anyway: she had had geotechnicians sent over to rob the tribal steppes of water. Now the Kurruds were held safely in his fief thanks to her, but he didn't acknowledge it and she began to be seriously alarmed. 'Oh, Bernardina, you are priceless! I trust you've had yourself recorded as a death-gift for your many friends? Don't tell me you're trying to call in what you see as old debts?'

The Matriarch of All Earth found a smile deep inside her and attached it hypocritically to her face. She said nothing, taking control by allowing the silence to dapple through the sunny grove. Rehearsing mental mantras, she radiated the outward appearance of relaxation until it began to sink inwards into her being as well.

The Crown stirred more honey into his tea, letting the spoon tinkle on and on. But it was he who spoke first. 'Information is power, da?'

Bernardina tilted her head sideways, raised her wispy

brows a fraction. It could have meant anything from disparagement and disbelief through to 'Not only is that self-evident, but everyone else knew it long before you did'.

Another silence reached out to pool into quietude the shivering of leaves in the breeze and the hum of insects among the primroses and anemones scattering the clearing. Bernardina had no intention of putting him into power over her by asking what information he meant. She allowed her purplish lips to thin into the vaguest of smiles while the sylvan scene passed its pretence of peace into her by osmosis. Not for a second had she forgotten the archers behind the battlements.

At last the Crown said, 'Bernardina, you play this game passing well. But in forty-something years you've never found out my name, have you? And the scales of the World Council are shifting. Beyond the sea Oceana is aligning with Li Chan to put the Sinans on top in Asiapura. For once the Saharistanis are united under a call for a holy Jihad. And our little Minnehaha is gluing together all the economic groups of the Americas under her gaudy condor. Soon I will have potential enemies on three of my frontiers. I never take liberties with the Bering Sea.'

'Then don't!' Bernardina retorted. 'But if you take liberties with me I could freeze it hard enough for all the Aleut Armies to stroll across at midsummer.'

The Crown clicked his tongue. 'Threats? My word, you are suffering from paranoia.'

'Just because I'm paranoid doesn't mean you aren't all out to get me.' The ancient quip helped lance her festering anger.

'Me?' A boyish grin slid ill-fitting over the Crown's pudgy, middle-aged face. 'I'm not out to get anyone. But

I should think twice about that Carandis of yours. I don't think you'll find your temples across Northern Asia are quite as infectious as you've been led to believe. Agents don't always like to admit they haven't come up with the goods as promised.' He leaned sideways across the divan, propping himself on one arm like a fat porpoise lolling on its flipper. 'I need to know two things: what is it you want from me? And is it worth my while doing it?'

Looking up through her ragged, stumpy old eyelashes, Bernardina saw one of the archers on the battlements scratch his chest with the tip of his recurved bow.

22
TENTACLES OF THE MATRIARCHY

Pilar Jímenez dropped her lambent gaze, slumped her shoulders, pulled the rags of a serape around her as she climbed out of the stagnant shallows. Her feet were bare now and seemed too broad for the sandals, made out of tyres, that she slung into the choke-cherry bushes along the draw. She put her foot down and a cracked nutshell from last year scraped her ankle; she cursed by the Inca gods, but the blood mixed with the dust on her skinny heel and she felt her disguise was complete.

Just as well, since her destination lay before her under the low-hung amethyst sky. She had forgotten how enervating true poverty was.

The San Antone Mission stretched sleepily to the lullaby of the wind in the cottonwoods. This had once been live-oaks country somewhere in the hinterland of the Gulf of Mexico, a prey torn between the cattle-barons and the hidalgos; now it was mostly a dust-bowl retreating from the drowned coastline and the hulks of dead refineries. But Santa Ana was not forgotten, not when the whitewashed walls of adobe carried the lines of Spanish architecture and the ancient graffiti of wetbacks. Comforting odours of chilli and beans reached out to her. In her nostrils was the remembered scent of the mud Under-Mexico-Fields.

Yanqui music came tinny from cheap Yanqui power-packs. Poor yellow lights came from here and there, but they could not dim the stars overhead or the red glow on the horizon that came from the ribbon-road.

Pilar stumbled up the crooked trail from the dried-up riverbed, and not all of her exhaustion was faked. She walked slowly up the dirt road to the gates of her enemy and raised her hand to knock the huge iron ring.

She didn't have to. As soon as a sensor detected her, it broadcast a gentle light over her, brightening the crystal stars, brushing away the smell of the stagnant pools with the perfume of firs and roses and hibiscus. Some subtle olfact strengthened her, and the blue of purity laved her soul. No wonder the poor had spoken to her of magic.

All before I open the door, huh? Pilar thought, and hid her smile behind her look of Indian impassivity. Because the saints carved so assiduously on the ancient wooden gates bore not gringo but Mayan features, and Christ on Calvary looked more like the sun-god Huitzilopochtli on a sacrificial ziggurat. *Two European religions have been here but they still can't steal my people's hearts.*

A junior matriarch opened the small door cut into the gate. She smiled and said, 'Welcome,' and her skin was so smooth and fine that the smile was like Mary's on the gate. Suddenly Pilar felt very old.

'Come unto me, all you who are weary and heavy laden, and I will give you rest,' the girl said, and the knots of obedience at her waist flounced with her modest walk as she took Pilar's arm and led her inside. *All she needs is a crucifix,* Pilar thought, *to go with the Biblical quote*, but the

Indian girl was leading her between areas of tomatoes and pepper-plants that were rich and sap-scented in the moonlight, and she never mentioned the Lord. *Well, she wouldn't,* Pilar knew, since she'd spent almost five years herself under the matriarchy's blue mantle. *It's only the structure and the persuasive power Bernardina's stolen from Christianity, not the heart of the faith.*

'Would you like to tell me your name?' the girl asked.

Pilar had been expecting that. Calmly she said, 'No.'

'Then you needn't. But I will call you Sister Dolores, if you don't mind, to avoid confusion.'

Pilar missed a step. *Is she playing games with me? Surely she doesn't know? Or is it just coincidence, Dolores, the pains of my Three Americas?* It took her back to her years of sanctuary; oh how sweet the hurt of nostalgia!

But the girl went calmly on, 'I am Junior Matriarch Catalina. Would you like to wash while I fix you some supper?'

The girl took her under the cloisters and into a spartan room where she turned on a power-pack for lighting. 'There's a bath and towels behind that curtain,' the junior matriarch said, nodding her capped dark head at an alcove.

But Pilar was more impressed by the little shrine glowing above the bed. *A very simple piece of technology*, she thought, *but no doubt choc-a-bloc with subliminals and olfacts and subharmonics on a narrow band. Calm to the spirit and a good night's sleep guaranteed. It's almost as impressive as the hardware in my teeth.*

Junior Matriarch Catalina saw the Indian woman stop and stare at the little blue glow. In her simplicity she obviously thought the newcomer was even more simple. Pilar forgave her, because it meant that her own sufferings over the last month had been effective. It proved that starving and driving herself to the point of exhaustion had been worth it. And letting her glorious black hair grow matted and grizzled until she looked like a crone. And having a doctor ulcerate her leg.

Catalina said, 'That's the symbol of our Founder. She loves us all. She wants the best for us: peace, and harmony, and sisterhood.' She spoke reverently and with pride, but she didn't betray the Founder's name. So far this was like any Christian mission near the skeletons of dried-up oil-wells, native converts rising through the lower ranks. 'But I expect you're hungry. I'll go and get you some supper, Sister Dolores, unless you want to eat with the rest of us?'

Pilar shook her head. 'Not tonight, girl. Tonight I just want to eat and sleep.' *And spy before I meet my enemy.*

Though it was wonderful to soak in a steaming tub, hearing through her maxillary receptor the ultra-harmonics massacring the fleas and the nits in her hair that were the little brothers of the poor. Letting this outpost of the Matriarchy relax her in its familiar gossamer tentacles, Pilar Jímenez pondered what she had learned anew in her walkabout through the underside of the Three Americas of which she was president. She had learned that you didn't have to be a Yanqui to be rich, or a Native American to be poor.

Pilar smiled as she wondered how Bernardina was enjoying the hospitality of the Crown.

On Harith the Matriarchy was having a field-day. Twiss sat in a calm, green room in the Hospital, holding Irona's hand. It was warm under his fingers, but unresponsive, nerveless. She hadn't moved since her twin guards Declan and Malambé had found her crumpled on the floor of the

Synod Tower. They had brought her to this place of clinical smells, naïve enough to think that Jai and the doctors could cure anything. Twiss had been at her side almost ever since.

Tubes fed her; hidden away under the soft metallic sheet, other tubes cleaned her. Behind her head, monitors showed the deep alpha-rhythms of sleep as lazy as the waves on the sunny beach outside. Her hair shone with its rich gold curls haloing her tranquil face. Twiss had forgotten how much he had loved her. As slow as seasons, her ribs rose and fell to her breathing.

So slowly that Twiss could not believe she was really alive. He shifted his grip, thumb on her wrist, and when he had found the beat there he cried out in alarm.

Instantly Jaimindi came running. 'What is it?'

'Her pulse! It doesn't show on the scanner but it's going like the clappers.'

Jai swiftly checked the link-ups then glanced down at Irona's pale arm. 'I'm not surprised, Twiss. I told you not to take her pulse like that. Use your fingers, see? It's your pulse you were feeling, not hers. She's fine.'

Twiss looked at his erstwhile lover Jaimindi, her curls like blackberries clustering around the smooth coffee-colour of her face. She didn't look a day over sixteen, plump and healthy. For some reason it annoyed him. 'If she's fine, Jai, why on Harith doesn't she wake up? The planet's going to hell in a handbasket. Doesn't she know how much I need her?'

Jai twisted one cheek in resigned irritation at Twiss's insensitivity. After almost twenty years of mothering him and the children she had borne him, she couldn't pretend any more that it didn't exist. Some days she asked herself how Irona would feel if she woke and saw her friend and rival over her. Some days she wondered what would happen if she pulled the plug and Twiss's wife slipped over the edge into oblivion.

But Jaimindi knew about Lowena too. 'I wish you wouldn't say things like that,' she told him.

Twiss wasn't listening. 'It's my fault,' he was saying, and he bowed his head over his sleeping wife's hand. The nape of his neck was pale and defenceless where the sun hadn't reached through his hair. His ex-lover could have smacked him as she sometimes smacked a wilful toddler.

'Twiss ...' but she stopped, not knowing what to say. Besides, he was too busy with his internal world to notice her.

Into this domestic tableau came Regenerator. 'What you up to then, boy?' he asked his king.

Twiss raised his woebegone face, more round and plebeian than ever without its cheerful smile. 'Just sitting here,' he said hopelessly. Not even the magical powers of Harith could erase the lines of strain that pulled his cheeks down and puckered the skin beside his eyes.

Regen clapped him hard on the shoulder and perched one hip on Irona's bed. Twiss sketched half a gesture of protest but Regen said, 'She wouldn't mind. I ain't on no wires or nothing. But this won't buy baby a bonnet. Twiss, you got to do something. Entirely.'

'What can I do?'

'Well you can stop arsin' about in here, for a start. You look like a spilt ice-cream, droopin' about like that. Arias, he's been trying to call you for the best part of some time.'

'Well I don't want to talk to him.' Twiss couldn't help but sound petulant.

'Oh, very mature. Look, our Synod's been waiting for you but you never came. Half a dozen Second Wavers out in Rainshadow Valley swear the Arms've been buzzing they, the *Thistle-up*'s crew won't unload or take off or nothin', we've had another two murders, and there's snake-worms in the third granary. There's somethin' bumpin' off they poor little fisherchildren in Eastcliff. The whole of Harith's under attack but you won't wake up and see it. They call you Arcturus Rex, don't they, and you lap it up.' Regen's knobby face could hardly disguise his contempt, though he tried. The little man's reedy voice was harsh as he said, 'You've had the game, Twiss, now live up to the name.'

Twiss gazed up at him with his hazel eyes red-rimmed, then dropped his head. He wouldn't actually say it but Regen knew anyway: Twiss didn't know what to do. Things had got too far out of hand.

'Don't you go bullying Twiss,' Jai began, but Regen chopped his hand viciously through the air. Underneath it all she knew Regen would never hit her, but she backed off anyway, then said from the door, 'I'll – er – check in on her later. See you.'

'Look, Twiss,' Regen said. 'You can do it. All you got to do is take one thing at a time.'

'But I don't know where to start!'

'Yellin' at me ain't it. 'Sides which, you're smart enough to take counsel. Ain't that why we got a Synod in the first place? What you're good at is gettin' people going once we got a plan.'

'What d'you reckon, then?'

'I reckon no-one ain't going to do your thinking for you no more. Entirely. Bet you're sorry now that you buggered Irona about, ain't you? But it's too late for that. Between they Arms and that stupid First Wave – Second Wave ruction you don't do nothin' to improve, the place is about ready to explode. If you want to hold it together you'll have to set about it now.'

Twiss pulled out a hip-flask that never seemed to be very far away from him these days. He took a swig, spilling some on his beer belly, and Regen all but snatched it from him to take a short pull for himself. Then he tossed the shell-inlaid plastic on to the windowsill behind him and said, 'Come on, boy.'

The leader of Harith stood, hesitated a moment as Regen watched him, then turned to walk out of the door. He didn't go back for the flask. That would have been too great an admission.

Twiss came out into the hot sunshine, brushing aside a cluster of red air-plant seedlings that were almost as fine as mist. They clouded the gleaming surface of the Eye which had been waiting patiently outside for him.

He turned automatically towards his palace of Tingalit. Its tall glassy spires soared above the curving roofs of Kifl, gleaming so brightly that they hurt his eyes, and as ever the sight of the dream he had realised put some steel into his posture. He went down the steps two at a time, striding diagonally across the gravelled square, heedless of the designs some recovering patient had so painstakingly raked into its surface. Normally such pointless expense of energy would have driven him wild.

Regen, more ungainly but far more determined, caught him up and swung him round. 'You need to go to the airfield first.'

'Why's that, then?'

' 'Cos Arias is calling you about the tariffs. So you need to see the captain of the *Thistle-up* so's you know where you're bargaining from.'

Twiss tossed back his head to look arrogantly down his

nose. No doubt he was unaware of the double chins which made it a somewhat silly pose, as far as Regen could see. The King said, 'I ain't bargaining with Arias. I tell him what to do and he does it, and that's it.'

Regen nodded wryly. 'Yeah, if he feels like it. In the meantime you make a right prat of yourself. You need to go to the airfield first, take my word.' And the little man set off in a different direction, the sunlight reflecting off the sweat on his thinning pate.

Twiss followed him, reaching him in a couple of his long strides. 'Why don't we call a tractor?' he said, fishing for his pocket remote.

' 'Cos if we're going to see action against they Arms and their controllers, which we entirely are, then we need to get some of that fat off of you.'

'Fat? Me? You're kidding yourself!'

Regen chuckled. 'Tell that to your shadow.'

Both men were glad of the shade the olive-groves cast along the sides of the dusty road. The noon sun was hot above Kifl, and the airfield was on a patch of barren, sandy ground some two kilometres outside the town. As Regen had known he would be, Twiss was red-faced and puffing by the time he passed through the tethered nets of air-fruit and came out on to the rock-strewn wasteland.

It was dominated by the silvery length of the *Thistle-up* anchored, unusually, a hundred metres above the ground. In its oval shadow a knot of dock-workers were arguing with a group of young fisherfolk. Against the bright tunics and trousers of the crowd of Kiflians, the unclothed fisherchildren stood out with their sombre-coloured fur fluffed out against the heat.

The hubbub of angry shouts spread out under the fierce blue of the sky. Heat-haze robbed the scene of detail, the vagueness of the threat making it even more menacing.

As Twiss and Regen strode across the lifeless sand, one thing was clear, though. The amoebic mob grew a pseudopod of angry Kiflians who moved to one of the balloon's anchors. They began to wind the curving cable around the rock bollard despite the fisherfolks' protests.

Quick as a needle winking in the sun, a fishergirl snatched a case-knife from its scabbard on her belt. She slashed at the cable and the mob overran her. Not before she made another cut and the great silver airship broke free of its mooring to swing around its other anchor-line.

Twiss and Regen broke into a run. In seconds they burst into the angry crowd, and Regen watched in admiration as Twiss took control. He never stopped to think.

'The Eye! Use the Eye!' Regen called to him.

Twiss didn't hear. He charged ahead, leaping the jagged rocks, and it was this recklessness that carried him through. It was in situations like these where he was at his best, and for the first time in years Regen felt the rekindling of admiration for him.

Pushing the Kiflians aside, the leader of their Synod shouldered through to the front. Even the scared fisherfolk stopped their fruitless attempts to drag their comrade clear of her attackers when they felt the anger radiating from him. His face now was as merciless as the sun overhead.

Besides, the fisherfolks' actions were unnecessary now. As soon as the Kiflians saw their leader, they edged back, afraid. Many of them had felt his uncertain temper before. All of them knew how he had once emptied an ocean on to their town.

The trouble was, it looked like they had already accomplished what they had set out to do. The fishergirl, her virgin breasts still budding forlornly, lay motionless on the ground. Beneath the auburn fur, her skin was pale and mottled as a new-born infant's. An unnatural dent hollowed one side of her skull. It seemed that she would never reach maturity.

'Check her,' Twiss ordered, flicking his eyes at one of the down-skinned lads she had travelled with.

The youth knelt beside her, but instead of feeling for a pulse he probed the gill-slit below her ear. Inserting the tip of his finger, he touched one of the coral fans of flesh, and Twiss saw it jerk in a reflex. The boy looked up at him. 'She lives,' and his breath hissed the end of the word.

'Good.' Twiss snapped his mouth shut, holding the crowd with the spell of his anger. It was just as well that most of them didn't know that he was stumped. He was good at sounding decisive. 'Regen?'

'Of course I'll send her to the Hospital. Pass me the remote and I'll call a tractor.'

The fisherboy, slim as a stickleback compared to the King of Harith, said, 'It would be quicker to send her in the airship.'

Twiss and Regen exchanged a glance. Regen nodded all but imperceptibly, distracting the mob by kneeling beside the girl and stretching one hand out to brush the bare skull above her wound.

The Kiflian leader summoned the crew of the airship. 'Captain Hoojer? Can you come down and take this girl over to Jai's Hospital?'

Hoojer's face, recorded from below the chin, looked ugly. Her tone wasn't much better. 'No problem, so long as that's all I'm doing. I don't want to get caught up in no riot. Hang on while I reel the line in and fix another anchor.'

It didn't take as long as Regen had feared. All the same, the seconds dragged past, time moving torpidly, like air-bubbles in molten glass, like the glassy heat-haze imprisoning the crowd. Regen could feel it: the scent of sweat and fear and dust was strong, and the volatile anger still simmered beneath the illusion of tranquillity.

Two of the larger fisherfolk, a boy and a girl from the same hatching, carried their wounded comrade tenderly aboard the moment the *Thistle-up* lowered its gangplank softly beside her. Naturally everyone else had moved aside as the transparisteel hull sank down above their heads. Regen was pleased to see that the factions had separated automatically.

'Tell Jai I sent you,' Twiss called, and from the clear deck Hoojer waved a hand in salute.

Before the dock-hands and fisherfolk could completely cast off, the captain had her propellers whirling. Dust flew, blinding their eyes, stinging their skin. Regen, squinting, saw Twiss's Eye blown off course for just a moment, then it spun upon its axis, looking for a target.

Regen jogged Twiss's arm, jabbing his thumb upwards. Twiss was quick to take the hint and call the orb to his side, calming it almost as if it were a pet.

Then the huge cylinder of seasilk was clear. The dust settled and people cautiously stood up. They found Twiss ready for them, upright and commanding, his own shirt of the precious material scarcely dimmed by the flying grit.

'You,' he pointed at a man who had been amongst the first to swarm over the fishergirl. 'What do you mean by attacking citizens?'

The man gaped, his eyebrows twin arches of astonishment. 'I never! All I done was—'

'I saw what you did. The fisherfolk are citizens of Harith too.'

Regen hid a grin at hearing Twiss repeat the words Irona

had tried so long and hard to din into her reluctant overlord, with him arguing every step of the way.

Twiss went on, 'I'll be having words with you later,' and the man squirmed under the threat. 'But why did you attack her?'

'Me? You saw what she did! She were cutting the cables on the *Thistle-up*. I couldn't let 'em get away.'

'The *Thistle-up* is free to go wherever it wants, same as you,' Twiss said. Then, glaring at the man from under his brows, he added, 'For the minute.'

A tense silence spread its claws through the Kiflians.

Twiss turned to the fisherfolk. 'And what have you lot got to say for yourselves?'

He was surprised to find that the one who answered his sharp question was a young brown-furred girl from a late hatching. She stood away from her larger companions and said, 'We wanted to get away because these landfolk of yours were robbing us. The Creator said—'

'Who?'

The girl answered Twiss's question, not a whit abashed. Instead she seemed both patronizing and surprised by his ignorance. She flapped a webbed hand at him. 'Arias Tang, of course. He created us, didn't he? He said we needed more foodstuffs and seeds and that the *Thistle-up*'s load of seasilk was more than enough to pay for it. He said to bargain, and we were doing, only that load of hotskin oafs didn't like it and they tried to push us out of the way. When we wouldn't go, they started threatening us. So Captain Hoojer took the *Thistle-up* aloft, and then this lot tried to pull it down, and Maerika tried to cut the aft-line like an idiot, and then those men started beating her up, and then you came.' She finished all of a rush, her statements naïvely jointed in her shrill voice.

Regen could see that Twiss was finding it a strain to take this young, hairy child seriously. In fact, he was looking downright embarrassed by the nakedness under her brown fur, no doubt prompted by that weird modesty the Admin had enforced.

Twiss scratched at his tousled hair. 'What did you ask for in your bargain, then?' he asked, still directing his question generally at the fisherfolk.

The girl fluttered her webbed fingers across her face, fanning herself. Regen caught a whiff of the fishy scent that oiled from her pores instead of good, honest sweat. With remarkable self-possession, or with the immediacy of a child, she said, 'Look, it's hot here. Can't we find somewhere shady to sit so we can talk about this?'

The leader of the Kiflian Synod shrugged. 'Why not? I'll be glad to get out of the sun myself. I'll take three of you, and three of this rabble. Regen, go and commandeer that tractor over there, will you? And have a couple of guards waiting for this murderous fool.'

Before too long they climbed on to the hot plastic flatbed of the tractor to ride into Tingalit. The townsfolk in their gaudy robes were drifting aimlessly towards their siesta, and Twiss would have expected the fisherchildren to be giggling and pointing out the strange sights to each other, but they sat quietly, riding into the covered alleys and out into the bright squares of Kifl with not a word passed between them. What with their silence, their domed skulls, their fur and their flapping hands and feet, they didn't seem like normal children at all. Once or twice he opened his mouth to comment on it to Regen, but under the fisherfolks' grave regard the words dried up on his tongue. Even the three Kiflian dockers barely whispered to one another.

Twiss had the driver go through the gates and cross the palace gardens to the Amber Wing of Tingalit. In the heat of afternoon, the yellow glass spread a hot, sticky light like syrup through the halls. Bobbing over the heads of the party, the Eye looked like a roc's egg of gold. Garwin and the guards on the doors trooped along at the back, obedient to the jerk of Twiss's head.

Regen saw the way Twiss glanced at the children as he told Regen to demonstrate the grav-shaft. Obviously the king expected them to play with it, to be excited, to react as Arno might have done when he first came across something new. But as the little man wafted upwards, smiling down encouragingly, the fisherchildren solemnly followed him without a word. There was more reaction from the dockers, even though they had heard of such wonders.

Twiss came last, catching them all up and passing through them to swing wide the doors to the Ocean Room. Regen looked at his face; it was expectant, waiting for them to love the room they way Arno had. But they gave him no link with his past. And the three Kiflians from the airfield were too overawed – or perhaps too guilty – to express an opinion on décor.

The guards were sent for drinks. Twiss wandered up and down a little, restless, peering out through the rose-scented air-plants at the cheerful sailboats on the blue waters of the bay, while the rest sat, the fisherchildren still and apparently at peace, the dockers ill at ease.

When the two guards came back, they brought honey-cakes, fishballs in a spicy sauce and a jug of opalescent lily-wine. It wasn't strong, and bubbles sparkled on the surface when the men poured it, filling the room with its sweet, nutty perfume. Regen knew it had been one of

Arno's favourite drinks when he came back from an afternoon's hunting on the slopes of Heralia.

After the thanks, voices subsided.

And that was where the Matriarch's plan broke down.

23
THE SEASILK NOOSE OF LOVE

Bernardina said to the Crown, 'You won't find it.'

Her lips moved thickly; the eyes lolled in her head as she strove to focus on the servants carrying something briskly from the gateway. Birdsong reverberated from the walls of her skull, filling the convolutions of her brain with maddening, lilting echoes. Anemones and bluebells shrieked their perfumes at her, sharpened by the drugs that must have been on Bernardina's side of the silver rim of her glass.

The Crown simpered at her. 'Oh, I think we will. Everybody has a lever. And this is where we put the handle on yours.'

The servants came closer, three of them, staggering under the weight of the something. Bernardina had no idea what it was but it scared her. She shifted on the divan, trying to move away from the threat. She toppled, unable to help herself, and the Crown's laughter was jewelled scintillations and thunder in her mind.

'Prop her head, someone,' he ordered, and a woman as broad as she was tall hauled the Matriarch of All Earth on to a pile of silken pillows.

'Happy now?' she said familiarly, and the Crown

nodded. 'Yes, Babushka. Can the old witch see?'

The square-set figure that had to be Babushka replied in a voice laden with stretched vowels, 'Of course, heart,' without even glancing down at the helpless Matriarch.

'Then we'd better get on with the program, da?'

'First level only,' Babushka said strictly.

'Of course, of course. I only want Bernardina to see what she's doing now.'

The voice was a peasant's, all diphthongs and triphthongs and swallowed consonants. At the best of times Bernardina would have had difficulty understanding it. Now, though, was not the best of times. Babushka said, 'There's a sensible lad.'

The Matriarch of All Earth tried to centre her mind to form one simple question: *Where is my ring-car talker?*

Focusing on the monitor was like looking down a tunnel rimmed with cartwheeling lights. And at the bottom of the tunnel was Bernardina herself.

The Matriarch shook her head to clear it, but waves of nausea were the only result. Still her own face looked back at her from the monitor in the Crown's sunny glen.

She was in her own eyrie, her private sanctuary at the very top of Camelford Tor. She was giving orders to the computer that angled out of the wood-panelled wall between the windows. She was dressing in her finest robe of celestial blue – thank Synod that her flat, empty breasts swung decorously clothed in undergarments! – and a junior was nervously arranging the simple pieces of jewellery that were eyes and ears and sensors to look like a gemmed hairnet and rings for ears and fingers.

She was making arrangements to go to a Summit with Oceana. The arrangements were last-minute ones. She was walking down through the trap-door, leaving her windows wide to the wild roses of June.

She was saying, 'I have other business to attend to. I will be back in time for the next full Synod.' Then the junior shut the trap-door and the marble floor was intact again.

Intact.

Untouched.

But violated by the Crown and his agent.

But who was his agent?

It was as well that Bernardina couldn't move her tongue, her palate, her teeth, or she would have spilled words of inanity whose memory might have shamed her later. For she was thinking, *But that's me! And I'm here!*

But the Crown snapped his fingers and Babushka shut off the power. The monitor opaqued in a diminishing iris of colours, and Bernardina was speechless, her mind inchoate.

Babushka was as shy and insecure as a schoolgirl fishing for a compliment. 'What do you think, heart?'

The Crown beamed happily at her. 'It's wonderful. You are wonderful.'

The thickset woman cast down her eyes and brushed her thick, red, peasant's fingers over the embroidery on her skirt. From someone with the sere eyelashes of age, it was a horrible travesty of youth. 'I shall remember your delight to my dying day, heart, and beyond.'

'So now we can pass to the second level, Babushka,' the Crown said, full of optimism. 'You have worked another miracle.'

Babushka twisted a fold of her crimson skirt between her fingers, and a layer of white linen showed above the thick stockings. Her hair was grey, with tragic locks of auburn intermingled. 'I think you will find that the second level is even better,' she said.

From the Crown's point of view, it was. Bernardina didn't want to believe it. Because, when the scarlet-garbed Babushka first gelled and then taped electrodes into place, the Crown's handmaid ensured that Bernardina could see exactly what was going on.

There, on the screen, was exactly the opposite of what Bernardina wanted to see: her own thoughts, detailed and filed and recorded second by second. Even her reactions to them. Even where the blocks were, that should have stopped an enemy doing exactly what her enemies were doing: pulling out her innermost secret.

That innermost secret was Irona. Irona, who shouldn't have existed at all, who like all the other offspring of those elevated to Synod should have been brain-wormed and turned into a sleeper, never to be a lever or a threat. Irona at seventeen was what Bernardina saw, the way she had been in the sleeper-room of the spaceship: at peace, slim-waisted, yet with softly-rounded hips and breast, her long eyelashes sweeping the bloom in her cheeks, her hair tumbling around to crown her head with gold highlights glinting in the brown of her curls.

'And where is this paragon?' the Crown asked, smiling his fat, lascivious smile.

Not for all the worlds she sought to pacify would Bernardina have said a word. But she couldn't stop her mind, not with all the drugs they'd given her. Even her years of training could not block out her thoughts, and only later would she wonder why.

Irona, her sweet, heart-shaped face translucent on the cedar and citrus fragrant world of Harith, creating an army to oppose the force of Arms which had lain dormant until a hidden, automatic signal on the *Starbird* had woken them. Irona, who must have overcome Gundmila, and who would now be a colossa, a matriarch of power; her battle-skills honed on the Arms and her political skills – after the defeat of Gundmila – obviously sharp and strong. She'd be a mother, and Bernardina saw her genes march on to destiny in a flock of children a whole new planet could support. And still as beautiful as she had been at seventeen. On Harith, not a mark would be on her face, not a blemish or a wrinkle or a hint of sag about the neck. (Bernardina saw her own jealousy on the screen with her rheumy, age-shrunk eyes, and embarrassment of her mind's nakedness burned her as Babushka and the Crown watched gloating.)

Irona, whose mind-blocks would have worn off, leaving her soft with love for her mother. Bernardina saw her daughter with arms outstretched to encircle her mother in a loving embrace. In Bernardina's thoughts her daughter was desperate for a reconciliation after all this time.

She'd been preserved off-world, uncontaminated by Carandis, the Liga Mediterranea, Bill Peach of Oceana, Li Chan, white-eyed Nanuk of the North and South, that whorebitch Jímenez . . .

Irona. Soon, soon Bernardina would summon her across the starless void. Then Irona would take up the reins of empire so Bernardina could die in world peace.

In delta five the lights blacked out, then pulsed a feeble, dying rhythm.

Toni struggled out of his creaking chair.

'What is it?' Irona asked, struggling to grasp wakefulness in the uncertain gloom. She hadn't realised that her exertions had pushed her over into sleep.

'Eletacatricity.' Shutting her out of his awareness, he propelled himself through the flimmering shadows across the diagonal of the room. His tall frame waded through the sheafs of old-fashioned paper fanning still from the humming computers. He leaned across one bank of machines, jackknifing his arms to push his head up close to a square of fine grey mesh she hadn't noticed before.

Irona too came to her feet, watching him intently. 'Air-supply?' she said quietly.

'A-huh.' He straightened his long arms. 'Nothing to worry about though, for the minute. Can't you hear it?'

'Hear what?'

'The air stopped.'

Knuckling the crumbs of sleep from her eyes, she said, 'What?'

'The air stopped. There are huge great turbines down at the root of the mountain.'

'I know,' she said dourly, remembering when she and Regen had dived through the slashing blades of the fans.

'Nothing's supposed to interrupt the power-supply to them. And something obviously has.'

The floor of delta five began to vibrate. Piles of paper rustled like the leaves of a forest in a gale; his bottle started a dance on the counter between the consoles. Dust as fine as fog dropped from the ceiling, making it even harder to see. Instantly air-filters began to whirr, sucking a breeze through the hub of Camelford's computers, cleaning the air so that no damage was done to the heart of the Admin.

But the rumble was audible now. It sounded like an earthquake approaching. Irona felt fear building inside her and looked to the tall man for reassurance, but he had none to give. The smell of his nervous sweat wafted past her to be drunk by the thirsty extractors.

'Didn't one of these go through the Mountain a while ago?'

Toni nodded, not really listening. He was scanning ranks of glass eyes that looked like the psychicators and scanners and monitors Irona had known up in the Watchtower. Except that she couldn't read half the shooting peaks of light.

Miles of air-ducts began a clamour like ten thousand war-trumpets. The air-grid rattled savagely; one of its rivets burst loose, ripping the metal. A filthy gale swirled outwards. The grille tore itself free, scything across the room with its jagged edges.

Irona ducked, throwing herself face down behind the chair. The grille stabbed into the seat back where her head had been a second before. Wind howled through the grille-hole, black and formless as a demon. Her eardrums all but ruptured under the fierce change of pressure.

Clasping her hands to the sides of her head, she was assailed by helplessness. There was nothing she could do. Not even open her eyes fully against the sickles of grit. The wind rose to a crescendo, and paper flew whirling through the air like a swarm of albino bats. As the storm passed, the paper settled on her, layer upon layer of it, heavy, smothering.

When the gonging had died away, she forced a hand up through the mess, then another, until she could come to her knees, her feet. Squinting against the sandstorm still haunting the flickering air, she looked for Toni and found him struggling up too. He was black from head to foot, only one paler patch showing where he had flung an arm up to protect his sight.

'What did you mean by eletacatricity?' she tried to say, and broke into a paroxysm of coughing. Toni was in no better case. Finally she managed the question again.

'That's what they call it when the system goes wrong.

Not just the computers . . .' Toni stopped, looking round at the sparking, dust-blackened wreckage of his beloved machines. Few were still chattering away. The lights went off again, leaving few of the screens with anything but the eerie glow of stored electrons. By the reflected light she could see the hurt and anger in his face.

'Not just the computers,' he repeated, 'but the whole thing. The whole electrical network. It's kind of like a germ eating away at power-packs and lighting and heating and cooking and transport. The pulses seem to form some sort of manic code—'

'Sounds like you've given that lecture before,' Irona said.

'Well, you get the picture. That's what I used to warn my trainees about, otherwise they'd never take the job seriously.'

'Well, where are they now?'

'Up in the Watchtower itself if they have any sense. They know that once an attack starts they'd never get through the defences alive.' He brushed the question aside with a tired flap of his hand. 'But what I don't understand is how anybody managed to get the supply to the air-pumps. It's on a separate shielded circuit. That's not supposed to happen.'

'But it has.'

'Yep. And now there'll be people in the middle rows of the middle levels who are suffocating.'

'At least it'll put out the fires,' Irona said glumly. 'But what are we going to do?'

'Do? How should I know? Eletacatricity has never spread this far before. We've always managed to contain it. All the back-ups have failed. That means the barriers between the Warrens and the Watchtower must be down too. Any minute now the Waking is going to break through the entrance from the accommodation levels and spill into Synodland here.' He spoke as though the Waking were some monstrous animal, and in a way Irona supposed it was. A ravening, mindless beast with tentacles writhing to noose the Admin.

'Do you suppose—' she began, and stopped.

'What?'

'Do you suppose someone's done this on purpose?'

'Of course they have. Ionising the electrics to a rhythm, that takes skill, time, dedication, and purpose.'

They stared at each other in horrified silence.

'Then once the wakers are in control—'

'They won't be in control. There's nothing to make them cohere to any one purpose, is there?' he said hopefully.

'I don't know,' she said slowly. 'Maybe they just wanted to stop the Arms and the olfacts and the way we kept them half-asleep.'

Toni stared down at her, his heavy eyebrows lifting in surprise and disbelief. He was obviously too entrenched with the thinking of the Watch to comprehend what she was saying. 'It's not as though they were slaves or anything.'

'Well I know that,' Irona said, and groped through her years on Harith for the words to express what freedom meant. Knowing it was impossible, she still had to try. 'But they were more like animals caged in a zoo, don't you see? What did they have to live for?'

'What does anybody have to live for? Come on, for Synod's sake! We haven't got time for a philosophy class. Get real, will you? We've got to get out of here. Assuming we can, that is.'

'You mean like the lifts won't work or something?' Irona asked, half-hopefully, but knowing all the same that the situation was far worse than that. Already there were curls of smoke feathering in through the grille and the temperature had distinctly risen, yet when Toni had tried the door before, it hadn't budged. Sweat had begun to trickle between her breasts and stick her bodice to the small of her back.

'Don't be moronic!' Toni tried again, keying in a command-pattern on the LED panel beside the door. A second time he tried it. A third.

The door stayed firmly shut. He slammed the palm of his hand against the panel. 'Lifts? Who cares about lifts?' he yelled. 'I can't get the damned door open!'

Perspiration was dripping in her hair. Toni's announcement seemed to make it suddenly worse.

'What's the matter with it? Is it the Waking?'

'No. Yes. Maybe. It's the eletacatricity. Seems to have armed the defence system. Even if we got the door open we'd be dead before we crossed the threshold.'

'There's no wakers out there, are there?' she said, not wanting to believe they were trapped by a simple door when at any moment the air might be full of smoke and fumes, the heat might set light to the papers, the computer-controls might go even more haywire ... 'They can't be here yet, surely? How long was I asleep?'

'As far as I can tell, there's no wakers. If there were, they'd be dead anyway, same as we're going to be. Because of delta five's defences.'

'Why don't we just stay until someone rescues us?' she asked in a small voice. 'Don't tell me. Because even if we survive the fire and the wakers, the ones who woke them will be on their way.'

'You've got it, girl,' he said. 'In spades.'

The air grew denser with carbon dioxide and the residue of distant conflagrations. Darkness flickered over them in irregular waves. Now and then, batches of screams flared up the air-duct and a fine black rain of dust settled over everything.

Toni tinkered desperately with his broken toys, trying to coax certain of them back into line. He had long since given up any hope of getting in touch with the Watchtower. Instead he was concentrating on disarming the array of weapons that battened the door against all comers, no easy task with half his machines inert and some of the others inimical. He didn't even notice when she charmed one of the other computers into a semblance of function.

So he was astonished when Irona suddenly said, 'I've got something!'

He barely glanced round. So intent had he been on his own labours that it had never occurred to him she too would set to work. He hadn't seemed to connect the idea that she had once been a warden with the obvious corollary: she too could play the game.

'What is it?' he muttered, not really interested.

'Something from the Watchtower!'

He straightened, surprise making twin arches of his heavy brows. Behind him, the emergency generators were wheezing to pour power along the computer circuits. 'You sure?'

'Who else would it be? Read this.'

It was a long irregular line, broken apparently at random, that marched across one of the cracked screens.

'What's that then?'

'Morse code, obviously.'

'Doesn't look like any code to me. Just short strings of pixils that fade and relight.'

'You have to learn how to read it.'

'And can you?'

'Sort of,' she added, dismay bringing her down from her excitement. 'Only I think I've forgotten most of it. It's going too fast for me to make much sense of it.'

With no obedient microphone at her command, Irona twiddled with the Record key, but as half the functions on the monitor were out of commission she had no idea whether the recorder was actually working or not.

'D'you read the spaces or the lines?' Toni asked, rubbing his gritty eyes.

Irona supposed his head ached as hers did. The toxicity of the air was increasing at an alarming rate now that the air-filter pumps had ground into stillness. 'The lines,' she said, and groped around in the strobing dimness for a stylus to copy the patterns. Only gradually did she realise that it was almost identical to the rise and fall of the lights.

'Where is it from?' Toni asked her.

'Ssh.' Irona scribbled, then sucked her pen. After a while she said, 'Well, it's not the Watchtower, that's for sure. But who sent it I can't quite make out. Or where it's from. Does the name Aleph mean anything to you?'

'Aleph?'

'Aleph-13, to be precise.'

Toni was peering over her shoulder at the transcript. The damp heat of his flesh through her robe was gluing grit to her skin. 'It's the first letter of the Sanskrit alphabet. It's the name of a machine.'

She nodded in disappointment. 'It would be.'

'What do you mean?'

'A load of service machines have caught the disease of

eletacatricity. Aleph-13 isn't coming to rescue us. It wants us to go and rescue it.'

Toni still could not unblock the door.

'Oh come on!' Irona said, feeling her blood throbbing with the dark poisons building inside her. 'It can't be that dangerous, surely?'

He whirled on her with frustration. 'You don't get it, do you? If you're so damned precious, why do you think those machines sent you here in the first place? Because it's impregnable, that's why.'

She arched her brows in disdain. 'I was in the Arms' sanctuary before. That's pretty impregnable, wouldn't you say? I mean, you can't even see it. So why did I need to be cooped up in a room full of immobilised software?'

Toni went on, 'There's lasers out there that would cut you in two. Micro-wave patterns that would kipper your guts. Nerve-paralysers. Fear-ghosts that don't just hop up your adrenalin-levels, they knock your mind out permanently. You might want to be a gibbering wreck but I certainly don't. So shut up and let me get on with it, all right?'

He didn't seem to mind her not answering. In any case, he turned his back in a pointed manner, doing his best to close her out of his concentration, so she thought he would probably be pleased that she didn't answer.

But Irona had had an idea. Why had the machines sent her here, of all places? They must have known she could die in any number of unpleasant and implausible ways if she stirred beyond the Arms' invisible hideout. Why risk her life in fire and riot to put her in delta five?

So there must be something in here for her to find. Something hidden in the electrical labyrinth of the computers.

She started with the most obvious thing. As if she were still back on Watch, she keyed her identity into the console before her. For a time nothing happened, and she was on the point of giving up and trying to solve the riddle of the door when the monitor-screen in front of her began to jump with the familiar mandalas of her own psych-profile.

In wonder she touched her hand to the scanner, letting it read her fingerprints. She had hoped that one by one, unsteadily, the familiar words would trace themselves over the swirl of colours that made up her identity.

But of course, they wouldn't. *This isn't your body, remember?* she told herself savagely. *None of your ID cues are valid. Body-mass, scent signature, retina pattern, cell-structure – they all belong to the big-bosomed curvaceous body my mind's in now. I'm not me any more.*

All the same, not knowing what else to do, she hoped against hope that maybe some mind-scan would know who she was, locked in this construct.

And somebody did. The somebody who had summoned her across the leaping void and put her in this alien envelope of flesh.

Though the whorls of her fingerprints glowed in strange shapes, though the dancing graphs of the body's identity were stronger than hers since the body had not yet learnt how the icicles of insecurity could tear its cells apart, the mind-patterns were her own.

In wonder, she said, 'Irona,' and gave the date and the year in which she was born, typing them in with trembling fingers.

That information scrolled itself jerkily through the appropriate database until her own name was highlighted. Scent-signature curves and a request for a voice-print flickered on to the screen and answered themselves instantly. The machine said, 'Ready.'

Leaning over the voice-receptor and speaking very quietly because she felt rather silly, she said, 'Cross-reference Irona and Bernardina, Matriarch of All Earth, and find any messages.'

The machine hummed away in the dust-shimmered, faded gloom. It was obviously doing something, but she didn't know what. *Maybe it's going to shoot some kind of death-ray at me*, she thought, but on balance decided that that was mere paranoia. How had anyone – or anything – been able to say that this was the machine she would eventually use? Except that she had been summoned to delta five. But the Arms had done that, and she wasn't used to thinking of good things coming through the Arms. Maybe this was the only machine she could use. Despite her efforts not to, she managed to think up any number of ways, from lethal harmonics to mind-numbing mandalas, that a computer could use to dispose of her.

The lights flimmered faster than ever. She had to crane forward to see anything even though the screen was supposed to be non-reflective. Swiping dust from its surface, she read the message it printed: 'One further cross-reference is needed since parts of the pattern have been recoded.'

Irona racked her brains for the password she needed. Then it came to her: Elditch. Her father's name, or rather, the name of the man who was supposed to be her father.

The strobing steadied almost to normal. Just being able to trust the light was a relief. Across the room Toni looked up, grunted, and went back to skimming through the sheafs of print-out.

The computer drew letters on the screen almost too fast for her to follow. Casting a hasty glance back at Toni to make sure he was still busy, Irona read the words her mother had written her.

My darling daughter,

And Irona sat back, stunned. Even with the passwords she had had to find, she hadn't quite believed that the message was for her. But underneath the writing on the screen appeared a young woman's face, a woman just entering her thirties, and it tugged apart the reluctant surface of Irona's mind. That face was warm, and smiling with tender love. It penetrated to the wells of subconscious memory inside Irona. For it was the mother the child in her remembered from that glowing keyhole of peace she had never since been able to unlock.

'When did you write me this?' Irona's mouth framed the syllables but could not voice them. And the message didn't answer her.

Hollow, shattered like an empty pot, Irona stared at the screen and let the words fill her.

How I have missed you. I hope by now all the mind-blocks have worn away and you can remember the loving family we were. We were a nice family, weren't we?

Irona's frozen lips split to let out the icebergs dammed inside her for so long: 'But you abandoned me.' Her voice was so low that Toni didn't hear it. Irona read the next words that her mother, her very own mother, had written her.

And will be again. I had to block out parts of your memory to get you past the psych-profiles and on board the Admin's ship to Harith. I knew you'd be safe there, and prosper. I wasn't Matriarch of All Earth then, and I couldn't have done it any other way, not with the trail of havoc you and your companions left all over the security system. Nor could I let anyone know that you were related to me. It would have been too dangerous for us both. Too much of a lever. Then I never would have got you back.

You have always been nestled in my thoughts the way you once were in my arms. I have sent you messages over the years through the ansible to the Synod tower in Kifl, but I don't think you can have received them. Certainly you never sent me a reply back, and that hurt. Although I know you are too loyal and caring to ignore an appeal from your matriarch – or your loving mother.

But if you are reading this, instead of where I can embrace you and speak to you face to face, then we are in danger once again, and I must give you the weapons to fight back.

Don't trust Carandis. She daren't kill you outright but she'll use you if she can, then stab you in the back. She's one I'll brain-worm when the time is right.

Irona had to stop reading. Tears starred her eyes because she remembered the moon-face that had swum over hers when the drill bit into her skull. The pain sprang fresh and new as though her blood were weeping for her, because it had been the Matriarch herself who ordered the brain-worms poured inside her head. Memory was bright as diamonds: the betrayal had been complete.

Only Bernardina went on, *I gave you the best weapon then that I could. I knew the Synod would be recording everything that went on in Tau Seven, so I let them think I had brain-wormed you and your waker friends in case some day Synod viewed it. Elditch and I, we made it look as though we enjoyed your pain.*

Something inside Irona screamed, 'You did!'

But you weren't brain-wormed, were you, any of you? I slipped an enhancer into you, that was all, and I'm sure you're smart enough to have used that artificial empathy to take control. You're here because you beat Gundmila.

Again, Irona couldn't go on. The world was a phantom around her, because nothing she had seen or touched or been was real. She felt as though she herself were a ghost, a galaxy of unconnected atoms whirling in a random void. But her eyes would not deny the writing that scrolled in front of her while Toni muttered and cursed over the innards of the door-panel.

Don't go to the Watchrooms, my darling. Make your way straight up to my sanctuary at the peak of the tor. Anyone you see may belong to Carandis, so don't let them catch you. If they move fast enough, they may even be beyond my power to stop. Come to me, Rirona. Come back to your loving mother.

24
TENDRILS OF TREACHERY

In the Ear and Eye room of the Watchtower, Carandis watched in mounting horror as even her artificial night failed to calm the sleepers. Darkness and chaos surrounded her. She could smell her own stink; Roger's, compounded as much of stale beer as of terror, was much sharper in her nostrils. And it wasn't all due to the olfactory alarms, either, or the atavistic terrors called up by the feculent fear-ghosts. Reeling a scanner from level to level, she watched mohocks slaughtering innocent sleepers against a background of fire and wreckage.

'The night should have worked,' Carandis said, and was so far from her normal control that she didn't realise she had spoken aloud in the flickering gloom.

Roger must have been reading her lips. He slicked back the sweaty strands of hair across his skull and smiled nastily. 'I could have told you that artificial night crap wouldn't work. They're not sleepers any more, are they? Not all of 'em are nice fat sheep who'll follow where you lead.'

Carandis drew herself up, still in defeat keeping the image of the stern and noble matriarch. The trouble was, both she and Roger knew it was a shell. A smear of soot twisted like a scar across her cheekbone and eyebrow. Trembling, she said, 'I had to try.'

She needed nothing to tell her that her term as Matriarch of Camelford hadn't heralded a new day. Instead, the Admin's central city was doomed. All that remained was to see what she could salvage from the wreckage. At best, it might rescue her own career. At worst, it might just save her from being brain-wormed.

The worst horror, that another nation might invade, was something she refused to contemplate.

But Roger wasn't fooled. Raking her with a sneer that flushed her with humiliation, he said, 'If olfacts, Arms and sleep-gas won't work, how you can kid yourself a bit of darkness would is beyond me.' Then he thrust her bodily aside. She barely glanced to see what he was doing. The thoughts were hurtling like ring-cars in her brain. But they kept crashing in the circles of fire.

Here, too, in the heart of the Watchtower, the darkness was split by random flashes of spectral lightning. The few consoles that were still working spattered flaming images of looting and slaughter. Two of the last psychicators were flooding a hideous light of deathly maroon. Carandis felt nausea heave at her stomach.

Roger straightened a little. He was still propping his back against the wall, hands on his knees, trying to steady his breathing.

'What are you doing?' Carandis shrieked at him.

He raised his heavy, sweat-polished head. 'Nothing, can't you tell? But I've just managed to switch off the scent-suite in here. I thought the alarms were a bit unnecessary at this stage. Now I'm practising breathing, so leave me alone.'

Carandis inhaled. It was true. The virulent stench of putrefaction was fading, though the fear-ghosts still glowed evilly in the darkness. But she could breathe without gagging. Now all she had to worry about was the throat-scratching reek of burning cables and scorched plastic. Around her, frantic wardens coughed in the alkaline fumes of extinguishers. The sound and stink of vomit made the air even more wretched, but at least the olfactory alarms had gone.

Roger said, 'Call Bernardina. Or I will.'

Trapped, Carandis said, 'No you don't. I will.'

For she knew what Roger would get if he used any of the normal channels: a hologram of the old witch dressing to go to meet the Crown of Novaya Zemla, not a wispy ancient hair out of place, not the slightest hint of stress tightening the sag of her cheeks. Bernardina was a thousand klicks away, having her sharp edges filed into docility. If Roger made the call, all he would see was something recorded in a yesterday that wouldn't respond to the present. And not even Bernardina's self-control was good enough to pretend a Waking wasn't about to wreck the Mountain.

The Matriarch of Camelford put up one hand to catch a flying microphone. She was clumsy; it knocked her thumb backwards and it was Roger who caught it on the rebound. He slapped it hard into her palm, meaning it to hurt, and it did.

Carandis spoke a code pitched to a distinctive sonic key, a series of tonemes gauged at precise intervals in a weird quarter-tone scale. She held her breath, praying that she had got it right – self-doubt was new and acid in her mouth – and that the disease of eletacatricity, wherever it was coming from, wouldn't disrupt the command that went higher than Roger could reach.

She breathed again. It was a picture of Bernardina moving about, all right, the recording Carandis had faked yesterday from stock-shots. But the Crown must have had that weirdo Babushka over-speak a message using syllables taken from Bernardina's own speech. The microphone spoke tinnily, so that Carandis and Roger had to strain to hear against the chaos in the dark E & E room: 'The Matriarch of All Earth is unavailable. She is on a secret mission until next Sabbath.'

Roger's dismay was good. It hid the triumph that gleamed in Carandis's green eyes, giving her time to turn away before he saw it.

Stepping past a pool of puke, Carandis seized command of a console. She tried to control the Eye it linked to, but the orb was busy about some program of its own.

In micro-seconds she was drawn into the sights it showed. Its Earthbound plunge paralysed her diaphragm. The dizzy scream of pictures that whirled from the killing machine all but short-circuited her mind, for it had been too long since she had ridden the Eyes as a warden.

The monitor's image spun headlong, seeming to dash Carandis into the madness of the Warrens. Falling. Spilling downwards. Plummeting to her death.

She was in a vaulting central chamber, up where the sun-relays honeycombed the granite arches of the roof. But there were no sunbeams now to brighten the aesthetically tranquillizing plaza. No friendly golden daylight to sparkle on the fountain that was a dried-up heap of junk. There was only darkness lit by the flaming red torches below, and the sick green and purple of dying neon signs. Around her albino starlings wheeled and crashed into one another, trying to clear the death-path of the Eye.

It sliced through the air until the air itself shrieked in pain, but it didn't drown out the screams and wails of the mob. Shop-names fleered past her vision as she tumbled from a height to the all-too-crowded concourse below her.

'It's a single-letter level!' she whispered to no-one. Terror-struck, pointing upwards at the Eye and her, the crowd scattered. It seemed that her head was about to be crashed into the solid granite.

Just in time she wrenched her mind from the dizzy swoop, for the Eye shattered above the panicked flood of humanity. Carandis didn't know if it was sabotage or suicide. One last sensor cartwheeled out from the dead-ground of its explosion. It showed wakers dying in their hundreds, screaming as the fire lanced through them and boiled the flesh from their bones. Around them, fragments of transparisteel fell like razored rain. Broken, bleeding bodies of rats and enormous cats burst as the mad crowd stampeded.

Then the monitor went dead too. Dimly now from the terraces of the Mountain the sounds of the rioting came into the E & E room, not only as recordings but as a hideous, living echo of themselves.

'Silence!' bellowed Roger. 'Silence now! Cut the volume on everything to zero. Do it!'

Looking sideways at one another, the wardens obeyed, glad to have a simple, clear order that they could follow, however mad it seemed. In the E & E room, nothing moved. Not a console murmured in the flickering light of eletacatricity. No-one spoke.

The muted animal roar carried on.

Roger turned to Carandis, Matriarch of the Admin. He said baldly, 'The Eyes have been subverted. Most of the Arms are overwhelmed.' His voice was deliberately loud.

'The power's contaminated. The wakers have reached the inner entrances to the Watchtower.'

Now the silence in the E & E room was the calm before the storm, the sleep before death.

Roger said, 'Most but not all have been turned back, but that sound you can hear now is the waking streaming up the terraces from the Warrens.' Every warden stared at him with horrified eyes. His words were punctured only by sizzling plastic as he added, 'Carandis, unless you ask for help from the Liga Mediterranea or some other nation of the World Council, the Admin is dead, and us with it.'

'But I can't do that without Bernardina.'

'Then find her.'

Carandis realised how her treachery had impaled her on a barbed hook. For she knew that she had delivered Bernardina into the hands of the Crown of Novaya Zemla while pretending she had gone straight to the Three Americas. Unconvincingly, Carandis stuttered, 'But I don't know where she is!'

'Then call the last of your Arms' – at Roger's words, Carandis knew that her undermining of the Arms was common knowledge, and she blenched – 'and ask them to get us the hell out of here before whoever started this shows up.'

'What about Synod?' she asked. Hope flared suddenly in her: if she could save them, at least, maybe—

The old Watchwarden killed her lifeline. 'They're below us. There's no way we can save them. They'll have to take their own chances.'

'But the lifts and everything are off!'

Roger said, 'Too bad. But we can't put any more tranquillisers into the masses. The systems have been subverted anyway. We should have pumped out enough drugs by now to knock out a herd of elephants.' He shrugged. 'The only result seems to be a few thousand wakers frying in artificial sleep. But that's not the point. We don't want to die for nothing. If you'd get your finger out and call your personal Arms, some of us might actually survive, so do it!'

But an idea of monstrous simplicity had just imploded in Carandis's brain. If Roger had known, he would have killed her then and there even though all the wardens would have witnessed it.

For the idea that had come to her was cold and clinical as diamonds: if she blocked off the air, all life in the Warrens would die. Or at least be blacked out and immobile. So she could stop the Waking. True, a few hundred thousand sleepers might be sacrificed, but so what if she stopped the contagion reaching Londover and Undersea and Tiger Bay and all the rest of the Admin's territories? It was even good. It would solve decades of demographic problems at a single switch.

When Bernardina came back, she'd hail Carandis as a heroine. And even if she didn't, Carandis still had that dagger the old witch had stupidly put behind her own back: Irona. Safe in the Arms' roost. Bernardina didn't even know where she was. The Matriarch of the Admin would come out on top, where she belonged. Especially if Roger and his mental pygmies weren't there to rat on her. And even more especially, if the E & E recorders were destroyed by the Crown's eletacatricity, say, or wakers. Or even Arms. Afterwards, who could tell?

Carandis felt the icy beauty of her ideas flowing into place, hardening into crystal perfection.

As it was, Roger didn't know. Looking at her haggard, spent face with its sooty cicatrice, hearing her increasingly desperate plans, he thought Carandis was a spent force.

So he didn't notice the unusual meekness with which she accepted his suggestion. 'Triad and Wilderness,' she commanded, accessing the Matriarch's personal channels, 'bring a squad to the Watchtower at once. Assemble outside the E & E room.'

When she left, he thought she had merely gone to await them.

Elditch, Chair of the Synod, pushed his tottering frame through the corridors as fast as he could, shoving aside the members of the Council who rushed panicking past him. Not a one of them would do as he said. For too long, he realised, he had been a puppet on the Synod. At least when his Bernardina was Matriarch of the Admin people had listened to him as she spoke through his mouth. With Carandis ever more boldly showing her open contempt, he wasn't even a loudspeaker any more. He was an old man whom people shunted aside.

Stumbling as someone stepped on the heel of his shoe and never even apologised, he cursed his years and the way he had let others pull his strings. He wasn't as big as he had been; shrinking now with age, his strength wasn't enough. With never a word Brereton of Indemnity straight-armed him aside and dashed on.

Elditch cannoned into a lacquered cabinet, turning it to matchwood. Dark eyes baggy now, he stood in its lee, hating his withered flesh. Twenty years ago they'd never have dared to treat him this way. But the past was closed to him, with all its glories. Catching his breath as the tide of people washed past him in the flickering gloom, he wondered with a kind of desperate plea where his Bernardina was. Or if she were watching him even now, enjoying his dependency. 'Come on, you old witch,' he mumbled. 'Save me, for Synod's sake.'

But Synod was rivering past in a hundred seething bodies and a thousand hangers-on. Some gathered treasures. Others, burdened already, scarcely noticed as priceless statuettes fell from their makeshift bundles. One woman overtook him then suddenly knelt right in front of his feet to sweep up the little trail of gold and gems she had dropped. It was all he could do not to stumble over her, but he managed to straddle her kneeling body. He knew that if he went down, he would be trampled underfoot.

And with coils of oily smoke smarting in his eyes, he hadn't gone a few paces when he heard a cry and the thud of flesh against flesh. When he looked past, there was a knot of tumbled figures on the middle of the flowered rug where she had been, and men and women thrust themselves past on either side, ignoring her screams for help. Abruptly the woman's pleas choked off.

Everyone was heading for the elevators at the end of the curving row. Until a man at the front yelled, 'The wakers are only two levels down!'

Immediately those at the front began to barge their way back, while those furthest away hadn't heard. They continued to surge forward. The dim air was meaty with their fear-laced breath. Flattening himself in an alcove, Elditch could only watch the destruction of all he and his wife had worked for. He knew death was as close as the scratches on his shin.

Carandis eeled her way out through the exhausted throng in the Ear and Eye room. Let them play their role as guardian angels! It wouldn't change a thing.

She palmed the control that slid the doors closed behind

her and leant on the thick coating of steel. Eletacatricity tingled round the hairs on her arms, stung like thunderflies around the incipient moustache she so assiduously depilated every day that Camelford wasn't waking.

As soon as the Watchroom's taken care of, Carandis told herself, *I'll cut that damned eletacatricity*, and tried to rub the sting of it from her top lip.

Side-stepping into the corridor, she sucked down the cooler air, feeling it glaze the sweat on her forehead. Out here, with not even the emergency lights working most of the time, the blue glow limning her skin seemed stronger. Or maybe it was stronger.

And for what Carandis planned, that might be all to the good. What if somebody was jamming most of the Eyes? They wouldn't be able to touch her own personal one. That was safe where it always was, in the Arms' roost.

Using the remote in her pocket, she summoned her Eye, relaying the rest of her message at the same time, still on the private channel only the Matriarch and the Arms could receive: 'Assemble outside the Ear and Eye Room. Then destroy everyone inside.'

In the glimmering darkness, she put her mouth close to the door mechanism. With Bernardina elsewhere, Carandis's voice-print was the single most powerful force in the Admin. She said, 'This door to remain sealed until Triad and Wilderness arrive.'

Almost immediately someone inside tried to follow her into the row. Soon they were beating a panicked rhythm against the solid steel panels. Dimly she heard a chair or something crash against the inside.

Smiling grimly to herself, Carandis left them to their futility. Feeling her way along the walls of rough granite, allowing her toes to probe each dark step in the hollowed limestone floor, she left the sounds of outrage to die away behind her. Within minutes she was at a cross-rows, partially concealed by the bulge of a transplanted stalagmite. If her skin was still oozing that weird blue gleam, it didn't matter. It was mostly obscured by the flimmering emergency lights.

Her Arms had their orders, though. And her personal Eye would find her.

Down to the Weather-Control room, the real nexus of power in all of Camelford. The room that was disguised in the double-speak she and Bernardina had fed to the wardens. Its name was the innocuous delta five.

Irona read and re-read her mother's message, feeling as though she were disintegrating. The spaces between one nerve-ending and the next were as astronomical as the chances of finding a given electron at a given point. The world dimmed again, and for a time Irona thought it was merely the erratic play of the lights. Then a reflex forced her to draw in air, and, as the room spun and steadied, she realised that she had been on the point of blacking out because she had forgotten to breathe. Icy sweat tightened on her skin. Her teeth were dancing some crazed fandango of their own and her hands wouldn't stop shaking. That neon-blue light still ghosted from her flesh.

Madness lay in ambush, ready to leap out and rend her identity into charnel doll-rags. Wells of memory gaped treacherous at her feet. Her whole universe was atilt. Nothing was as she had thought it was. Nothing. Everything she had believed in for decades was skewed out of true. Concepts had ceased to have any meaning for her.

Out of the cacophony in her brain, one question re-printed itself until finally the words cohered enough to have meaning: *Why did I ever come to delta five? What am I doing here?*

And, slowly, the mental picture of a delta formed to back the word. Delta. The mother of rivers. The mother of water. Water that fell from the sky. The idea burst over her like a typhoon.

Drawing air deep enough to speak, she coughed as acrid fumes burnt in her throat. 'Didn't you say this is where the weather-shield controls are?'

Trying not to breathe, Toni growled assent.

'That's why there's so many blocks on the door?' she persisted.

'Yes, for Synod's sake! What does it matter why they're there? We still can't get out. And if we don't, we're going to die in a sea of poisoned gasses, so shut the hell up, will you?'

'Trace where the orders for this eletacatricity virus are coming from and I'll get us out of here.'

Toni snarled wordlessly, knee-deep in the printed dumps that he searched for clues.

Irona slithered across the paper mountains to him. She shook his arm, saying, 'Find me where the eletacatricity is being controlled from! Or you'll never get out of this.'

He wrenched his arm from her grasp. Red veined his eyes where the smoke was sharp in the air. 'What do you think I was trying to do before you came in? But we haven't got time to waste saving the world now because we're the ones who are going to die, so shut up and let me fix this bloody door!'

'Never mind that! You'll never break down the blocks. Find the source of that eletacatricity and we're out of here. Because the ones who've orchestrated the Waking will be heading for delta five. And we'll be right in their sights.'

25
A DEADLY EMBRACE

Nona pulled open the door of the Ocean Room of Tingalit, all but flooring Garwin, who was leaning against it.

'What do you mean by keeping my people locked up here all day?' she said fiercely, throwing a dramatic gesture towards the three dockers from the airfield.

Twiss got up angrily. He leaped towards Nona, who, for all her arrogance, backed up a few hasty steps before the hostility he exuded. He raised one fist as if to strike her, then mastered himself. Striding restlessly to the curtains that framed the view of the bay, he yanked them shut against the purple dusk. Above him, his personal Eye stirred in the draught he'd created. It attracted the attention of everyone else in the room, but he didn't notice. The dockers and Nona were terrified, the fisherchildren curious and Garwin first alert and then indifferent, but the Eye bobbed less and less as the sea air settled. Finally it stilled.

Twiss turned to stare at her. 'Look, woman, I've been with the factions all day, all right? I've about had it up to here. One of your damned dockers – and who gave you jurisdiction outside the harbour is anybody's guess, because I certainly didn't – one of they pieces of scum nearly murdered a child, and all for a few poxy pieces of shell and a metre or two of seasilk. Meantime, I've about had enough of your trying to throw your weight about just 'cos Less is your cousin, and of folks rowing about who owes who what and what it's all worth. Plus we've got Arms raging around and about a million other little details, so back the hell off, woman; and, unless you've got anything constructive to say, shut the hell up.'

With an effort Twiss stopped his tirade. His throat had that empty itch in it that only a drink could still. It wasn't so much the night he wanted to block out, but the way the situation would go on and on until somebody did something about it. With Irona a mindless husk on her cold couch in the Hospital, that somebody could only be him. The trouble was, he hadn't got a clue what to do for the best.

Ferociously he muttered, 'But I'm not going to be robbed by that bastard Tang!'

Behind him, the fishergirl Tesserae knelt up on the couch. Innocent in her nakedness, she had no idea how much she disturbed the Kiflian leader. 'Oh, it's not like that!' she said. 'The Creator would never do anything bad. You see, it's just that if you don't help us with more food, we're never going to be able to move away from spending all our resources on cash-crops like seasilk that you *will* trade us food and supplies for. So then you'd have to send us even more food, and you haven't got it. You wanted us to farm the Eastern Ocean for you, and we're trying to, but we need your help to do it or we'll never be able to support you instead of you supporting us. At least, that's what the Creator—'

Twiss snapped. He roared, 'Bugger your almighty sodding Creator! Garwin, get me Regen!' and the stocky, stubble-chinned guard sketched a hasty salute and moved towards the door. The fishergirl paled to her gill-slits, and one of her companions mouthed 'You've done it now' at her.

The Kiflian leader caught Garwin up in a couple of strides and swung him round on the polished glass floor as though he were a toy. 'I don't mean you personally go and look for him, you idiot!' Anger corded Twiss's neck as he yelled. His face was suffused under his tan until it looked like he was about to erupt like the crater of Heralia. 'Use the Eye, for Synod's sake!'

Striding up and down, he flooded the room with his rage, the power of it touching everyone in it with a force that urged them to discretion. Not a one of them dared speak, not even the surly female mouthpiece of the dockers. The King's black moods could be fatal – for somebody else.

The violet skies blazed with stars and still the hapless Garwin couldn't locate Regen. As night solidified, the sea-breeze flapped the drapes in an irritating rhythm. None of the people dared to say anything, except maybe to chance a quick whisper with a comrade.

The youngest of the fisherfolk, a lad who couldn't have been more than ten years from hatching, subsided into sleep. His version of a snore was a whine of air through the little pink slits under his ears. Twiss found himself waiting for the next one, his own breathing suspended until he knew the lad still lived.

'Right, I've had a belly full of this. I declare this meeting adjourned,' he said finally. 'We'll reconvene in the morning. Once I've got this thing sorted, Tesserae, I'll call your damned Creator, but not till then, so don't ask. Garwin, show them where to sleep. You kids can go – but not outside the palace. It ain't safe.'

As the dockers stood, wriggling their shoulders to get the kinks out of their backs, Twiss said, 'Not you. You ain't leaving Tingalit till I say so.'

'But my husband'll give me hell!' the chunky dock-woman exclaimed.

'Then call him up. Call anyone you like up. But you ain't going nowhere until I'm good and ready to let you, so put that in your olfactory and smoke it.' Twiss touched keys on the remote in his pocket. 'And just to make sure, I'll be keeping an Eye on you.'

The dockers remembered how Twiss had used an Eye to drown Kifl. They might mutter covertly, but they subsided, casting fearful glances at the orb shining balefully above their heads. They didn't dare do anything else.

Stamping along the corridors to the peace of his own green suite of rooms, Twiss kicked the door open and headed for his drinks cabinet. A plump white arm beckoned him from the doorway to his bedroom, but he didn't see it, or the way Lowena pouted.

Plastering another seductive smile on her vapid features, Lowena pulled the strap of her diaphanous gown just a little lower over her muscle-padded shoulders and oozed across the rugs to kiss the back of his neck.

He started; the carafe clattered on the rim of the goblet. 'Synod, you stupid cow! You made me jump.' Dark wine stained the green of his tunic and he brushed at it in annoyance. 'Where the hell did you spring from?'

Even Lowena could tell that he was in no pleasant humour. Cooing, she said, 'Here, let me pour you a nice cool drink.'

Twiss spun on his heel and threw himself across a contour chair that wasn't big enough for two. 'I've already got a drink,' he informed her brusquely, and took two long, long swallows.

'My poor dear, I can see you've had a terrible day—'

Again Twiss interrupted her. 'And I'm going to have a terrible night, too, so clear off and leave me to it. I haven't got time for pratting around.'

Lowena showed her blush all the way up through her short, frothy gown, but it was the colouring of pique, not embarrassment. 'Is that what you call all the time I spend making love with you?' she asked, and there was a thin thread of acid in the way she spoke. To Twiss, from years of practice, it was clear that she believed she'd soon have him back at heel.

'I don't care what you call it,' he said, and his lips were thin with barely-checked tension. 'I got rid of that slob of a Hesperion for you, didn't I? And promoted you. You've had your reward. So get the hell out of here before you say anything you'll regret.'

'Listen, Twiss,' she said. 'You talk to me civilly and I might—'

He drained his goblet and flung it across the room. The chased silver gonged against the heavy carved jade glass of the door. 'There's the way out,' he said, gesturing peremptorily with his chin. 'Take a hint. I've got enough on my mind without you gumming the place up.'

'If I go, Twiss, I'm not coming back.'

'Who wants you to? There's plenty more where you came from. I was getting tired of your everlasting yapping anyway. You're OK on the parade-ground but off of it you ain't got a brain-cell in your body. Find some other poor sucker to batten on. Don't call me and I won't call you.'

He scarcely even noticed when she'd gone. Standing up to pour wine into another goblet, Twiss dimmed the lights because his head was throbbing tightly. He thumbed the controls on the remote.

Poor Garwin answered, his stubbly face, in the tiny flat screen, looking pinched and somewhat misshapen. 'I'm sorry, sir, I can't find him,' and Twiss didn't know whether the lad's nervousness made him want to laugh or slap the young fool. And Arias Tang's been trying to get hold of you again.'

'Bugger Tang. Tell him I'll call him when I've got something I want to say to him. How's that fisher deve in the Hospital?'

'The doctor finished operating on her a while ago. Jai's with her now. She called to say the girl's going to make it. She doesn't think there'll be any brain damage.'

'Well that's one good thing to come out of today's mess, anyhow,' Twiss said gloomily.

'Yes, Twiss. But Jai wants to call Tang. They're not quite like normal people and she wants his help.'

The Kiflian leader sighed. 'She would. Tell her I'll call him first thing. And make sure there ain't no Arms loose in the city. I don't want they harming a hair of that fishergirl's head, whatever her name is.'

'Maerika.'

'Yeah, her. I don't want a war with Tang's lot on my hands an' all. Give me a shout about nine, will you? I'm knackered.'

'Right. I've got the deve kids—'

'Don't you start!'

Garwin swallowed his amazement at this change of heart. 'Sorry. I've got the fisherchildren and the dockers bedded down. Good-night,' Garwin said.

'And a good night to you, too.'

Twiss switched off the remote and tossed it casually on

to the couch. It slid off the silken material and clattered to the floor. Kicking it moodily with one foot, Twiss eased his boots off and leant back, wishing Irona were there to sort everything out like she always did.

That was when the walls to his chamber began to glow as some fierce light burst outside the glass walls of Tingalit.

Staves of fierce emerald light beat at him. Twiss could feel the heat even through the thick transparisteel walls. Down below, in the gardens, a guard cried out. Her voice bubbled for a moment and then was gone. Darkness spread. The air was sharp with ozone when the heat thinned.

Twiss reckoned the focus of the light was out there at ground level. After-images of the glow burned orange in his vision. He stumbled to the doors on to the balcony and just stopped himself hurling them open. Instead he eased the catch and dropped to the floor.

Through the crack he could hear wild swirls of locust-lizards, frightened by the explosion of light in the darkness. Somewhere in the tangle of houses beyond the palace gardens he could hear a child crying. For a moment he thought it was Arnikon.

Irritably Twiss shook his head. Then he looked round for his Eye.

'Damn! Left it spying on they dockers,' he mumbled, and crawled across the room to his remote. He groped around and found it tumbled amongst the seasilk pillows on the floor.

Still making as little noise as possible, he crept across his state-room and opened the heavy, carven door. Nothing was moving out there in the hallway. He left the door ajar so his Eye would be able to come to him and entered his orders on the slim black remote.

Shoving the gadget inside his tunic, he eased across to his balcony once more. Here the glass was swirled with patterns of bubbles as tiny as sand. Trying to line his gaze up with a curve of clear jade so that he could see what was going on, he cursed himself for putting beauty top of his list of requirements for the builders of Tingalit.

He heard the rush of feet below as guards arrived, some from across the lawn by the gate and others from different wings of the building.

'Careful! Careful!' he whispered to them, the brave men and women with whom he had worked for so long on the drilling-fields.

But nothing happened to them. He heard Lowena say, 'All right. Nothing we can do for Keri.' Lowena's voice was shaking, and outside the bedroom she was as tough as ironwood. 'But we've got work to do. We know it was an Arm or Arms. Spread out and tell me what's going on. Search-pattern. And cover each other like we do in practice. You know how to do that.'

Twiss heard his guards pattering off. As he stood, his Eye circled in front of his face, letting him know that it was here. He keyed it to round up any intruders. When it left, he leaned on the balustrade that was still warm to the touch despite the night breezes.

Lowena knelt below, vomiting on to a flowerbed that was white with narcissi. On the gravel path beside her lay something black and twisted that he couldn't make out. But his imagination filled in the details: Keri, a hearty brunette with whom he had enjoyed a bit of sport last summer, was calcified as Thebula had been. Amongst the ozone, the sea-spray and the perfume of the flowers he could smell the stench of burnt meat. She had been fun.

Only when Lowena had turned handfuls of soil over her

embarrassment did Twiss call down to her. She made a play of examining the scene and he did her the courtesy of not asking her if she was all right. 'Call a tractor to take her – to take her to the Hospital, OK? Then let me know if you find anything else. I'll be in the Synod Chamber.'

She said thickly, 'Good idea. Did your Eye get anything?'

'Not yet. I'll see you up there in twenty minutes, OK?'

'Fine.'

He left her to it and went inside, splashing cold water on his face and wishing he hadn't had quite so much wine on an empty stomach. The thought of Keri being dead, and worse, dead like that, made him feel nauseous. Fear shivered through his guts too, wondering where the Arm was and if he were next on its list.

He pulled on his boots and ran up the ramp to the Synod Chamber, thinking about what he and Lowena had said. As the conversation replayed in his head, he also wished he hadn't kept saying, 'OK?' as though he wanted her approval.

The trouble was, he did.

Twiss felt the ghosts of the past as he walked into the dark, echoing chamber. Soft-footed and watchful as a cat, he approached the circle of high-backed chairs that ringed the Synod table. He remembered all too well how Gundmila, Red Lal and Arias Tang had once lain in wait for him there. In his hand was a flechette gun he had taken from them all those years before; the very gun that had threatened his son's life when Arno was still a baby.

But the spike-backed seats were empty. Gundmila was dead, and Red Lal, and Tang was safe on the other side of the planet. This was a far more subtle enemy.

With a sigh Twiss sat in the place Irona normally occupied. Just being in the place where she should have been tightened his anxiety another notch until it was a band of pain around his skull. He didn't call the lights on, though. Without his Eye keeping watch above him he had no wish to advertise his whereabouts.

Even though he had far less skill on the thing than she did, Twiss knew enough to power up the computer let into the stone of the table-top so he could call the Hospital.

It was Jai who answered. Twiss groaned to himself.

'You had a call from the guards yet?' he asked.

Jai yawned. 'Yes, I have. They wanted a tractor for some accident. And no, of course I don't mind you disturbing me. I've only been looking after people' – he knew she meant Irona by the acid in her voice – 'for you all blasted day. Why should I need any sleep?'

Twiss hissed out an irritated breath but managed not to shout. 'Being sarky ain't going to get us nowhere, Jai. But I called to warn you there's Arms about again. You take care now, hear me?'

The drawn coffee-coloured skin flushed; the lines of her face softened with tenderness.

Until Twiss said, 'Make sure that Eye's right over Ro every minute.'

'Oh, wonderful! I'm supposed to take care of your damned wife and never mind what happens to me?'

Twiss shook his head like he was trying to drive away a stinging fly. 'Oh, come on, Jai. It ain't like that. Only she's unconscious and under threat, and you ain't. Look, put Sticker on, will you? I'm sending a couple of guards over to keep a watch on that fishgirl Maerika.'

Jai was already reaching for the keyboard. He watched her hand coming towards him like a fist as she said shortly, 'He's not here.'

'Find him then!'

But he had no idea whether or not she had heard. No Irona. No Regen. And no Sticker. With a growing feeling of being trapped in a quicksand, Twiss called what was left of the Synod. And Irona's capable friend Tebrina.

The red-faced woman answered sleepily from her farm. Behind her Twiss could see her husband Sinofer dozing in his chair.

Twiss explained what he wanted, and added, 'You don't mind, do you, Tebrina? Only with – with Ro the way she is, I need all the friends I can get.'

Twiss was staring at the epidiascope. Across the table-top rose the 3-D light-sculpture of Kifl Bay, so accurate that he could clearly see tiny figures hauling nets of fish from the rippling charcoal sea. Here and there were the warm glows of windows in the curving walls of the houses; out past the moon-shimmered olive-groves hung the cylinder of the *Thistle-up*, a black cloud against the stars. Dangling below it, the transparisteel hull of the basket warped the celestial designs of the heavens.

The leader of Harith took off his crown. Wearily he laid it beside the console and absently fiddled with the great kistle gem gleaming darkly against its setting. *What was it Regen said? I've had the name and now I've got to have the game.* With no-one left on his team, the thought was like a burr rasping at his skin. He was glad when the rest of the Synod arrived in a wave of chatter and lights. Even Nona's bitching was better than the silence that let him hear his own thoughts.

'Another attack by the Arms?' Less was saying when Lowena came in to report.

Twiss silenced Less with a wave of his hand. Baika the squat builder and Irona's friend Tebrina leaned forward to listen.

'Dr Darien's found another message like the first one,' Lowena said. 'He's recording it now, then he'll bring it over. The first part of it sounded pretty much like the one they left with – with Thebula.'

Twiss found it incredible that Thebula had been murdered only a few short weeks before. Not letting himself get lost in the maze of thoughts and emotions that opened before him, he dragged his mind back to his captain's report.

'Irona's Eye is still guarding her. I checked its functions. They're fine. The fishergirl's asleep normally. And everywhere's quiet. Most people are still keeping to the new curfew though we've had to goose a few youngsters – including your Fessbar, Tebrina – who were having a barbecue on the rocks at the end of the bay. No sign of the Arms, and Sticker's finished burning out those snake-rat larvae who broke into the granary.'

'I found where they'd got in and reinforced the walls,' Baika said.

Tebrina said, 'You might start a patrol out on the slopes of the Moon Mountains where our farm is. We've had quite a few of them popping up but they ain't quite an epidemic yet. Don't want 'em to be neither. Makes me wonder, though, if it's going to be a migration year. Don't want 'em swallowing up the farms in Rainshadow Valley.'

Twiss, pulling a face at the unwelcome news, nodded his thanks but turned back to face Lowena. 'Anything else?'

The tall, slender blonde with the well-muscled shoulders looked him straight back in the eye, as expressionless as though she were on the parade ground. 'No, Twiss.' She lifted her helmet so that the air could cool her head. Her long, oat-pale hair was plastered around her face but her eyes were bright as fever. 'Oh yes, I almost forgot. I found Regen's spare Eyes—'

'You didn't find him?'

Lowena shook her head. Her helmet cast weird shadows over her forehead and below her cheekbones. 'Sorry. Not a sign. I hate to disappoint you. I thought he might be out at the airfield talking to Captain Hoojer, but she hasn't seen him. Anyway, I spread the Eyes out over the town, all four of them.'

At that moment Sticker entered precipitately, letting the door slam back against the wall. 'Oops, sorry, folks,' he said. 'Only just got your message off Jai. Me and my squad, we was electrifying they snake-rat larvae out by the silo. Be done in a couple of hours, most likely.' He trotted to his seat beside Twiss, slapping down a pair of heavy gauntlets on the table. Twiss could smell the sweat on him, the grease in his hair. And worst, the faint odour of burning that brought back the horror of what had happened to Thebula and Keri.

Oblivious, Sticker said, 'Hope I haven't missed too much. What's going on?'

In a few brief words, Twiss sketched the situation for him.

From the way Sticker closed his eyes and swallowed, he thought his friend must have known Keri, too. Twiss wondered what Jai might have to say about that.

On the subject of the Eyes, though, Sticker said, 'Synod Tower, definitely better leave one there, don't you reckon? Otherwise it's our weak spot. Don't want nobody else gettin' hold of that there computer, do we?'

'Declan and Malambé still there?' Twiss asked.

Lowena nodded.

'Well done.' He flashed his famous charismatic smile at

her and, tired as she was, she pulled back her weary shoulders. It thrust her flat breasts out towards him.

'Right away, King.'

Lowena, his captain of guards, was one of the few people who could call him King without it sounding like a slur. Before she had time to leave, he touched her lightly on the arm. 'Thanks, Lowena. I knew we could count on you.'

He was genuinely grateful. But more than that, even without Irona's heightened empathy, he knew she would fight for him till her last breath. For a moment it heartened him.

Then he began to wonder if she had misplaced her faith. What if he let her down?

The impromptu Synod ran its course. Twiss brought them up to date on the crisis out at the airfield and said, 'I can't stop much longer. I've got to deal with those dockers who attacked the fisherfolk—'

'I don't know how you can call them folk,' Less said vehemently. 'They're deves, they're mutants, just as inhuman as these Arms you seem to have brought down on us. They're a danger to everyone on this planet. I'll never understand why you let Tang build them in the first place.' He drew breath for another tirade.

'Because we needed someone to harvest another food-source, that's why. I'd like to see you swimming about tending fishbeds.'

'Well they're not doing much of a job if we keep having to squander our own pitiful supplies on them, are they? More power to the dockers, that's what I say. At least they're good human Kiflians.'

Twiss flicked a glance over Less's shimmering tunic of buttercup and his smooth grey jacket and trousers. All of his clothing was made of seasilk that must have cost at least a sack of grain. Twiss continued his raking stare until its acidity had registered even on Less's thick skin. 'I notice you don't mind wearing the stuff they send over to us, though,' he said. 'How much did you pay for that?'

Less flushed, but he wasn't to be drawn. 'We should milk them for everything we can get.'

Twiss saw that Tebrina was even redder in the face than usual. He could tell she was about to explode. To forestall her argument he flashed her a beseeching look – Tebrina had never liked being told what to do – and said smoothly to Less, 'I'd of said the same thing, once upon a time. But that's like saying you ain't human if you got different coloured eyes, or two-colour hair.'

'That was below the belt,' Less retorted angrily. His own hair was black with wings of white at the temples, as it had been ever since the First Wave of settlers had landed forty or more years ago. 'At least I don't have feet like a duck's.'

'Well stop puttin' 'em in your mouth, then, and let's deal with the situation as it is.' The leader of the Kiflian Synod drew a breath because it cost him to admit he wasn't infallible, and went on with a rush, 'What am I going to say to Arias about the tariffs?'

Tebrina said, 'Get him over here.'

'Nah. Just fob 'un off.' That was Sticker, blunt as ever. 'What with they Arms, we got trouble aplenty to deal with without mixing all that up in it.'

Twiss turned the idea over briefly in his mind, as though it were a rock he'd just found hiding a snake-rat larva on its underside. 'No good. I don't trust him.'

Tebrina smiled triumphantly. 'All the more reason to get him over here, then. That way you can keep an eye on him.'

Slowly Twiss began to nod. ‘Yeah, you might be right. I’ll do that. In more ways than one.’

As soon as the meeting dissolved, Twiss confirmed with Jai that the injured fishergirl’s position was stable and called Tang. It was fortunate that there was a weather-window, but something somewhere disrupted the transition. It seemed to Twiss that Tang’s hated face was flickering at him as though he were a demon speaking from Sheol.

Shaking off his goosebumps, Twiss said baldly, ‘You found out anything about they Arms, Tang?’

‘No, Twiss. I’ve found out about what your fine strong Kiflian rabble did to one defenceless young fishergirl at the airfield, though. I hope you’re proud—’

‘I’m dealing with it. Tang, you’ll have to come over here.’

Tang’s chisel-pointed face came briefly into clarity. ‘I think not, Twiss.’ Before the Kiflian leader could protest, he added, ‘Because I’ve found out something even worse than the Arms.’

26
DAMOCLES AWAITS

The all-too-solid muscles of her legs had grieved Pilar Jímenez when she was younger. What man would want a woman with legs like cartons of milk?

Lying in the clinic of the Mission, though, Pilar was no longer worried about the great bulges of her calves. For one thing, she had long since ceased to care about men who only wanted pneumatic nubile dolls with empty heads, flash cookers and a hole between their legs. That had been a great stride forward, leaving behind her adolescent anxieties about her body: her terracotta-coloured skin, her high-bridged Mayan nose.

But the other thing was simpler. In six weeks she had walked thirty kilometres a day, every day, keeping going long after her food and then her body's fat resources had run out. So her system had cannibalised its own flesh to power that poignant, never-ending pilgrimage through the wounds of two of her Americas. She had dredged the lees of her land. Her legs no longer looked like earthenware pots. They looked like dried brown spaghetti.

For now, at least, they had stopped hurting. The Matriarch's Mission had accomplished that much, anyway.

Pilar lay back, staring at the holy pictures marching across the ceiling while the mission doctor worked. Comforting drugs wrapped her much more softly than the fluffy white cotton-bolls she had walked through could have done. They burnished her memories of the stops that had barely punctured her awareness of the baking blue sky.

Pilar's one-woman procession had kept her moving from aggressive, arrogant towns who boasted of sky-scrapers as though the planet's sky was something they wanted to hurt. At first, when she had been clean and sleek and well-fed, the descendants of oil tycoons and shipping magnates had wined and dined her in penthouse luxury while they told her how much better things had been in the old days. Not that she told them who she was, of course.

A lot of the time it wasn't the descendants of gringo rich men who fed her. Here in the South there were still oases of atavism despite centuries of co-operation. Still people who subconsciously thought that the only good Indian was a dead one. If the Indians were poor and hungry and ill-educated because they cleaned shoes for coppers when they should have been at school, that was because there were no other good Indians.

She remembered that lesson from the time she lived Under-Mexico-Fields. There, of course, it wasn't so much the white-eyes who looked down on the destitute grand-sons of Aztec kings. It was the children of Spanish mothers who could afford to live on the surface, or even above its blankets of pollution.

Religion. No.

Nationality. No.

Whatever the tycoons and the magnates and the mothers in shiny cars picking up their kids from ballet-classes and frat dances said, it was what it had always been: the conflict between those who wanted to hold on to everything against those who would like to have anything.

Pilar's husband was white and she loved him. When he was tanned from working outdoors and she was pale from councils and bureaucracy, his skin was darker than hers, but their love was equally bright. Pilar smiled just at the thought of him. Caught here in the sucker at the tip of one of the enemy's tentacles, she hoped she would see him again.

The doctor's probe stung and she jerked away, not so much from the actual pain but from the pain her body thought was coming. She and the young man exchanged a twitch of the lips that meant: I'm sorry, I couldn't help it, it won't happen again.

'Soon be done,' the blond man said. 'Once we've got the synthetic flesh on you, you'll be as good as new.'

They both looked down at the end of the sonic probe. It was vibrating so fast that neither of them could see it move, and the sound was so high-pitched they couldn't hear it either. But it was breaking up the necrotic tissue round the ulcer that spread wide as four fingers and almost down to the shin-bone. Pulverising dead cells into little bits that her boosted immune system could carry away. He had assured her, once he knew she understood, that the little bits were too small to clog her arteries and stop her heart.

He was kind. He wasn't some patronising imported round-eye bastard. He was an orphan of what he said himself was 'poor white trash from down the road a ways'.

Pilar liked him. She said, 'Tell me about the Mission. Take my mind off my troubles. How long have you been here?'

'Since I was a snotty little punk full of piss and vinegar.' He winked at her, checking that he hadn't offended her.

Sometimes it could be hard to tell, but Pilar grinned at the big blond man and said, 'I can imagine.' She kept her accent strong.

He drawled, secure in himself. 'I never had no family. There was just me and my big sister and whichever shit – 'scuse my language – she lived with. Had me out foraging for stuff soon as I could wipe my own ass. My sister, she went clear to Galveston Inner one time. Told me she'd be back in a week or two, but she just had to see the drowned city and the roof gardens and the treasures they were salvaging from all them high-class sunken apartments. She'd seen it on a disk she'd stole and when she got hopped up one night she just had to go see it.'

Sliding the probe to a new site under Pilar's skin, the doctor checked that he wasn't hurting her and that her instrument readouts on the panel behind her head were all clear. 'She was gone for most of a summer. Her boyfriend, him and me got along fine most of the time but ever' now and then he'd just naturally get pissed at me and whale me with whatever came to hand. One night, I can remember them big ole stars looking down at me, kind of circlin' round my head 'cos he'd hit me that hard I was in like my own private planetarium. So when he went to sleep, I just naturally whanged him one back. Got him right on the bean with a frying pan he'd stole.'

The man's big, strong hands in the sterile gloves moved carefully about their work. ''Scuse me a sec, honey. Difficult bit. Gotta think.'

Pilar stole a glance up at his face, feeling like a peeping Tom when she saw that his concentration had robbed him of any social mask he might have had. His face was homely, marked by the kindly grooves his frequent smile had left behind. Pale crow's feet showed where he squinted against the southern sun, and twin vertical lines above his nose were deep now as he kept most of his mind on his job. She put his age at thirty-four or thirty-five.

Pilar nodded just fractionally. She was getting to like him more and more. He wasn't one of those men who had to hide himself from others. They always flagged their weaknesses by the very ways they tried to disguise them. It was good to have men like him in the Americas. Huitzilopochtli knows, they needed him and his kind. She could wait to hear the rest of his story.

'Anyway,' he said after a while, 'sis snitches a ride on the ring-road and gets burnt pretty bad, but she finally makes it home only her feller, he didn't take too kindly to me beaning him when he was asleep so he'd lit out. Took ever'thing we'd got. I brought her here but she didn't like it. Said it didn't feel right, the way the matriarchs kept looking after her and feeding her and all, whether she worked or not. First she told me she was milking the system. Then she got kind of mad because the folks at the Mission, it didn't seem to matter a damn that she was taking the piss. Then she got jealous 'cos I was fittin' right in – 'cept for my language, of course – and she upped and walked out one night and I ain't never seen her since.'

He hitched his stool back on its castors and wiped his forehead with his forearm. A quick spray from an aerosol – she felt only its coolness – then he tore his surgical gloves off and slapped them against his thigh. 'Well, that's it. What did you say your name was?'

'Nice try, doctor, but I didn't. The matriarchs round here, they call me Dolores.'

'Well now, I ain't going to call you any name that ain't your own. I ain't going to tell you my name till then, neither.'

They shared a grin. Wasn't his name on the badge on his chest? On her notes? On his graduation picture tacked up on the wall?

'Think I don't know your name, Tom?' she asked, liking his humour.

Then he shocked her out of any pose she might have assumed. He said, 'Think I don't know yours?'

In Eastcliff, Seriathnis was still child enough to want to go exploring. Unfortunately, the Creator had expressly forbidden it. Nevertheless, as she sat fiddling with the computer in the communications room, just waiting there in case a call came through, a certain element of boredom crept into her.

She sighed, and realised that far from studying, for the last twenty minutes she had been staring at the rippling creepers on the wall. Still, at least her watch was almost over. There was so much else she could have been doing: swimming free in the caress of the ocean, or tending the seedlets of life down in the breeding-pools, or just grooming and being groomed. Yet the Creator had told her to stay on watch until he came.

As ever, his approval filled her with a gentle pleasure when he finally opened the door and smiled at her. These days, though, ever since the last visit of the Irona-one, the Creator's smile had been small and far away. Seriathnis had always liked the Irona-one since she was little, but still she wished that the Irona-one had not made the Creator so sad and distant.

Released from the melancholy of his company, Seriathnis raced off to the Seasilk Garden and dived straight in. Oxygen caught and bubbled silver in her fur, its movement a sensual pleasure. Catching a passing fish, she nibbled it daintily from its bones and tossed the skeleton tidily over the rim and into the ocean.

Only then did she acknowledge the presence of her hatch-mate Ehrlatch. He didn't mind, of course. He was smaller than she, ruddy brown with mischievous eyes, and though the Creator used to try to stop his fisherchildren selecting a pecking-order by strength, they all thought it was normal. In the end, that was a battle which the Creator had had to give up. Seriathnis protected the shorter boy, and his patent admiration made her feel good about herself.

Now Ehrlatch said, 'Let's go exploring.'

Disobedience.

But the Creator was on watch, probably, Seriathnis realised, waiting for a message from the Irona-one or that arrogant, angry hotskin Twiss.

With the wisdom of an old eel who knew when it was safe to come out of its cave, Ehrlatch said, 'Come on. The Creator will never know.'

They had been brought up in the same slowly-growing knot of tunnels all their lives; there was only one place they could go exploring. Not beyond the horizon, because they were not permitted so far in the unfathomed sea, and razor-fish and lightning-eels from the deep currents had told them it was not a good idea.

But in the tunnels where the twitchy hotskin had rescued the Irona-one, that would be all right, wouldn't it? Who could touch them there? Nobody, now that fool Hesperion had gone. It was another knot of tunnels, wasn't it? So it would be almost like home, only the entrance was higher up. And the Irona-one had warned them of the low, dark, foul-smelling pool where the sea-corals ate living flesh.

'Promise me you'll stay away from the smelly place,'

Seriathnis said, and Ehrlatch nodded, his inner eyelids blinking rapidly in a horizontal wink that acknowledged his plan had won.

It didn't take long to shinny over the boulder and up the cliff to the entrance. Though the air-threads were a nuisance if you went barefaced, they were no problem at all to two children with thick fur, transparent inner eyelids and nostrils that closed. All they had to do was comb their thick neck-fur over their gill-slits. And the sharp rocks couldn't get through the pads of toughness between their webbed fingers and toes.

They crawled in through the hole in the black rock face. Eyes that could accommodate to the lower density of light under the surface made it easier to see than the hotskins would have found it.

Besides, Ehrlatch suddenly produced a piece of glow-coral from his loin-pouch. Seriathnis was in front of him. When he tapped her on the shoulder and held the coral's pinky light under his chin, she turned. His underlit face made her squeak.

He laughed, knowing that he had scored a point.

She laughed, acknowledging his fractional rise in status. She let him keep the glow-coral though she could have taken it from him. He walked proudly in front, using the faint cyclamen light to peer into dark corners, but their senses of smell and air-pressure were so acute that they could have found their way with no light at all.

Here too there were nodes of quartz, and luminescent air-anemones that sifted the air for microbes. There were signs in a rock-fault that adult snake-rats migrated through the upper levels before they hurled themselves into the sea, and Seriathnis couldn't stop her fur fluffing out in a shudder. Another loss of face.

Which is why she didn't suggest they went back as soon as she meant to. It was one thing defying the Creator, but overdoing it would be stupid. Only she couldn't afford another drop in status before Ehrlatch.

Following the narrow, webless footmarks of the Irona-one, the twitchy hotskin and Hesperion, they saw where tiny creatures had crumbled away the edges of the indentations. Without the constant comings and goings of the tunnels up above, this place seemed quiet, and strange. Seriathnis began to feel uncomfortable in the brooding semi-dark where the smells of the pools were unfamiliar. Only she couldn't say so. She wished she had obeyed the Creator after all.

Little by little, Ehrlatch's wanderings led them to the decaying under-cliff forest. Dimly, by the peony glow, they saw the span of rock-wood rising like a rib-cage to cross the smelly pool, and they heard the chitinous fronds of hungry plants rubbing together at the wind of their passage. The hungry corals were just waiting down there in the dark for them to fall and be food.

But Ehrlatch didn't suggest going back.

He stepped on to the bridge that was like a spine, taking the comforting warm colour of the light with him. He began to disappear around the curve, behind the giant upreach of the ribs, and step by step, testing her way, Seriathnis followed him. She didn't want to abandon the smaller lad and she was too scared of something going wrong to leave him on his own.

She caught him up where he crouched to read the story of the Irona-one's escape. Glancing at it with little of his curiosity, Seriathnis finally said, 'Don't you think we ought to go back now, in case the Creator finds out we've gone?'

'Yeah, well, maybe. But wouldn't it be great if we were

the ones who discovered where those Arms are being grown?'

Seriathnis repressed a fur-lifting shudder with difficulty. 'The Creator might forgive us then,' she said, acknowledging her guilt out loud, 'but if we do find the Arms, what are two kids like us going to do about them?'

Ehrlatch shrugged. 'Tell a grown-up, of course. The Creator can deal with that if it comes to it.'

'I think we'll give it another five or ten minutes,' Seriathnis said, rubbing her webbed fingers together thoughtfully, 'but after that, Arms or no Arms, we're definitely going back.'

Ehrlatch bounced a little in his joy, and immediately felt the bridge shiver under his feet. The pink glow leaped a little, making the upward-growing branches crackle and twitch like branches in a fire. He laughed aloud. 'Hey, it's just like a see-saw! Have a go.'

Seriathnis said, 'Don't be so childish. If we're exploring, let's explore.'

'Killjoy!' He gave a few more little jumps. Seriathnis felt the bridge sway, shifting her balance from under her. She clung to one of the ribs, exposing her fear. She didn't hide her anger, either.

'Ehrlatch, I'm telling you . . .'

At last Ehrlatch saw the different possibilities: not fun, but a plunge to the people-eating corals below. Coming to rest, he said, 'I'm sorry, Seriathnis. I didn't mean to scare you.'

'You didn't,' she said shortly, and untangled her hands from the curving branch that hadn't quite given her the illusion of safety. 'Come on.'

Stepping off the bridge, they moved side by side now, ducking to check that no footprints were in the grit and dust beneath their feet.

Seriathnis kept muttering to herself, 'How long is five minutes?' and in acknowledgement of her nervousness, recognised that her time-sense was probably warped out of its customary accuracy. When Ehrlatch's hand ruffled the fur on hers, she folded her webbed fingers around his. It wasn't much, and neither of them said anything, but they didn't let go and somehow it was a comfort, that plugging in to another person's life-warmth in the dark.

The tunnel constricted, the roof coming lower so that they walked bent almost double on the black sand. There were plants here, and moisture that was a relief to their dessicated gills, vast growths climbing up from the sea through fissures the stalks forced in the rock. The walls glittered with some crystalline deposit.

'Look!' Ehrlatch pointed at a mass of webless footprints, some so fresh there was no crumbling around their edges. There were handmarks too, unwebbed ones, where big people had had to crawl.

Then, abruptly, the sides flared out and they were in a horizontal gash whose walls they couldn't see. On hands and knees, ducking below the stippled rock above them, they crawled further forward.

Which was how they found it.

Tang's rock, the crystal that was between animate and inanimate, the prize which Hesperion had stolen. His bargaining-counter, if only he had known it.

Perhaps he did. But he had died before he could use that knowledge.

The children looked at each other, the same thoughts in both their minds: 'If we take it back,' Ehrlatch said, and Seriathnis finished for him, 'the Creator will know where we've been.'

The boy's face suddenly split in a grin that seemed very pale against the russet of his fur. 'Not necessarily. We can say we found it somewhere in Eastcliff.'

'Why wasn't it found before, then, when we were all told to search?'

Ehrlatch had the answer to that, too. 'Because it was in a seasilk cave or something.'

'OK, you win.' Seriathnis stooped to pick up the greying, translucent quartz. 'We'll take it back.'

They turned back, Ehrlatch almost tiptoeing across the rock-wood bridge. Seriathnis held her breath until they were both safely across.

Faster and faster they went, knowing that every second's delay meant a greater chance of the Creator catching them out. Finally a change in the scent of the air, a fractional change in the colour of the light, let them know that they were nearly out of the cave.

Throwing the glow-coral joyfully aside, Ehrlatch put his head up and ran, elbows pumping, feet flying, towards the outside.

And fell. Went sprawling headlong, the webs on his toes catching in something on the ground.

A merchild, just like he and Seriathnis.

Except he and Seriathnis hadn't had the tops of their heads ripped open and the brains scooped out.

27
FLYING BEFORE THE WIND

Carandis shivered in the darkness as strange howls crept down the corridors to her ears. Not all the time, but every now and then. It would have been more reassuring if at least they'd been constant. If she had known anything at all about weather, she would have recognised that the sounds came closer or retreated depending on which way the draughts were blowing. But then, until she had come to hide herself in this angle between rough granite and bare limestone, she had never felt a wind inside the Mountain, and certainly not a hot, smoky one. There had never been any to feel, only the regular throbbing of the air-pumps hundreds of metres below in the roots of the Mountain, a womb-music so faint and so familiar to her that it had never once consciously registered on her mind.

Then, somewhere much closer at hand, she heard the whine of jets and knew that her Arms were coming.

At least, she hoped they were her Arms. What if it was some of the rogues? What if it wasn't Arms at all, but some weapon the mohock makers of eletacatricity had devised? How could she tell in this maddening power-down?

She laughed at herself. The mohocks, make anything?

The very idea was absurd. No, the lighting was playing tricks with her mind as it strobed faint and then non-existent, a flicker at a frequency that played havoc with her nervous system. And the wakers would come with that hideous, mindless growl she had heard in the Ear and Eye room. Still, she was too scared to laugh out loud. She only wished her personal Eye would get here so she could put as much distance as she could between herself and the locked E & E room. When the Arms destroyed it she wanted to be good and far out of blame.

Out of nowhere a light played suddenly full on her face. She pulled further back, cowering into the shadows of the niche until the tines of the granite dug into her shoulders.

The light went out but for the moment it had seared her retinas. Sightless, she waited for pain and torment, but none came. When the dazzle had faded, she saw her Eye hovering overhead. At least, she hoped it was her Eye.

'No,' she muttered, 'I'm not going down that road again.' Louder she said, 'I am going to delta five. Precede me. Find me a safe route and protect me from attack or from being monitored by anyone.'

Like a good little Eye, the shining globe bounced along in the air, retreating the way it had come. It led her onwards through the dim, uneven row, sometimes scything round angles at ground level and sometimes pouncing high at the corner of the ceiling. The Eye, too, was surrounded by the same reaching blue fingers of lightning that writhed from her skin. They wriggled like a cobweb in a draught. Or like a spider's web with a giant spider running out of hiding along the crazy strands. Carandis found it hard to concentrate.

The scream of jets whined sharper. Around a bend roared half a dozen Arms in a solid phalanx. They were huge. Their sound clapped over her eardrums, its backwash echoing on after they had cut their power.

Triad was only a microsecond away from knocking into her; she fell back, but there was no need. Triad's amplified reflexes threw him in a somersault over her head. He caught her as she stumbled. His grip was as hard and gentle as a tractor's claws picking up an egg. Yet he seemed untouched by a near-collision that had left her panting with fear.

The rest came to a stop at the same instant as though they shared a single mind. Silence was a vacuum where their noise had been. An odour of metal and oil and musky, drug-scented sweat assailed her. They were all around her, filling the row in three dimensions of transparisteel. The teeth of Synod, and she was a soft-shelled toy between them. Solid black against the gloom, they did not need to move to be menacing. Even the pale lightning that licked around them seemed under their control.

Yet Carandis had seen the three-pointed gleam of Triad's eyes. She was still safe. The Matriarch of the Admin said, 'Report.'

One after the other the Arms spoke as if they had been numbered. The voices boomed along her bones.

'Power supplies are disrupted—'

'Not randomly but in a pattern we are trying to identify.'

'Many machines have gone berserk.'

'Ear and Eye systems have largely been negated or destroyed outright.'

'Tranquillising systems are ineffective or inoperative on levels KK to single R. Also in some peripheral areas above that. There are some breaches in the gates between the Warrens and the Watchtower, but these are too dangerous for all but the most foolhardy wakers. The Waking is much safer doing what it is doing: slithering up the sides of the Mountain.'

There was a pause. The news was bad enough, but there was a hideous expectancy about the Arms that spoke of worse to come. Though the bulky figures in their carapaces never moved, Carandis could have sworn that they were looking at each other in fear or in shame, not wanting to be the one who gave the worst news of all. The pause could not have lasted more than a second or two, but coming from the mechanical, inhuman perfection of the Arms, it drew out ominously.

It was Destroyer who finally said, 'Seventy-three Arms do not respond. Some are killed. Some disabled. But some' – her voice was so low it tickled unpleasantly inside Carandis's ears – 'have been subverted.'

Carandis did not have to ask who by, but her next question revealed her suspicions.

'Does anyone know where Matriarch Bernardina is?'

'Only rumours,' said Triad lightly, as though he had been waiting for punishment that never came.

'Then destroy all the wardens within the Ear and Eye room. Make it look like wakers. But leave no evidence at all. None, do you hear me? Nothing to connect you or me with what you are about to do. Not even in the recorders. Clear?'

'Transparent.'

'Then go.'

Carandis snaked her arms up to muffle their departing roar before it ruptured her eardrums. The force of the sound stunned her momentarily and she glared at her Eye for not warning her how close the Arms had been. But the Eye had troubles of its own. It was wallowing in the turbulence they had left.

With the Eye to lead her through this benighted, lonely part of the Watchtower, Carandis moved much faster. It peeked around every bend, sprang out opposite recesses, circled behind her to check she was safe from attack. It even lit the unevennesses of the stone floor. Just having it there made her feel much less alone. Even now she couldn't quite believe this wasn't all some deep plot and that Bernardina was going to leap out on her from the next door, or the next.

After a minute or two Carandis came cautiously to a junction where the third north-west circular row intersected with a radian. She tried to blend into the wall while her Eye spun low around the angle.

The Eye jumped back on itself. Almost, she tripped over it. It startled Carandis, making her mouth drop open because suddenly there was no breath in her lungs. Her diaphragm tugged; the hot, dry air jabbed into her, scratching her throat with the chemicals of ash.

Out of the darkness ahead something rolled rattling along the ground. She strained to see what it was. The thing wobbled and clicked as it fell into a hollow worn by generations of feet. It spun around on itself, a thick, fat disk that clattered as it fell to rest.

Her Eye danced above and in front of her, protectively. All of a sudden she felt a fierce downdraught and there was a flash that momentarily seared her vision. Something exploded noisily. From beyond came the sound of racing footsteps, terrifying when she couldn't see what was going on.

Rubbing fiercely at her eyes, Carandis blearily saw and heard the crepitation as her Eye shot a thin bolt of lightning where the simple explosive had come from.

Her Eye would have followed but she called out in fright, 'Don't leave me!'

The footsteps faded but from the secret place they had gone there came a peal of ugly, mocking laughter.

Her fright lasted long after she got her sight back. Carandis proceeded even more slowly along the route to delta five. Her Eye took her right to the perimeter wall which arched inwards here above her head. Between partitions of granite there was a flow of veined limestone. She was in some sort of gap between two outside apartments and she stared at the Eye's peculiar behaviour. It was bobbling stationary above two bushes, and she couldn't immediately puzzle out what was going on.

From within one of the apartments came small, frightened sounds. From the other there exuded a feeling of abandonment she didn't even question. What mattered was that the apartments here had windows, doors, terraces on to the great world beyond the Mountain. Terraces that scaled from the Warren to the Watchtower. Weaknesses where the howling rioters could break in.

Through them, faintly, came the sounds of the mob in full-throated roars.

'What do you want me to do, you stupid idiot?' she hissed at the Eye.

In answer it shot out a pencil-beam of light. Through the leaves she saw a small sigil carved into the limestone. It was just for a moment, then she knew.

Blessing the thing, she pushed her way through the mock-orange blossom, not caring that leaves and twigs fingered her hair. Then she touched the carving.

Nothing.

The sounds of the riot were coming closer at frightening speed. Inside the left-hand apartment she heard a crash and a sob of terror. Carandis stopped, holding her breath, but around her now was silence but for that formless distant roar. Urgently she probed the rock, tried to twist the carving, thumping the wall all around it, heedless of the cold, slimy feel of the limestone.

The Eye spat light again, pointing dead-centre on a vestigial stalactite above the insignia. And Carandis found the door-control in the stalactite's shadow.

In seconds she was inside the limestone, at the top of a tight spiral that was slick underfoot. The door to this service-passage clunked shut behind her, cutting out all sound. There was no light at all here, not even the insane flicker of eletacatricity, but the Eye glided above her like a torch, and she could still feel the mad static tickling at the hairs on her lip.

She sped downwards as fast as she could, dizzying herself with the endless downturns. At one point she missed her step. Her ankle twisted beneath her. She fell, rolling downwards, her elbows and hips and knees colliding painfully with the central column and the hard edges of the stairs. Her head crashed into the outer wall.

Even though she knew it would hurt, she spreadeagled herself, trying to curl her head into her chest for safety while she wedged herself against the walls. Another metre or two and she brought herself to a painful halt.

Battered and tottering, she got back her breath and shakily set off again, always following that one comforting light in all the dark, oppressive, silent world. Her legs trembled with the constant strain of going downwards, and with the mad dance of eletacatricity stuttering over her flesh she could hardly think, let alone plan ahead. Still, that didn't matter. All she had to do was follow her Eye.

Until it stopped. 'What's the matter with you, you stupid thing?' she muttered, the savagery in her voice sharpened if anything by her need to whisper. 'Get on with you! I haven't got the rest of my life.'

She stopped, wondering if the rest of her life was going to be very short.

But the Eye stayed where it was, a beautiful iridescent orb that reflected the manic blue flares of eletacatricity in its pearly surface. And despite the pain still ringing in her head, she realised all at once that she had reached level delta.

The sigil here was plainer to see. She went to touch it but it reacted to the nearness of her hand. Before she laid her fingers on it, the door control parted the stone wall in front of her.

Darkness gave way to greater darkness as the Eye's light reached out along the row before her. The reek of smoke sawed across her dry throat and stung her eyes, but she could hear nothing that sounded like a human being. She went out cautiously, testing her footing, keeping her hand against the slick limestone wall. Little by little, groping her way through the gloom, she felt her way along.

By the flickering neon gleam of eletacatricity that streamed from her fingers she saw that the next door was delta four.

'I've made it!' she whispered to herself, triumph flooding through her. She took the next few paces. Writhing wires of blue flared from her skin so brightly now that she could see several metres ahead. Yet nausea and disorientation struggled inside her for control so that it took a little while before she could make out the sign upon the stone panel before her.

She had reached delta five.

Since she had heard from her mother, Irona's impatience to

get out of delta five equalled Toni's. It was not just the idea of a death that she didn't quite believe in, though she had to admit the fumes were not just a nuisance now, and the heat was a crushing pressure that evaporated the sweat on her skin as soon as it formed.

Glancing across at him, though, through the thick, acrid air, she had no idea what he was doing. His monitors were sending out olfactory messages and harmonic patterns as well as scrolling weird peaks and troughs across their screens. He obviously understood them, which was more than she did. It made her feel an outsider.

As she watched, he threw himself back in his chair. The chair's pneumatics protested.

Well, he obviously hasn't got very far, she thought, and in some ways that was obscurely comforting. It didn't solve their problem, though. She tried yet another way of keying in an order on the console in front of her. Yet again she rubbed away the tears that smoke stung into her eyes. *If only there was a mike-link working I might get somewhere*. Never mind that she felt light-headed, as though her brain were stuffed with the cold wet density of the clouds she had known over Eastcliff. There had to be a way of tracking down the source of the eletacatricity —

'There's someone trying to get in!' Toni said.

Irona leaped out of her seat, bruising her leg in her haste, but she hardly noticed. Crossing to him, she saw him stab his finger at a starburst pattern on a screen.

'I can't read it!' she said.

Clicking his tongue in disgust at her ignorance, Toni trilled three tonemes and the screen became a mirror of what was happening outside. And there, in the dim, now-steady light of the innermost delta row, was a figure with a fulminating corona of blue lightning.

'Carandis!' Irona exclaimed. 'Look! She's talking! Turn the sound —'

'Ssh!'

'... recognise my signal? I am Matriarch Carandis. Open this door at once! I demand access to delta five.' And over her head, in the smoke-wreathed air of the corridor, hung a moongleam sphere that was an Eye.

'We recognise your signal, Matriarch,' said Toni, 'but the door mechanism has chosen to override it.'

Irona signalled frantically to Toni. He palmed a sensor-switch and glanced at her, still keeping half his attention on the Matriarch outside. 'What now?' he whispered at Irona.

'Can she' – Irona nodded at the image on the screen – 'hear us?'

'Not for the minute.'

'Well don't let her in!'

'I can't. The door won't let me. But I would if I could. She is the Matriarch of Camelford, after all, and I still don't know who the hell you are.'

Irona rolled her eyes upwards in disgust. 'I'm Bernardina's daughter. Didn't you hear?'

'As a matter of fact, I didn't. Bernardina's daughter, huh? A bit bloody convenient, aren't you? Especially when Matriarchs aren't allowed blood-offspring. No-one on the Synod is. Now shut up and let me—'

'Just don't let her in!'

Toni turned away from her, palming his switch again so that the sound came back up over the pick-ups from the hall outside. '... because if you don't,' Carandis was yelling, 'I'll have your guts fed to the badgers in the Park, do you hear me?'

'I'm doing my best, Matriarch,' Toni said, drowning out Irona's protests.

'Well do it faster or I'll brain-worm you personally.' Then Carandis, scorched and blackened like the scarecrow remains of a queen, flipped one blue-fire-clad hand at her Eye and it opened fire.

It was a mistake. The door mechanisms retaliated. They flashed out an eruption of sheet lightning of their own. Carandis fell back, the incandescent fury concussing her, sending blood fountaining from her nose, leaking from her ears. Only a protective curtain of force from her Eye saved her from the full blast.

All the same Carandis staggered backwards, cannoning into the opposite wall, her head cracking hard against an icicle of limestone. Flittering fear-ghosts sprang fully-formed all down the row, their images faithfully relayed over Toni's monitors.

They paralysed Irona's breathing. Their terror staggered her heart, seemed to drop the bottom out of her thorax. She slammed shut her eyelids, but rot and death seemed to have scored the inside of her eyelids even in the fraction of a second she saw them.

'Don't look!' Toni yelled, and blanked the visual display, though an ocean of sound flooded into delta five from the corridor outside.

Irona retreated before it. Hands over her ears, eyes squeezed shut, she fell, battered to her knees by the unearthly sounds from outside, all the worse because she couldn't see what they meant.

Wave upon wave of sound pounded her. Sibilant screams from Sheol overborne by the distillation of a baby's dying wail. Hatred hissing disdain until her mind was a fiery lake of self-contempt. Subsonics that vibrated her internal organs until her own ears gushed blood and reason was crowbarred from her brain.

All that in the aeon of micro-seconds it took Toni to block out the aural weapons' resonance that poured in from the row.

In blessed release silence came. Irona found herself sobbing on her knees, her arms around Toni, his weeping as deep as her own. Soot-smeared, mind-scarred, the two of them clung together, but what comfort they found was pale and insubstantial compared with the havoc of a moment before. The horror was still inside her eyes.

It seemed a long time before reason returned, though when Irona could see anything beyond the ghosts of terror, the monitors' multi-facetted gaze winked out the message that only minutes had passed. Smoke gleamed where it caught the light and rasped at her breathing.

Eventually Toni said, 'I told you so,' and his whisper was a distant thread to which she could cling.

'Yeah. You didn't have to be so right, though,' Irona replied. 'What's happening outside?'

'Synod knows. Or at least, it will do eventually.' His words seemed to spasm, or maybe it was that her head ached so badly that reality phased in and out. The fear-ghosts hadn't quite gone from her mind.

Irona rubbed her ears to clear them. Her fingers came away covered in blood. When she looked, Toni was no better. Clots of crimson clung to the beard either side of his sooty face, already drying in the appalling heat.

But she had to know about Carandis. 'Do you think she's still alive?'

Toni shrugged, 'Do you want to look?'

Neither of them did. Dimly, through the walls, came the sounds of massive shocks. The door rattled in its frame but held. A crack split the partition wall and snaked across the plastic coating. Trickles and tributaries and rivers of dust burst inwards, spraying across the machines, and the sounds of battle were louder now, though the wall did not give way.

Choking, Toni plunged his hands downwards into the filthy fans of print-out still littering the floor. He found some relatively clean bits and flung them protectively over the surfaces of his beloved machines. The paper crackled, shivering like a sheaf of flowers in a nervous boy's hands, transmitting the knowledge that explosions were still occurring in the row.

'She's still alive, then,' Irona observed drily.

'Look, will you stop babbling?' Toni said. 'If she's still alive we've got to save her. For Synod's sake, she's the Matriarch!'

'Use that relay-pattern I couldn't read to see what's going on.'

Toni smacked the heel of his palm against his forehead. 'Stupid! Why didn't I think of that?' he said, and spoke to his machine.

Irona went back to the one she had been working on. Recorded dots and dashes told her Aleph-13 had died, angry at being abandoned. Still remembering the magma of self-hatred, Irona felt guilty for not saving the machine, but she brushed the feeling aside and cleared the screen. She found that, untouched by the fear-ghosts, it had been labouring to fulfil her previous command: to find the source of the eletacatricity.

'The Matriarch's retreated,' Toni told her. 'But her Eye's still out there. And a couple of Arms. They're trying to blow the door-mechanism. With a bit of luck we'll be out of here in a couple of minutes.'

Give me just a little more time, Irona prayed to a deity she didn't believe in, but what she said to Toni was, 'Have they got through to the control-panel yet?'

He shook his head in disgust, and sweat flew from his heavy eyebrows. The heat was worse than ever. 'Nope. But they will,' he said staunchly. 'We might get out of here before it's too late.'

Then I might finish this in time to show you what's going on, she thought, and offered Toni a distractor. 'How come the Arms aren't affected by the fear-ghosts?'

'What do you care?'

'Because if they're not, maybe the fear-ghosts are gone and we can get the hell out of here.' Irona carefully didn't say that she wouldn't let Carandis loose with the weather-control systems in delta five. 'And see if you can get through to the E & E room now, will you?'

'I couldn't before.'

But Irona knew that half the problem with the eletacatricity had been the system trying to contact her, and that was gone now. 'Try it anyway.' She held out a lure. 'Maybe they can do something from up there, now, before delta five's defences kill your precious Matriarch.'

Toni made no answer but she heard him give the order. She had punched the right buttons in his psyche. Now she had a job of her own to complete. It was not in her to give up. She turned wearily back to the screen in front of her.

And there, suddenly, was the answer to her problem: the source of the eletacatricity, just what she had expected. A 3-D schematic of the Mountain rippled like a fisherman's net in the tide and there was one pulsing glow.

Another tremor from the row outside. Paper whispered in answer to the crump of an explosion, but there must have been something in Irona's voice because when she said,

'Have a look at this, Toni,' he strode straight through the sheaves of paper to her side.

She didn't have to explain to him. Keying in the order to display all the cables, she showed Toni what she had found out.

Each strand of the sickly green glow showed the skeleton of the Mountain, a lattice that kept all its ant-like folk alive. The slightly off-centre peak of the tor crowned the matrix of power-lines that passed through every single room and ramp and row.

Before he could grow impatient she tapped in another order, the current state of the system. Shadows bled darkness into parts of the gridwork where the Waking had killed that section of the Mountain.

Then she blanked out all the 240 cycles per minute that the generators produced. What was left was a red stain, throbbing like a spider above its prey, pouring its venom down along the strands of its web to poison the Watchtower, the Synod, even the very heart of Camelford: the generators, and the lungs: the air-pumps.

And the ruby spider hung at the tip of the Mountain.

'But – Carandis – Matriarch Bernardina – that means . . .' Toni croaked.

'It means one of them's putting the eletacatricity into the system, yes,' Irona said, wondering still what her mother's involvement in all this was. She could not ignore the fact, though, that Carandis was the Matriarch of the Mountain. 'But there's nothing up there could generate the amount of ionisation she needs. She's getting it from somewhere else.'

'But she'll be in here in a minute!'

'Yes. Did you find out what's happening in the E & E room?'

'No.'

'Then do it, quickly. We haven't got much time.'

'Maybe she's doing it to stop the Waking,' he said, wanting to believe it.

'If she'd left the control systems alone the Waking would have been over before it started. Look, find out what's happening in the Watchtower, will you? We haven't got time for this.'

The door rattled again, as from some heavy concussion outside, and parts of the metal bulged ominously inwards. Toni stared at it through the smoke, aghast.

'Do it!' Irona yelled, shoving him back to his console while she tried to backtrack from Carandis's power-nexus to find where the eletacatricity was coming from. Though the air was rank and its toxicity was making her feel like an iron band was clamped around her temples, she still didn't want the doors open. She didn't want Carandis getting her hands on the most powerful man-made force in the world: the weather.

Minutes passed. Irona was panting now, her lungs thirsting for oxygen, but still she hadn't traced Carandis's ally. Or maybe, Carandis's controller. It was in the East, though. Definitely in the East, and somewhere to the North. It looked like it might be coming from New Estocolm, or maybe even Novaya Zemla. But Irona didn't know enough of the politics of the world to say for sure who it might be.

Toni gasped.

Then thunder and lightning blasted Irona against the far wall. A mighty wind tore at her hair, ripped at her shredded clothing, spattered her face with debris even as a light too fierce to withstand seared her vision. The temperature swooped so suddenly that her fear-sweat rivered glacially down her shoulders and between her breasts.

When the air cleared, she risked a squint.

Flanked by the black, solid bulk of two Arms, Carandis stood in a golden halo cast by her Eye. Blue wires of light danced from her flesh. She was swaying, holding herself up by extreme effort of will, and on her face was madness.

28
IN THUNDER, LIGHTNING AND IN PAIN

Twiss stared Arias straight in the eye, his face so near the Creator's that each could feel the other's breath on his cheek. On many a Kiflian, the trick of such closeness worked, especially when Twiss was as angry as he was now. Most men – or women – would have flinched at Twiss's invasion of their personal space, but not Arias Tang, not even on Twiss's territory, and they both knew it. Arias might have come across half the planet to find Twiss in the hospital right in the heart of Twiss's capital, but that didn't mean Twiss had the upper hand. Slowly Arias winked one of his blue-grey eyes not a handspan from Twiss's tired hazel ones.

Twiss made an inarticulate noise and flung away to sit down again at Irona's bedside. Ducking to avoid the banks of scanners and careful not to interfere with any of the wires and tubes running in and out of her body, he held her hand and leaned possessively over her inert form as though staking his claim on her in front of Arias. It was almost as though he knew how much that might hurt his adversary.

But Arias had more sense than to react. It wasn't that the

shimmering globe above Irona frightened him, as it did so many Kiflians. Arias knew better than most the havoc those Eyes could wreak, but he wasn't afraid because he knew he could never be a threat to her. It was more that his concern for his lost love was too deep. He just asked calmly, 'Any change?'

Twiss had to admit that there wasn't.

'Has Regen or anybody had a good look at that disk they found by her body?'

'He better have or I'll swing for 'un.'

'Ah, yes. An excellent solution,' Arias said drily. He leant against the wall, folding his arms and crossing one leg elegantly before him. 'And did Regen have time to report before you battered him senseless?'

'O' course I han't hit 'un! But—'

'But what?'

Twiss made his admission with his eyes still fixed on Irona's face. Of the three of them, only she was not clad in the luxury of seasilk. Only she could not move, or speak. In her mind were neither dreams nor dreads. Twiss listened for a moment to check that she was still breathing. 'But no-one don't seem to know where he is.' Then added hastily, not quite an excuse, 'You know what he's like, always shootin' off somewhere without sayin'.'

'A true original.' Arias nodded. 'I don't suppose you'd let me see what I can find out in the old Synod Tower?'

Twiss didn't ask him how he knew that's where Irona had been found, rather than in Tingalit's glassy grandeur where Twiss's Queen should be. He rubbed at his red-veined eyes and scratched under the shirt that was almost the same colour. 'Go ahead,' he said. 'Help yourself.'

Arias smoothed his fingers over the sleeve of his silver-grey tunic. 'I will in a minute, thank you. But first I ought to see Maerika. I'd hate her not to know how much I care about her. About all my people.'

'Your creations.'

Even Twiss felt the anger blazing from Arias's slatey eyes. Arias sprang upright, ready to do battle, and though he was slender compared to Twiss he was no less dangerous, a rapier to a cutlass. Not moving forward, he still radiated cold, threatening rage. 'You created a child with Irona. I created my children with the help of many people. Your child is dead. Do you think I want that to happen to mine?'

Twiss dropped Irona's hand as though it were nothing. He rocked to his feet in one fierce movement, stepping the two paces over to Tang. All the mistrust and hatred of the long years boiled up. His body was vibrating with the urge to punish the other. 'You leave my Arnikon out of this, you piece of shit!'

'Then don't lay a finger on one of mine again! Call yourself a king? Then look after all your people, not just the few who happen to have found favour for the moment. You're leaving my people to starve—'

'I'm doing no such thing!'

'You wanted me out of the way and you wanted new lands opened up. I wanted to get the hell away from a man who could slaughter innocent children by calling up a flood. We both want Eastcliff to feed the rampant population Harith's suffering from thanks to you and your Second Wave, and we both know it'll take time before we can even be self-supporting, let alone rich enough for you to cream off. But while you numb-headed Kiflians only send supplies in exchange for baubles, my folk will continue to grow cash-crops rather than food for their own bellies! Can't you get that through your thick skull?'

Frustration congealed around the tableau, its force challenging that of the sunlight that poured into the hospital room. Unspoken between them lay the power-struggle for Irona, for her ability to lead, for her intelligence and compassion – for her body and her mind. Arias wouldn't move to strike the first blow but he had no doubt that if it came to it, he could beat Twiss. It showed in every line of his whipcord body. And Twiss stoked up his anger towards killing-point.

Into this wordless, deadly confrontation came Jai, running through the arched doorway. Meek as ever where anything else was concerned, when it came to her patients she held nothing back. 'Be quiet, the pair of you! This is a hospital, not a playground! Now get out of here! And don't come back until you've learned how to behave around sick people.'

The two leaders stayed locked eye to eye in challenge until Jai seized them each by the arm and thrust them bodily towards the exit, saying, 'Out! Out! Out!' in a theatrical whisper that could have splintered glass.

Not in unison, the two men thundered down the corridor and out into the bright gold of a spring morning. They slammed out through the doors and into the fertile landscape of Kifl.

Sprays of lilac and rhododendron burst their breath-taking colours either side of the steps, and violets and late narcissi gave out their fragrance to the warm sea-breeze. Somewhere was the spicy scent of green-ball plants, and the musk of ground-covering native vegetation. Somewhere the silver thread of locust-lizard song stitched the cloudless sky.

Twiss and Arias pounded down the shallow steps and along the paths of white marble chips that First-Wavers still raked into decorative patterns, an activity that was so non-productive Twiss considered it almost treason. The elongated green lace of bamboo wove above the gentle clash of the stalks, but neither man noticed.

Then a locust-lizard swept round a bush towards them, its translucent gilded wings almost brushing their faces. Both of them ducked, though the creature made no move to plunge its blood-sucking belly-razor into them. Instinctively both men turned as if to track the threat, but the jewelled insect circled harmlessly in an updraught, its ruby eyes winking in the sunlight, and chimed its almost-melody upwards until they could no longer see it in the depths of the sky.

'Twiss, we beat them,' Arias said. 'Subharmonics, remember? Regen and I discovered them. We've staved off the snake-rats too. Rainshadow Valley is covered in farms now. We're winning, Twiss, we're winning. But it takes time. That shirt you're wearing—'

'So are you!'

'Save your belligerence. Yes, I know seasilk is great. And the shells are beautiful. But I've only got so many caverns I can farm and so many people to farm them with. If we have to grow seasilk to trade we can't be growing food at the same time, don't you see? I need access to your gene-library so I can culture some fish and some more edible seaweeds. My children are growing. Don't you know how much children eat?'

A smile of reminiscence pulled Twiss's face into pleasant lines. His hazel eyes were soft as he said, 'You should see how much Arnikon used to pack away at a sitting! Irona used to call him the eating-machine. And Jai's lad Beris – always on the go, he is. The only time he sits down is to stuff his face.'

Both of them knew that Beris was also Twiss's son, but it wouldn't help to mention it now. Arias held in the anger that wanted to burn out through his blue-grey eyes and said, 'Then you know what I'm talking about. Even the exiles you send me have to fill their bellies if they're going to be able to work. Twiss, I know it's hard for you. But out there we've got no cropland at all where we could grow grain or fruit, not where the snake-rats can't get at it anyway.'

Twiss began to interrupt but Arias held up his hand and plunged on, 'We will have. Oh, we will have. I'll fix those snake-rats yet, see if I don't. All it'll take is some more harmonisers, when you can spare some. We have found some more things we can eat, but Twiss, I need grain and fruit. For two seasons more, at least.'

'What about my people? Don't we deserve to eat too? After all, we're the ones who are growin' it.'

'And breeding faster than you can clear the land to grow it.'

With no answer but a grunt that might have meant anything, Twiss moved off along the pretty path, moodily scuffing at the designs with his boot-heels.

Arias turned the corner with him and leaned on the parapet of a bridge over a stream. Below him the water chuckled over its stony bed, and here and there fish flashed as they turned between the brown and yellow pebbles.

Twiss came to lean beside him, his elbows close to Tang's but not too close. A truce, not the cessation of hostilities. 'Irona's idea. The stream has like nets across it every hundred metres so's we can cultivate the fish.'

'You miss her, don't you?'

The Kiflian leader nodded slowly. Across his back the sun drew shifting patterns on the deep red of the seasilk. He kept his gaze on the sunlight glinting in the soft, peaty water. 'I do. I didn't think I would, but I do.'

'You know it has to be the Matriarch, don't you?' Arias said suddenly.

'Why does it?'

'Well why else would Irona be dragged away from her body?'

Twiss shifted his elbows, turning his face to stare at Arias. 'What you on about, boy?'

'Well you surely didn't just think she was unconscious, did you?'

'In a coma, that's what that quack Darien said.'

'How come there's no dream-activity at all, then? You saw the monitors for yourself.'

'Must of hit her head when she fell,' Twiss said thickly.

'Wrong. There's nothing of her left in that body, I'm sure of it.'

'How would you know?'

The sun was hot now, dappling down through the leaves in dizzying patterns though it still lacked several hours to noon. As if to cover up his feelings, Arias made a great play of rolling up the sleeves of his tunic while he said, 'I just do, that's all. The only one with resources enough has to be the Matriarch. It happened not long after there was a package from Earth, didn't it?'

Twiss shrugged, stared back down at the fish in the stream, and nodded. 'How did you come to hear about that?'

Tang didn't answer that one. He said, 'There you are then.'

'What for?'

Arias clicked his tongue in irritation. 'How would I know what for? I'm not the Matriarch. But if I can get at that disk, I might be able to find out.'

Twiss straightened rapidly. He clutched at Arias's forearm, his hand brown and strong on Arias's ivory smooth skin. 'Well don't just stand there, boy. Get on with it!'

Arias smothered a smile. 'I'm going to. As soon as I've seen my poor little Maerika. And as soon as I have your assurance that my people will be properly fed. But get it into your skull, Twiss, I'm not staying here long. You might have Arms, but we've got something worse. There's something stalking the corridors of Eastcliff and it's killed seventeen of my people. Then' – he stopped, a look of deep pain and horror darkening his eyes – 'then it eats them.'

'It eats them?' Twiss repeated, unable to take it in.

Tang nodded. 'Plus three of your dissidents have conveniently gone missing just when I wanted to ask them a question or two.'

Twiss rocked his head in what might have been a nod. 'Right. Well you come to the Synod then. Through the front door, this time.'

Arias glanced across at him, not quite sure that Twiss was attempting humour about something that had hurt him so deeply. But that was the way it seemed. The Creator smiled his thanks at the alliance, knowing all the same it might be temporary, but said, 'Just one thing, though. Do you think it's a coincidence that Arms suddenly start appearing right when Irona's out for the count?'

Speculation lit Twiss's eyes, then died. 'Yeah. It's got to be a coincidence, 'cos they come afore the spaceship dropped that package.'

They began walking again, the white marble chips crunching beneath their feet. 'That's what I thought,' said Arias. 'But if I'm not making the Arms, and you're not, who on Harith is?'

*

Arias, careful to show no sign of triumph, left the Synod shortly after eleven. He walked back through the hospital, passing the small side-wards where children played with bright toys after operations, or languished in the grip of illness that the natural healing properties of Harith couldn't tackle. Women cried out in childbirth or grieved for the stillborn; old men mumbled toothlessly of past glories and the chronically depressed ghosted through the wards, faces blank with the sorrows that overwhelmed them, and Arias found it oppressive.

Jai bumped into him as she was carrying a tray of instruments. They greeted each other warily, each of them knowing of the convoluted relationships that linked them, but unwilling to speak of such things openly.

'How can you do it, Jai?'

'Do what?'

'How can you work with all this pain and suffering?'

'Because I know it's going to get better. If I can help them heal more quickly, that's all I want.'

'Even those ones with the mental sicknesses?'

Jai smiled, her blackberry curls clustering low over her bright eyes. 'Especially them. Half the problem is they think it'll never get better. Once they know it will, that's it. They're OK.' She changed the subject adroitly. 'Come to see Maerika, have you?'

'Yes, and Irona.'

'Twiss won't be back now till about an hour before sundown. He'll be off drilling his guards and shouting at the administrators. Dr Darien has gone down to the beach with his boyfriend.'

'Thanks, Jai. I won't be too long.'

'Call if you need anything.'

*

Arias Tang carefully shut the door, seeing the protective Eye hovering like a bubble in the air above his lover's head. He ignored it and sat beside Irona, stooping forward to kiss her forehead, to brush a finger gently over the slack lips. Then he cupped the side of her head in one hand and lovingly stroked the soft curve of her cheek.

'Ro?' he whispered.

There was no response. He checked her carefully, using every scruple of the skill he had acquired over forty years and more of genetic engineering. She was breathing without assistance, her heart-rate was slow and steady, but there was no brain activity other than the autonomous functions which kept her body alive. Even the monitors could detect no sign of Irona's bright, affectionate personality inside that empty mind.

Tang's shoulders slumped. Even though he had known she was like this, seeing it was different. Seeing it hurt to the point of despair. He slid his arms carefully under her, cradling her head, but it made no difference. She never heard his loving words, his confession of his need to have her beside him. Her head lolled back, inert.

Gradually anger subsumed his pain. 'I'll kill that old witch Bernardina,' he said. 'I promise you, if she's hurt one hair on your head I'll tear her apart. Never mind what Twiss thinks, or what you thought. It wasn't him that held this planet together, it was you. You and your skill. And she's not having you back. We need you here. I need you. And so do your six babies. I made them, just for you. I wanted them to be a surprise. A compensation for Arno. They're all growing, some a part of you, and some a part of me, and some a part of – of Twiss, because you'd want that for Arnikon's sake. Nothing's going to hurt them. I'll take good care of them, my love. I promise you that. My people will too. They'll love your children just as they love you.'

Arias leaned forward again until he could feel Irona's breath fanning his cheek softly. 'You take care of yourself, my love, until I can get there. I'm coming for you. I'll get you safely back, don't worry, my darling Irona. Nobody's going to leave you alone ever again.'

Arias laid her tenderly down on her pillows and tucked the covers about her as tight as the arms of a lover. Swiping the tell-tale brightness from his blue-grey eyes, he stood, making his farewells, imprinting her beloved image on his mind. Then he strode out of the room.

Jai heard the transparisteel slam of the hospital doors behind him. He had already given Maerika Twiss's reassurances, and a neat puzzle-glass that delighted the simple fishergirl. What Jai thought of his visit she kept to herself.

Arias Tang walked swiftly through the heat of noon towards the old Synod Tower. Normally he would have delighted in the beauty of the pastel town by the sea, its gentle landscape such a contrast to the harsh black cliff where he had made a home for himself and his people. Now, purpose in his slim, elegant form, he made quickly through the bowery curves of the rows. Light and shadow slid over his sculpted face with its high cheekbones but no-one who had seen him could have doubted that he meant business.

But it was the siesta. There was no-one to see him. Even the caged locust-lizards were too torpid to sing on their flower-hung balconies. Not a soul was out on the streets.

Only two large, black forms who had cut out the sound of their jets. They stepped from behind the swag-bellied pillars. Jags of blue fire spun around him. Before he could so much as cry out, Arias Tang was their prisoner.

29
THE EYE AND THE HURRICANE

'Kill them,' Carandis said.

Toni couldn't believe it: good, pure-hearted Toni. From where the blast had knocked her against the far wall, Irona saw him staring in utter disbelief at the vision in the corridor beyond the torn doors of delta five. Toni was still sitting in his swivel-chair, soot and blood drawing watersheds in his beard, and above his dark pupils seemed to eat his eyes.

Triad blinked in triplicate and a grimace of pleasure cracked his inhuman face and the eletacatricity was reflected in rivers on the black map of his carapace. 'Fast or slow?'

Irona understood the implications as well as Carandis did. She couldn't help the sudden urge to relax in her bladder, and she couldn't make her lungs suck oxygen from the smoky, dust-wreathed air that all at once seemed too solid to breathe. Standing was beyond her. But she scrabbled seemingly at random amongst the smouldering papers in the angle between the console and the wall.

Carandis, still gold-lit beyond the entrance like a saint in some old triptych of the doors of hell, said to her Arms, 'You deserve your reward.' From her flowed a sick hot emptiness that she wanted to fill with Irona's pain. The Matriarch looked at her rival's daughter. She smiled and said to Triad, 'I can give you ten minutes.'

Irona forced a shallow movement into her chest and said in a strained, high voice, 'Toni will do anything you ask him to because he's loyal to you. Don't hurt him. And you need me for a bargaining-counter.'

Once again each of Triad's three eyes blinked and, on the other side of the Matriarch, Wilderness bared his rows of inward-facing shark's teeth.

Carandis said, 'You're right. I could have used you. I was going to. You were important enough once that Bernardina would have risked it. If you had stayed in Arms' Roost you would have been safe. But you didn't. You came here. Therefore you know something. Therefore you are a threat.'

'But if Bernardina knows you've killed me . . .'

Carandis too was a Matriarch. Carandis had empathy. She chose her words like knives to soak up the rich taste of Irona's anguish. 'You do know something. Plus you over-rate yourself. Bernardina has lived without you for forty years and more. Didn't she give you up once? She might have a momentary pang but she's too old. She's lived too long for you to matter that much. I'll be safe.' Carandis turned her head sideways and it seemed that the lightning wires of eletacatricity spat like snakes' tongues from her mouth. 'Triad' – Irona was that unimportant to her that she took her eyes away and looked at the chronometer scaling away on the monitor – 'get on with it.'

Irona sent a message down to still the frantic scrambling of her fingers so that she could pour all her force into her words. 'At least tell me where she is! She is my mother, after all.'

'How touching!' Carandis blew a parody of a kiss that turned her face into a sickening pout beneath the mad green eyes. 'Your dear little motherkins is in Novaya Zemla with her ring-car driver. The Crown's putting words into her mouth for me before she goes to see that bitch Jímenez. Now stop distracting me. Triad, Wilderness, you may begin. But make it hurt.'

Each of the black cockroach figures was half a metre taller than Irona. Triad's thighs were thicker than the waist of Irona's borrowed body. Hanging from the harness over his black carapace was his jet-pack with its store of solid fuel that could propel him forward to crush her faster than a flechette, and he winked open the round mouths of toxin-catheters in the knuckles of the hands which could have crushed her skull. But he flexed his hard-shelled fingers because that was how he wanted to tear her apart.

Irona saw it all in slow motion as though her mind wanted to expand each of her last moments so that she could never die. Fear was a pit of vertigo that wanted to suck her down and down and down.

Carandis smiled and raised her eyebrows and tilted her head in a little shrug that meant, 'You've lost, I've won,' and the gilded halo from above hooded her eyes in shadow. The fanged edges of the blasted door spiked high and low around her.

Triad lifted his leg ponderously to step over. The transparisteel toe of his boot clanged as he put it down on the floor inside delta five. Wilderness behind him and to one side was just beginning to move forward. Carandis smiled. Hatred and contempt battered her prey.

Irona looked for a weapon but there was none. Even the air-grating was buried out of sight in the sea of smoke-wrecked paper. Leaning heavily on the wall and the console, she levered herself upright.

Triad ducked to get below the steel icicles that still clung to the frame. And his fuel-pack triggered the door-defences. He exploded. Behind him Wilderness was caught in a chain reaction. Between the black flying scrawl of fragmented carapace, crimson and ruby fire shouted its triumph as it hurled ribs and skulls and toasted guts around.

In one last horrifying microsecond Irona saw Carandis's hair aflame then a sheet of fire and force tore the matriarch into fragments and flung them all away. Irona threw herself downwards, trying to bury herself in what safety the angle could give her. Glass screens imploded one after the other and the Eye droned and crashed like a damp squib. The sharp reek of fuel and the deep stench of excrement fell on her with the ugly red rain.

Finally, finally came silence. Only Irona could hear crying. It took her some time to realise that it was her. Then she could deal with it. All the same, like a child hiding under the bedclothes she stayed in her niche. It was too much. It was all too much. In her mind she was saying: *Make it stop please make it stop* over and over again as though there were somebody who could make it stop, some deity or some lover who had the power to put an end to the treachery and pain and deception; someone who cared enough to do it.

But there wasn't.

She didn't understand why her wounds didn't hurt. Burns and cuts and contusions, they should all have hurt.

She wanted them to. Deep in the oily swamps of her subconscious a part of her believed that if everyone hated her so much that they caused her all this, then she must deserve it. She wanted a knife to stab herself, or a hammer to break her fingers. She wanted to watch her own blood running out through the white skin and pink muscle, because she knew she must be evil.

Yet the kindly shock caught the physical pain before the neurons could fire across the gaps between her nerve-cells.

Head rocking, she pulled herself up to her knees and crawled across to the console seat where Toni had been. What she saw was not what she had expected. The high back of the chair had saved him from the worst of the blast and though he was unconscious and bleeding from a hundred superficial cuts, though his right arm now had an extra crook in it where the humerus was broken, he was still breathing.

Irona's guilt relaxed. She put her head on his lap and waited for the shudders to pass, and when he began feebly to stroke her hair tears came to her eyes again.

'I'm sorry,' he said. 'I should have believed you.'

She still rested face down against his legs. Her shoulders shook with bitter laughter. 'It's not your fault. You can't believe anyone, Toni. They all lie. You can't trust anything.'

'I didn't tell you, did I? What I saw in the Watchroom. Her Arms killed them all. She tried to block it but she couldn't. The Waking's still on. She must have started it.'

'We don't know that for sure.'

'Who else could it have been? Who else had the power?'

Irona sighed. Little by little she knew that she was going to have to start doing something; in a minute. She said, her words still muffled in the blood-smeared fabric of Toni's lap, 'You saw where the eletacatricity's coming from. Who else can get into the eyrie?'

His answer was indirect. 'How are we going to get Matriarch Bernardina back?'

'How are we going to stop the Waking? How are we going to take that weapon out of somebody else's hands? Why can't somebody else do something for a change?'

In what the Indios still called Texas, an old-looking woman came back towards the mission gates. Here outside, on the scrubland leading down to the river, hundreds of campfires were already starting and there was that smell of woodsmoke she always associated with sewers. Folk were singing out there, and laughing, and talking, and couples were sneaking off into the bushes, all the normal life between birth and death, but quieter, somehow; as if they were waiting. Many of them surreptitiously tipped their hats to the old-young woman, or nodded a greeting as if they didn't want to be caught doing it but couldn't help it.

She walked in through the wooden gates in the high adobe wall. Wearily she crossed to the clinic, though she knew it was empty, and wiped away the perspiration under the headband that held her greying hair. After a drink from an earthenware olla hanging in the breeze, she sat in a rocking-chair on a wide verandah under a bright and beautiful blue sky. As she rocked, taking pleasure in the breeze she made, she glanced down at her legs that were still thin and brown. Not like milk-bottles at all. And Pilar was so tired of talking it was a relief to be on her own.

It was the *hora de paseo*, the time of coolness that came before sundown, the Mission was waking up. Young men leaned against corners, watching the groups of girls stroll by in their colourful clothing, calling remarks that sent the girls red with shy, proud blushes. A bevy of plainly-dressed juniors passed by the brightness of life, capped heads down, eyes fixed modestly on the ground.

Something clouded the face of the woman in the rocker, a poignancy that her mind tasted like the sweet and sour pulp of a tamarind, but she returned her gaze to passivity and absorbed the sounds of the south-west. Waiting – like all poor people – was something she did well.

Children were running in and out between the almond trees, shouting happily about their games or arguing in knots about the rules that any adult had long forgotten how to understand. There were more of them now than there had been. From across in the old chapel that was now the shrine-room floated the soft chorus of response and antiphony from the matriarch and the juniors, and a drift of peaceful olfacts wafted towards her. The young-old woman felt the tug of subliminals; her fingers twitched with annoyance but she resisted it, focusing on the joyous trivia of living. Plump peasants used brushes to flick water from buckets on to the tomato plants, the beans and the squashes, so that the rich scent of moist earth rose up in benison.

Dr Tom came in through the old wooden mission gates, even his broad shoulders bowed beneath the weight of the two black bags he carried. He stepped back out of the way of two racing girls who hadn't even noticed him in the throes of their game. Smiling, he hefted the straps of his bags into a more comfortable position and started for his surgery. Only then did he see the old-looking woman called Dolores sitting on his porch.

She let her gaze wander across the open space with its tubs of flowers and the antique well-housing. Soon enough the big, blond man climbed the wooden steps. Nodding as he went past, he dumped his bags inside and came back out into the rosy freshness of the evening.

'Lot of people out there the last few days. Most be more'n a thousand. Ain't a bed to be had in the town. Me, I'm bushed.' He stretched, and Dolores stared at him in frank appreciation of the way his muscles filled his bright Navaho shirt. He caught her looking and she grinned at him, not the slightest bit abashed.

'Even an old woman enjoys looking,' she said. 'It's all we can do.'

Tom crinkled his eyes against the slanting copper rays of sun. 'You are forty-two years old,' he said, but he didn't stop his catlike stretching to get the kinks out of his frame.

'You peeked,' she answered as he came to sit on the bench beside her.

'Hardly peeking when your life-story has been on the holodisks all over Central America.'

'How is it that you know, Tom, when nobody else here does?'

'President Jímenez—'

'Call me Pilar.'

'Partly it was the actress – she didn't look a hell of a lot like you, and partly it was that nobody would expect you to be here. Anyway, who in this neck of the woods would remember seeing you when you first walked through all those years ago telling the poor that together they were strong? How come you don't do that no more?'

Breath escaped Pilar in a quiet sigh. 'That was when I thought it would be different for me. That I wouldn't have to be faceless like the old presidents because nobody would want to execute me.'

'Nobody does, much, else you couldn't of walked

halfway across the Americas. Talkin' to those folks out there, there's some clear from Ottowa or down to Yucatan. You should be proud of yourself. 'Sides, you didn't look much like yourself when you came in.'

'She didn't look much like me either, though, that actress, did she? She didn't have legs like milk-bottles.'

'There's nothing wrong with your legs, though I suppose even a President is entitled to her own insecurities.'

'You don't appear to have any.'

Tom touched the toes of his outstretched feet together in a little rhythm of his own. 'Appearances,' he said with a wry look at her, 'can be deceptive.'

'You didn't tell anyone else who I am, did you?'

He cocked an eye in her direction. 'Did you think I would?'

'No.' And neither of them spoke the threats that might have been.

'So, *señor médico*, I've shown you my insecurities, now you show me yours.'

Bats flittered high in the amethyst dusk. Stars began to gleam through the trees. From the kitchen came the homely smell of onions sizzling, and Tom talked.

'So I do good for these people because the Mission gives me the money and the space to do it, but they don't own me. They're a good thing, these missions, all up and down the world they do good.'

'Except in the Sahara Communes,' Pilar-Dolores said with dry humour.

'Except in the Sahara Communes. They got their own equivalents, of course. Pilar, stop throwing red herrings at me. I want to tell you this.'

'All right, I'm sorry. What do you want to tell me?'

The bench creaked as he shifted, and Pilar heard the fabric of his shirt brush softly against the whitewashed wall in the dying warmth of the evening. She waited, knowing that silence could be strength. That he, like her husband, could be trusted. But he didn't answer her directly, and his words were thickened with emotion.

Eventually Tom said, 'The Matriarchs, they use good as coinage. When folks come here, the lonely and the destitute, even if they steal, the mission gives back goodness for evil. But the Matriarchs, they don't do it out of love. They do it to buy power. In their goodness, they're lying to these people, manipulating them. If the Matriarchs were nothing but good, they wouldn't pretend that the Missions ain't theirs. Nor they wouldn't need to block people from travelling to the Admin Territories, would they? But I know. They do.

'Over there, the other side of the Atlantic, after the floods stopped rising, the Matriarchs stepped in to help what was left of the government, but they weren't helping. They were taking. Pretending they don't run the Synod. Pretending that's man's work, all the hard things like keeping folks down and half asleep. They put the people in nice, easy cages where they don't have to starve or to work or struggle or do nothing for themselves. All those people pay is freedom and the power to have children when they want.'

'You know better than that, Tom. We can't just go on having children who'll end up starving under the streets because if they come up into the light they'll be shot.'

'So they should do something better with them! Send 'em out to the star colonies. They should teach people, not blag their minds with drugs. And if the people do try to think for themselves the Matriarchs steal their brains.'

'And you still work for the Matriarchy?'

'I still work with the people who come here. I could have bought myself a clinic in DC knee-deep in carpets and ass-lickers if I'd specialised in diseases of the rich. You know that, Dolores-Pilar. I could have had women crawling over me, or men either, for that matter, only I'd never have known, would I, if it was me they wanted or my money. But I wouldn't sell my soul and the people who need me come here so I'm here where they can find me. Anyhow, you've brought me a fair number of patients, ain't you? I'm bushed.'

In the darkness, now, where mothers were beginning to shout for their daughters to come in away from the dangerous young men with their flashing smiles and shining eyes, Pilar listened, waiting still for what he had to say. But that was the end of it and when she had let the silence linger so long that he knew she had taken control of it, she said, 'And that, in answer to your next question, is why I'm here. By the way, I'm sorry you're so tired because in the next few days there's going to be a hell of a lot more people here. In six weeks of walking – and cheating, because I have to admit I did hitch the odd ride – I've seen more of my people than I have for years.

'I'm sorry, Tom. That's not what you wanted to know. It's where to start . . .

'Churches have always wielded secular power. They've had a hand in politics but I'm not letting them do that to my peoples. I'm not into religion as an opiate for the masses. If we work together, we don't need any opiates. All of us together, not just some crazy old woman on the World Council, that's what this is about. All the people that you have talked to and I have talked to. The Three Americas aren't perfect, Huitzilopochtli knows, but at least we don't gas the sewer-children any more.'

She knew Tom had heard the undertones of passion though she had kept her words calm. He said, 'I haven't told you anything you don't already know, have I?'

Tilting the rocker back as far as it would go, she stretched back her hand to pat his knee. 'You've told me you are an even better man than I had thought. That you can walk from temptation. What we have to do here is to keep the good and – ah – excise the bad. We need the infrastructure in place so that Missions can help our people. We're at the tip of a tentacle, Tom.'

'And that's so you can pass messages up to the brain?'

'You're right.'

'You're the President of the Three Americas. Why didn't you just call her?'

'I have called her. The Matriarch of All Earth is meeting me here.'

Bernardina heard the Crown say, 'The words you must tell her are in your mind, do you understand?'

Behind him, in the glade outside the ruined castle in the south of Novaya Zemla, Babushka nodded.

But Bernardina didn't understand. She heard the syllables only as sounds, saw the flowers only as colours and couldn't have said what the colours were. The Crown knew, because he could see in the psychic imager exactly what passed for thoughts in her brain.

'The words you must say to President Jímenez are in your mind,' the chubby man repeated, his sharpened tone reflecting his annoyance. He looked at Bernardina but she was still too far gone to make sense of it.

Babushka ducked an apologetic half-courtesy and started fiddling with Bernardina's controls again, saying,

'I'm sorry. I won't be a minute.'

Clicking his tongue in annoyance, the Crown rolled his eyes to the heavens. But he didn't notice the first faint traces of cirrus flecking the pale sky.

In Tau-53 in the Watchtower of Camelford Mountain, a body in a jar stirred. It was the perfect figure of a man, and it stared with empty black eyes at the other bodies with their hooks and wires and filters. If his head had happened to be under the surface of the nutrient fluid he would have died because he didn't know he had to breathe. But the genetic engineers knew, for Bernardina had selected them well. The body couldn't sink.

The trouble was, the engineers had fled the Waking that spread like a column of soldier-ants up the sides of the Mountain. The body had to come to fruition alone.

Arms and Eyes fought the wakers; raging fires broiled them; the death of the air-pumps starved them of oxygen; falling masonry flayed them; Arms and Eyes fell on them in their thousands; and thousands of wakers died. It didn't matter that some of them had started out in the sombre hues of sleepers and others in the skin and warpaint of mohocks. The common deaths had united them. The blood had stained them with the same uniform and their target was revenge. Most of them didn't know on what or on whom, but some of the sleepers and more of the mohocks knew exactly what they were doing. They just hadn't said yet.

Meantime, the body in the jar in Tau-53 kept breathing. All of a sudden it convulsed. Noises too formless to be screams escaped from the throat and the man's spasms tore out his own hooks and wires and filters, but not until they had held his face above the liquid so a personality could leap in with the air. He was violently and comprehensively sick.

But after that he climbed out, amazed at the strength in his muscular arms. He stood dripping on the tiles, cataloguing the sights and smells and sounds, including the communications relay that showed the Waking. Then, as he seized a sheet from a basket to dry himself, he suddenly halted.

Stock-still, he realised that he was thinking straight. That there was no flashing in his mind to splinter the thoughts. That he was for the first time in his life whole. That he had been well and truly regenerated himself.

Then Regenerator grinned and polished the moisture off his strong brown limbs and his full head of hair. He felt strong, and powerful, and – and majestic. He relished the smooth workings of the muscles that let him walk without jerkiness, that kept his head from twitching forward and his eyelids from blinking like a heliograph.

But most he loved the freeing of his mind. To have the hands of his brain reach out and snag ideas quicker than fish from the inflow of data. To be able to meld the ideas into long chains of thought without the shackles that had always held him back until people—

But they couldn't do that to him any more. He could see the eletactricity hovering in the fringes of the air, but it seemed to roll off his new body. It was joyous to be alive. To be Regenerator and alive.

As he slid into borrowed clothes he simultaneously slid into the communications network, looking for traces of Irona. It was like a sixth sense, an extra arm that worked perfectly despite the scars of the eletacatricity. The nausea didn't bother him because even feeling sick he still knew he was better than at any time in his life. Power was in him.

Traces of Irona lay all over the matrix, clues to her

existence for anybody who knew who and what she was. He saw what had happened to the E & E room, tracked her to delta five and saw what she was doing to the weather-control system, and in replaying the workings of one of the surviving computers, he scan-read the message her mother had left her.

'Poor kid,' he muttered to himself, hearing his deep, scratchy voice for the first time. 'No wonder she was going off her head back on Harith. And that bastard Twiss was no help.'

Then he found the yellow skeleton of the power-lines, saw the red throb of the eletacatricity. It started in the Matriarch's eyrie that Irona had told him of so long before. Two sets of computer activity down there in delta five. That meant there was Irona and somebody else. And if the weather-system was on the move, that meant the somebody else was its controller. So Irona would shortly be leaving. Heading to kill the cancerous eletacatricity so the Waking would crawl back into hibernation.

Regen almost turned to go, thinking he could catch up with her when she faced her oldest adversary on her enemy's own ground. But he didn't.

It was no trouble to slip down a message saying, 'Hi, Ro. Regen here. Meet you up at *her* place.' The trick was to do it without screwing up the program she was already writing. So Regen watched and waited a little until there was a hesitation in the duplicate of her program that he had called up.

Because even with his brains unscrambled, even with this wondrous smooth body, there would always be some part of Regen that couldn't trust anyone to love him. He had to let her know he was coming in case she didn't wait for him. And if he told himself it was because she needed to know she'd got back-up, it didn't stop him doing the thing that flagged his weakness.

Irona was scared so she tried to make a joke of it. Toni cracked gags of his own but she could feel the fear in him, the guilt and the uncertainty. Still she needed him, whole and working at what he did best. The cuts on her face hidden by synthflesh, she leaned over from her monitor and said, 'Are you OK, Toni?'

He swivelled sideways, careful not to knock his splinted arm. Nodding briefly, face grey and drawn with pain, he said, 'Are you sure you know what you're doing?'

'Yep.' She checked the controls with their weather-Eyes already in position. Oily black nimbostratus clouds were heaving into leaden formations that were continually ripped to shreds and reformed by the vicious gusting winds. Below, the gilded spires of Tallinn rose from the sea to flash in the livid sun and to the north tiny black dots moved like water-beetles, ferries taking tourists around the drowned city of Helsinki.

Irona tried hard not to think of the tourists, or the sea-farmers in their floating fields, or the marine-life in the cold salt sea. She said, 'It's a simple enough recipe, isn't it? Take a shallowish body of water like the Baltic Sea.'

'But they don't have hurricanes there.'

'Wrong. They didn't have. Maybe they don't have solid Sky there because they're right on the edge of the Admin Territories but it doesn't mean to say we can't bake them a little hurricane all of their own. It'll be a bit of a surprise, that's all.'

She gripped her hands together as if to hold in her patience and gave him the same arguments all over again. 'Look, Toni, either you do it or I do it, but one of us is going to. The Crown's got Bernardina, right? The only reason he'd do that has to be he's trying to take over the World Council. When he does, he'll impose his very own brand of censorship – mass slaughter of anyone who speaks out against him. Look what he's already done to Camelford. Look at the monitors, for Synod's sake! Haven't you seen what he's doing out there?'

He had. Unwillingly Toni's gaze slithered across and away from the images of murderous warfare in the Mountain. Not three levels below delta five, the Waking was battling a phalanx of Arms and the Eyes were slaughtering wholesale. A sea of fire was rising inexorable as the nova-death of the sun. He glanced down at his injured arm and looked at his own vulnerability with the door smashed to nothing.

Irona said, 'There's people dying in their thousands, Toni! I don't actually want to drop this little storm on the Crown's head, I just want him to know that I can. So don't make life harder for me than it is already, OK?'

She took a deep breath, ignoring the catch in it that was the echo of her sobbing from before. 'Take a warm sea and still air, and cook it a bit with half a dozen or so weather-Eyes for speed, so the air becomes humid and rises. As your warm air rises with its water-vapour, the space is filled by the cooler air rushing in from the sides. Especially if you start up near the Arctic Circle. Then you get some nice cool winds that are already spinning a little because of the Earth's rotation, and start rotating them faster over the sea because that'll give us a head-start. We'll soon have a nice steep pressure gradient that'll fuel itself for a while.'

Toni looked round wildly, trying not to think about the terrible thing they were doing. Also he didn't want to meet her gaze. Then something on the monitor where she had been sitting caught his attention.

'What's that?' he said.

She whipped round, ready to be overwhelmed by another burden of disaster. She glanced, stumbled across to her screen. Thumping down her chair, she leant forward, stunned.

And Irona felt tears come to her eyes, good ones, because there was Regen's message. He had found her. She was not alone.

Half-laughing, half-crying, Irona whooped and hugged Toni's good side. The emergency olfacts she had found in another room further down the corridor had put a lambent glaze on his eyes but he still knew what was going on, and laughing like a maniac didn't fit into it. Hc stared at her suspiciously, the sounds of her exultation battering his ears.

Irona saw it and didn't care. 'That – that's the winning factor. It's a friend of mine. Now I know everything's going to be all right. Look, do you absolutely promise me I can trust you? All you've got to do is put the frighteners on the Crown and then Regen and I, we can get down to business. The Waking'll be stopped and everything's going to be all right – so long as you don't let me down.'

'Huh. So long as the Waking doesn't get here before you've done your bit of dirty work.'

'It's not dirty, Toni. It's clean.'

She stopped talking because outside in the nest of rows sounded a distant crash. The scream that came next was so distant that it seemed like a programme on a distant neighbour's holodisk. But the faint roar that came with it was the sound of the living beast that stalked them: the Waking. 'Shut up and let me finish this reconnaissance, OK, Toni? And you hurry up and finish cooking me a good storm because I need it yesterday.'

So Irona sat, reaching into the system through her mother's control-codes, checking and re-checking that it really was the Crown who'd brewed sedition and terror . . .

While all the time the pseudopods of the Waking reached nearer and nearer.

30
THE EYES OF THE HURRICANE

Irona had run out of time to research. For once she was thankful for her empathy. She was sure it had shown her the way.

Now she finished her own program and told it to run. She only hoped she could trust the poor battered machine, especially when the others were shattered trash. Away somewhere in the gridwork of rows outside she could hear the gnome-screams now, hideous and shrunk by distance, and a thin bass roar punctuated by the tiny crump of explosions.

Now that the door was reduced to swarf, the air in delta five was clearer though smoke still puffed in sporadically through the ventilator shaft. Being able to breathe, plus finding the olfacts, had meant her headache had gone, and her nausea. She relished the recuperative powers of her new body, feeling a moment of longing to follow the sensuality in its heightened responses, but there wasn't time. Adrenalin buoyed her.

Toni said, 'What do you think of this?'

She stepped swiftly over to him, laying her hands on his shoulders and giving him a quick backrub because she could tell he was as close to exhaustion as she was. Lines of strain lay like nets on the pale cheeks above his beard, and sweat beaded the roots of his hair.

Reading over his shoulder she saw that he had indeed cooked her up a good storm: a pressure gradient of 80 millibars over a diameter of a little less than 100 kilometres. She looked through one of the Eyes.

Below the swirls of cloud that raced across the face of the Earth was the land-bridge between the Gulf of Finland and Lake Ladoga, a land-bridge that was a fraction the size it had been before the sea-level rose and drowned so much of the world. There were Tallinn and Helsinki on the curve of the horizon, St Petersburg and Viipurj, and the marshes between the rolling hills flashed livid in the sickly sun.

No numbered creatures there, with all the span of Asia a safe knowledge at the back of their minds. Freedom to live and hunt and die. Irona could almost smell the dank green ponds with the light sifting down to bless their depths. The frogs sang for her, and the dragonflies darted neon needles on their diaphanous gleaming wings. Children ran around the tractor-talkers who were walking their mechanical beasts back to the farmsteads through the fields of beet. Only now they weren't plodding with the weariness of day's end. They were anxious, flinching at the daggers of lightning, and the rolling thunder rolled the laughter out of the children until women and men and children were running in terror through the drowning rain.

Irona swallowed. She thought of the thousands maimed in the burnt-out caverns of Camelford, and she thought of the Arms roasting Thebula into a blackened calcified stick-woman. She thought of the shifting balances of power and the millions and millions of sleepers sacrificed to keep the Crown's Juggernaut. And she kept her gaze on the screens.

'Move it faster, Toni,' she said. 'Steer it this way.' And her Eyes let her see what she would sooner have forgotten.

From the drowned towers the miners were climbing out of the water. Amazement pulled their faces out of shape. They asked each other, 'Where has the storm come from?' and in the same breath shouted against a peal of thunder, 'Never mind! Let's get out of here!' They didn't say 'before the storm kills us', but it was what they were all thinking.

They started hauling up their golden salvage of the past but it was taking too long, too long. They abandoned their livelihood to the soaring walls of the waves. Under the whiplash clouds she had made, Irona saw them order their boats ahead through the canyons and peaks of the sea, and the wind sliced off the white crests of the water and spun them back against the miners' faces, and the miners tied themselves to life-lines and squinted through the salty lances of the spindrift to reassure themselves that their homes were still waiting for them though the dense clouds bellied down to attack in a threat built of purple and blue and black. But the rain crashed upon the waves and the waves leaped up in pain. Then the darkness of the storm swallowed it all and she had no way of knowing whether their homes embraced them in the end.

Thousands of tonnes of hot air were rising, and when the air reached cooler levels it inevitably began to condense as rain, losing heat in the process. That heat was picking up vapour from the sea again, so the whole thing was growing almost exponentially, with the air spinning faster and faster to fill the vacuum left by the centrifical force of the winds.

'You did it, Toni,' Irona whispered.

'I'm scared. Look at all those cities on the plain there.'

'Toni, don't you think I'm scared? I can see them just as well as you. Narrow it down a little, will you, and steer it down towards Kalinin. I've done all I can. I've got to go.'

'We're killing people, for Synod's sake!'

Howls shrieked down the corridor outside the mother of waters, delta five. 'Hear that?' Irona said. 'They're already killing people. We're just going to stop them.'

Pelting out of delta five, she headed straight for the Eye-store which was only a couple of levels above. Leaping obstacles and going as fast as her new body would take her up the spiral of a staircase, she outpaced the animal roar of the Waking.

It didn't take her long to open the inconspicuous door. It was right where she had found it on the screens downstairs, and the electronic lock seemed to take ages to function as she had programmed it. She filled in the interval by thinking, *Time spent in reconnaissance is never wasted*, though subjectively it felt like aeons were passing.

The door opened on to a narrow passage lined with slots. Each of them contained an Eye's remote control. It took her a while to realise that the darkness of the room was just that: the neon tongues of eletacatricity no longer rose from her skin. Picking a control at random, she discovered that technology had moved on while she was away in Kifl. She backed out into the corridor for a moment, using the ambient light there to see by.

The control was still a thin black pad as long as her hand, with a little screen at one end to show her what the Eye was seeing. But there were many new pressure-pads whose purpose she could only guess at, and since anyone who used them was trained up for it, there was nothing to show her which did what.

Huddling around the corner, she aimed at the mass of globes inside. On banks of shelves the Eyes lay like glistening eggs, but what they would hatch was death. Trying to see them without being in their direct line of fire, she rotated a kind of marble in the remote. It seemed the most likely guiding mechanism.

The trouble was, she hadn't got a clue which of the death-eggs it would touch; or if there were any charge in the remote; or power in the globes; or if it was the wrong button and she would blow them all up with a force that would rip open the flanks of the Mountain. There seemed to be a long time to wonder because nothing happened.

Then, from one of the lower racks, was a clittering sound. She peered and ducked back. Something gonged and rolled across towards her hiding-place by the door. But nothing attacked her.

Sticking her head out, she found an iridescent Eye trundling straight past her. It banged into the wall opposite, deflected into a new direction across the tiles that had it rumbling out into the corridor with never so much as an electronic blink at her. It was inert. Harmless. Useless.

Oh well, it was a good idea while it lasted. Irona shrugged, straightened, and in a shock of fear saw an active Eye staring at her head.

It was an idea she had stolen from Carandis and the flight to the Arms' roost. Practising hastily with the controls, she discovered that the Eye would lift her. It was sluggish, perhaps, but it would hold her weight. She aimed herself out through the doorway. She was half afraid that she wouldn't have the strength to hold on, but her new body did fine. Her smooth arms rounded with the power of her muscles. She stepped back and the Eye buoyed upwards but not so hard that it clanged off the ceiling. Irona got the Eye to put her down gently.

And the sounds of the Waking were reaching up towards her now.

Ordering her Eye to keep watch outside, she activated several more to produce stun-waves that would not kill. She groped back in memory to find a power and timing that would knock the wakers out for half an hour or so because if she hadn't accomplished her task by then, she never would.

Then she sent them outside, her own little gleaming string of pearls that would fly through the Watchtower and immobilise one limb at least of the Waking.

That done, she scooped up all the remotes and buried them under the pile of sleeping eggs on the top shelf where anyone would have to climb even to find them. After that, it took only a moment to programme an Eye to keep guard further down the corridor.

Irona had already mapped her route on the machine in delta five. Reality, though, didn't look too much like the map, especially with dense smoke belching from the air-vents. Still, the plan of Camelford Mountain hadn't changed since her time there; even if she had never actively explored this level, it was the same in essence as all the others. She counted off the radials and followed one.

Finding an outside room, she hesitated before its steel-shuttered windows. This was the dangerous part. She had no idea if the talons of the Waking had reached this far up the sides of the tor, but at least she could hear its growl only as a background noise.

The Eye blasted apart the catch on the shutters with a blinding flash of energy. The frame of the transparisteel itself was easy enough to unlatch so she pushed wide the window and stepped outside onto the little terrace with its potted jungle of plants. And, clasping the Eye with her chest half leaned across it, she ordered it up to the windows of the Matriarch's eyrie.

Now that Toni had taken control of the Sky, dawn was creeping blearily over the smoke-shrouded fields around Camelford. Except that this time, the dawn was the Sky going back to its normal daytime translucence and the sun appeared midway up the western quadrant towards zenith. Through the haze and the transparisteel it looked like a smear of blood.

Irona held tightly to the Eye as it fell upwards into the air. It pushed upwards against the place where her ribs divided and her heartbeat rocked against it, but it would not be for long. She watched the ground dropping away from her.

She glanced below, hearing the shouts, flinching as she saw the Waking throw stones up at her after the curses. Their rage barged up to meet her, but they couldn't touch her and the new light was dousing the fiery sparks of their torches. Suddenly the Waking seemed diminished and there was a tiny shoot of hope in her that reached out its radicles to enlarge her soul.

At the crest of the Mountain, all was as it had been all the times she had seen the Matriarch's sanctuary from the E & E room in the Watchtower, a room that opened on to all four compass-points. Its windows were open under bowery June roses, and now the sun had come out there were fat, sleepy bees bumbling their way into the nests of golden stamens.

Soaring up towards sanctuary, she breathed in the perfume that plumes of lilac spread: her mother's lilac; her mother's sanctuary. All the wood-masked shutters of the windows were folded back and a soft, golden glow welcomed her. She only hoped that the commands she had given the computers had killed the force-fields over the openings where so often, hiding in her Eye in the darkness of the night Watch, she had glimpsed the tired Matriarch leaning out to see over her Mountain, her crop-fields, her Park, her Earth.

Irona hovered cautiously where granite pillars held up the spike of the tor. Peeking sideways she saw a man in the eyrie: a tall, dark-skinned man with black, steady eyes. Strong and attractive, he held features that were the best of all races, a sort of glow of perfection that matched the stereotyping of the body she herself wore. Apart from Elditch there had never, as far as she knew, been a man allowed in sanctuary.

She still couldn't think of Elditch as her father.

The times were perished but even so, the Matriarchy would never allow a man up into the heart of their domain. Synod could be a government and a power of men, but not the Matriarchy. It had to be Regen; she hoped.

Irona reached out with her empathy, using it as a tool now to identify the personality under the smooth, tanned skin. His emotions held the warm glow of friendship, the broken shards of fear. Could it be him?

But the twist of his emotions was different. The doubts, the staccato shifts of feeling, they were all but gone, shrunk so small they no longer gave the acid taste of Regen. Yet strength was there, expectation and purpose and a total absence of malice. It had to be Regen.

She hoped.

Trusting that she wasn't blocking her Eye's defences, she glided in through the south window and landed on the acres of marble floor. The man watched her, calm and steady, lacking the vibrating tension Regen had always had. He wore only a sheet kilted firmly about his waist. The old Regen would never have dared such nakedness, not because of modesty but out of self-consciousness for his spindly, knobby limbs and little pot-belly. Not this man, though, sleek and strong, with the sunlight polishing his high cheekbones and the beautiful curve of his lips.

'Ro?' he said, not quite a question.

'Yes.'

A broad, creamy grin slid over his face, radiating such joy that Irona could hardly believe it. He said, 'Like your body.'

'And yours. Feels good, doesn't it?'

'You don't know how good.' In him were depths of passion that she had never heard before. 'Ro, meet Regen mark II.'

'I like your style. But I liked the old one too.' She caught the tips of his fingers. 'Thanks for coming for me.'

Pulling her into a hug that was fierce with his care, Regen said, 'Any time. Entirely. Except there isn't any time. Know where the transponder is?'

Sweeping the room with her gaze, Irona went to kneel under one of the window-seats where the machine in delta five had promised it was. 'Here.'

Together they went to peer at the mechanism hidden behind an oak panel. Crouching there in an angle, she could smell the strong, vital scent of him. It was musky, masculine, clean, with an underlying tang of nutrient chemicals. And for the first time ever when she touched him even accidentally, there was no tremble to his limbs.

'How's the Waking?' he asked.

'I've reconnected the fire-extinguishers – I hope.

Hopefully there'll be calmants starting to take effect because I think I've knocked the eletacatricity out of the olfactory system. And I've found out where it started, the Waking, that is.'

'What level, do you mean?' His voice was a pleasant basso profundo.

'Don't care about that.'

'Just to let you know, I've subverted some of the Eyes to knock the riot-leaders out.'

'So have I,' she said, happiness giving her strength. 'But what I meant was, the eletacatricity isn't coming from here, it's coming from Novaya Zemla. This should be the relay if I've got it pin-pointed right.'

'Do you know, I hate that stuff. Even in this body I can feel it prickling on my skin, but it can't get through this nervous system. Do you have any idea what that means to me, Ro? My last body, it vibrated at just the right frequency for the eletacatricity to play havoc with it, but this one's got more resistance entirely, 'specially since I reckon you must of damped it down.'

'Well, I've knocked it out of some of the grid. I felt like I had a nest of something crawling all over me and inside my brain. I don't think Carandis or Bernardina would have had the transponder installed here unless it was well-shielded though. I can't feel it, can you?'

'Only a bit. So what's the next part of the plan, Ro?'

She grinned as though it were all a game and not a shard of glass that twisted through her muscles and sinews and blood. 'I've plundered my mother's knowledge of the Crown. If I can't read a psych-profile now I never could. Only will you check out what I'm saying to him?'

'Will he listen?'

'I think so, Regen. I'm using a little idea I've pinched

from Twiss. I've sent the Crown of Novaya Zemla a storm.'

The Crown huddled against the massive grey stone walls. In this angle by a ruined chimney-breast there was still some remnant of a wooden roof to keep off the worst of the rain; nevertheless, the water pounded his balding head and beat rivulets against his eyes. Though he tried to keep them back, his servants were more scared of the storm that rampaged around them. Their closeness oppressed him as much as the fringes of the hurricane did.

Lightning daggered almost continuously. The roaring gale carved massive limbs off the trees to send them whipping against the stonework. A chair clattered past, spinning end over end, but in the growl of the hurricane and the lash of the deluge, nothing else could be heard. Babushka was on her knees in the weeds and the mud, clinging tightly to a huge block of masonry for fear that she might be swept away. The cube of stone had fallen so long ago that only the top of it showed like a tombstone. She looked like she was weeping over her own grave.

Bernardina thought her body could take no more. Each crash of lightning sent a judder through her heart and the tachycardia was making her dizzy. Some degree of logic had returned but when she groped for thought there were obstacles shattering reason and her thoughts burst away from her as though they were frightened hens. Even facing away from the slanting rain it was hard to catch her breath because the wind sucked at it and tattered her clothing into pennants which threatened to take flight and sail her up into the bruised and broken belly of the skies.

Away across what was left of the courtyard, a shaft of blue fire hit a ruined tower. The noise was deafening, drowning even the wind for a moment or two, then the stonework crashed to the ground, its delicacy gone as the carvings shattered into shards of rock.

Bernardina saw the Crown do something strange. A ritual gesture from some borrowed memory. He traced a vertical line and two horizontal ones on the air, and the sleeves of his sodden tunic seemed to glow the colour of blood against the background of lightning. In the pauses of the lightning came stroboscopic darkness.

From the trailing black curtains of the storm she saw a bird come whirling headlong out of control. She wanted to call to it, *Don't come here! The Crown'll get you*, but the thought remained as feeling because she didn't yet have words to form verbal concepts.

In pity she watched it come closer. It jagged and snagged erratically, but that, she saw, was because of the ragged lash of the wind. And it wasn't a bird. It was smooth and round as an egg.

It was an Eye.

Words came out of nowhere to slot themselves back into their places, waiting in the convolutions of her brain to make chains of meaning that could lay a handle on the world. Words, she saw, were power.

One of the servants saw the shining crescent of the Eye in the hurricane's night. He tried to shoot it with his recurved bow but the wet string slapped like an out-of-tune guitar and the arrow flew barely a dozen metres.

That was all it had time for. The Eye made a microcosm of the hurricane and the arrow burned turquoise before bursting into crocus-coloured flame that the cascading rain doused before it hit the tide of mud. Circling curiously, the iridium orb zoomed in close to each person's face, sending the servants yammering to their knees.

Then the Eye threw out a beam of light that was cinematic against Babushka's tombstone. It was the picture of a woman who seemed brushed still by the memory of girlhood. The curve of her cheek bloomed peach beneath the capless cloud of hair.

Bernardina caught her breath at the sight of that face from her past. She couldn't remember how many times she had visited the Tau-level laboratory to see how the girl was growing, the girl that would one day house her daughter's spirit.

What Bernardina couldn't understand was how the girl came to be here, now.

The girl's eyes were blue and seemed more made for laughter than for the bitter controlling words:

'Crown, your waking of Camelford has died. Your tool Carandis has died. Your scheme for upsetting the balance of power has died, and you will too unless Bernardina my mother walks out of here alive. Because what you have done to Camelford, I will do to all of Novaya Zemla. I have shackled the lightning and harnessed the wings of the wind. The old god of destruction, Hourah-acan, is charging down upon you, the god whose chariot wheels are of fire and who left the plains of Gehenna littered with lifeless bones. He will sweep the trees from your orchards and the housing from your mines. In one night the sea will rise up and swallow the rest of your towns. There will come no ark to save you, for he has read the evil in your heart. Not a shock of corn will stand and of your palaces, not one stone will stand upon another. The rivers will burst their banks and wash away the bloated bodies of your cattle and your sheep. If anyone is left alive, the cholera will come and they'll rot around this ruin that you thought was so secret. You'll watch your Babushka swell and blacken until her heart stops.'

The Crown held his hands in front of his eyes as though he couldn't bear to look. But he couldn't stop himself parting his fingers just a little to peep. Now he was just a little fat man with flags of hair flapping over the bald spots on his skull. The blood had drained back to engorge his heart so that Bernardina, looking at him in wonderment, knew he felt death inside him as well as out.

He tried to speak, couldn't. His mouth worked, the tongue probing behind his teeth for spit that wasn't there. Finally he forced his lips to say, 'You wouldn't. Wouldn't kill a nation for the sake of one woman.'

The girl was too young to be saying such things. But Bernardina knew, perhaps, that you have to be young to hold slaughter in the palm of your hand, and suddenly shame pierced her with agony. *Haven't I done the same? Haven't I driven my daughter away and made her a demon?*

But Bernardina's daughter said, 'For the sake of the nation I was born to, and all the other people who would be crushed when you topple the axis of power, I would do anything.'

Bernardina held her breath, wanting Irona to say, 'Yes, and for the mother who bore me in the baptismal fires of birth.' But that was too much to ask for.

All Irona said was, 'In a little while there'll come the eye of the hurricane. When the clouds have gone and the sky is calm, when the dead birds have stopped tumbling from their roosts in the trees, send Bernardina down to the carriage that waits for her in the ring-fires.'

Genuflecting, making obeisance, the boy whose nurse Babushka had been recalled all those tales of brimstone, and prostrated himself, hoping to appease the death that came nigh him.

*

The tractor-talker woke Bernardina, Matriarch of All Earth, when the ring-fires had given way to darkness. 'Matriarch?' said the talker in a small, scared voice. 'Matriarch?'

'Mmm?' Bernardina opened her eyes but there was no light to see by. None at all. It felt like the inside of her head was inhabited by a large black cloud. There was something she was supposed to remember but for the life of her she couldn't think what it was.

'Matriarch, wake up! Please,' the woman added belatedly. 'I don't know where we are.'

Bernardina felt less like a personage of power than like an old woman whose shoulders were growing humped with age and whose hands were warping with arthritis. Her mind wouldn't come clear and her head ached to the heavy throb of her labouring pulse. 'Where should we be?'

'I don't know.'

'What do you mean you don't know? You're the talker for the ring-car, aren't you? I gave you orders, didn't I?'

'Well, I'm sorry but I can't remember what they were.'

On the point of shouting, Bernardina stopped. Slowly she said, 'I can't either. Is there anything on the console to tell us?'

'The console's not lit up.'

'Ah.' It was a little dry sound, like a cough in the distance. Cautiously, Bernardina searched her own memories, but they seemed to skitter away at her approach and she couldn't pin them down. There was something she had to do, something she was supposed to say . . .

The air seemed dead and too dense to echo. She felt the weight of the planet poised over her and she knew she was somewhere in that hollow dragon of light far underground.

A pity the dragon's fires were dead and they were caught inside it as though they were leaf-mould inside a worm. Bernardina's head throbbed faster. 'Where have we been?'

'We went to . . . to somewhere there were birch trees and anemones in the grass, and it was kind of rainwashed and sunny.'

Bernardina nodded and wished she hadn't. 'Novaya Zemla. This is your ring-car, isn't it? Can you remember getting into it?'

A small, scared silence. 'No, Matriarch. I don't even know if it's mine. It feels like mine, but . . .'

'I can't, either. It's like there's a big blank in the middle of my head. What happened out there? Are you sure this is a ring-car?'

On that the woman obviously had no doubts. She said 'Yes' very firmly, as if that would help her to orientate herself, but it didn't seem to.

'Is it switched on?' Bernardina asked.

The woman groped about under her console. 'Er . . . no.'

'Then wake up and talk to your damned machine, for Synod's sake! Pull yourself together, woman!'

Voice-commands didn't register until the ring-car talker had connected up three or four cables by touch. Then the navigator-screen painted a picture of a simple, spindly web. Without warning, before the talker had time to decide where to go, let alone give the command, the machine lurched into motion.

'Slow down, girl!' Bernardina yelled, almost thrown to her knees by the lurch of acceleration.

The talker tried, by voice and manually. 'It won't stop!'

'Well, where is it taking us?'

'I don't know,' the talker said, her voice thick with the unshed tears of fright.

'Well, at least it saves us making a decision. I just hope it's not to that sick bastard Li Chan.'

31
KNOTS AND SCISSORS

When Arias Tang came to consciousness, he found himself in a chamber that shifted in his vision as though it were underwater. At first he thought the shimmering was a result of his unconsciousness, but his hearing stayed steady so he realised it wasn't that.

It really was the light moving, throwing rippling reflections on the floor, on the walls. On the door.

Door.

A way out.

From beyond it came a muted rumble of voices, deep, so deep that though the sound carried to the pallet where he lay, the words didn't. There was the smell of river-water, of mud and sweet decay that carried a hint of musk and metal and machine-oil. What he was doing here he had no idea, but the last flash-memory was of the Arms coming for him . . .

Arias needed all the strength of his wiry body to push himself up. First he achieved a sitting position, then verticality. His head ached abominably and he thought to himself, *It's a toss-up whether I vomit*, the faint ironic humour of which gave him enough force to explore his prison.

Its ceiling and walls were some sort of crysteel, hard, translucent but not transparent, radiating that faint illumination by which he could see. Peering more closely, he realised that he really was under water. He was under the bed of the river, and as far as he knew there was only one river on this side of the continent: the one that rose in the Moon Mountains and ran to the estuary around which Kifl was built.

No wonder Ro could never find where the Arms came from!

Tottering to the far side of the room where the door was, Arias was just about to put his hand out to open it when it opened inwards, knocking him down.

He scrambled back, trying to get out of the way of the attack he saw in the monster's face, for the Arm was monstrous. It dwarfed him. A fearsome beak took the place of its lips, and when it opened its mouth, he saw that the tongue and palate were formed of rows and rows of spikes.

Clawing to get to his feet, at least to die upright, he saw the armoured hands as big as shovels reaching for him.

The bed was in his way. He couldn't get up.

Vast grey-black tentacles were its fingers. It reached for him, the tentacles waving, and he closed his eyes . . . Only to find that it lifted him from the floor to place him gently on the bed. Arias opened his eyes.

'The fisherfolk tell me you are called the Creator,' it said, in a tone as hollow as Heralia. 'We had a Creator.'

Arias licked his dry lips with a tongue that was just as dry, and had to make do with a nod.

'Then help us for we are dying.'

Ten minutes later, the fear-sweat still drying on him, Arias was led to the ansible. The Arms had fed him dried fruit, and river-water to drink, but he still didn't understand why they hadn't killed him.

The tentacle-fingered Arm sat him on a chair before the machine set into the wall. 'From here is come our orders,' the Arm said. 'The Matriarch sends them. She woke us from our long long star-sleep and told us to frighten some of your little people in Kifl.' There were pauses between its words as though it was having trouble thinking, but it drew in a breath that let Arias know there was more.

It gathered its thoughts together and went on, 'To stir trouble. To frighten, to kill, so that your people will make a battle-force and your leader Irona will be strong for when she must will come to Earth to make the planet-peace, for Bernardina.'

'And you did. There's a militia – a guard,' Tang added, seeing the incomprehension in the indecisive movements his captor made. 'But Irona's already gone to Earth. So what do you want me to do?'

'I want you to tell us first how not to die, then—' The vast Arm looked down at Arias. In its eyes there was a shadowy look of puzzlement. 'Did you say' – it paused – 'that Irona is gone to Earth already? This should not have been.'

Again it sucked its breath in to let Arias know it wanted to say something else when it could catch the thought. Arias could see how hard it was trying; he waited patiently, consumed by curiosity. At last it said, 'And, and I want you to talk to the little matriarch on Earth and tell her not to make us kill.'

'Just don't do it,' Arias said in wonder.

'She puts the thoughts in our brains. Our bodies are made to obey her. We can't not do it. But now we can't make our minds work. We can't direct our flying. We are falling into mountains, trying to breathe under the sea. Our bodies are falling apart, brains like mush. Look at my hand hurting.' The creature stretched out one massive limb and put the hand, with its scaled tentacled fingers, right up to Arias's eyes. The scales were pulling away, thick, greenish pus oozing from the gangrene beneath. A stench of putrefaction wafted strongly upwards.

Arias didn't know what to say. He had to turn his head not to gag. Groping for words, he asked, 'How old were you when you were put on board the ship?'

'We hadn't been grown very long. We were young and strong. We were young and strong when we landed here, but Harith is not a good place for us. For you, it makes your bodies good, the fisherfolk say. We saw them once, children who were not frightened of us, when they were down at the river-mouth. This world makes your bodies last. But we are not good here. It makes us get older by the day.'

Suddenly a light winked on the ansible, a flashing, wordless pattern that had no meaning for Tang. Yet it must have had meaning, for immediately the Arm jerked upright, heading for the exit, the floor clanging under his boot-heels. It was checking the circuitry in its limbs for that lethal discharge of lightning . . .

With all his strength Arias picked up the huge, Arm-sized chair and smashed the panel.

The Arm jerked again, unbalanced. It caught itself against the wall and slid slowly to a sitting-position, cradling its injured limb against its chest.

'So simple. So simple,' it said, shaking its head. And died.

Arias walked dazedly out of the ansible-room. Other Arms were outside in a larger chamber. Their enormous bodies were sprawled every which way, slumped over tables and piled in the doorway leading to the corridor beyond, as though when they too had felt the call they were heading for the exit to execute some murderous command. Now, no longer linked to that central control, they ceased to exist.

Not quite believing, Arias took his time picking a way over the heaped-up corpses. He had to climb; it was not hard to find toe- and hand-holds on the black, matte-scaled carapaces, but it turned his stomach. Despite the destruction he had witnessed on Irona's viewdisks, he felt something akin to pity for the death of these monsters.

Slithering awkwardly down the other side, he looked back at them. 'Whoever made you is the real monster,' he said.

Arias was world-weary when he finally staggered out of the mud of the estuary. His head ached and his body felt disjointed from the electric shock which had captured him, but how he felt emotionally he could not tell. It was as well that he had to concentrate on crossing the distributaries, heading for the largest, southernmost stream which led up to the docks at Kifl. The walk back was hot and long.

There was a tractor at the quayside beside a fishing-smack. A talker and two fisherwomen were unloading their catch on to the tractor's rear flatbed. They weren't hurrying; the heat of late afternoon and their cheery gossip made sure of that.

The Creator simply walked past the vehicle on the other side, climbed in and ordered it to take him to Jai's Hospital. Too surprised even to call the tractor back, the three of them stood flat-footed and open-mouthed and watched the tractor's balloon-wheels rolling up the slope into town.

Tang was almost sure that the Hospital was where he would find Twiss.

He was right.

The Kiflian leader didn't even look up as Arias walked in. Twiss sat on the edge of Irona's bed, holding her hand, stroking it, leaning forward to whisper something, his mouth close to her ear.

'Twiss, the Arms are dead.'

That did make the Kiflian leader look up. 'What did you say?'

'I said the Arms are dead.'

'Then I was right!' Twiss said. 'You did make them.'

Arias sat heavily on a chair and put his feet up on another one. 'Try not to be more stupid than you usually are, Twiss. Of course I didn't make them. I told you that. No doubt Irona and Regen did too, and your blasted Eyes that you sent peering all round Eastcliff.'

'Well who did then?' Twiss asked pugnaciously, disbelief still written all over his face.

'The Matriarch.'

'Oh, very likely.'

'Stick your sarcasm where the sun doesn't shine. You must have realised that we haven't got that sort of capability – or the inclination – to make Arms here. Why the hell do you think most of us came to Harith in the first place? To get away from crap like that.'

Twiss paced across the room to the counter under the window, where he stood thinking, his fingers drumming an irregular tattoo on the flat surface. 'What makes you think it was the Matriarch? The Arms' attack started before the last ship came by.'

'They came on the ship before that. Your ship. I was wondering whether maybe the *Starbird*'s approach had anything to do with their waking, but apparently not. Apparently they got their instructions by a primitive ansible that fed straight into their brains.' Tang explained the whole thing while Irona's empty body breathed quietly on its own in the gathering dark.

Over Camelford too the sun was setting, the real one, not some Sky-induced illusion. Though the Watch was dead, crushed and maimed by Carandis's Arms, Irona and Regen had a plan to save what was left of the Admin's capital.

The first thing was to cut off that eletacatricity from Novaya Zemla. Unfortunately Carandis had had the transponder surrounded by all sorts of protective devices, not least of which was a small force-field that crackled whenever Irona or Regen attempted to touch it.

But Regenerator, in his strong, non-vibrating body, relished the challenge. 'Oh, you don't know how good it feels, Ro, being able to think straight for the first time in my life. This ain't difficult,' he said, kneeling near the machine and looking up at her.

'It isn't?'

'Hah. Piece of cake. Entirely.' He stood, not a little man any more but a tall, bronzed warrior with a cheeky, white-toothed grin. Grabbing her wrist, he pulled her over behind the Matriarch's flotation chamber. 'Don't just stand there, girl. Shove!' he said.

When she added her muscles to his, the dense, black oblong began to slide over the marble floor. Once they had overcome the inertia it went faster and faster, slamming into the force-shield. Wild waves of light flared from the collision, sheafs of colour blaring in a crash of sound. The fluid inside the box sloshed out, first drowning the circuitry then splashing back over the couple from Harith.

'How's that then, Ro?' Regen beamed.

'Pretty good! What's next?'

'What's next is to get in touch with that Toni feller and get a lid on this panic. Plus making sure the Crown ain't cheated and got no troops storming up from the ring-cars or somethin'. You coming?'

'I'm not staying.'

And, with the flotation fluid still dripping from their soggy clothes, the couple from Harith headed down for delta five.

It wasn't hard. Tom followed Pilar Jímenez Costanza from his clinic in San Antone Mission across the midnight shadows of the compound to the huge double gate. They opened it.

Alarm bells started to ring immediately, though as calming olfacts were poured into the air at the same time, the one counteracted the other. The Matriarch and her juniors flooded out of their apartments; the orphans and the vagrants pooled out of their dormitories.

But outside, on the dusty plain, thousands of people started forward the moment the gates opened. One, two, hundreds, the defences could have coped with, but not the sheer number who had answered the call of Pilar Jímenez on her walk across two of her Americas. All night they had been arriving, coming to join the thousands who had already arrived.

Now they walked in through the gates and there was nothing the Matriarchs could do about it. The capped, blue-clad figures fled in bewilderment to their shrine. They barred the door, desperately trying to put in a call for help to the next nearest Mission.

Before they could, though, Pilar gestured and a hundred

volunteers broke down the door. They thronged into the room, seeming to fill it, then somehow, miraculously, they cleared a path through their numbers.

Pilar smiled and said, 'Thank you,' walking along between her peoples, the Whites, the Blacks, the Indios, the Asians. At that moment she felt very proud.

'Tom, can you open a channel for me to Camelford?' she asked.

In answer he came to stand beside the contour-chair a junior still occupied. The girl looked around nervously then slid out of the seat. Tom, with his lifetime spent in the Mission, had no difficulty putting the call across the ocean.

With the eletacatricity gone, there was still the damage the Waking had caused. More and more, though, the trio in delta five managed to bring the control-systems on line, because whatever freedoms were right, still wholesale murder was not the way to achieve them. Too many people were dying.

All the same, Irona found it hard to trigger the olfacts, the Ears' body-harmonics, all the ways the Matriarchy had made the Synod and the Watch keep the sleepers asleep for so long.

'Not to worry, Ro,' Regen said cheerfully. ''Least we ain't got to brain-worm no-one.'

Irona shrugged dismissively. 'What worries me is where on Earth has Bernardina got to?'

'Er, I don't want to worry you unduly,' Toni said, instantly achieving just that, 'but there seems to be a call coming in from the President of the Three Americas. Who shall I send it to?'

They looked at each other. No Carandis. No Bernardina. No Watch. And no Synod.

'Erm, I suppose I'd better talk to her,' Irona said.

Pilar spoke directly, not having sent a message-disk this time. After introducing herself from what looked suspiciously like a Centre Shrine, she said, 'I'd like to speak to the senior Matriarch present.'

'That would be me.' Irona was acutely conscious of her filthy, bedraggled state.

'Have you been having problems?'

'The Crown of Novaya Zemla sent us a Waking and kidnapped my mother, Matriarch Bernardina. But we've handled it. What do you want?'

'Ah. I wondered what the delay had been. We'd actually expected Bernardina here a while ago. Did you say you were her daughter? I thought that was against your Matriarchy's rules.'

'It is.'

'Ah. And where is Bernardina now? I don't quite see how you fit in.'

'My mother was put back on a ring-car. I assumed she was heading back here. Apart from anything else, she needs treatment because the Crown appears to have done something rather nasty to her head.'

Pilar said, 'Ah,' again, unwilling to commit herself until she knew which way the wind was blowing. 'Hold on a moment.'

For a minute or two, Irona, Regen and Toni were left staring at a screen that displayed not the bland blue mantle of the matriarchy but a ferociously-coloured condor winging above the world.

'At least they ain't playing none of that crap music,' Regen said. 'Why don't you see if you can track down your mother's ring-car?'

'I've tried. Toni's got nowhere with it either. That part of the system's either blanked or inoperative.'

So they waited, tension gathering in knots in their muscles, while Toni continued to try and patch together the remains of Camelford's life.

The screen flickered into stillness once more, and there was the flat Indio face of Pilar Jímenez. 'It seems that the Crown has sent Bernardina straight to us. I don't think this is good news if he has implanted something.'

'Oh, he's done that all right. Where are you?'

Pilar said, 'San Antone Mission. Are you coming over?'

'Right now. I'm on my way.'

32
IN LIGHTNING'S WAKE

When Bernardina and the talker awoke again, not knowing how they could both have fallen asleep in the fire-ringed tunnel, the car was slowing of its own volition as it pulled to a halt in what was recognisably a station. The crysteel walls curved to part in a tunnel-mouth that let in the sky. For there was no smear of the heavens being excluded by transparisteel. The sense of displacement grew. Above, where they had expected to find daylight, was a night lit with stars and flares and shooting rainbow sparks.

'What are they doing to my Admin?' Bernardina asked. She didn't expect an answer, and got none, for the talker was gazing as if hypnotised at the fireworks.

The talker opened the door. It let in the noise of a crowd watching transient fiery beauty with ooh's and aah's that somehow held a different quality than those at Carnival back home. A quality of bright life and sharp joy.

Shakily, the two women stepped down from the car. Bernardina found herself so weak that she actually had to ask the talker to support her. It felt strange to find another woman's arm around her waist – and worse, to need it.

They walked feebly towards the exit. Out here the air

had a strangeness to it that Bernardina had never experienced: dusty and fragrant with trees whose pollens she had never known. Over it all, though, was the sharp, disquieting odour of woodsmoke and burning chemicals. Dread rushed over Bernardina: *is it a Waking?*

But as they came to the lip of the cutting, it became clear to them that they weren't in the Admin at all. The first thing they saw was a building of adobe, tiled roofs and semi-circular arches, that wasn't native to the Admin's Northern Isles. Nor was the compound, with its coloured lights strung beneath silver-leaved trees, and the gates flung wide showed thousands of campfires glowing friendly in the dark. Only the stars were anything like the same – *but then,* Bernardina realised, *I've never really looked at the stars in the first place. They were just a blurry mass that held my secret dream – Irona.* The winking gems overhead absorbed her mind since the shock was too great to bear.

In all the thousands upon thousands of people, nobody seemed to notice the tottering women. Everyone was too busy looking at the shooting rockets, the roman candles and the golden rain.

Bernardina had never been ignored before. Feared, hated, envied, admired – but never ignored. She didn't like it.

Then someone in loose white trousers and a colourful tunic stepped regretfully away from the display and came over. As the woman neared them, Bernardina saw the high-bridged Mayan nose, the dark eyes, the braids that should not have been streaked grey.

'Jímenez!'

'Matriarch.' Pilar nodded briefly, a courtesy that Bernardina failed to return.

'Why have you brought me here?'

'Firstly, to tell you that I had nothing to do with whatever mischief the Crown has tried to carry out. Secondly, to offer you hospitality.'

'No thanks.'

'Oh, you needn't fear poison from me. But if you want to go hungry and thirsty, that's up to you. And Dr Tom – wherever he's got to – can sort out quite what it is that the Crown has done to you. Your daughter's very worried.'

'My daughter? Here? On Earth? You've seen her?'

Pilar smiled gently and shook her head. The braids pulled a little against the bright, coarse fabric of her tunic. 'No, only by com-link. But she's on her way. She's most concerned about you.'

Bernardina couldn't think of anything to say. She found herself mirroring Pilar's headshaking, and stopped, but no word nor gesture came to fill the gap.

Pilar linked her arm through the Matriarch's, saying, 'You look like you've had a terrible time. Well, in fact I saw a viewdisk of part of it. Your Irona's a most resourceful young lady to have extricated you, wouldn't you say?'

A battery of flickering images assailed the Matriarch of Matriarchs: green, flowered woodland scents; red silk; sugared cakes; pain and the forlorn drooping tail of a hanging squirrel, a storm that flung her against a gravestone, a Valkyrie who didn't look like her daughter . . .

But as Bernardina couldn't pin down the false memories from the true, she declined to comment. Somewhere a recollection was fighting to burst through into awareness. Something she had to do.

A large, male figure detached itself from the crowd on the steps of a low annexe. His eyes glowed briefly in the darkness as a rocket exploded in a shower of purple light. Pilar passed the aged Matriarch to his care and said, 'I will come to see you later. My home' – the Mayan's teak-coloured features split in a sudden grin of humour – 'is your home.'

The President of the Three Americas walked back down the steps, but Bernardina didn't look at her. She felt instead the soothing powers of a shrine coming from inside the softly-lighted building. The tall, blond man came down a step or two to stand beside her on the old, creaking wood, and take her arm comfortingly.

'Ma'am, you ain't looking too pert,' he said to Bernardina. 'Whyn't you come into the clinic here and let me fix you up a bit?'

So, little by little, Bernardina let herself be charmed by Tom's transparent simplicity. The reassurance of the familiar olfacts, the very atmosphere of the Mission, made the Matriarch feel at home. And if Dr Tom used the Mission's sublims on her too, well, that was only to the good. After all, hadn't Bernardina originally written them for herself?

It never even occurred to ask her where the matriarch-incumbent was. But that worthy lay where Dr Tom had put her, hypnotised by her own shrine.

Noontide in Kifl.

Twiss sat solemnly in his Synod Chamber, wearing his kistle crown and presiding over what was left of his council: Sticker and Tebrina for the Second Wave and Baika, Nona and Less for the First. For the first time in fifteen years, Arias Tang was there too, but nobody dared ask Twiss or Tang why. In the doorway Garwin stood with the ugly shape of a flechette gun across his muscled chest.

The aqueous emerald light was slashed across Twiss's face by spars of bright sunlight coming in through the shattered dome, but at least the 3-D town on the table before him was as it should be. All the broken glass had been cleared away; the tiny mirrored figures were coming home. They should have been sauntering home from their morning's work, or gathering in the shady courtyard of some tavern for a drink before the siesta, but they weren't. They were pushing themselves through the gathering heat, making sure they were somewhere they could see the strange announcement.

Twiss hardly noticed. He checked himself in a broadcast monitor. His shirt was a shimmer of gold, his jacket and trousers a rich brown that might have lent colour to his pale face – if the green light hadn't swamped it in a sickly hue. He passed a hand over his unruly hair, using the monitor as a looking-glass, and said, 'Do I look all right, then?' One tuft of hair on the back of his head stuck up, glided like a feather by a bar of sunlight.

Baika nodded.

Nona was more forthright. 'No, you look like death warmed up. You must have lost about half a dozen kilos in the last few weeks.'

Less smoothed his badger-striped eyebrows with one knuckle and said, 'It doesn't make any difference anyway. Synod knows what you're up to. Rearranged everyone's schedules and wouldn't even tell us what for, frightening half the people to death. Noon's when you said the message was going out, so send it out and have done. You might have told us what it was,' he added grumpily.

But there was no time for that, for Baika had turned on the recording disk. Out in the town, over the Rainshadow Valley, Kiflians everywhere had come in from their normal routine to watch the special broadcast Twiss had insisted on.

Nearly everyone tuned in. They expected news of hundreds of Arms slaughtering the population, or for Twiss finally to call the Second Wave to massacre the First. They didn't get what they expected.

Twiss said, 'It don't matter whether you're First Wave or Second. They Arms have gone, and it weren't none of us what made them: not First Wave nor Second. Them of you as won't believe me, you might believe Tang. And I been with Lowena and the Guard to check it out.'

Arias told what he had found: the rotting, mindless hulks of the Arms Bernardina had planted when their colony was young. Teacher-disks showed it all compellingly, even the shattered machine Tang said was an ansible, so that those with the fanciest sets could smell the gangrene in the dankness of the river-bed. And there, at the end, was the heap of monstrous corpses blocking the doorway.

Then Arias gave his confirmation. He was dressed in cool, pale grey that shone like a starlit sea when he moved. He was calm, slightly remote somehow, the random sunlight polishing his cheekbones. Looking at his sleek, dark hair and his blue-grey eyes, a new generation of Kiflian women found a fantasy figure to beguile them.

'So you see,' Twiss said, when Arias gestured at him to speak, 'it ain't none of usn that's doing it. First Wave and Second Wave, we got somethin' real to worry about now. We got the Matriarchy.'

In delta five, in the heart of the Admin, Irona and Regen saw that everything was gradually coming back under control, and made their decision. The President's words might be a trap – but then again, they might not.

'Regen—' Irona said, and stopped.

''Sall right, girl. I'll come with you. 'Fact, you couldn't keep me away. Entirely. I ain't never got to meet no like real royalty before.'

'Don't let King Twiss hear you say that.' Both of them grinned.

Neither Irona nor Regen had ever ridden the ring-cars before. Yet both, through their spying from years before, knew exactly where to go.

'Are you sure this is a good idea?' Toni asked sleepily, across the Ears' subsonic calmants. He blanked them off from delta five, but still echoes of the body-harmonics came in through the blasted doorway. 'I mean, it's not as if there isn't plenty here for you to do.'

'Toni, now we've got the Crown tied up and the eletacatricity off, all you have to do is call the relief watch and see if you can round up a few survivors of the Matriarchy and the Synod. Elditch, even' – her voice caught at the memory of her father – 'if he's still alive.'

'Yeah, but—'

'But nothing.' Irona finished plaiting her red-gold hair into a neat wreath around her head. 'With the eletacatricity gone, the Zemlan Arms are dead. You find your trainees and get them the hell up here, or wherever you need them, and get the aftermath tidied up. I've got to get hold of Bernardina before she accidentally wrecks the balance of power and some other rising nation steps in here to fill the vacuum.' She turned to Regen. 'Do I look all right?'

The little man, who was little no longer, glanced at the patches of synthflesh, the char on her torn blue robes, and said, 'You look fine. Let's get on with it.'

So now Irona and Regen stepped down from the ramp

into the shadowy station and across to the small shed. Peering in through the glowing windows, they saw the talker quietly meditating in the sun-and-rose light of the station shrine. Automatically, Irona's hand went down to pray along the knots of obedience on her belt, but Regen's fingers caught her wrist. She nodded.

Opening the door to the peaceful smell of the shrine's olfacts, Irona said, 'The Matriarch Bernardina needs me. I am to go to San Antone Mission.'

The talker, a woman in her late sixties whose face shone with tranquility, scarcely started. She bowed her head and said, 'I am the Matriarch's to command.' Not once did she ask about the Waking, but as she closed the shed door behind her, the couple from Harith noticed that she left the shrine running and the mystery was explained.

Irona was dreading the questions the woman might ask about the tall, wide-shouldered man walking calmly by her side as though he belonged in this matriarchal environment. But when he stepped from behind the corner of the hut, Irona merely said, 'The Matriarch has imprinted a message on his brain for delivery to the Mission.'

The woman merely bowed her head again. 'The Matriarch's will be done,' she said, and ordered the car to open its door for them. Irona tried to look as though she travelled in ring-cars all the time, but at least she had the experience of Kiflian tractors to show her which was the talker's place and which the passengers'.

At first both Irona and Regen had a tendency to duck as the circles of fire seemed to suck them out of the darkness. Irona clutched Regen's hand, wincing a little as his fingers pressed the synthflesh over her burns, but the ruby and gold and diamond flares yanked them unscathed through the burning hoops and pushed the car out along the darkness behind.

The talker hadn't even noticed. Down here, where the ring-cars burrowed deep beneath the earth, no wakers would ever come. Because how could the sleepers think the cars were anything but legend? Her security was complete.

Irona made a mental note to warn Bernardina about it.

She didn't notice that she had been asleep until the talker said, 'San Antone Mission.'

Irona raised her head from the muscle-padded warmth of Regen's shoulder and rubbed her neck. She felt well, and strong, and hungry – until she realised that at last she would be meeting her mother for the first time in more than forty years. Nervousness assailed her, quivering in her stomach, and she was glad to have Regen by her side.

He smiled at her, swiftly brushed a wisp of hair from her forehead; but, because of the talker, he said nothing. Irona smiled back at the momentary tenderness, and she noticed that in this body he no longer smelled of fear. She wondered what she smelled of herself.

The talker ordered the car to stop. To open the door. From miles away Irona heard her. The woman's simple, almost lineless face was serene beneath the symbolic cap. She knew she had done her job well.

Irona could hardly breathe. She kept forgetting to, and consciousness brightened and faded, brightened and faded. The trembling wasn't just in her stomach now, but through every part of her body and in her mind. She could feel prickles of sweat starting on the arches of her feet and under her arms. Sickness began to gripe inside her, and her tongue seemed to swell in the desert of her mouth.

Regen nudged her and stood. 'Thank you,' she muttered to the talker in a voice that was not her own, and descended from the round, glassy car into the ruddy light that flooded from the tunnel mouth. She would have fallen if Regen had not been there to steady her.

As they walked towards the red light outside, Irona wondered if it was fire like the Waking had brought. But once they had stepped out of the lips of the tunnels, she felt a smile tugging at her borrowed face.

For just as in the maternal peace of Centre Shrine, there was the rosy light of dawn. To the west the sky was still freckled with friendly stars above the sheltering purity of the white walls, and overhead there was the promise of blue in the sweet, endless air. But over the sleepy buildings, clouds were nets of pearly gold and soft cushions of pink that invited her to comfort and to rest.

In the blossom-ripe trees, birds were beginning to sing a hymn to the dawn. There was no-one abroad. Irona stepped free from Regen's support and raised her arms to the freedom of the air. He folded his smooth-muscled arms across his chest and smiled, but the smile was the sweeter for the sadness in it.

At last she twirled, a serenity in her gaze that steadied them both.

'You all right now then, girl?' Regen asked gruffly.

She nodded but it was a while before she spoke. All the time the day was brightening. 'It's like – it's like I had to go through my fear to come out into – into this. Like I had to make lightning and dare myself to bathe in it.' She closed her eyes, and saw the blue flares of eletacatricity spiking from her skin, and the lightning-bolts of her hurricane whirling through the storm above her mother and the Crown. Softly she said, 'I was so scared it would kill me. Who was I without the Watch to shape me? Without – without my mother to love me? Or Twiss? And I had Arno' – tears starred the blue-green of her borrowed eyes – 'till

I lost him to the volcano. And Arias, though he never loved me enough to brave Twiss's anger – but was I any better? I had happiness, Regen, oh, I've had great happiness. It was the sweeter because I knew it couldn't last. And I've always had one good friend.'

Irona patted his arm, looking up through the lashes where tears still gleamed like pearls in the gilded morning. 'But I've died a thousand deaths, and love has burned me like lightning because it's never stayed. And this – this is the fiercest storm I've ever had to face.'

She sighed, and from beyond the wall the first signs of sunlight speared across the courtyard. Sweet bells chimed to call the Matriarchs to their shrine, and Irona looked about her at the first threads of smoke spiralling from the chimneys, the first blush of colour coming from the geraniums hanging in their pots.

A woman, greying braids held back by the beaded thong across her forehead, came out of a door, shutting it carefully behind her. A colourful blanket floated around her shoulders as she crossed to them. 'You are the Matriarch's daughter?' she asked.

Irona nodded.

The woman smiled a welcome that was deepest in her dark brown eyes. 'Then come. You are welcome here.'

It was something Irona had dreaded time after time after time. Rejection, humiliation, a sudden love bursting the dry stream-bed it had abandoned so long before. Though her legs shook and her fingers would not still their trembling about the coffee-cup, it was nothing like she had feared. *All those dreads. All those imaginings – all wasted. So much of my life wasted in defence against terrors that were never this shape.* What she felt, more than anything, was exhaustion.

The withered old woman lying back in a padded rocking-chair looked her up and down with sharp eyes, and finally nodded. 'You are my daughter.'

Irona inhaled the pine and lavender and rose designed to give peace in the clinic of San Antone Mission. She was scarcely conscious of anything but the figure with its purple lips and wispy down-tugged eyebrows, yet in the background she felt the sublims. On the corners of her vision she saw Regen, the big gentle doctor and the woman who was President of the Three Americas. None of them were as important to her as the Matriarch, but the Matriarch was a shell of the woman who had drilled a hole in her skull and put the empathy-enhancer inside her.

Irona sipped the coffee and nibbled at a piece of sweetened corncake, hearing the tinkling of spoons as the ritual of courtesy that channelled pain deep below the surface like a sunken stream. The birds were still threading their song through the morning-light; the matriarchs were chanting and somewhere two kitchen-helpers were hurling extravagant insults. Finally she acknowledged, 'I was your daughter.'

Bernardina rocked back and forth, back and forth, in the padded chair, its runners creaking rhythmically on the floorboards. 'I'm glad you've come home to me, Irona. I've missed you.'

Irona spread one hand in a shrug, the corncake still crumbling between her fingers. 'I missed you, too, once. Do you know what it was like to go home and find it wasn't my home? To stare at where my family lived and know I wasn't even part of it—'

'But you were!' the old woman said so forcefully that Tom leant forward to lay a hand on her wrist.

'Not enough to be asked to go with you,' Irona said.

'Not even enough to be told you were moving. I got back and all that was left was empty spaces on the walls where our pictures should have been. Even my stuff had gone out of the cupboard and I never saw any of it again. What could I ever have done that was bad enough to deserve that?'

'I had to do it!' Bernardina shouted, and Tom rescued her cup from her violently-gesticulating hand. 'I couldn't take you up to Synod and the Matriarchy with me, and if I hadn't blanked your memory they'd have brain-wormed you. I did what I did to keep you alive.' The old woman sounded indignant now. 'Your memory's come back now, hasn't it? You've been the Matriarch of a whole planet. Isn't that enough for you?'

'I wove a hurricane and plaited lightning and brought you out of Novaya Zemla,' Irona shouted.

'I've sent you across the stars to grow strong enough to inherit the Matriarchy. Now you're back to receive your destiny.'

'Yeah, but it wasn't even you that called me back, was it? It was Carandis, and she tried to kill me.' Irona was panting with emotion, her hand gripped so tightly around her half-empty cup that Regen feared she would shatter it.

'That's why I hadn't called you back yet,' Bernardina yelled. 'But now you're here I can give the Matriarchy over to you. Who's that with you?'

'I don't want your damned Matriarchy. I'm sick of my life being a payment for everybody else's wellbeing. I don't want the weight of another planet on my shoulders, thanks very much!'

'Who is he?'

'He's a friend. And now we're going home.' But Irona stopped suddenly, because she no longer knew where home was.

Bernardina said, 'But you can't! Who's going to look after the Earth?'

Pilar had said nothing for so long the two Matriarchs had forgotten her existence. Now she leaned forward to take the cold cup from Irona and said, 'I think if we took a little air, we might find out the answer to that one.' She stood up decisively, and the positivism in her tone and action led the others to follow her. She it was who linked arms with Bernardina, and once they had gone down the board steps of the clinic, Irona came sheepishly up to take Bernardina's other arm. They seemed somehow to be drifting towards the open gates.

The Matriarch had never seen anything like it. Thousands of people were camped outside the Mission, a whole seething township not under anyone's control, and Bernardina was frightened. The babble of voices seemed to her to be threatening, so voluble was it, not at all like the sleepers she had watched over so long.

But there was no threat. Tortillas sizzled on flat rocks around the cook-fires, children played noisily, and women gathered fish in the river below the flats, while men scavenged wood or carved sandals out of abandoned ground-car tyres. Yet, at Pilar's approach, all movement stopped. Then the crowd parted, to fall in behind the President and the two Matriarchs in a silence that strained to hear every word the leaders might drop.

'These,' Pilar said as the Matriarch and Irona drifted to a halt at the edge of the clearing, 'these are the people who will take care of the world. Come here,' she beckoned to a child of five or six who could have been boy or girl in leggings and bound braids. 'This is the future.'

Bernardina breathed hard, and the air whistled through her mouth. The child, black-haired and blue-eyed, sidled round her and slid a hand into Pilar's, keeping a wary watch on the elder Matriarch.

'This is your son?' Bernardina asked.

'No.' Pilar squatted to embrace the child on level terms. 'Not more than any other. But these are all my children, or my mothers and my fathers, all the brotherhood and sisterhood of our world. We are responsible for each other, aren't we?' she added to the little one, who put a finger in his mouth and stared at her from big, puzzled eyes. It was still early enough for the morning to throw long bars of shadow from the trees over the gold-lit sand.

Bernardina pushed her hands into the wide sleeves of her blue robe. It was obvious she felt hurt that the child had gone to her rival, not come to her.

Pilar looked up at her. 'The only power—' And she broke off.

It was the word 'power' that had done it. That was the seed that the Crown's Babushka had planted in her brain.

Bernardina, ruler of the single most powerful force on Earth, head of the World Council with a power-web stretching beyond the black void between stars, crushed a porcelain tooth-cap in an involuntary spasm and dashed a hand to her mouth to gather the venom on a nail. Bright turquoise as the stones that decorated Pilar's headband, sick blue as copper sulphate, the poison gleamed evil on Bernardina's nail in the instant that she reached to claw Pilar's eyes.

But the child pulled her sleeve, then Bernardina was pressed to the trampled earth by a thousand people. Irona tried to move but they immobilised her as well, and her friend.

They let Dr Tom through, though, to stop Bernardina

dying of the Crown's poison, then they let her up at a sign from President Jímenez.

Pilar said, 'These people, and you, and me, and all the people of all the worlds, we are more strong together than any force you can name. Even the Crown and his brainwashing,' she said with humour. 'We can boil up lightning and pass through its fire, and spin words between the worlds, and the only thing that makes any of it work is that we work together. Not fighting, not suppressing and killing, not having factions on councils run by ambitious men. Together, my sisters, together we will be all right.'

The people patted her – Bernardina, Irona, Regen, and even Dr Tom; then hands reached out to embrace and be embraced.

It was two days later, then, that Bernardina and Irona, arm in arm, went to the secret room cut out in the granite of Camelford Mountain. Regen stayed on guard outside, for there were still a few dazed mohocks wandering around even up here in the Watchlevels.

'And this really can speak between the stars?' Irona asked, looking at the ansible's lights start to flicker as Bernardina powered it up.

'Yes, my love, it really can, if there's nothing in the way between here and there.' She made no mention of the Arms.

'I wish I'd known it was there sooner,' Irona said.

Knowing what she knew, Bernardina replied, 'It's probably just as well you didn't. Anyway, we can see if—'

'What's the matter?'

'Look, somebody's trying to call us.'

Across the light-years glowed the loving face of Arias Tang.

33
FIRES AND ASHES

'Arias?' Irona's whisper rode the wild spaces between the stars. From the secret, sparkling granite womb in the mothering walls of Camelford, he heard her, and the old Synod Tower of Kifl tiptoed out of his sight.

'Who's that?' he asked, peering at the screen, and Irona felt a new wound in her, though she knew in this artificial form her once-lover couldn't recognise her physically. But he hadn't known her mentally, either.

'It's me, Irona. I'm in a borrowed body in Camelford.' She turned her head to one side, spoke to Bernardina whom Arias could not see. After a moment she said, 'It's all right now, Arias. I'm alone.'

Alone. The word echoed like the closing of a door.

Arias said, 'I told Twiss that's where you were, but he didn't believe me. I'm coming to get you now.'

With a sad smile she said, 'I'm all right, Arias. I'm coming back soon. Regen came to get me. Have you been looking after his body?'

An expression between distaste and regret crossed over Tang's features. 'I would have done, Irona, but I've only just this minute found it.'

'But Arias! He must have been there days!'

'I'm sorry, Ro. I was on my way up here to Synod Tower but the Arms captured me, and Twiss never thought to come up here. I got here as soon as I could. When I found him, I put a little water in his mouth. There hasn't been time for me to do anything more. I've sent your two bodyguards for help.'

'But he's still alive? Tell me, his body's still alive?' Irona couldn't keep the anxiety out of her tone.

'Oh, yes.' Tang swallowed, stretched his neck briefly towards the open window that showed the cone of Heralia snowy against the blue, blue sky of Harith.

She watched the way he breathed the fresh, inflowing draught of cedar and snow-winds. Irona closed her eyes a second, knowing the noisome state her friend must be in had stirred all Arias's fastidious disgust.

'Don't take him to the Hospital, will you, Arias?' she asked. 'He'd hate that. Get them to clean him up and put him in my bed downstairs, all right? We'll be back very soon.'

Arias's face lit. The planes of his cheeks curved into a sudden dazzling smile. 'You're coming home to me, my love?'

For a long, long moment Irona could not answer. She saw Arias lean forward, twiddling with the controls of the ansible; only then did she clear her throat and say, 'Arias? My love?'

At her tone it was as though a shaft from a flechette gun had hit him. 'What?' he asked in a choked voice that sounded nothing like his normal, clear tenor.

'Arias, we have hurt each other too much. You always said we could be together, but you never did anything to make it happen. And nor, let's be honest, did I.' She drew a deep, sharp breath and let it out in a sigh. 'I can't face it, being alone with you like we were sometimes before, not at the moment. You've been wonderful to me. You've kept me sane when life has burned me, been an anchor against all the lightning that's speared me. But you never made a move to be with me forever.'

'You know I'd do anything—'

'Anything but leave your creations at Eastcliff to be with me. They need you. It was the same for me. All we were to one another was an oasis; a shallow reflection of how it should have been. And if I stay on Harith long, Twiss'll be leaning on me again and I can't go through any more.' A sob thickened her voice. 'I can't. Maybe one day, but not right now. I'm sorry.'

'But I grew you those children!' he said, as though that would bring her to him.

'I know. You always said you would, but I never asked you to, did I? Children need both parents and I can't split myself between you and the fisherfolk and the Kiflians and Twiss and Earth and—. I'm sorry, Arias. For a little while I've got to go somewhere just to be me. But we have all eternity, or at least you do on Harith. Synod knows' – she laughed, because that was another thing no Synod could possibly know – 'if I'll have eternity too. But the *Starbird*'s coming back for me.'

'Then I won't see you at all?'

'Oh, yes, you'll see me. I'll see everyone who cares about me, Tebrina and Declan and Malambé and everyone. We'll have time to say our farewells before the *Starbird*'s shuttle lands. But I can't hurt you by giving Twiss cause for jealousy. Not when he's got forever to think up some way of venting his spleen.'

It was Arias's turn to be silent, and she saw what might

have been a tear glittering on his cheek, but he swallowed two or three times and said quietly, 'What about the Arms?'

She smiled at a memory and said, 'There won't be any more, Arias. The Matriarch doesn't need to play with Harith any more.'

'What about you?' he asked. He meant to add, 'When are you coming home?' but Irona didn't give him time.

'No, I'm fine. She doesn't need to play games with me any more either.' To herself she went on, 'But I wish I'd seen Elditch before they got him.'

'What's that?'

Irona smiled, the rounded cheeks of her borrowed face flushed pink and healthy. As she shook her head, red-gold curls flounced free above the perfect, healed skin. 'Nothing. You just make sure the lads take care of Regen, all right?'

This time she knew what to expect. She and Bernardina exchanged a kiss, an embrace, a handclasp that slackened as the transfer package did its work. But when the envelope of flesh was empty of that personality, Bernardina still sat caressing the motionless fingers of the young and vacant hand.

With understanding, with free will, the swoop of flight between the eternal necklaces of stars was a rush of joy. Irona gloried in her mental wings that grew and grew around her until she encompassed it all. Awareness heard the music of the glowing spheres, saw the fountains of rainbow light as electrons danced a barcarolle between suns and gravity. Clear and bright, Irona felt each one of her own electrons join in the measure. Her individuality was a chord in the eternal melody and all the freedom of the cosmos transported her in exhilaration. It was as though she had swallowed the universe and its harmony flowed glittering through her. Irona wished the flight could have lasted forever.

Twiss had gone from Jai's Hospital when the pale figure rose up on the couch. She scarcely noticed the friction as she pulled the hampering tubes from her nostril. A sense of airiness pervaded her. In the moons'light sliding in through the darkened window, she kilted the silvery sheet around her and edged her feet over the edge of the bed in the darkened Hospital.

Her movement pushed waves of dizzy blood through her brain, but the sensation was fleeting. When she stood, her arms naturally rose towards the discs of light rushing across the heavens, spinning their shadows like spokes from her body.

Everything, everything was the universe. Particles of light, motes of olfacts and scintillas of the clinical odours of Jai's Hospital streamed through her as freedom exploded her being. Each atom of her body would have sung if it could. The tides of the stars' chant wanted to river from her mouth but she knew she could never do justice to the song that wanted to sing her. Arno was so close to her that she knew she could have seen him if only she could turn quickly enough round the corner of the next dimension. Just being was carillon enough.

The worlds above her and the worlds below her feet on the other side of the whirling sphere of Harith called out to her. A kinship deeper than blood serenaded her from every one of the shimmering crystal stars. The winds of space tickled her mind as gently as a breeze over the sunset orchards; life carried an excitement, a tingle, a perfume of metal and rock and soil and bone strewn with haphazard flesh that enclosed the reality of life.

Taking one tentative step after another, she ghosted through the Hospital whose walls and doors seemed intangible themselves. The patients were warm, glowing coals in her awareness. Their consciousness was lulled in alpha-waves. Even so, they seemed to be aware of her as she passed, and their souls flickered brighter for a second.

She passed the entrance to Jai's flat and pushed at the transparisteel doors. The reflection of the nightlights mirrored the corridor for her, but outside palm-fronds beckoned, and the soft clitter of bamboo-stalks rubbing in the snow-winds from Heralia was applause for her every step.

Stretching the wings of her spirit, Irona waited for the miracle she expected. She turned to face the old Synod Tower, feeling for that candle of light she knew was there. The light of her friend's soul. She knew he was alive, and waiting for her.

Her heightened sensitivity swooped towards his gleam and she drew Regen's presence into her. It was like a favourite tunic, warm and soft and comforting, or sun-kissed sand caressing her feet. A well-loved viewdisk where the scenes didn't just happen remotely but turned to face her and pull her into his life.

Regen was alive. Her mirror, mentally healed and restored, and in the same way that he had truly regenerated her so many times, now she had done the same back for him. Not as debt, but as love.

From inside his mind, she felt that his body was resting, although feeble, but she could not blame Twiss for what he hadn't known. Because now the mazes of Regen's mind were cleared, and his spirit pulsed strongly through them.

Fears and eletacatricity no longer shivered his judgment and twitched him every time he moved. The flight had expanded him too and even in his sleeping body, his dreams were of joys to come. Regen was whole – but she had something to do before she met him again.

Irona used the enhancers her mother had implanted to touch the minds of the two guards, Declan and Marlambé. Not quite knowing why, they yawned awake and soared obedient to her impulse up the grav-shaft to check again that Regenerator's body was growing stronger. They were such good lads, foster-sons more than guards, that she knew he was in safe hands. Regen would wake up to her in his own rooms in the morning, clean and wholesome now without his nervous sweat; pride intact. Her beloved friend was safe in mind and body and soul and hope. Their faith in each other had brought them through, and one day soon it would take them to the jewelled worlds that danced in the ebon harmonies of space.

Now she took another pace or two into the darkness beyond the doors. Out in the cool breeze, a locust-lizard sang as it wheeled over the graceful curve of the Hospital steps. Only now she understood its melody. Night reached out to encircle her in its loving embrace. The doors clashed gently shut behind her.

Jai heard the door. 'What's that?' she asked Sticker. 'Did you hear it?'

In the warmth of his sleep-fuddled bed, Sticker muttered, 'Never heard nothin'. It weren't me,' and went back to sleep.

Jai slapped at his mess of greasy blond hair. Still floating in alcoholic dreams, he thrashed a lethargic hand at her.

Rather than stay there, with him, Jai slid on her

dressing-gown with its embroidered cuddly toy and walked out into her Hospital to find out what had disturbed her.

In moments she had checked the sleeping wards. All life-signs positive, more positive than she had imagined. And all patients safely tucked in their beds. Even the little fishergirl, Maerika, was breathing more sweetly.

But something had disturbed Jai. With a grabbing presentiment of alarm, she began to run towards Irona's room.

The bed was empty.

'Oh, no! Twiss!'

And the nurse spun on her heel in despair, heading for her booze-fusty bedroom where the remote control for Twiss's Eye lay.

But Twiss wasn't in the Synod Tower, or the barren frosted palace of Tingalit. He was far beyond the reach of any Eye that Jai might drive.

The moons drifted her over the foothills wrapped in their gossamer gleams. Over the spiked crests of the Moon Mountains a lightning storm was playing, and the cold air broke like surf against Irona, filling her with an exhilaration like spindrift aspark with St Elmo's fire. The little tractor she had whistled from under the nose of the Palace guards skimmed merrily over the road. The secret, eternal joy of the night filled her. When the rain cascaded over her on the green shores of the Rainshadow Valley croplands, Irona laughed as wild as a Valkyrie.

Astonished farmers woke and shuddered at the cry. Sleepless children let their souls fly on the wings of fantasy at that clarion call. But the farmsteads lay unmoving, too frightened or too rapt to stir in the shifting moonlight under the beat of the scudding wracks of clouds.

Urging the little tractor to ever greater speeds, Irona outdistanced the rain. Looking back over her shoulder, she saw its silver lances pricking fertility into the rich earth. The lonely salt tang of the sea skirled and under it droned the heady potion it brewed from moist loam. This, too, she had made. The sight and the scent of it pulled her poignantly, but she knew she was leaving it behind. *Who knows what tomorrow brings?* she thought, and the wonder of it enraptured her. Speaking softly to her transport, she listened to its balloon-wheels humming along the road.

When she reached the river, its platinum threads were tangled by the jet spars of sandbanks. Ropes of diamonds flew from the wheels as the tractor jolted her across the rippling water. Within seconds she had ridden the jouncing streambed and was racing the moon-shadows again. Granfer's cave-tomb leaped past and behind her.

The bittersweet melody of a locust-lizard chimed from over the night-black Interior. Too late for spring mating, too early to die in sacrifice to the autumn sea, the gemlike creature flittered on sparkling wings. Its ruby eyes circled the fringe of the dunes and its song held the edge of the world in thrall. Its melody was a honeyed counterpoint to the sharp, edgy smell of the green-ball plants. Shadows that weren't shadows wreathed their incantations below the transparent fronds.

And the locust-lizard's promise was true.

With a whispered command, Irona stopped the tractor on the Valley-side of the dune. Beneath her bare feet, the sand still remembered the heat of the day. It trickled warm and soft between her toes.

Twiss sat, elbows on knees, staring out across the untamed Interior. The lullaby of the wind had drowned the sounds of her arrival. The first he knew of it was when miniature landslides from her footsteps nudged him into awareness.

'Irona?' he said incredulously.

She puffed laughter down her nose and nodded. 'Who else would it be?'

As if they were just out for a stroll, as if she hadn't been away from him in body for weeks and in life for years, she folded cross-legged beside him. 'How are you doing?' she asked him.

He turned to her, and in that moment the shooting moons swept beyond the crest of the dune. Shadows towered out before the man and the woman, sweeping them into darkness more cosy than the finest bedroom Tingalit had to offer. Twiss only nodded non-committally, swaying his head a little in the phantom of a shrug.

'Mmm.'

The wind turned cool and the silver-limned clouds blanketed the sea of sand, but the rain had spent itself before it left the croplands. Irona felt her skin turn chilly, but the touch of Twiss's elbow on her forearm was as hot as the leaping sparks of an arc-weld.

'How did you know I was here?' he asked eventually.

'I followed a locust-lizard like we did before, you and I. This is where it started.'

'Did it?'

But Irona knew suddenly that it hadn't started here. It had started with her oppression in Camelford and the joy of a warrior unchained; with the touch of his hand on the moon-silvered flank of a stallion; with her mother, and her father, and their offering the daughter they had loved on the altar of their plans; with her acceptance of being oppressed.

In the dunes, in the new covenant the open blue skies of

Harith had promised her, Twiss had taken her gift of herself, and held it ever since, because he had never been brave enough to say he didn't want it any more. He had been a warmth, a comfort better than a child's family embrace in the midst of a night of terror. He had said, 'I've got you. You're safe,' and her heart had bled out of her and into him in tenderness at such love.

He had offered her an oasis, and she had thought it was an ocean with no shore.

She said, 'Well let's say it recharged its power-packs here, remember?'

He half-chuckled, and all at once she knew that the pressure of his arm against hers was not an accident. She leaned into him, gently.

Twiss responded by slipping his hand around to rest on her shoulder above the twisted folds of the sheet. He pulled her gently to him, nuzzling her hair, then he touched her tenderly along the curve of her throat and cheek to turn her face towards him. Irona resonated to his touch, but this time her mind remained her own. With a passion as slow and deep as an ocean, he kissed her.

His love lured her into herself, and with astonishment she felt the breaking of her waters over him, as though she were the hyacinth ziggurat of the sea that they had once unleashed over Kifl. In her love he was reborn. Now they would be free to say goodbye.

He eased her back on to the sloping warmth of the sand. In wonder he touched her, hardening his belief that she was really there with him; that she had wanted to be with him; that she had known him well enough to know where he would be.

Her breath rose when she felt the warmth of his fingers. The King and Queen of Harith kissed again, languourously tossing aside his clothes, her sheet. Then they came together like an endless horizon where the earth meets the sky.

Afterwards she lay in the crook of his arm, closing her mind to the faint cramp in her shoulder, not wanting to disturb his rest. But Twiss wasn't asleep either. He tucked the sheet more securely around her and pulled his shirt of seasilk that he had lent her closer up to her chin.

She smiled, her eyes dark with the night. Soon dawn would come, knives of apricot and peach and gold slashing them apart. But for now they were together.

'I'm sorry, Ro.' His voice was a whisper, though there was no-one to hear them. 'I never meant to hurt you.'

'Why did you, then?' and the question wasn't pointed, but fuzzed with affection and a desire to know without malice.

He was silent for so long that she thought he wasn't going to answer. Mentally she shrugged. Now it didn't matter any more. Besides, she thought she knew what he would have said anyway. The smell of him was on her skin, permeating her. His quiet breathing entwined with hers, and that was all she needed.

'Just jealous, I guess,' Twiss said finally, when the sky began to furl pale wings across the glittering stars.

'Of me?'

He kissed her nose, then pillowed his head on the dune once more. 'Yes, of you. I thought I could do it. I thought I had a gargantuan appetite for life. Even in the Admin I knew I was going to live forever. Full of juice, I was.'

'I know.'

'You would, wouldn't you?' Admiration enriched his tenor voice. Too late he had discovered just who and what she was.

'Mmm. How you thrilled me and horrified me that

moment when you brought the rabbit down. It was barbaric – and magnificent.'

'I thought I could get away with it forever, see? Do whatever I wanted. Poach and beat the Arms, pass the psych-profile and get me and Granfer out of Camelford. Arcturus Rex, that was me, straight out of the legends from before the Sky.'

'You got your palace, though, didn't you, Arcturus Rex? And you beat the Arms and Wave sectarianism. As long as you stay on Harith, you've even beaten death. Then there's Jai's children. You've got it all, Twiss.'

'And the crown Granfer always promised me. Don't forget the crown.' He gestured to it, his bare foot peeping out of the bottom of the soft, metallic sheet. The circle of metal lay half-buried in the sand, the green kistle sleeping darkly.

'How could I?' Sadness crept into her voice. 'Nobody else did.'

His lips brushed her ear, and she felt him gentling her hair. The glacial fragments of the stars melted in her vision at his tenderness.

'Don't you get it? That was part of it. Spoils of conquest, like.' He stopped, cleared his throat. 'But they never meant nothing. None of 'em.'

'Not even Jai?'

'Well, maybe Jai, a little.'

'Neither of us really believed in eternal life enough to live without having children.'

'Have some more, Ro. Get that Arias feller to grow you some from cells or something.'

'He has. I didn't want him to. But it's not the same. We're not the same. Look after my little ones for me, Twiss. Please.'

She saw the whites of his eyes gleam. His face was

strong and lean now, toughened by his battles.

'Don't go, love,' he said.

Irona smiled at him, and she felt the love radiating out of her and into him. For once her own emotions were clearer than anybody else's. Even his.

Trying to hide his desperation, he let his words tumble out like a mountain stream over a waterfall. 'See, I was so scared of you. You'd got it all. Brains, education – you always had a plan. I never did. But I couldn't let it be you. I wanted them to love me. I'm sorry, sweetheart. I never meant to hurt you.'

'I know you didn't. You just sort of couldn't help it. I just got caught under your chariot wheels.'

'Hmm?'

She shook her head against his arm, and sand cool as daybreak slithered to cushion her neck. 'It doesn't matter.'

'But the whole planet needs you.'

'No, Twiss. There's another ship coming. A common enemy to link both waves behind you. The planet doesn't need me any more.'

His voice dropped, as if he didn't want to hear his own admission. 'I need you. It'll be different this time. I promise.'

'Twiss, I can't ask it of you. On Harith a promise lasts forever, literally. You couldn't keep that promise for eternity. You'd try, I know you would, but it would choke you. And I couldn't stand an eternity of wondering whether this would be the night that you didn't come home to me. Let's face it, Twiss: eternity's a killer.'

Their laughter joined, balanced on the pivot of harmony, and the sun burst the gladness of the new day upon them.

But the ship she had summoned darted glinting through the wells of space, speeding to take Irona and her friend to their destiny among the stars.